DATE DUE	BORROWER'S NAME	ROOM NO.

Toenails, Tonsils, and Tornadoes

Toenails, Tonsils, and Tornadoes

Bonnie Pryor

illustrated by
HELEN COGANCHERRY

Morrow Junior Books • New York

Text copyright © 1997 by Bonnie Pryor
Illustrations copyright © 1997 by Helen Cogancherry

Printed in the United States of America.

1 2 3 4 5 6 7 8 9 10

Library of Congress Cataloging-in-Publication Data
Pryor, Bonnie.
Toenails, tonsils, and tornadoes/Bonnie Pryor; illustrated by
Helen Cogancherry.
p. cm.
Summary: Martin weathers the fourth grade while suffering through
the prolonged visit of a difficult aunt and enduring the trials of a
classic "middle child."
ISBN 0-688-14885-9
[1. Family life—Fiction.   2. Aunts—Fiction.   3. Schools—
Fiction.]   I. Cogancherry, Helen, ill.   II. Title.
PZ7.P94965To 1997   [Fic]—dc20   96–30637   CIP AC

To my newest grandchild, Sharon,
who doesn't have red hair,
and her father, Rick, because he does

Contents

1. Weird Relatives and Toilet Flushes   1
2. Dog Barks and Smelly Sneakers   8
3. Do Families Grow on Trees?   16
4. The Great Paint Disaster   27
5. Getting Rid of Aunt Henrietta   36
6. Tonsils and Troubles   43
7. To Kiss or Not to Kiss . . .   50
8. Cousin Agnes   59
9. Girl Problems   65
10. Tonsils and Toy Soldiers   79
11. Be My Valentine   84
12. More Tonsils   93
13. Capitals and Sympathy   100
14. Tonsils Again   106

15. Tempers and Toenails   113
16. Water Balloons and a Pen   119
17. Even More Relatives   128
18. Tornado   138
19. Martin the Hero   147
20. Another Surprise   152
21. Another Kind of Brave   157
22. Home Again   165

1

Weird Relatives and Toilet Flushes

DID YOU EVER wonder if you were born into the wrong family? I think about that a lot. It's as if some angel decided to play a practical joke on the day I was born. "See that Snodgrass family down there on earth?" he said to the other angels. "They live in New Albany, Ohio. Everyone in town knows they're special. The dad's a doctor, and in a few years the mom's going to be mayor. They have a sports star son and a brainy daughter. Now baby number three is coming along. Let's put an *ordinary* kid in the family for a change and see what happens. Then later we'll give him a really cute little brother."

Some joke.

When I was little, friends of my parents adopted a baby. For a long time after that, I was sure that I had been adopted, too. One day I finally got enough courage to ask my mom about it. She just pointed to our family picture that's sitting on the coffee table. There we all were, lined up. There was my brother Tim, my sister, Caroline, my little brother Robbie, and me. All of us with our red hair and freckles just like Dad's.

"What do you think?" Mom asked.

"Maybe I just got put in the wrong body," I said.

I know I could never be like my brother Tim. His whole room is about to sink with the weight of all his sports trophies. I'm pretty good at math, but that's nothing compared to Caroline. She's eleven, only a year older than I am. But she is two years ahead of me at school because she's so smart. When I look in the mirror I see a fairly nice face, but of course Robbie, my little brother, is much cuter.

My sister, Caroline, has a theory about it. "If you ordinary, boring people weren't around," she said, "how would anyone know he or she was amazing? Take me, for instance," she added brightly. "Next to you I positively shine."

I have to admit her theory does make sense.

I guess I really don't have much to complain about. I have a new puppy named Sam, and he's finally housebroken, so Mom and Dad let him sleep in my room at night. He's supposed to sleep on the floor, but every morning when I wake up, he's on the bed beside me.

My fourth-grade teacher, Miss Lawson, is the prettiest teacher in the whole school. When I started fourth grade, Jamie was my best friend. He decided that this was our year to be popular, but I got bored hanging around with the cool kids. I ended up with a new best friend named Willie and even a girlfriend named Marcia—although sometimes I wished that I hadn't. So mostly, things were going along pretty well.

Then one Saturday a letter came. I was on the couch, miserable with a sore throat and cold. It was my third cold that winter, and it was only the middle of January.

Dad carried the letter in from the mailbox. He held it between his fingers as if he were holding a piece of moldy bread. "I suppose this is from one of your crazy relatives," he teased as he handed it to Mom. "Henrietta Somebody? The name is pretty smudged."

Mom fingered the envelope. "Henrietta," she repeated. "I do have a cousin Henrietta. But why would she be writing from a post office box in Washington, D.C.?"

Dad got a strange look on his face. "Cousin Henrietta. Is she the one who gave our wedding present to a perfect stranger?"

"No," Mom said. "That was Aunt Abigail. And she didn't mean to give our present away. She got mixed up and went to the wrong wedding."

Caroline looked up from the thousand-piece puzzle she was putting together on the dining room table.

"Your aunt went to the wrong wedding?" she asked. Mom's weird relatives were the subject of many family stories.

"Not on purpose," Mom said, a little defensively. "She hadn't seen me for years, and the other wedding was only a block away."

"So which one is Cousin Henrietta?" Dad asked. "I can't seem to place her. Where does she live?"

Mom was a long time answering. "Nowhere, really."

Tim tore his eyes away from the basketball game he was watching on television. "Your cousin is a bag lady?" he screeched. Actually it didn't start out as a screech. Tim's voice has been doing strange things lately.

"Of course not," Mom said. "Most of the time she stays with Aunt Abigail. But they don't always get along. So every now and then Cousin Henrietta visits people. The last I heard, she was visiting my brother John."

Dad had a wild look in his eye. "Just how long has she been visiting John?"

"About six months," Mom mumbled.

"Read the letter," Dad ordered. He looked grim.

Mom meekly tore open the envelope. We all sort of held our breath and stared at her as she read.

"Well?" Dad asked after several minutes.

"She's on her way," Mom said in a small voice. It was quiet for a minute.

"On her way *now*?" asked Dad.

"There is one thing, though," Mom said. A smile twitched in the corners of her mouth. "It's not my cousin Henrietta. It's your aunt Henrietta."

Dad grabbed the letter and stared at it. "I haven't seen Aunt Henrietta since I was about twelve years old. I don't remember very much about her. She's my father's sister. She works for an international relief organization of some sort. Come to think of it, it *was* based in Washington. I know she was teaching school in India. Before that, she lived in South America. I can't imagine why she would be coming for a visit after all these years."

"She says in the letter that she has been away so long that she wants to get reacquainted with her family. I think it's a good idea," Mom said in her no-nonsense mayor voice. "The children should know more of their relatives."

"I suppose she's a real prim and proper old lady," Tim said. He sighed. "We will have to drink tea and look at slide shows."

"Hey, wait a minute," Caroline said, examining the letter. "Why is her name Jones instead of Snodgrass, like ours?"

"That was her husband's name," Dad answered. "He died a long time ago."

"How long is she going to stay?" I asked.

Mom consulted the letter. "She doesn't say."

"Where is she going to sleep?" Caroline asked.

Mom looked thoughtful. "That is going to be a problem." She frowned. "Martin, you could sleep in Tim's room, since he has the extra bunk bed. And Aunt Henrietta can sleep in your room."

I groaned. In the first place, there was hardly enough space in Tim's room for Tim and all his trophies. In the second place, after a night in a room with Tim's sneakers I might never wake up again.

Just then Robbie came toddling into the room with his pants down around his ankles. "I pooped," he said proudly. "Come see, Martin."

"I'll go," Mom said. Robbie just started going to the bathroom by himself. But someone always has to go admire it and tell him what a good boy he is.

Robbie stuck out his lower lip. "Want Martin to see," he said.

With a sigh, I followed him down the hall to the downstairs bathroom and looked in the toilet. "Wow, that's great," I said automatically. "You're a big boy," I added as I reached for the handle.

"Robbie flush," he yelled. He pushed the handle just as I noticed something bright green swirling around in the water.

"Dad!" I shouted. But it was too late. Robbie's favorite green car disappeared down the hole.

2

Dog Barks
and Smelly Sneakers

THE PLUMBERS DIDN'T get to our house until Sunday morning. Aunt Henrietta arrived just as they were leaving. Dad was waving his checkbook around in the air. "Two hundred and fifty dollars! The next time someone messes up the plumbing, please don't do it on the weekend. That has got to be the most expensive flush in the history of mankind."

Robbie stuck out his lip. "Robbie likes to flush."

"Of course you do," boomed a voice from the door.

I stared in amazement. The speaker was at least six feet tall. Her hair was gray, with just enough red left to identify her as a Snodgrass. It was piled up on her head, making her look even taller. Under all that hair was a nice face with a rather large nose. Bony elbows poked out from under the rolled-up sleeves of an old sweatshirt. Bright red plaid pants and sturdy brown shoes covering the largest feet I had ever seen completed the picture.

There was a moment of awkward silence. Everyone sort of froze in place, staring at one another. "Weren't you expecting me?" the weird-looking woman finally said.

"Aunt Henrietta," Dad exclaimed in a strangled voice. "It's so good to see you."

"And there's a lot of her to see," Tim mumbled from behind me.

Aunt Henrietta waved at the taxi driver. He started unloading the taxi and carrying an amazing assortment of suitcases, boxes, and bags into the house. Dad's face looked a little more glum with each piece of luggage.

"This is an awful lot of luggage for a short visit," he whispered to Mom while Aunt Henrietta paid the taxi driver.

Aunt Henrietta didn't seem to notice Dad's concern. She wrapped her long arms around him in a big hug. When he introduced Mom, Aunt Henrietta hugged her, too.

"These are our children," Mom said, and she introduced us one by one. Each of us in turn was smothered in a huge bear hug. When it was Robbie's turn, he barked.

9

Mom looked embarrassed. "Sometimes Robbie likes to pretend he's a dog."

Aunt Henrietta bent down to Robbie. "Woof, woof," she said solemnly.

"Woof," Robbie replied. He was obviously pleased to find someone who spoke his language.

Suddenly Sam woke up from his nap and discovered there was someone in the house. Sam is not the world's greatest watchdog, obviously. He bounded into the room and added his "Yip yip" to the chorus of barks.

Aunt Henrietta pulled a huge men's handkerchief from her pocket and sneezed. "A-choo. A-choo." She smiled apologetically. "Sorry. I guess I should have warned you I was allergic to dogs."

"Martin, take Sam out to the garage," Mom said.

"But he'll be lonesome," I protested.

"He'll be fine," said Dad with a look that told me I'd better not say any more.

I picked up Sam and stalked out to the garage. Behind me I heard Mom clear her throat. "Why don't I introduce you to Mrs. Albright," she said cheerfully. "She's our housekeeper." Aunt Henrietta followed Mom to the kitchen. Dad picked up four suitcases and grimly headed for my bedroom.

I found an old piece of rug for Sam and made a bed for him near the back door. When I sat down on it, Sam whined softly and put his head on my knee.

"It's not fair, is it, Sam? You were here first. I already have to give her my room, and now this. I hope she doesn't stay very long."

Sam just looked at me with mournful eyes. When I went back in the house, the grown-ups were talking around the kitchen table.

"Robbie likes Dog Lady," Robbie said. He trailed past me into the kitchen.

I found Tim and Caroline in the living room. Caroline rolled her eyes. "Weird!" she said. "I wonder what Mrs. Albright will think about her?"

Everyone in the family loves Mrs. Albright. She's more like an extra grandma than a housekeeper. She and Mr. DeWitt, our next-door neighbor, go to concerts and movies together. Right now they are really good friends. But Mrs. Albright told me if they ever do get married, we'll still be like her own family.

"Maybe Aunt Henrietta is barking at her," Tim said.

We listened, but the conversation coming from the kitchen seemed to be friendly.

Dad left to visit patients in the hospital, and Mom came back into the living room. "They're chatting like old friends," she said. "This is a good time to change the beds around. And we will have to vacuum thoroughly to make sure we get all the dog hair out of Martin's bedroom."

11

Mom rolled the vacuum into my room and started cleaning everything in sight.

"Mom's getting all your cooties out of there," Caroline said with a smirk.

I ignored her as I carried my things to Tim's room and tried to find a place for my clothes in his closet.

"You can sleep in the top bunk," Tim said.

"I don't like the top," I said. "What if I fall out?"

"Tough," Tim said cheerfully. "It's my room."

Tim plopped down on the bottom bunk, his sneakers only a few feet from my nose. Suddenly I felt better. At least up on the top bunk I would be that much farther away from Tim's smelly feet.

Aunt Henrietta was busy unpacking when I passed by my bedroom door. Mom had already cleared off my dresser and shelves. My fuzzy bedspread had been replaced with a quilt, and a stack of old-lady clothes was on my bed. The room had turned into her room. It was as though it had never been mine.

"Nice room," she said. "Yours?"

"It was," I said grimly. "I have to sleep in Tim's room while you're here."

Aunt Henrietta didn't seem to notice how unhappy I was. "I appreciate it," she said. She stuffed an empty suitcase in the closet. "Sorry about the dog. Although I have to admit that I never understood why people want to have animals in the house. Messy creatures. Always drooling and dropping hairs about."

"Sam is a great dog," I shouted. "He never drools." I stomped downstairs and threw myself in a living room chair.

"You look like a thunderstorm about to happen," said Mrs. Albright. She arranged some magazines on the coffee table she had just dusted. "What's the trouble?"

"I hate her," I blurted out. "First she takes my room and messes it all up. And I'll bet she just pretended to sneeze to get rid of Sam. She thinks dogs don't belong in the house."

"I'm sure she wouldn't have done that," Mrs. Albright said. "I don't think Sam will mind being in the garage that much if you take him out for walks. I have an old laundry basket. If we put an old blanket in it, I think he will be pretty comfortable." She patted my arm. "It's only for a few days."

Mrs. Albright helped me make up the bed for Sam. I carried his food and water dishes to the garage. When we went back inside, Aunt Henrietta had just come downstairs. "Like to run?" she asked.

"Run?" I echoed.

She ran a few steps in place to demonstrate. "You know, run."

"I'm not very athletic," I said, not looking at her.

Aunt Henrietta snorted. "You don't have to be athletic to run. I run every day. It's good for your heart. Young people today don't get enough exercise." As

13

she spoke, she pulled on a beat-up pair of running shoes. "We can take it easy today. Just a few warm-ups and a short run. We won't go far."

"No thanks," I answered crossly. "I'm just getting over a cold."

Dad walked in just in time to hear the conversation. "I think you are well enough for a little run, Martin. Aunt Henrietta doesn't know her way around the neighborhood. We wouldn't want her to get lost on her first day."

I tried to think of another excuse. "I don't have any running shoes."

Aunt Henrietta frowned thoughtfully at my shoes. "Those will do for now. I'll talk to your mother about getting some proper ones."

Miserably I put on my jacket. The last thing I wanted to do was go running, and certainly not with an old woman I didn't even like.

Then Caroline came downstairs. "Robbie and I are going running," Aunt Henrietta informed her.

"I'm Martin," I protested. If she was going to kill me with embarrassment, she could at least remember my name.

"Of course you are," said Aunt Henrietta.

Caroline's grin went nearly from ear to ear. "I'll bet you have a wonderful time," she said. "All that fresh air and exercise."

"Why don't you join us, too," Aunt Henrietta said.

"Yeah, Caroline," I said. "Then you can get some of that good fresh air and exercise yourself."

"I would really love to," Caroline said, almost convincingly. "But unfortunately I am going to my friend's house to practice for the spelling bee. I was last year's state champion."

"You got that from your great-grandpa Snodgrass," Aunt Henrietta said. "He won the state championship in 1927. He would have won for the whole country, but he got tripped up by the word *logistically*."

"L-o-g-i-s-t-i-c-a-l-y," Caroline said.

"Nope. Same mistake your great-grandfather made. There are two *l*'s."

Caroline's face looked dark as she hurried off to look it up in the dictionary. "Don't bother," Aunt Henrietta called cheerfully after her. "I'm pretty good at spelling myself."

She reached for the door. "Ready?" she asked.

"I wanna go, too." My little brother left the pile of cars he'd been racing across the dining room floor.

"Not this time, Martin," Aunt Henrietta said.

"I'm Robbie," Robbie shouted.

Aunt Henrietta patted his cheek as we went outside. "Of course you are."

3

Do Families Grow on Trees?

ON WEDNESDAY, MISS Lawson passed out some papers. "We've been studying United States history," she said. "Families have histories, too. As a matter of fact, the histories of all our families make up the history of our country. The founders of our country were somebody's great-great-grandfathers." She stopped and stared at Willie. He was leaning back in his chair, whistling the song "Dixie."

"Willie, why are you whistling when I am talking?" she asked.

Willie sat up straight. "I was listening," he protested. "But I thought maybe some of our ancestors might have come from the South."

"This is just a paper, Willie. It doesn't need sound

effects." Miss Lawson's pretty face looked stern.

Willie shrugged. "Sorry, but I'll bet it would be more fun with music."

Miss Lawson sighed, but I thought I saw her lips twitch as though she were fighting a smile. I looked at the sheet she had handed me. It was labeled "My Family Tree" and showed a tree with spaces to write in names.

"One of my ancestors came over on the *Mayflower*," Marcia said.

"Too bad," Lester said loudly. "I heard it was a pretty nice country until then."

Miss Lawson frowned. "I'm sure that everyone has some good *and* some not so good characters in their family tree. Sometimes learning about our families can help us understand ourselves. For instance, Jason is a very good artist. It may be that somewhere in his family tree is an ancestor who was very artistic."

"My mom and dad came to America just before I was born," Brianne said shyly. "All my ancestors come from Italy." Brianne was the new girl. Her hair was so curly that it bounced when she moved her head. She always smelled like vanilla. "My parents miss Italy," she continued. "All my grandparents live there. But I miss California. We lived right near the ocean, and it was almost always warm."

"Is Brianne an Italian name?" Marcia asked.

"No, my parents wanted me to have an American

name," Brianne answered. "The lady who lived next door to us in California helped my parents a lot when they came to this country. Her name was Brianne."

"We are going to be studying the states for the next few months," Miss Lawson said. "Why don't you plan to tell us about California?"

"Do we have to turn these family tree papers in?" Willie interrupted.

"No, you don't have to turn these in," Miss Lawson said. "I just thought it might be fun for you to see how much information about your family you can find out. If there's anything interesting you want to share, let me know."

"I'll bet I have all kinds of interesting ancestors," Marcia said smugly.

"I'll bet you have all kinds of ugly ancestors," Lester mumbled.

"Miss Lawson, Lester is making fun of me again," Marcia complained.

"That's enough," Miss Lawson said tiredly. She started our math lesson, so I tucked my family tree paper in my notebook and forgot about it until after school.

At lunchtime I hobbled to the cafeteria. I walked past Jamie and his friends Steve and Lester and sat down by myself. Willie Smith slid his tray on the table.

At first, I hadn't liked Willie very much. He'd been

left back a year at school, and he always seemed to be causing trouble. But Willie turned out to be a great friend. We both joined the community Youth Theater, and Willie got the lead role in a musical play based on *The Adventures of Tom Sawyer*.

"What's wrong with you?" Willie asked as I groaned. Every muscle in my body ached.

"I had to run about ten miles last night," I said. "Trying to catch up to Aunt Henrietta."

Willie's mouth froze just as he was about to bite into a peanut butter sandwich. "Your aunt was trying to run away?"

"Exercise running," I explained, laughing at his confused expression. "She said we only ran about a mile." I rubbed my sore leg muscles. "But it sure seemed like more."

"Why does she need so much exercise?" he asked.

I shook my head. "Because she's crazy."

"You'd better put her in your family tree. Then your tree will have a crazy branch. Like a crazy bone. Get it?" Willie hooted at his own joke.

"Are you ready for tonight?" I asked him, changing the subject. Tonight was the first dress rehearsal for *The Adventures of Tom Sawyer*. Then we were having another run-through tomorrow night, which was Thursday, and then three performances over the weekend. Suddenly it was all happening very fast.

"I'm pretty nervous," he admitted.

I grinned at him. "I would be, too, if I had to kiss Caroline."

Caroline, of course, had the star part of Tom's girl-friend, Becky Thatcher.

Willie shuddered. "I don't want to even think about it."

When we went outside to the playground, Marcia followed. Her round glasses make her look cute, like an owl, but she could be a real pain. "How's Sam doing?" she asked. Marcia had given me Sam when her dog had puppies.

"He was doing great," I said. "Now my aunt is staying with us, and he has to stay in the garage."

Marcia looked sympathetic, but she shrugged. "My mom won't let our dog in the house either."

She was starting to say something else when I noticed Brianne standing nearby. A few flakes of snow drifted down.

"Did you have snow in California?" I asked.

Brianne pulled her coat around tighter. "Not where I lived. Once it snowed when we went to the mountains."

"You'll see lots of it here," I told her.

"I can hardly wait to make a snowman," she said.

"This snow is too dry," I said. I stuck out my tongue and caught a flake. "You have to have just the right kind of snow to make a snowman. I'll show you how when we get a good snow."

Willie came over and sniffed loudly. "You smell like cookies," he announced. A lot of the girls liked Willie, with his curly black hair and blue eyes.

Brianne giggled. "It's my sister's new perfume. It's called Tropical Vanilla." She held out her arm for us to smell. "Do you like it?"

Some of the girls called to Brianne and she ran to join them. Willie and I walked across the playground. Marcia didn't follow us. I looked back and saw her standing by the swings. She did not look happy.

Willie grinned at me. "Looks like your girlfriend is jealous."

"I wish I had a magic wand," I grumbled. "I'd make Aunt Henrietta and Marcia both disappear."

Our neighbor Mr. DeWitt was sitting on his front porch when I got home after school. I let Sam out of the garage, and he bounded around the yard while I talked to Mr. DeWitt.

"Sam probably thinks no one loves him anymore," I said glumly.

"How about my keeping Sam until your aunt leaves?" Mr. DeWitt suggested. "Daffy and I would love the company."

Mr. DeWitt's yellow cat was sitting on the windowsill washing her face with her paws.

"What if Sam forgets me?" I said.

"How could he forget you? You can come over and

see him every day. And you can still take him for walks. You might even bring something of yours he can chew on to remind him of you."

I thought for a minute. "There's an old pair of slippers in my closet."

"Why don't you give them to Sam?" he asked.

"Thanks, Mr. DeWitt. That's a good idea." I ran inside and found the slippers and an old shirt. I put them in Sam's bed and carried them all to Mr. DeWitt's house. Daffy arched her back with alarm, but Sam settled right down in his basket, chewing happily.

"Dinner smells good," I said when I walked in the kitchen. We were having an early dinner because of the rehearsal. Mrs. Albright was fixing spaghetti, my favorite. Her sauce is really special.

"I hope it tastes all right," Mrs. Albright said. "I couldn't put any onions in it. Your aunt says they give her indigestion."

"I wish she would leave," I grumbled. "Next I suppose we'll have to eat prunes for breakfast."

Mrs. Albright patted my shoulder. "Give her a chance. She's really a pretty nice lady."

I sighed. "Mom says she's spent her life serving other people and she deserves being treated specially for a while. I suppose that's true. But why did she have to pick us?"

"That spaghetti smells delicious," Aunt Henrietta

said as she came in the kitchen. I gave her a guilty look, wondering if she had heard me, but she just smiled and sat down at the table.

I have to admit that even without onions, the spaghetti was delicious. Caroline only put a few strands on her plate. She pushed them around, not eating.

"There are children in some of the schools where I've taught who would be awfully glad to have some of this spaghetti," Aunt Henrietta remarked.

"I'm not very hungry," Caroline said.

"Are you feeling all right?" Mom asked.

"She's probably on a diet," Tim said gleefully. "She is looking kind of chubby lately."

"That is not a very nice way to talk about your sister," Aunt Henrietta said.

I gritted my teeth. It was true, but what right did she have to say it?

"I was only teasing," Tim mumbled.

"Maybe she's nervous about the rehearsal," I said.

"Will you all quit talking about me as though I wasn't sitting right here?" Caroline shouted. "I am just not hungry." She glared at Tim. "I may be chubby, but at least you can't smell me coming a mile away." Then she turned her glare on me. "And I am not nervous. I know my lines perfectly. I just don't feel like eating."

"I know my lines, too," I said. "And I'm still nervous."

"You only had a few lines to learn," Caroline said in a sour voice.

"I could have learned more. I even know your part—including the songs. I've had to listen to you practicing so much." I sang a few bars to show her.

"Your great-uncle John used to say that every part in a play is important," Aunt Henrietta said.

Robbie rattled on his high-chair tray. "All done," he said.

"Who was Great-Uncle John?" Tim asked.

"He was my grandfather's brother. He traveled all around the West doing Shakespeare's plays. He was quite famous in his day."

"Hey, I could put him in the family tree," I exclaimed. I explained about the paper Miss Lawson had given us.

"All done," Robbie repeated.

"Just a minute, Robbie," Mom said absently. "I can help you with my side of the family, Martin. I'm sure Aunt Henrietta could help you, too. She knows everything about the Snodgrasses."

"These children should know more about their ancestors," Aunt Henrietta said. She snapped her bony fingers. "We should have a family reunion. They'll hear a lot of family history there."

I thought Dad would turn down that idea immediately, but he seemed to be considering it. "It has been a long time since we've all gotten together," he said.

"All done." Robbie banged on his tray with his spoon, but everyone was busy talking.

"My family had a reunion about a year ago," Mom said. "I was so busy with the garbagemen's strike that we couldn't go. I think it would be good for the children to meet more of their family."

"Exactly how many people are we talking about?" Caroline asked.

Aunt Henrietta did some rapid mental math. "We would have to make a list, of course, but I would say fifty to one hundred."

"What do you do at a family reunion?" I asked.

"All *done*," Robbie said.

"Talk mostly," Dad answered. "Get to know people in your family you didn't even know existed."

"Sounds boring to me," Tim said.

"If we wait until the weather gets warmer, we could have it right here. Maybe like a picnic," Mom said.

"That would be a lot of work," Dad said.

"Not if everyone helped," Mom said. "Tim, you could help organize some activities."

Robbie banged his plate on his tray. "ALL DONE!" he roared.

"My goodness," Mom said. "Why is Robbie so excited?"

I got up and unfastened the tray to release him. The grown-ups hardly noticed, they were so busy finalizing the reunion idea. Tim, Caroline, and I went outside on the porch. Robbie tagged along behind us. I went next door to get Sam and brought him back to our yard. I tossed a ball for him to fetch while we talked.

"I don't know about this idea," Caroline said. Her voice was sounding really scratchy. "Probably some of them will stay at the house. We'll end up sleeping on the floor."

"Aunt Jane and Uncle Dave are pretty nice," Tim said. "We haven't seen them for a while."

"I'll bet Grandma and Grandpa would come from Florida," I said.

"What if there are a bunch of weird relatives like Aunt Henrietta that we don't know?" Caroline asked.

I pointed to Tim's shoes. "If there is anyone we don't like, we can just put a pair of Tim's sneakers in their room. Believe me, the relatives will be gone the next morning."

4

The Great Paint Disaster

MOM HAD A city council meeting after dinner. Some people in town thought that the intersection near the new shopping center was dangerous. They were going to present a petition to have a traffic light installed.

Mrs. Albright had taken Robbie for a walk with Mr. DeWitt and Sam. Dad was going to drop Caroline and me off for our rehearsal on his way to the hospital. That left Tim as the only one at home to go running with Aunt Henrietta.

"Why does she run so much anyway?" Tim grumbled.

"I thought you knew," Dad said. "Aunt Henrietta wants to run in the Boston Marathon."

Tim laughed. "That's ridiculous. She must be sixty

27

years old. She doesn't have a chance of winning."

"Aunt Henrietta has already qualified. But I don't think she cares about winning," Dad said. "It's just something she always wanted to do. Simply to finish would be great."

"I don't understand," I said. "What is the Boston Marathon?"

"Don't you know anything?" Caroline said, shaking her head. "It's a big race held every year in Boston. Thousands of people run in it, but a lot of them don't make it. It is over twenty-six miles long. It's one of the hardest marathons because of the hills at the end."

"That's stupid," I exclaimed. "Why would anyone want to run that far? Especially an old lady like her."

"I don't think you had better let Aunt Henrietta hear you call her an 'old lady,' " Dad said. "Actually, Aunt Henrietta has competed in several big races all over the world. She has won some trophies, too. But this is the first chance she's had to run in the Boston Marathon. I'd like you kids to help her train. It's good exercise for you." He gave Tim a playful poke. "Running is good training for sports."

"What if somebody sees me?" Tim complained.

"He means, what if any girls see him," Caroline said.

"It's not just the running," Tim grumbled. "Aunt

Henrietta is a real pain. Yesterday Mary Ann Masters called. Aunt Henrietta told her I couldn't come to the phone because I was in the bathroom."

Dad looked puzzled. "Where were you?"

"I was in the bathroom," Tim explained. "But you don't tell that to the prettiest girl in the seventh grade."

"Ah." Dad nodded wisely. "Well, perhaps Aunt Henrietta didn't realize she was talking to the prettiest girl in the seventh grade."

"She really *is* a pain," Caroline agreed. "Every time we talk about something we've done, she knows some kid halfway around the world who did the same thing."

"Only better," Tim mumbled.

Dad turned to me. "I suppose you've got something to add?"

"I miss my own bedroom," I said. "And I hate it that Sam has to stay next door until April." That's when we were having the reunion.

Dad sighed. "I'm sorry you are all so unhappy, but Aunt Henrietta is a guest in our house. The Snodgrass family is always kind to guests. I'm counting on you all to make her feel at home."

Dad dropped Caroline and me off at play practice and headed to the hospital. For months we had been practicing in a church meeting room. Tonight was the first time we were in the theater where the play would be performed. It was a great old building, with a large stage and a huge seating area, that the town used for special events. This was also the first time we'd done the play all the way through with costumes and orchestra.

Marcia Stevens's mother was the director of the play. She looked like a general ordering around an army of parent volunteers. "Everyone go to the green room to get your props and costumes," she shouted over the noise.

We followed the crowd to a huge room in the basement. "This isn't a green room," I whispered to Caroline.

"You are so dumb," Caroline said. "The room where the cast waits during a play is always called a green room."

"Calling a yellow room green sounds pretty dumb to me," I retorted.

Caroline gave me a scornful look. But before she could say more, someone whisked her behind a curtain to help her get changed.

Someone else handed me a pair of bib overalls and showed me where to change.

Marcia was waiting when I was finished. She was wearing a gray wig and old-fashioned glasses, and her clothes were stuffed to make her look plump. She was playing the role of Aunt Polly.

"You look really good," I said.

"Thanks," she said. "You do, too." She paused. "You were talking to Brianne an awful lot today."

"I was just telling her about snow," I said.

Marcia sniffed unhappily. Just then Willie grabbed my arm and pulled me away. "They are putting lipstick on all the boys," he whispered in alarm. "I don't want any of that stuff on me."

Several mothers were rubbing makeup and lipstick on everyone. We stood in line waiting our turn. "I think it is so the people in the audience can see your face," I said.

Willie's grandmother was helping with makeup. She motioned to me. *"Buenas noches,* Martin. *¿Como está usted?"* She rubbed some makeup on my face and dabbed some red color on my lips.

"Grandma is learning Spanish," Willie explained. "She listens to tapes while she is sleeping."

"How can she learn if she is sleeping?" I asked.

Willie shrugged. "I don't know. But it must work. Grandma talks Spanish so much I'm going to have to learn so I can talk to her."

"They're called *subliminal* tapes. Even though you are asleep, a part of your mind hears and remembers," his grandmother explained.

"Why can't we just do that for school?" I asked.

" 'Cause grown-ups like to torture us," Willie said. He looked as if he were being tortured now. His grandmother had finished with me and was smearing

31

makeup on Willie while he squirmed with embarrassment.

"How can girls stand to wear this stuff?" he groaned.

"It will wash right off," his grandmother assured him. "Don't worry, all actors have to put this on."

"I'll bet Arnold Schwarzenegger doesn't," Willie grumbled.

"Oh yes he does," his grandmother answered cheerfully.

Willie still looked doubtful, but he stood still until his grandmother finished.

"You look positively beautiful," I teased.

Willie started to make a fist. Then he grinned. He took his hand and wiped off most of the lipstick. "So do you."

Mrs. Stevens came rushing by. "As soon as you are done here, go see the prop lady," she said.

The prop lady was passing things out in a corner of the yellow "green" room.

When we told her who we were, she checked her list and handed me a straw hat, a fishing pole, and an apple and Willie a can of paint and a brush.

"There's a little bit of real paint in here, so be careful. Just barely dip your brush in. We don't want any dripped on the stage."

My part was of a boy who is tricked by Tom into whitewashing Aunt Polly's fence. I was in the first scene of the play, which was lucky because I was starting to get nervous. My stomach was shaking and my hands were sweaty. I saw Caroline sitting by herself in a corner. She was so pale her freckles stood out like polka dots.

The New Albany High School Orchestra began tuning up, and then it was time for the play to begin. I picked up my pole and tried to look cheerful as I walked out onstage. Willie was there, busy painting the fence and whistling. A long planter filled with flowers sat in front of one end of the fence to make it look more real.

"Too bad you have to paint that old fence. I'm on my way fishing," I said. I reached in my pocket and pulled out the apple.

As Tom, Willie pretended he was having a wonderful time. "This is much more fun than fishing," he said. "Why, I'd choose this to do any day."

"You'd rather paint that fence than go fishing?" I asked.

"Sure would. Why, my aunt Polly picked me special to do this. She wouldn't let just anyone do it."

"Can I try it?" I asked. "I'll give you this apple."

"Well, maybe just for a little bit," Willie said. He handed me the bucket. I dipped my brush very carefully. From where I was standing I had to stretch over the planter to reach the fence. I leaned over, but the can of paint I was holding pulled me out of balance.

33

I reached for the fence with my other hand, trying desperately to stop myself from falling. Too late I realized my mistake. The fence was only a prop, and of course it couldn't hold me. Slowly the fence tipped over, taking me with it. At the same time the paint can slipped out of my hand and hit the stage with a loud thud. As it rolled away, white paint splattered on me and on Willie, making a big puddle all around the broken fence.

5

Getting Rid of Aunt Henrietta

THE REST OF the dress rehearsal was almost perfect. Willie managed to kiss Caroline without throwing up, and by the time Dad arrived most of the paint had been cleaned away. I still had some sticky spots where paint had dried in my hair.

"You won't believe what Martin did," Caroline tattled to Dad. "He almost managed to wipe out the whole theater production." She told him the whole story while I huddled miserably in the backseat. "Why do I have to be related to him?" Caroline finished with a dramatic wave of her hand. "It's so embarrassing."

"Mrs. Stevens said it could happen to anybody."

Caroline shook her head. "She was just being nice.

36

No one else in the whole world could be that clumsy. Our second run-through is tomorrow night, and that fence is a disaster!"

"I'm sure Martin feels bad enough without your rubbing it in," Dad said. "I'll call Anne Stevens and see if I can help repair the fence tomorrow," he added. "That should make up for it."

At home, Caroline repeated the story again for Mom and Aunt Henrietta.

"Oh, honey," Mom said to me. "You must have been so embarrassed."

Aunt Henrietta leaned back in her chair. "You don't know it yet, but that was one of the best things that ever happened to you."

"How can you say that?" I sputtered. "It was the worst thing. Everyone laughed at me."

Aunt Henrietta chuckled. "It does sound like it was pretty funny. You would have laughed too if it had happened to someone else. And one of these days you may laugh about it yourself. The Snodgrasses have always loved a good story. Fifty years from now, your children may still be talking about the time Dad almost wiped out the whole production of *Tom Sawyer*. Only by then the story will be that you set off a chain reaction that wiped out the entire set, sent three people to the hospital with broken legs, and spilled a fifty-gallon drum of paint over the entire theater."

I had to smile. "Like when Dad tells us he had to walk five miles to school in snow over his head?" I asked.

"Is that all?" Aunt Henrietta asked. She winked. "One time I had to ride my horse to school. The snow was so deep the poor horse could hardly walk. When I got there, the school was closed. That poor horse of mine was so tired I had to carry him twenty miles back home."

I laughed. "That beats Dad's stories."

"Well, I'm older than your father. My stories have had time to get bigger."

The next morning Willie was waiting for me when I got off the bus. *"Buenas días,"* he said. "That means good morning in Spanish. Grandma is kind of hard of hearing. She plays those tapes so loud I guess I'm learning it, too."

I stared at him. "Say that again."

"Buenas días," Willie repeated.

I waved my hand. "Not that. Tell me about the tapes."

"Grandma listens to her Spanish tapes while she sleeps and in the daytime, too," Willie said patiently. "I guess I'm learning some myself." He shrugged.

I snapped my fingers. "That's it. That's how I can get rid of Aunt Henrietta."

Willie looked blank for a moment. Then he slowly grinned. "You mean that we could make a tape telling her to go home."

"Exactly. If it works for your grandmother, it should work for Aunt Henrietta. I'll just wait until she's asleep and turn it on."

"You had better make the tape at my house. That way no one will find out," Willie said. "Call Mrs. Albright and see if you can come over after school."

Mrs. Albright agreed to pick me up and take me to the rehearsal, so as soon as school was over, Willie and I headed for his house. "Are you sure your grandmother won't mind?" I asked.

Willie's mother had left home when Willie was five. Now he and his father lived with his grandmother not very far from school. At first Willie and his grandmother hadn't gotten along very well. But working together in the play had brought them a lot closer.

"She won't mind," Willie said.

It had snowed the night before, just enough to make a pleasant crunch as we walked. Willie sang some of his favorite commercials, changing the words to make them funny.

"Wait up," Marcia called, running to catch up. She lived close by.

We waited for her. "Are you going to Willie's house?" she asked.

When I nodded, she added, "Why don't you both come home with me? I've got a new sled we could try out on the hill behind my house."

Willie's eyes lit up, and he looked hopefully at me. I thought about that hill. It was perfect for a sled ride. "Maybe for a few minutes," I said.

We stopped to pat Mitzi, Sam's mother, while Marcia took her book bag into the house. Mrs. Stevens made Mitzi stay outside in a little storage shed, but Marcia had made a warm box with rugs and blankets, and there was a little swinging door so Mitzi could go into the yard whenever she wanted to. "We found homes for all of her puppies," Marcia said happily when she returned. She pulled a shiny new sled out of a corner of the shed.

"Wow, that's great," I said. We spent the next half hour taking turns flying down the hill.

"I think my toes are frozen," I finally said.

"I know my fingers are." Willie laughed.

"Mom will make us some hot chocolate," Marcia said as we put the sled away.

We took off our boots and left them outside the door. Mrs. Stevens was pretty fussy about the house. Everything was always perfectly in place. She made us steaming cups of hot chocolate and set them on the kitchen table.

Marcia's family tree paper was displayed on the refrigerator door with a magnet. She noticed me looking at it. "I've almost got everyone filled out," she said. "See, one of my grandfathers was a judge."

"One of my great-uncles went to jail," Willie said cheerfully. "Maybe your grandfather was the judge who sent him there."

Mrs. Stevens's lips set in a disapproving line, but Marcia grinned. "That would be funny, wouldn't it."

"My great-grandfather died in World War II. He got the Medal of Honor for courage," Willie said.

Mrs. Stevens looked relieved. "Maybe you take after him," she said hopefully.

"I don't think so," Willie said. "I haven't noticed anything brave about myself. I think I am just me."

We sipped the drinks while our fingers and toes stopped tingling. "This was fun," I said. At times like these I didn't mind having Marcia for a girlfriend.

I looked at the clock and jumped up in alarm. "Mrs. Albright's picking me up at Willie's house at five," I said.

"You could watch for her from here," Marcia offered.

"I told my grandmother that Martin was coming," Willie fibbed as he pulled his coat on. I thought Marcia looked disappointed that we didn't ask her to come, too, but she didn't say anything. "See you tonight," she said as we left.

Willie's grandmother had fallen asleep watching TV. We tiptoed past her and up a narrow staircase. The house was old and the floors creaked, but I liked Willie's room, which had once been the attic. The ceiling slanted down on each side so that you had to duck your head, but Willie's father had paneled the walls and built shelves and dressers into the small spaces. Willie reached into a drawer and pulled out a tape recorder and a blank tape.

"What should I say?"

He shrugged. "Go home?" he suggested.

I hesitated. Aunt Henrietta had been awfully nice about my making a fool of myself at the dress rehearsal. Still, three more months of her was just too much. Determinedly I spoke into the recorder. "You are terribly homesick, Henrietta. You don't like New Albany. You really want to go home. Home is best."

I repeated it over and over until the tape was full. I switched off the machine.

"That sounded great," Willie said. "This has got to work."

I heard a honk in front of the house. I slipped the tape into my pocket and said good-bye to Willie. I was smiling when I got in the car. "You must have had a good time," Mrs. Albright remarked.

I nodded. I didn't tell her the real reason I was smiling. In no time at all we'd be rid of Aunt Henrietta.

6

Tonsils and Troubles

OUR SECOND DRESS rehearsal was pretty smooth. I managed to get through it without falling or spilling paint on anyone. I came home, dropped my things in Tim's room, and went back downstairs. Aunt Henrietta and Mom were sitting at the dining room table, busily writing invitations to the family reunion.

"I haven't seen Uncle George for years," Mom said. She looked up at me and smiled. "Do you remember Uncle George? He's a geologist. He travels all around the West looking for oil deposits. He visited us a couple of years ago."

I nodded. "He gave me a rock collection."

"One of his daughters is grown-up and married," Aunt Henrietta said thoughtfully. "We don't want to forget her."

I went upstairs to get ready for bed. Tim was sitting on the bottom bunk listening to my tape. He took it out of the player when I walked in the room.

"Hey, that's mine," I said, trying to grab it back.

Tim held it just out of my reach. " 'You want to go home,' " he mocked. He grinned finally and handed it to me. "That is pretty clever. Are you going to hypnotize Aunt Henrietta with it?"

I figured he was as anxious as I was to have Aunt Henrietta leave, so I explained.

"That's a great idea," Tim said thoughtfully. "But how are you going to know when she's asleep?"

"Caroline says she snores. She can hear her through the heating vent. I'm just worried that Aunt Henrietta might wake up and catch me when I turn the tape on."

Tim was silent for a minute. "I just thought of something gross," he said. "When you sneak into Aunt Henrietta's room, what if you see her in her nightgown? Or her underwear?"

"Oh no," I groaned, thinking about the possibility.

Then Tim snapped his fingers. "We'll put the tape recorder in Caroline's room, right by the vent. When she hears Aunt Henrietta snoring, Caroline can turn on the tape."

"Then we'd have to tell Caroline," I said reluctantly. "What if she tattles?"

Tim thought about that. "She can't. If she lets us

do it, she'd be in trouble, too. And if she says no, we'll deny the whole thing."

We took the recorder and knocked on Caroline's door. She agreed immediately.

When I looked surprised at how easy it had been to convince her, she shrugged. "She's driving me crazy. This afternoon after school I was watching TV. Aunt Henrietta spent ten minutes telling me about all the chores she had to do when she was my age."

The sound of Aunt Henrietta's voice drifted up the stairs. "I think I'll go to bed," she was telling Mom.

"Here we go," Tim said. " 'Operation Get Rid of Aunt Henrietta' is about to begin."

"Be sure to wait until you hear her snoring," I said.

"Unlike you," Caroline said in a haughty voice, "I am not a dimwit."

Tim and I scurried back to our room just as Aunt Henrietta started up the stairs. We listened for a while, but Tim's room was too far down the hall for us to hear.

The next morning I was awake before the alarm even went off. I jumped in my clothes and hurried down for breakfast.

Aunt Henrietta was already at the table, calmly spreading jelly on her toast. "Good morning, Martin," she said brightly.

Tim staggered into the kitchen and plopped down in his chair.

"Did you sleep well?" I asked.

Tim gave me a look, but Aunt Henrietta smiled. "Like a baby," she answered.

I ran back upstairs and caught Caroline before she came down. "You didn't play the tape, did you?"

Caroline was holding her throat. "I did. We will have to do it more than once. What did you expect? That she'd be packing her bags, ready to go?" She brushed past me and continued downstairs.

"You look kind of pale this morning," Aunt Henrietta told Caroline. "Are you feeling well?"

"I'm all right," Caroline said.

"Your voice sounds scratchy," Dad said. "Does your throat hurt?"

"A little," she admitted.

Dad felt her head. "Better come in the office and let me take a look," he said.

Dad's office was at the back of our house. I followed them into his examining room, hoping I could help. Lately I've been thinking that I might like to be a doctor when I grow up. Dad switched on the lights and told Caroline to climb up on the examining table. He looked down her throat and took her temperature. "Hmmm," he said.

"What does that mean?" she asked nervously.

"I think we need to take out those tonsils," he said. "You had trouble all last winter, and they really look bad."

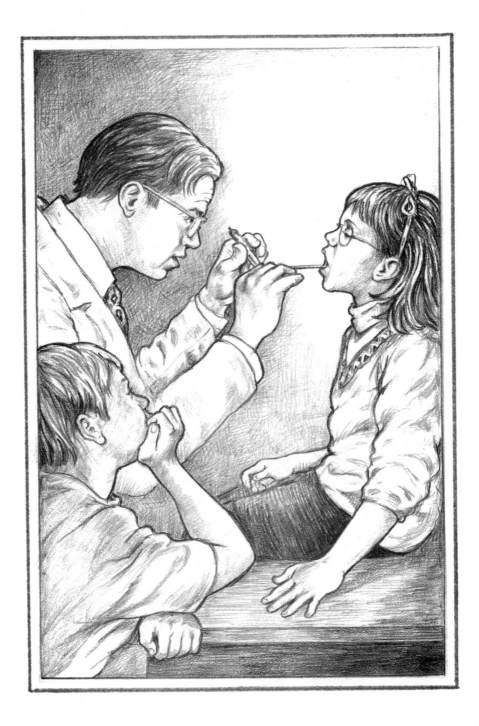

Caroline grabbed her throat with her hands. "You mean an operation?" she gasped. "It will hurt."

"Only a little," Dad said. He patted her back. "It's really not that bad. You won't even have to stay in the hospital overnight. It's certainly better than being sick all the time."

Then a worse thought struck me. "The first performance of the play is tonight," I said.

Dad shook his head. "Caroline's fever is a hundred and two. I'm sorry. The only place she is going is bed."

"I can't miss the play. Everyone is counting on me," Caroline wailed. "I've got one of the main parts."

"If we can get that fever down, you might be well enough to do the play tomorrow night and the Sunday matinee," Dad said as he gave Caroline some pills. I got her a drink of water and handed it to her. "But not tonight. Maybe someone else can do the part," Dad said.

"There isn't anyone," Caroline cried. "The whole play will be ruined. Everyone will hate me."

Dad hugged Caroline. "They won't hate you. You can't help being sick. Don't you have an understudy?"

Caroline blew her nose on the tissue Dad handed her. "I did. But she broke her leg in a bike accident!"

Dad made Caroline go to bed. When I passed her room a few minutes later, she was staring up at the ceiling, too unhappy to sleep. Dad told Mom the news, and a minute later she came into Caroline's room and felt her head. "How are you doing, honey?" she asked.

Caroline sat up. "Awful," she croaked. "It isn't fair. The whole play will be ruined—all because of my stupid tonsils. Nothing like this happens to other people."

"I missed the trip to the zoo last year when I had the chicken pox," I said.

"That's not the same," Caroline wailed. "Nobody hated you afterward."

"Marcia Stevens did," I said, grinning. "I gave them to her."

"It is a tough break," Mom agreed. "But no one is going to hate you for it. I'd better call someone at the Youth Theater."

"It's too late for anyone to learn my part," Caroline said.

"It's not that hard," I said without thinking. "I know it all from listening to you. I'll bet I know every word."

Caroline stared thoughtfully, making me realize what I had just said.

"Oh no," I said. "I'm not doing it. It's a girl's part."

"You and Caroline do look a little alike," Mom said. "You are almost the same size, so you could wear her costume."

"Absolutely not!" I shouted. "I'd have to kiss Willie Smith. I wouldn't care if you gave me a million dollars. I'm not doing it, and that's final."

7

To Kiss or Not to Kiss...

MOM HAD DECIDED to call Mrs. Stevens. She went downstairs to give her the bad news.

"You've got to do it," Caroline said. "Otherwise they'll have to cancel tonight's show."

I just shook my head.

Caroline changed her tune. "I wonder if Mom would like to hear about that tape and how kind you're being to Aunt Henrietta?"

"You wouldn't dare. You'd be in trouble, too."

"I don't think so," Caroline said. "I am awfully sick. And if I confess because I feel so bad for helping you . . ."

"I left a message," Mom announced as she came back into the room.

I glanced at Caroline. She smiled serenely and sank back on her pillow.

"I have to get ready for school," I said, backing out of the room. I brushed my teeth and scurried downstairs and out the front door.

Willie was nervous. I could tell because he just couldn't sit still. Miss Lawson scolded him several times. I decided it was best not to mention Caroline's problem. No need to get Willie upset. Maybe the grown-ups would have it solved by the time we got out of school.

During silent reading, Willie climbed up to the reading loft and sat beside me. He made jungle bird noises.

Miss Lawson peeked over the floor of the loft. "This is silent reading, Willie," she remarked. "You might find that a more interesting book if you read it right side up."

"Oops!" Willie said, turning the book. "I thought this was kind of a boring story."

"Perhaps we can forgive Willie for being so fidgety," Miss Lawson said to the rest of the class. "Tonight is the opening of the Youth Theater's production of *The Adventures of Tom Sawyer*, and Willie has the starring role. I dropped in at the dress rehearsal last night, and I can tell you it is a marvelous play. Several other students are in it, too. I hope you all are planning to see it."

51

At recess, Willie was still worried about kissing Caroline. I didn't tell him that he might be kissing someone else. "Just bend your head down and sort of kiss the air," I suggested. I puckered my lips and bent over to show him what I meant.

Two fifth-grade girls walked by. I turned the pucker into a whistle and bent over as if I were tying my shoe. "Fourth graders are soooo immature," one of them said.

"Good thinking," Willie said. "But next time you want to show me how to kiss, don't do it in school."

Caroline was bundled up on the couch watching television when I got home. "The surgeon can't do the operation for three more weeks," she said, sniffing. "That means it will be right before Valentine's Day."

I almost felt sorry for her. Then I remembered how she had threatened to tell about the tape. "Willie said when he had his tonsils out, the doctor just reached in and yanked them out," I teased.

"That's not true," Caroline gasped. "They put you to sleep. Willie doesn't even know what they did."

"Well, they did try to put him to sleep. But it didn't work. That happens sometimes, you know," I added wickedly. "Rrrip!"

"Mom!" Caroline screeched. "Martin's trying to scare me."

Mom came out of her study. She was frowning.

Just then I saw Mrs. Stevens's car pull up in our driveway.

"Why is she here?" I asked suspiciously.

"Well, she is the director of the play," Mom said. "We need to decide about what to do. We can't cancel the performance tonight. Every ticket has been sold. It's too late for anyone else to learn the part. But Mrs. Stevens thinks she's heard Caroline enough to do it. We've got the costume here."

"Oh no," Caroline groaned. "She'll ruin the whole play. She's too . . . old."

"There doesn't seem to be any other choice," Mom said. "Unless . . ." She looked at me hopefully.

"No!"

Aunt Henrietta had come into the living room. Even though I was saying no, I guess I already knew I was going to end up playing Becky Thatcher. I've only lived ten years, but there is one thing I've learned. A guy doesn't have a chance if a roomful of females want him to do something.

"I'm not kissing Willie Smith, no matter what," I said as Mrs. Stevens walked in the room. "And you have to promise that you won't tell anyone. And Caroline has to swear, too."

"Caroline has been so worried about the show that I'm sure she will promise," Mom said. "Tim will be out of town at his basketball game, so you don't have to worry about him teasing you."

Mrs. Stevens beamed at me. "I promise." She made a zipping motion with her lips. "Mum's the word," she said. She ran through the script with me to see if I really knew the part. "Oh, you are such a dear boy to do this," she said, practically gushing with relief. "Mayor Snodgrass, your children are just wonderful. You must be so proud of them."

Mom put her arm around my shoulder. "I am pretty proud of them. But we haven't got much time. We'd better try on the costume in case it needs to be altered."

I felt myself getting pale. I hadn't thought about that. Not only was I going to play a girl, I was going to have to dress like one. "Couldn't she be like a tomboy and wear jeans?" I pleaded.

"Girls didn't wear pants in those days," Mom answered.

"If you're going to do this thing, you might as well do it right," Aunt Henrietta put in. "Try to imagine yourself as a girl. Caroline's name is in the program. With a wig and some makeup, most people won't even know that it's not her."

"Do you think so?" I asked hopefully. "I wouldn't mind doing it so much if no one knew it was me."

"Let's see," Mom said. She pulled the dress over my head. Mrs. Stevens reached into a bag she had brought with her and produced a wig with long blond braids. Mom tugged it on and tucked in my own hair.

"It itches," I complained.

Mom looked thoughtful. "You don't really look like Caroline. But we might be able to convince them that you are somebody else. A cousin, perhaps. We could put makeup on to cover your freckles."

Mrs. Albright came into the living room to say good night. She was going out to dinner with Mr. DeWitt. She had agreed to stay with Caroline later while Mom and Dad went to the play.

"Could we borrow your name?" Mom asked.

"Agnes?" replied Mrs. Albright.

Mom nodded. "You could be Cousin Agnes from Columbus," she said to me.

Mrs. Stevens clapped her hands. "Oh, this is sooo much fun. I know just how we can do it, too. There is a small room next to the ticket window. Martin, you'll go to the green room with everyone else. They will all see you do your part. But instead of your going back to the green room, we'll say you are sick and had to go home. Then you go to the other room and change your clothes."

"Won't people wonder why Cousin Agnes is not in the green room?" I asked.

"Just say that she needs the time to look over her part, since she hasn't had a chance to practice," Aunt Henrietta suggested. "Actually, you probably could use the time to look over each scene."

For the next two hours everyone worked frantically

56

to turn me into Cousin Agnes. I had to practice walking and sitting like a girl. Robbie got up from his nap and watched. He liked my wig.

"Martin has new hair," he said, reaching up to pat it.

"It's pretend," I said. "I can take it off, see?"

Robbie tugged at his own hair. "Ow. Robbie's hair is stuck."

"That's real hair." I laughed.

Robbie stopped pulling his hair and patted the dress. "Martin has pretty dress. Like Mommy."

I groaned. "What if Robbie tells?"

"He'll forget all about it by tomorrow," Mom said. "If he says anything tonight, people will just think he's playing."

At last Mrs. Stevens looked at her watch. It was 5:30. "I'd better get home. Marcia will be worried."

I looked up in alarm. "Don't tell Marcia."

"I can't tell her that your cousin Agnes is filling in for Caroline?" she asked, giving me a big wink.

After she left, Mom helped me take off the dress. We ate a quick dinner. We had to be at the theater at 6:30, even though the play didn't start until 8:00 P.M. Caroline was huddled on the couch, feeling miserable, when I left. I felt sorry for her until she opened her mouth. "Don't mess up, dinosaur breath," she hissed.

When we arrived at the theater, Mom took the costume for "Cousin Agnes" into the small room Mrs. Stevens had mentioned. "Now remember, as soon as you are done with your part, say you are not feeling well and come here," she reminded me.

Willie already had his costume and makeup on when I walked into the yellow green room. "Hey, where's your sister?" he asked.

"She's sick," I explained. "Don't worry. Our cousin Agnes is coming from Columbus to take her part."

Willie looked as if he were about to explode. "Oh, man, everything will be ruined."

"Don't worry," I repeated soothingly. "Cousin Agnes knows the part. Really."

Willie still looked doubtful. "I never knew you had a cousin named Agnes," he said. "What is she like?"

"She, uh, is kind of a tomboy," I said.

"Is she cute?"

I gulped. "A little."

Willie sighed. "Good. Maybe it won't be so awful to kiss her." Then he gave me a suspicious look. "How come she knows the part?"

"Her school put on the same play and she was Becky Thatcher," I said, thinking quickly.

"I don't know," Willie said. "It's going to be pretty hard doing the play with someone new."

"Cousin Agnes is real easy to get to know," I said. "I'll bet after a few minutes you'll feel like she's an old friend."

8

Cousin Agnes

WILLIE WALKED ONTO the stage and poked his head through the stage curtains. "The theater is almost full. I don't see your family," he said.

"Dad and Aunt Henrietta are coming at the last minute," I said. "They didn't want Robbie to get restless waiting for the play to start. Mrs. Albright is staying home with Caroline. She and Mr. DeWitt will be here tomorrow night."

Willie tapped his foot anxiously. "Are you sure your cousin Agnes is coming? Columbus is pretty far."

"Don't worry," I said. "She'll be here."

"Why isn't she in the green room?" Willie asked.

I shrugged. "Maybe Mom is helping her with her costume."

Marcia Stevens came out on the stage with us. I could hardly recognize her with her wig and granny glasses. It made me feel better about being Cousin Agnes.

"Mom says it's almost time. I am sooo nervous," she confessed. "I heard about Caroline getting sick. I wish we could meet your cousin. Are you sure she'll know what to do? I hope I don't forget my lines."

"Marcia," I almost shouted when I could fit in a word, "you'll be great. Calm down. You're making me nervous listening to you."

I ran back to the green room. The prop lady handed me my fishing pole, the apple, and the straw hat. I took my shoes and socks off and rolled up my pants legs.

Mrs. Stevens scooted us all into position. The lights dimmed, and the orchestra played while the curtains slowly opened. The spotlight centered on a part of the stage made to look like a little house. Aunt Polly was scolding Tom. For the first few lines her voice sounded nervous. But then she seemed to forget about the audience, and her voice grew stronger as she told Tom he had to whitewash their picket fence. Marcia was great. She sounded just like a grouchy old lady. Willie was perfect, too. Tom picked up his brush, and the spotlight swung to the other side of the stage, where the fence and window box props were set up. He gave a loud unhappy sigh and started painting.

"You're on," said Mrs. Stevens, giving me a little push.

I did my part just right. The audience laughed when Tom finally gave in and allowed me to do his work for him. I picked up the brush and very carefully started painting the fence. Several other boys joined us, each one giving Tom a bribe.

The audience seemed to be enjoying the scene. Out of the corner of my eye I could see Dad, Robbie, and Aunt Henrietta in the very first row.

I only had a few minutes, while Aunt Polly admired the freshly painted fence and then the scenery was changed, to transform myself into Becky Thatcher. I raced past Carrie, one of the scenery changers. "I'm sick," I moaned. "I have to go home." I knew Carrie had a big mouth. In a few minutes everyone would think I had really left. I raced to the stage door. Then, at the last second, I swerved and slipped through the door next to the ticket window.

The room was somebody's office, with a desk and file cabinets along one wall. Mom jumped up from the only chair and threw the dress over my head. "We have to hurry," she said. She buttoned the dress in the back while I pulled on the wig and tucked my own hair underneath. Next Mom made me up.

"Hold still," she warned, "or these rosy cheeks will be on your forehead."

At last she slipped on my nose a pair of old-fashioned glasses without any glass in them and stood back, giving her creation a critical eye. "Hmm," she said. "Not bad."

I looked in the mirror. "Do I look like a girl?"

"I'd never guess it was you," Mom said.

"Really?" I asked.

Mrs. Stevens came to the door. "Hurry," she said. "You look wonderful," she added as we hurried back to the stage.

Finally we got to the scene where Tom and Becky Thatcher are in the schoolhouse, and Becky promises to marry Tom. I watched carefully to see if Willie recognized me, but I could see that he hadn't.

"Now that we're engaged," Tom finally said, "we have to seal it with a kiss."

I hid my face behind my apron and pretended to be bashful. "Please?" Tom said. "Just a little kiss?" Willie's face was blazing red, even through the makeup. This close, I was certain he would recognize me, but he was too embarrassed to look straight at me. Instead he stared at the bow in my hair.

I leaned forward to kiss the air, the way we'd practiced. I thought Willie was going to do the same. But at the last minute he must have decided to do it for real. He turned toward me just as I turned aside. Fortunately, our lips never met. Actually, it was our heads that met. We banged our heads together so hard that we both staggered back.

Willie recovered first. "Wow!" he said, thinking quickly. "That was a powerful kiss."

The audience roared with laughter. Willie leaned over and whispered, "Sorry, Agnes."

I couldn't believe it. Even this close, he didn't recognize me. This might be fun after all.

"That's quite all right, William," I said in a sugary voice.

The rest of the play went perfectly. At the end the whole cast came out to the front of the stage. Willie bowed first, and the audience clapped and cheered. Then it was my turn. "Hi, Martin," Robbie shouted as I walked to the edge of the stage in my dress and wig. I saw Dad trying to hush him, but luckily the clapping drowned out the sound of his voice before he said anything more.

I noticed Willie giving me a strange look as the rest of the cast took their bows, but I needn't have worried. After the show, he came running up to me. "You did a great job, Agnes."

"Thank you," I said, looking around for a way to make a quick escape.

"Do you think you will be here tomorrow?" he asked. He gave me a shy smile. Willie was flirting with me!

"Maybe Caroline will be better by tomorrow," I said quickly.

Mrs. Stevens came along and practically dragged us toward the theater lobby. "Everyone is waiting to congratulate the actors," she said.

Parents were crowding around the cast, telling

them what a good job they'd done. I squeezed my way to the small office, keeping my head down. Mom was waiting to help me change. "You did it," she said, hugging me. "You were terrific. Are you sure you don't want to just tell everyone it was you? You did such a good job."

I thought about it. "Willie was flirting with 'Agnes,'" I said. "I think that it's better for both of us if Agnes just goes home to Columbus and is never heard from again."

9

Girl Problems

ON SATURDAY AFTERNOON, Aunt Henrietta bundled up in a bright purple jogging suit and tied bows in her running shoes.

Caroline's fever was down. Dad had reluctantly agreed she could be in the play that evening, even though her voice still sounded scratchy. However, he insisted that she stay in bed until then. Tim was at another basketball game. His team had won five straight games. I figured he'd have another trophy pretty soon. At the rate he was piling up trophies, there wouldn't be space for me in his bedroom much longer. I was really tired of sleeping in there by now. Every time I passed my room and saw Aunt Henrietta's things in it, I felt unhappy. My desk was covered with papers because she was writing to all the relatives, asking them to attend the reunion. Her fuzzy pink bathrobe hung on my door, and my closet was full of her clothes.

"Coming with me?" she asked.

I hesitated. "I don't want to get tired out before the play."

"You youngsters today," Aunt Henrietta said with a shake of her head. "None of you has any pep. Why, when I was a girl, we had to run a mile just to get to the outhouse."

"Why don't you ride your bike," Mrs. Albright suggested. "You could put a leash on Sam and let him run with you."

"That sounds like a good idea," Aunt Henrietta said. "Sam won't bother me outside. It's only when I'm shut up in a room with a dog that I start sneezing."

I was trapped again. I went upstairs to get my coat. Robbie was in the bathroom. "Come see, Martin," he sang out proudly.

I checked to make certain no toys were in the toilet, then let him flush. Robbie watched as the water swirled down the drain. "All gone," he said proudly.

Robbie followed me downstairs. Aunt Henrietta was finishing her warm-up stretches. He and Aunt Henrietta barked at each other while I zipped up my coat and went next door to get Sam. Robbie was rolling on the floor giggling when I returned.

I rode my bike beside Aunt Henrietta as she jogged along, slowly at first, then faster and faster. Sam tugged at the leash, wanting to examine every bush. I had to pull the leash to keep up. Aunt Henrietta was tall and bony, but when she ran, she no longer looked awkward. She ran smoothly, her feet hardly seeming to touch the ground. She was smiling, and I could tell she really enjoyed running. Even riding a bike, I was already huffing by the time we started back, but Aunt Henrietta was hardly panting at all.

After a quick dinner, Mom drove Caroline and me to the theater. Mrs. Stevens made a big fuss about how nice it was to have Caroline back. The play was a big hit again, but on the ride home Caroline was fuming. "Everyone kept telling me how great 'Agnes' was in the play last night," she said.

"Martin did your part to help *you*," Mom reminded her.

"He didn't have to do it better than me," she stormed. "He's such a show-off."

There was one more performance Sunday afternoon, and luckily by that time no one was talking about "Cousin Agnes" anymore. The newspaper ran a story about the production. In addition to praising Willie's performance, the article said that Caroline was the perfect Becky Thatcher. Marcia was also singled out, and there was a lot of information about the Youth Theater.

Everyone was sad to see the curtain come down

on the last performance. We had a cast party, and the parent volunteers bought pizza for the cast, musicians, and crew. "I hope you will all try out next year," Mrs. Stevens said. There was a lot of talking and laughing, but no one wanted to leave. We had worked so hard, and now it was all over.

"Too bad Agnes had to miss this," Willie said.

"She said to tell you all good-bye," I lied smoothly.

"I liked her," Willie said. "She was real pretty."

"How could you tell with all that makeup she had on?"

"I could just tell," Willie said. He leaned close to me. "Did she say anything about me?"

"Er, no," I answered.

"Too bad," Willie said in his best Tom Sawyer voice. "I sure took a fancy to her."

Plays are sort of like Christmas, I found out. The best part is getting ready. For the next few days everyone talked about our play, but then it was forgotten until it seemed almost like a dream— although Willie kept asking when I was going to see Agnes. The weather had turned even colder and drearier. It snowed a few times, but not enough to be pretty or even to make a snowman. At school we divided up in groups to research different states. I was hoping to be in Brianne's California group. California seems to be a pretty interesting state. They were looking up things about the Gold Rush and pioneers and earthquakes. I was working with Steve and Lester, and our state was Iowa. I'll bet the people who live in Iowa like it fine, but it was not the most interesting state to have for a report.

Nothing had been said about Caroline's tonsils, and I think she was hoping Dad would just sort of forget about them. But then both of us got sick again and we missed almost a week of school. Dad scheduled her surgery for the Thursday before Valentine's Day.

When I got back to school, everyone was working on a relief map of the states. I found myself next to Willie. "Hasn't the tape worked yet?" he whispered.

I shook my head. "We've been playing it right along. This morning at breakfast, Aunt Henrietta was talking about how much she likes it here."

Marcia crumbled some brown paper to make the Rocky Mountains. She leaned close and gave me a smile as though we were sharing a big secret. "Are you talking about Valentine's Day? I am sooo excited. It's next week, you know."

Miss Lawson had already decorated the room with big paper hearts. Mrs. Headly, the art teacher, had promised to help us make boxes to hold the valentines. I thought that was a great idea. In third grade, valentines were just passed out. I had worried about Valentine's Day for weeks before the big day. I even had a nightmare about it. In my dream all the other kids had stacks of valentines on their desks. I didn't have a single one. Of course, it hadn't happened. But I was still glad that this year we all had our own boxes. That way no one would know who got the most valentines.

Now there were only a few days left. Valentine's Day was on a Sunday this year, but Miss Lawson had promised a party on Friday afternoon, and Marcia's mother was making cupcakes.

I had a feeling Marcia was expecting something special for Valentine's Day. The problem was that I wasn't sure I wanted to give something special to Marcia. Actually, I thought I might like to give something special to Brianne. On the other hand, I liked Marcia, and I didn't want to make her unhappy. Besides that, I wasn't even sure Brianne liked me. Or maybe she liked me the way I liked Marcia. It was confusing.

Finally I decided to ask Tim for advice. I figured he knew a lot about girls. Every night at least three girls called him. Tim acted as if that really bothered him. "Again?" he grumbled when the phone rang. Then he'd sigh and roll his eyes. But I noticed that he never refused to talk. As a matter of fact, he always took the phone and hid in the bathroom so no one could hear, and he was usually smiling when he came out.

"I'd just let them fight over me," Tim said. "May the best girl win."

"That's stupid. What if you don't like the winner?"

Tim shrugged. "Girls are all the same."

"They are not the same. Marcia likes everyone to follow the rules. She also likes dogs and sledding, and she can be lots of fun. Brianne is quiet and sweet, and she has a funny laugh."

Tim didn't seem to hear. He examined his lip in the mirror. "Does that look like hair to you?"

Caroline suddenly appeared at the door. I supposed she'd been listening all along. "Everyone has hair on their upper lip."

Tim looked again. "I think it looks thicker than usual."

Caroline peered closer. "Nope. Just baby fuzz," she said cheerfully.

Tim's face fell. "You can see it, can't you, Martin?"

I looked again. "Well, maybe a little."

Tim danced with glee. "I knew it. I'm probably going to have to shave pretty soon."

"Pretty soon, like in three years." Caroline snorted.

"Forget shaving," I said. "What about my problem?"

"At least you can tell the difference between girls," Caroline said, sounding almost friendly. "Tim here has been so busy playing sports the only thing he knows about girls is that they're not boys."

The next morning everyone brought a shoe box to art class and covered it with foil and red hearts. Then we cut a hole in the top of each.

"Now no one will know who gets the most valentines," Rochelle complained. Rochelle was the most popular girl in class, so she wanted everyone to see how many cards she got.

"I'm cutting the hole in my box extra big," Marcia said, "in case anyone gives me an extra-special valentine." She gave me a big smile.

Brianne was working at my table. She had made little lace hearts on the top of her box. "That looks nice," I said.

"Thank you," she said. "So does yours."

I looked at my box. All my hearts looked more like red lumps than hearts. "I'm not very good at making hearts," I said.

"I've got some left over." She handed me some perfectly shaped hearts.

She started to help me paste them on. Marcia gave me a lacy white heart. "Why don't you put this one on," she said, glaring at Brianne. "Then our boxes will match."

Art class ended while I was still deciding what to do. We went back to our room, and Mrs. Lawson gave us our spelling practice test. Next we had math. Every time I looked at Brianne, she was looking at me and smiling.

Miss Lawson wrote some problems on the board. I saw Jamie pass Charles a note, and Charles passed it to me.

Jessica told me that Brianne likes you.

Do you like her?
*Yes*_____ *No*_____

I checked the "Yes" and sent it back.

Willie was humming a beer commercial. Miss Lawson turned from the board, where she had been showing us how to subtract fractions. "Willie, are you paying attention?"

Willie nodded. "I can think better when I hear music."

"I don't believe that is true for everyone in the room," Miss Lawson said. "Although that might make an interesting experiment for science class."

I sighed with relief. She hadn't seen the note. Miss Lawson was pretty strict about notes. Any time she found one, she read it out loud.

Miss Lawson turned back to the board. Then she turned around suddenly. "By the way, Charles, you dropped the note you were passing," she said. She walked to his desk and held out her hand.

Charles reached under his desk and reluctantly handed her the note. Miss Lawson unfolded it.

"Unfortunately, the note isn't signed. But it seems to concern a rumor that Brianne likes someone. This certain someone returns your affection, Brianne."

Several of the boys whistled. Brianne slipped down in her seat and covered her face. I felt my face getting hot, but I stared at the ceiling and tried not to look guilty.

"Friday is our Valentine's party," Miss Lawson said. "Perhaps that would be a better time to express your feelings."

Marcia twisted around in her seat and stared at me. I pretended to concentrate on fractions.

After lunch, Marcia was waiting for me on the playground. "Brianne was really embarrassed about that note," she said.

I nodded, dreading the next question.

"Who wrote it?"

"I'm not sure," I said truthfully.

"It must have been Charles," Marcia said. "The note was under his desk."

Luckily for me, Willie ran over to us at that very minute. "Hey, Snodgrass. Do you think your cousin Agnes will be here on Valentine's Day?"

"I-I don't think so," I stammered. "She doesn't come very often."

"Well then, could you give me her address? I want to send her a valentine," Willie said.

"I think it's unlisted," I said.

Willie stared at me. "Your cousin has an unlisted address?"

I thought frantically. "Her father is like an undercover investigator. He's probably put a lot of people in jail. So they have to be careful. No one is allowed to know their address."

Willie whistled. "Wow! You sure have a lot of interesting people in your family."

Willie was so impressed with my story that it made me feel guilty. But it was better than telling him he had almost kissed me.

Willie leaned close and whispered, as though telling a secret, "Are you sure you couldn't give it to her? It's really pretty. Lots of mushy lace and stuff."

I felt my face growing red. "Did you really like her that much? You only saw her for one play."

Willie held his hand over his heart. "That was enough. From the first moment I was in love. And when we kissed . . ."

My face was blazing. "Wait a minute. You didn't kiss. You bumped heads, remember?"

"How did you know that?" Willie asked. He was smiling broadly.

"Er, my cousin told me," I said.

Willie suddenly burst out laughing. "Was that before or after you put on the dress?"

"You knew all this time?"

"You should see how red your face is." Willie started laughing so hard he could only nod. Finally he stopped laughing long enough to say, "You fooled me for a few minutes. I was pretty suspicious, though. Then when Robbie yelled your name, I knew for sure. Actually, I had a little talk with Robbie one day when I was at your house. He told me all about your 'pretend' hair."

By the end of the day everyone knew that I had been Agnes. Surprisingly enough, although everyone teased me about believing Willie was in love with Agnes, no one said anything awful about my acting the part of a girl. I had done all that worrying about getting caught for nothing.

Mr. DeWitt was sitting on his porch petting his cat, Daffy, when I got off the school bus. "Did you come to see Sam?" he asked.

"Actually, I wanted to talk to you," I said. I let Sam out of the house for a romp and sat down next to Mr. DeWitt.

Mr. DeWitt picked up a seed catalog from the table beside his chair. "Are we going to plant a garden this year?" Mr. DeWitt asked. Last summer he had helped me grow a prize-winning pumpkin for the fair.

"Sure," I said. Then I sighed.

"You are looking pretty glum," Mr. DeWitt remarked.

"I have girl trouble," I admitted. "Marcia Stevens thinks I'm her boyfriend. She's expecting a really fancy valentine. But I sort of like a girl named Brianne."

"And you want to give her a fancy valentine," Mr. DeWitt finished for me. "Why don't you give them both one?"

"Then Marcia will be mad," I said glumly. "This boyfriend stuff is hard. I like Marcia. She's the one who gave me Sam. I just wish I didn't have to be her boyfriend."

Mr. DeWitt shook his head. "Hmm. You do have a problem. Have you tried explaining this to Marcia?"

I shook my head. "She'd be mad."

"Well, I have generally found it's best to be truthful with people."

"Maybe I should give them both a nice card, but not sign my name on Brianne's," I said thoughtfully.

"You mean like signing it from 'your secret admirer'?"

"That's a great idea," I said.

Mr. DeWitt stroked Daffy's soft fur.

"I wish I could figure out some way to make Marcia not want to be my girlfriend," I said.

"You'll have to figure that one out yourself," Mr. DeWitt answered.

"Did you get Mrs. Albright a valentine?" I asked.

Mr. DeWitt nodded. "I got her a big mushy one. And a box of chocolates."

"I'll bet she'll like that," I said.

"I hope so," he said.

Sam bounded across the yard and up on Mr. DeWitt's porch. He sniffed Daffy, wanting to play. Daffy hunched up her back and hissed. She growled low in her throat. Sam just wagged his tail.

"I don't think Daffy likes Sam." I laughed. I took Sam inside Mr. DeWitt's house and gave him his supper.

"Good luck with your problem," Mr. DeWitt called after me as I walked back to my own house.

I sighed. I had a feeling I needed more than good luck to solve this problem.

10

Tonsils and Toy Soldiers

MOM AND DAD took Caroline to the hospital very early Thursday morning.

"It's not that bad," I said when I saw her scared look. "Willie told me that when he had his tonsils out he got to eat all the ice cream he wanted."

Caroline made a face. "I don't even like ice cream," she said.

"You ought to tell the doctor to put your tonsils in a jar," Tim joked. "Then you could take them to school for show-and-tell."

Caroline rolled her eyes. "Oh, and wouldn't that make me the most popular girl in school." She pretended to be flirting. "Come on over here, handsome, and I'll show you some pickled tonsils."

"I'd think it was interesting," I said.

"Me too," Tim said.

Caroline looked back with a withering glance as she walked out the door. "Of course *you* two would."

"Poor Caroline," I said after she left. "She's going to miss Valentine's Day."

I followed Tim to the kitchen. "That's baby stuff," he said. "We don't do that in seventh grade." He rummaged though the cupboards looking for something to eat. "I wish Mrs. Albright hadn't taken the day off."

"She's going to Columbus with Mr. DeWitt," I said. "He's going to take her to the art museum and then to a show."

I took two bowls out of the cupboard and put them on the table. "You're lucky you don't have to worry about valentines," I said. "I have to buy two fancy ones."

Aunt Henrietta bustled into the kitchen just as Tim started to pour cereal into a bowl. She was wearing the fuzzy pink robe and slippers. She looked sleepy. "Wait," she said. "I promised your mother I'd fix breakfast."

"We like cereal," Tim said.

"No, no," she fussed. "Breakfast is the most important meal of the day. Now, you two go get ready for school. By the time you are done, I'll have something ready."

"If Mrs. Albright marries Mr. DeWitt, I'll bet Aunt Henrietta will stay forever," Tim whispered glumly as we climbed the stairs.

Robbie jumped off the toilet as we walked in the bathroom.

"I went," he said proudly. He suddenly looked guilty. "I flush now."

"Wait," I yelled. I checked to make sure there was nothing that shouldn't be flushed. Sure enough, a little toy soldier settled slowly to the bottom.

"He wants to go round and round," Robbie said, reaching for the handle.

I grabbed his hand away. "It will plug up the toilet," I scolded. "What are we going to do?" I asked Tim.

"I'm not reaching in there," Tim said, wrinkling his nose.

"Well, I'm not either." I sighed and said, "I'll go tell Aunt Henrietta."

I carried Robbie downstairs and explained the problem to Aunt Henrietta. I expected her to yell, or at least act upset. Instead, she chuckled and said, "That little rascal is sure stubborn." Then she calmly put on a disposable plastic glove and bounded upstairs.

Now that the crisis was over, I went back upstairs and got ready for school. By the time I helped Robbie get dressed and was back in the kitchen, Tim was already sitting at the table.

"I decided cereal would be all right," Aunt Henrietta said, "if we dressed it up a little." She had sliced bananas on the cereal, and there was a plate of bacon and another with warm blueberry muffins.

She poured us some orange juice, fixed Robbie's breakfast, and sat down.

"This looks good," Tim said. He wolfed down two blueberry muffins before I'd even poured milk on my cereal.

Aunt Henrietta smiled. "We are starting to get answers back from relatives who are coming to the reunion," she remarked. "Your cousins John and Vickie are coming all the way from Seattle."

"Do they have any kids?" I asked.

"I remember them," Tim said. "They stayed overnight one time. You were too little to remember. Cousin John snored so loud the house shook. They had a boy named Jason. He broke all my crayons."

"I don't think I have them on the family tree," I said. I'd hung the paper on the refrigerator, the way Marcia had hers, and I'd been filling in all the names I'd heard.

Aunt Henrietta peered at the tree. "I'm not sure they would even fit. John's father was the son of your grandfather's brother. So John is your father's first cousin, once removed, and your second cousin."

I shook my head. "It's hard to keep track of everyone. I never knew I was related to so many people."

"There are a lot of us," Aunt Henrietta agreed.

"Are Matt, Corey, and Tabitha coming?" I asked, naming our cousins from a nearby town.

Aunt Henrietta consulted her list. "Their parents

were some of the first to accept," she said.

Tim stuffed a last bit of bacon in his mouth. "Matt is pretty good at sports, too. Maybe we can organize some contests."

I looked at the long list of names that had accepted the invitation and sighed. I could picture it all now. It wasn't bad enough to live in a family of fabulous people. Now I was going to spend a whole weekend with fifty more of them.

"I didn't know it was so late," said Tim as he slid back his chair and grabbed his book bag. "I'm going to miss my bus." He dashed out the door. Through the window I saw the bus come to a stop just as he made it to the end of the drive.

I picked up another blueberry muffin. "Is there anyone in our family who is just ordinary?" I asked.

"I am," Aunt Henrietta answered cheerfully.

"You're not ordinary. You've lived all over the world."

"I have lived in some pretty interesting places," Aunt Henrietta said. "But I was just a schoolteacher. That is not *extra*ordinary." She smiled. "And I always wanted to do something extraordinary. I guess that's why I want to be in the Boston Marathon."

I gulped down my milk. It was almost time for my bus. "Do you think you will win?" I asked.

Aunt Henrietta chuckled. "I'm about forty years too late for that. I'll be happy if I just finish."

11

Be My Valentine

CAROLINE WAS JUST getting home when I arrived after school. She looked tired and pale and didn't answer when I asked how she felt. Mom helped her upstairs to bed.

"She doesn't feel much like talking," Dad said. "Her throat will be pretty sore for the next couple of days."

Tim walked in and overheard what Dad said. "Hooray," he exclaimed. "Two days without listening to Caroline."

I felt like cheering, too, but the stern look Dad gave Tim made me change my mind.

"Dad, can you drive me to the drugstore to get some valentines? The party is tomorrow," I reminded him.

"Why did you wait until now to ask?" Dad asked, throwing his arms up in the air.

"It's my fault," Mom said as she came downstairs. "He asked me two weeks ago. Dad needs to get back to his office, Martin, but we can go while Caroline is asleep."

Mom took me to the drugstore and I looked through the boxes on display. There wasn't much of a choice. I sighed, thinking about how easy it had been to choose when I was younger. But now I discarded box after box.

"These are nice," Mom said. She held up a box of superhero ones.

"Too babyish," I grumbled.

"Well, how about these?" Mom suggested.

I looked at them. "Too mushy."

I finally found an assortment of funny ones that seemed all right. "I have to buy a fancy card, too," I said as I started hunting through the rack.

Mom held up a pretty card. "Marcia would like this one," she said.

"It's not for Marcia," I mumbled. I had decided that if I didn't give Marcia a special valentine, she'd get the message.

"Oh." Mom looked surprised.

Just then I saw the perfect card. It had a glittering red heart. *From your secret admirer,* read the words on the front, just as Mr. DeWitt had said. I grabbed it before Mom could ask any more questions.

85

We bought some candy hearts to slip a treat into everyone's envelopes, then headed home.

Usually Mom helped me with my valentine cards. She would write each name on the envelope while I wrote *From Martin* on the card. But this year she was too busy running upstairs tending to Caroline. Now I had all these cards to finish in one night, plus a science test to study for. I also had a book report due in two days, and I hadn't even finished half the book. With a sigh I sat down with the list of names Miss Lawson had sent home.

"Would you like some help?" Aunt Henrietta asked. When I nodded gratefully, she picked up the list and started writing the names on the envelopes in her thin and spidery handwriting.

"Did you have valentines when you were in school?" I asked as we worked.

Aunt Henrietta read one of them and chuckled. "Not like these." She pointed to the card I'd picked out for Brianne. "What name do you want on this card?"

I grabbed the envelope. "I'll do that one," I said.

I looked through the pile of valentines for one to give Marcia. None of them seemed quite right.

"You haven't picked a card for Marcia," Aunt Henrietta said, checking the list.

"I think I will make her one," I said.

Aunt Henrietta's eyebrow went up a notch, but she

didn't say anything. She went upstairs and came back with a large white envelope. "You won't be able to fit a homemade card in those dinky envelopes," she said, pointing to the remaining boxed cards.

I stuffed the other envelopes in a paper bag and took a piece of colored paper to my room. First I drew a large heart. It turned out crooked, as mine usually did, but I guessed it didn't matter. I tapped my pencil against my teeth while I thought. Finally I wrote:

> *Violets are blue,*
> *Roses are pink,*
> *I'd be your valentine*
> *If your feet didn't stink.*

Perfect. Marcia would probably never speak to me again. I tried not to think about the day Marcia had let me pick out Sam, and the fun we'd had sledding. I slipped the card into Aunt Henrietta's envelope and stuffed it into my sack.

The next morning I rode my bike to school so I could be there early. I did a quick check around the playground as I parked my bike in the rack. I was in luck. There was no sign of Brianne or Marcia. But I had to hurry. Already the playground was starting to fill up.

"You are very early this morning," Mr. Higgen-bottom, the principal, said as I walked through the door.

"I, er, wanted to pass out these valentines," I said.

"Hey, Snodgrass," a voice said behind me. Mr. Higgenbottom frowned. Willie Smith was not his favorite person.

Willie held up an old beat-up sack and brushed off some streaks of dried mud. "Almost lost my valentines," he said cheerfully. "I dropped them while I was riding my bike."

Mr. Higgenbottom stared suspiciously after us as we walked down the hall. Miss Lawson was already in the room. "Good morning, boys. I was just going to the storage room to get the video player. I have a movie for the party this afternoon. Martin, do you suppose you could help me?"

I hesitated. "It will only take a few minutes," Miss Lawson said.

Willie was passing out his cards. I handed him my cards. "Will you pass these out for me? The big white envelope is for Marcia."

"Sure," Willie said, grabbing the sack.

I followed Miss Lawson to the storage room. It was locked, and we had to find the custodian to get the key. By the time we got back to our room, all the other kids were there, and it was almost time for the bell.

"Don't worry," Willie said. "I passed yours out. I figured the other big envelope was for Brianne, right?"

I nodded gratefully. "Thanks," I said.

Willie pulled a slightly grimy card out of his back pocket. "I bought this fancy card to tease you about 'Agnes.' But now I'll just throw the envelope away and give the card to somebody else."

"Martin, could you go back and ask the custodian for an extension cord?" Miss Lawson asked.

"Sure," I said. I ran down and got the cord. By the time I returned, the bell had already rung. Willie was in his seat making a paper airplane out of the old envelope. I wondered who had gotten "Agnes's" card.

"This afternoon we'll have our party and you can open your cards," Miss Lawson said. "But this morning we are going to review for our social studies quiz."

Willie let out a loud war cry: "Ahh, ahh, ahh!"

Mrs. Lawson frowned. "I don't think that will be on the test, Willie. But perhaps you could tell us what kind of houses the Iroquois people built."

Willie grinned. "Longhouses. They were made out of logs, and more than one family lived inside."

"Very good," Mrs. Lawson said.

Finally it was time for the party. Mrs. Stevens delivered the cupcakes, and another mother brought some punch. Everyone opened their boxes and looked through their valentines. I had just taken a big bite of my cupcake when Marcia came over to my desk. I gasped. She was smiling. And she was holding the fancy card. "Oh, Martin," she said. "You are so romantic. Every time I start thinking you don't like me anymore, you do something nice like this."

My stomach did a weird flip-flop. Willie had put the fancy card in Marcia's box. That meant that Brianne must have the other one. I realized I hadn't written a name on either envelope, and that both cards had big white envelopes. I groaned and put my head on my desk.

"Are you sick?" Marcia asked. "Do you want me to tell Miss Lawson?" She sounded worried.

I sat up. "I just have a little headache," I said. "I'm glad you liked it," I managed to choke out. Out of the corner of my eye I could see Brianne glaring at me.

Marcia hung around almost the whole party. She even sat next to me during the movie. Miss Lawson had gotten *The NeverEnding Story*. It was one of my favorites, but I couldn't concentrate. I looked over at Brianne. She was sitting very close to Willie, and they were laughing.

"Did you see the pretty card Willie gave Brianne?" Marcia whispered. "It was almost as nice as the one you gave me. He must really like her."

We took a break in the middle of the movie. Willie sauntered over. "Marcia must have really liked her card," he remarked.

"Why did you give it to *her*?" I said.

Willie looked surprised. "Wasn't that who it was

90

for? You were worried about getting her something special."

I nodded glumly. Willie didn't seem to notice how miserable I was.

"Brianne liked 'Agnes's' card, too," he went on happily. He pulled his too-short shirtsleeves down to cover his knobby wrist bones. "Brianne smells like vanilla. Did you ever notice?"

12

More Tonsils

ALL WEEKEND, CAROLINE kept everyone in the house running to wait on her. Mom coaxed her to eat with ice cream, Jell-O, and other goodies. Caroline talked only in whispers and tried to convince everyone she was practically at death's door.

Monday was a rainy day. It was a cold dreary rain. A layer of fog drifted a few feet off the ground, and the sky was dark and gloomy. All day I felt miserable and cranky. Usually the first thing I did when I got home after school was to play with Sam. But today all I could think of was how nice it would be to curl up on the couch with a cup of cocoa and watch TV.

When I walked in the door, I saw that Caroline had beaten me to it. She was tucked up on the couch sipping cocoa and watching some dumb soap opera.

"Could I have some cocoa, too?" I asked Mrs. Albright.

"I'm sorry, dear. I just made the last of it for Caroline. How about a glass of orange juice?"

It didn't sound as good as cocoa, but I accepted a glass and took a sip. It tasted good, but my throat burned when I swallowed.

"Where is Mom?" I asked.

Mrs. Albright put the juice container back in the refrigerator. "She couldn't stay away from the office any longer. She went to pick up some papers. Your aunt went with her."

From upstairs we could hear the sound of Robbie jumping in his crib. That was his way of letting us know he was awake from his nap. Mrs. Albright went upstairs to get him, and I wandered back into the living room.

"Let's watch something else on TV," I suggested.

"I suppose you'd rather watch cartoons," Caroline sneered. "That's about right for your brain."

On the screen two people were kissing. "I suppose you have to be pretty smart to watch that," I said.

"Look, dog breath," Caroline croaked, "I'm sick, so I get first choice."

"I heard your tonsils were so big and ugly they are going to put them in a museum so everyone can come and look at them," I said.

"I'm going to tell Mom and Dad you were mean to me when I was sick," she yelled, her voice suddenly stronger.

"So you *can* talk. Maybe I'll tell Mom and Dad you've been faking," I said.

"I haven't been faking," she said. There were tears in her eyes. "I've been sick, and you've been having all the fun."

"What fun?" I sputtered.

"I didn't even get to go to my class's Valentine's party."

"Believe me, you didn't miss that much," I said. My head hurt when I moved it.

Dad poked his head around the corner. I was surprised to see him. Usually he was in his office this time of day, seeing patients.

"It's a little slow this afternoon," Dad said. "I thought I'd slip over and check on Caroline."

Robbie toddled in. He was holding his throat. Ever since Caroline had come home, Robbie had been worried about her. "Caroline hurt," he announced gravely.

Dad pulled Robbie up on his lap. "Caroline's all right," he explained for about the tenth time. "She just had her tonsils out."

Robbie kept holding his throat. He gave Dad a suspicious look. "No hurt Robbie," he warned.

"No, no," Dad said. "You have good tonsils."

"Tonsils?" Robbie asked.

"Come over here, Martin," Dad said. "Maybe if Robbie can see your tonsils, he'll understand."

Obligingly I opened my mouth.

"Hmm," Dad said. "Hmm."

I didn't like the sound of Dad's "hmm." "What's wrong?" I asked.

"Is your throat sore?"

"A little," I admitted.

"Your tonsils look worse than Caroline's did. I think we need to take yours out, too."

A smile spread slowly across Caroline's face. "Now you'll see I wasn't faking."

Tim walked in just in time to hear Caroline's last remark. "Who's faking?" he asked.

"No one. Martin has to have his tonsils out, too," Caroline crowed.

"Tough luck," Tim said, giving me a friendly jab on the arm. "I'm glad I had mine out when I was little."

"What's the point of having tonsils if they just have to come out," I grumbled.

"Tonsils filter out germs," Dad explained. "We really don't like to take them out. But when they get infected and make you sick all the time, then it's best."

"Does it really hurt that bad?" I asked Caroline.

She smiled sweetly. "It's awful."

"It's not much worse than a sore throat," Dad said.

That was pretty easy for him to say. He wasn't the one that was going to feel it. Caroline grabbed her throat and made a terrible face when he wasn't looking. "It really hurts," she mouthed.

Tim looked around. "Where's Aunt Henrietta?"

"She went to town with Mom," Caroline said.

"Whew," Tim said. "I was afraid I would have to go running."

Dad glanced through the mail Mrs. Albright had stacked on the hall table. "Looks as if several more relatives have accepted our invitation. Here's one from Aunt Judith."

"Why do we have to have this stupid reunion anyway," I grumbled.

"In the past, people often stayed close to the places where they grew up. I think it gave them a sense of belonging. You understood your roots," Dad said seriously. "But today most families are so spread out that sometimes even close relations don't know one another. Look at our family, scattered all over the country."

I thought about the family tree Miss Lawson had given us. With Aunt Henrietta's help, most of the names were filled in. There were a few relatives I had never even met. Maybe it would be interesting to see some of those people. It was kind of nice to think about a family being a giant tree with branches growing clear across the country.

"Where are all these people going to stay?" I asked.

"We are reserving rooms at several motels," Dad said. "And a couple of people said they would bring camping trailers. Aunt Jane and Uncle Dave said they would pitch a tent in the yard. Thank heavens we have such a big yard."

Our house had a huge yard in front with lots of shady trees. The back was big, too, and it was surrounded on two sides by a cornfield.

"We could set up our tent," I suggested.

"That's a great idea. If you kids slept in the tent, we could put up a few more people in the house," Dad said. "We'll put the tents in the front yard, kind of off to the side. That way we can have the tables and chairs in the front yard and you kids can have the backyard for games."

Caroline looked out the window. "I hope it's warmer than this," she said just as Mom and Aunt Henrietta came in the door.

Aunt Henrietta folded her umbrella. "It *is* awful outside. I guess I won't be running today."

"I'll bet weather like this makes you wish you didn't live here," Caroline said.

Aunt Henrietta shook her head. "Oh no," she said. "I love it here. It's the strangest thing. A week or two ago I was getting homesick. But now I think I'd like to stay." She looked straight at me. "Sometimes I hear this little voice in my head."

"L-little voice?" I stammered.

"It keeps saying, 'Stay, stay. Make this your home forever.'" She smiled innocently. "Isn't that peculiar?"

I gulped. "That is strange," I agreed.

13

Capitals and Sympathy

CAROLINE GAVE ME the tape back the next morning. "She knows," she hissed. "You'd better get rid of this before Mom and Dad find out."

"I think Caroline is right," Tim said. "It was nice of her not to tell."

"I wonder why it didn't work," I said.

"Because you thought of it, dimwit," Caroline said with a sneer.

Tim looked at me and winked. "I see having tonsils out doesn't improve your personality."

Caroline sniffed. "Neither does living with bird-brains," she said as she flounced off to get ready for school.

I had to get ready for school, too. Dad had given

me some medicine. He said I wouldn't need to miss school, since I didn't have a fever. "Good news," he had announced that very morning at breakfast. "The surgeon can fit you in this Friday."

"Caroline got to wait three weeks," I whined.

"She had all that time to think about it," Dad said. "You'll just have it done quickly and it will be over. Since we are doing it on Friday, you won't even have to miss that much school."

I was feeling pretty glum when I went to school. It was hard to concentrate. Miss Lawson gave us a map and we had to fill in the names of the states. We had to memorize all the capitals. Then she let us divide into groups to quiz each other.

I was in a group with Brianne, Willie, Jason, and Marcia. Brianne sat close to Willie and didn't even look at me. They were holding hands under the table so Miss Lawson couldn't see them.

"What's the capital of New York?" Jason asked.

"Albino," Willie shouted.

Everyone laughed. "Albany," Marcia corrected. "That's so easy, since our town is New Albany."

"Oh," Willie said with a shrug. "I knew it was something that started with an *A*."

"I have to have my tonsils out," I announced.

Willie grabbed his throat, clowning around. "Arrgg," he gasped. He forgot he was holding Brianne's hand. He jerked his hand so fast that she was pulled off her seat. She teetered against him for a second. Then her chair fell over and both of them landed on the floor.

Miss Lawson was there in an instant. She did not look happy. "Willie and Brianne, would you please explain to me how two people can fall on the floor quizzing each other on state capitals?"

"It was all my fault," Willie said gallantly. "I got dizzy."

Miss Lawson looked tired. "Dizzy," she repeated.

Willie nodded. "I was so dizzy I fell into Brianne's chair and knocked her over."

"Perhaps you need to explain your dizzy spells to Mr. Higgenbottom," Miss Lawson said.

"It was my fault," I said. "I told him that I was going to have my tonsils out. Willie always gets dizzy when he hears about blood."

A smile twitched the corners of Miss Lawson's mouth. "Let's keep the conversation to state capitals. Maybe we can discuss tonsils in science class."

"Thanks," Willie whispered when Miss Lawson went back to her desk. "Mr. Higgenbottom said if he saw me one more time this year, I was in big trouble."

"Are you scared about having your tonsils out?" Marcia asked at recess.

"No," I said. "Well, maybe a little bit. My sister said it was awful."

"I had mine out last year," she said. "It wasn't really that bad. You just feel like you have a sore throat afterward. I could come over and make you some Jell-O."

"Mrs. Albright will make me some," I said. Then, seeing her disappointed look, I added, "That was nice of you to offer."

"How is Sam?" she asked.

I shrugged. "He's getting used to staying at Mr. DeWitt's house. I take him out a lot."

"You could bring him over sometime to visit his mother, Mitzi," Marcia said.

"Maybe," I said.

Marcia was the only one who was worried about me. You would think that someone facing surgery on Friday would get a little attention. But no. Mom was all upset over the meetings about the new highway. "I just don't know which side to take," she said at dinner. "One group would like the highway built because it would cut down on all the big trucks going through town. And they are right. The traffic is getting horrible and some streets are just too narrow for big trucks. But the other group says that all the shopkeepers in town would lose business because everyone would just pass by. And they are right, too. It doesn't matter which side I take, I'm going to make people unhappy."

In addition, there was the family reunion, which

was being held on Easter weekend. So far fifteen families had accepted. "Most people are off work, and the weather is usually pretty good," Mom had explained. "So the out-of-town people will be able to stay longer." She and Aunt Henrietta were busy making arrangements at motels and ordering food.

"We will have to figure out bathroom schedules, and we need lots of activities for the children," Mom said at dinner.

"Dad said I could organize some baseball games," Tim said. He rolled his eyes at me. "Most kids like to play baseball."

"Scavenger hunts!" Caroline suggested. "I could write some clues."

"Doesn't anyone care about me?" I exploded. "I have to have my tonsils out, and all anyone talks about is highways and baseball games."

There was a moment of shocked silence. "Oh, honey, we didn't know you were that upset about it," Mom said.

"It's no big deal," Caroline said breezily.

"Oh yeah," I retorted. "Then why did you make such a big fuss?"

"Dr. Michael will do the surgery," Dad said. "But I'll be right there watching."

"I'll bring you some ice cream afterward," Tim promised.

"I have an idea," Caroline said. "After dinner, let's

play Monopoly. You always win that. It will keep your mind off it."

Even Aunt Henrietta started telling me a funny family story, trying to cheer me up. It was almost embarrassing. A minute earlier I was unhappy because I wasn't getting any attention. Now I was getting too much. But that's the way it is with families, I guess. Sometimes they are a pain, but they are great when you need them.

14

Tonsils Again

FRIDAY MORNING CAME all too soon. "You are lucky," Willie had said on Thursday.

"Lucky?" I hadn't been able to believe my ears.

"You don't have to take the test on state capitals," Willie said.

"Ha," I said. "Miss Lawson will just make me take it when I get back."

"Well, at least you get a few days off school," Willie said.

"I'll tell you what," I said. "I'll go to school and you go get your tonsils out."

It was hard to feel lucky as I got ready to leave for the hospital. We were supposed to be there at seven

106

in the morning, and I wasn't allowed to have breakfast. Dad explained that food might make me sick when they put me to sleep.

"But I'm starving," I complained. As if to prove it, my stomach made a funny little growl.

As soon as we arrived at the hospital, a lady at the desk put a plastic bracelet on me. Then we were taken upstairs to a room with a bed. A nurse handed me a white gown. It had babyish little teddy bears on it. "That's our most fashionable outfit," she said when I frowned.

I didn't have time to think about it because as soon as I had changed, another nurse came in and gave me a shot. "Is that going to put me to sleep?" I asked nervously.

The nurse smiled. "It might make you a little sleepy. Mostly it will just help you relax."

Dad patted my head. "I'm going to go change and get ready to help Dr. Michael," he said. "I'll see you in a few minutes."

There was a television in my room. Mom and I watched while we waited, but that early in the morning there wasn't anything interesting on. "There is one good thing," I said. "I always wanted to see the inside of the operating room. I want to see if it's like the ones they show on TV."

At last I was wheeled into the operating room. I saw Dad with a mask on his face. Dr. Michael was there, and so was another doctor. "This is Dr. Abrams," Dad said.

Dr. Abrams explained that he was the one who would put me to sleep.

I tried to sit up, but he gently pushed me back down. "You won't let them do anything until you're sure I'm asleep, will you?" I asked.

"I promise," he said. "I'm going to give you a little shot. You just relax."

"All right," I said. "But remember. Pinch me or something. Make sure I'm really, really asleep." I took two quick breaths.

"I'm not asleep yet," I mumbled. My mouth tasted awful, and my throat hurt.

"Oh, you're awake," said a nurse, peering down at me. "Good."

"I haven't gone to sleep yet," I croaked. "Don't let them do it."

The nurse chuckled. "It's already done. It's all over."

I tried to focus my eyes, but I was too sleepy. "I forgot to look at the operating room," I muttered as I fell back to sleep.

The next time I woke up, I was back in the first room and Mom was sitting in a chair beside me. "Thirsty," I whispered.

Mom gave me some little pieces of ice to suck on. My throat felt terrible.

"When you're more awake, we can go home," she said. Her hand felt cool on my head. I nodded. As long as I didn't talk, my throat didn't hurt too bad.

After a couple of hours the doctor checked me and said I could go home.

I was surprised that it was so late. Tim and Caroline were already home from school and waiting for me. "How was it?" Tim asked.

I shook my head and pointed to my throat.

"He doesn't want to talk now," Caroline told Tim in her bossy voice.

For once she was right. All I wanted to do was sleep. Mom helped me to bed, and the next thing I knew, it was Saturday morning.

All day I sat bundled up on the couch and read or watched TV. Mrs. Albright brought me some ice cream. I was really getting hungry, but I only managed to swallow two tiny bites.

At three o'clock the doorbell rang. "There's someone to see you," Mom said.

"Is it Willie?" I whispered.

"No. It's Marcia," Mom said. "She says she has something for you."

I groaned. What could she want? Then I realized I was still wearing my pajamas. I pulled the covers up under my chin so she couldn't see.

Marcia came in the room carrying a small bowl with a lid. "I know you don't feel like talking," she said. "But I brought you something." She took off the lid. "It's vanilla pudding. I made it myself."

I looked in the bowl. It looked kind of watery.

Marcia made a face. "It's the cooked kind. It didn't get quite hard enough. But I thought it might feel good on your throat."

"Thank you," I croaked. "It looks really good."

We sat there a minute in silence. "Are you cold?" Marcia asked, pointing to my blanket.

I gave a weak nod.

"I could take Sam for a walk before I go home," she offered.

"He would like that." I looked at the pudding. "Could you ask Mrs. Albright for a spoon?"

Marcia went to the kitchen and came back with a spoon. "You don't have to eat it if you don't want it," she said.

"No, I want to," I said. I didn't really, but I knew her feelings would be hurt if I didn't. To my surprise, the pudding slid down smooth and cool on my throat. It even tasted pretty good. I ate almost all of it.

"That was good," I said, meaning it.

Marcia looked pleased. "I know you don't want to talk, but we could play a game. I could tell you about school yesterday," she said.

We played a couple of games. I didn't realize what a good time I was having until she stood and put on her coat. "I have to leave now if I'm going to take

110

Sam for a walk. My mom's coming in a few minutes."

She started for the door again and then suddenly ran back and kissed me quickly on the cheek.

I stared after her and touched my cheek. There was a snicker from the kitchen doorway. "Oh, Martin. You are sooo wonderful," Caroline said.

"You were spying on me," I whispered loudly.

"I couldn't resist," Caroline said. She clasped her hands over her heart. "Martin and Marcia, sitting in a tree, k-i-s-s-i-n-g," she chanted.

I threw my pillow at her.

"Touchy, touchy. I guess love does that to you." Caroline laughed as she ducked around the doorway.

15

Tempers and Toenails

MARCIA STOPPED BY for the next two days to take Sam for a walk. Afterward she would stay and visit. Caroline watched us like a hawk, but Marcia didn't try to kiss me again. By Tuesday I was ready to go back to school and Marcia had beaten me in twelve games of cards, two games of Scrabble, and one game of Monopoly.

Almost all of the relatives had responded to the invitations, and most of them were coming. Mom nervously read the long-range weather forecasts, but it looked as if even Mother Nature was cooperating with the reunion plans. Spring was in the air. Flowers were popping up, and the trees were in leaf.

The next few weeks Aunt Henrietta trained even

harder. Sometimes I ran with her, but I could never last as long as she did. Usually I would have to stop and rest until she caught up with me on the way back. Actually, I kind of enjoyed the running. With all that practice, I had even come in second when we'd run laps around the gym at school.

On the last Saturday in March, Willie was eating dinner with us. He took a bite of lasagna and rolled his eyes with delight. "Mrs. Albright, you are such a good cook."

Mrs. Albright beamed at him. "Save some room for the strawberry pie I made for dessert."

"Don't worry," Willie assured her.

"I have to go potty," Robbie announced. He jumped down from his chair. "I'll be right back," he said.

"It's not fair," Caroline said, picking at her own dinner. "Willie and Tim eat like horses and both of them are skinny."

"That's because both of them are growing so fast," Dad said.

I cast an envious look at Willie. He had grown a lot this year. The shirt he'd gotten for Christmas was already too short to cover his wrists.

"I wish I'd grow," I said.

"Don't worry," Mom said. "One of these days you'll just start shooting up."

"I wish I'd stop growing," Caroline said. "All my

friends are skinny. I'm just a blob." She put down her fork.

"Going without eating is not a good way to lose weight," Dad said gently. "And anyway, you are at a perfectly healthy weight."

"Plump," Tim mouthed around another bite of lasagna. "That's a good word. Pl . . . ump."

"That's enough," Dad said sternly.

"Be glad that you have all this good food," Aunt Henrietta began. "Children in the countries where I've taught—"

"I don't want to hear about other countries. And I don't want to hear about being healthy," Caroline raged. She stood up and pushed back her chair so hard it almost tipped over. "I don't want to be healthy. I want to be beautiful." She ran out of the room.

There was a moment of stunned silence at the table.

Tim calmly stuffed another bite of lasagna in his mouth.

"I'll go talk to her," Mom said.

Aunt Henrietta looked stricken. "I feel so awful. Caroline wanted to hear that she was pretty, and instead I start telling her about starving children."

"Caroline is just going through a stage," Dad said.

"Caroline's whole life is a stage," Tim said.

Dad held up his hand. "Do I hear water running?"

From the downstairs bathroom we heard a small voice. "I flushed," Robbie called.

Everyone ran to the bathroom. Already water was pouring out into the hall from the clogged toilet. "Robbie," Dad said grimly, "what did you flush down the toilet?"

Robbie hung his head. "Car."

"Robbie's going through a flushing stage," Tim said.

"Never ever flush again!" Dad roared.

"I'll call the plumber," Mom said as she came downstairs and saw the mess.

"You are lucky to live in a big family," Willie said later after the plumber had done his work and gone. We were out in the yard tossing a ball for Sam to catch. "There's always something going on at your house."

I shook my head. "Sometimes I wish I was an only child."

Willie rolled on the grass with Sam. "It's boring, believe me."

"I think I'd like to be bored. It's like a zoo around here sometimes. And it's going to be even worse when all these relatives come. What if Robbie flushes something down the toilet then?"

Willie shrugged and grinned. "I guess your dad will call the plumber."

After Willie left, I went back inside. The whole family was sitting in the living room talking about the reunion. Caroline was there, too, although she still looked unhappy.

"I just hope the weather is nice," Mom said.

"Since the reunion is on Easter weekend, we should have an Easter egg hunt," I suggested.

"Good idea," Mom said. "That would be a nice project for you."

"I could help you," Caroline offered. "We could mark some of the eggs and have prizes."

Aunt Henrietta sat on the couch and kicked off her shoes. She rubbed her big toe.

"You haven't gone running for three days," I said. "You might get out of shape."

"I hurt my toe a couple of days ago," she answered ruefully.

Her toe was purple and swollen, and the toenail looked strange.

"Gross," Caroline whispered.

"Let me see," Dad said. "How in the world did you do this?"

"One of the workmen at the new post office was walking by with a stack of bricks. The top one slipped off and landed right on my toe."

"That looks pretty bad," Dad said. "Better come in the office, and I'll tend it for you."

Aunt Henrietta hobbled after him.

"What if she can't be in the race after all this work?" I said.

"I have a feeling it will take more than a smashed toe to stop Aunt Henrietta," said Mom.

After a while Dad and Aunt Henrietta came out of his office. There was a bandage on Aunt Henrietta's big toe. "Well, it's not broken," Dad said. "But she's going to lose the nail, I think, and it's badly bruised."

"All this fuss about a toe," Caroline whispered under her breath.

"I had an ingrown toenail once," Tim said. "It got infected and it really hurt."

"You probably got the infection from those smelly shoes you wear." Caroline sneered.

"I'd rather have stinky feet than stinky breath like you," Tim retorted.

Robbie zoomed his cars around the living room floor. "Stinky, stinky, stinky," he chanted.

I thought about Willie going home to his nice quiet house. Some people just don't know when they are lucky.

16

Water Balloons and a Pen

EASTER WEEKEND FINALLY arrived. There wasn't any school on Friday. A lot of the out-of-town visitors were arriving, and we all had to help with the last-minute preparations. Tim and I were still picking up branches that had fallen during the winter, and then we had to rake the yard.

"How am I going to play baseball if my hands are all blistered," Tim complained to Dad.

Dad was up on a ladder cleaning leaves (and making more raking for us) out of the rain gutters on the porch roof. He climbed down and walked around inspecting everything. I thought the place looked pretty good. It seemed to me it was silly to clean so much before the relatives came. I mean, with all those people tramping around, it was not going to stay clean for long.

Dad finished his inspection tour and nodded. "You boys did a good job."

"You mean we can go?" Tim said hopefully.

"Not yet," Dad said. "We need to set up the tent."

We dragged the tent out of the garage and started pounding in the stakes in a shady spot at the side of the house. The tent had a faint musty odor. The last time we'd gone camping, Dad had gotten sprayed by a skunk.

Mom called us in for lunch just as we finished. "I want to get the dishes done before anyone comes," she said.

After lunch, Willie rode by on his bike. Some men were just delivering the picnic tables Mom had rented for the weekend. Aunt Henrietta dragged three new garbage cans from the garage. With everyone eating off paper plates all weekend, there was bound to be a lot of trash.

I noticed she was still limping slightly. All day she had been charging around like a human dynamo. I wondered if she was going to change before people arrived. Right now she was wearing neon-orange baggy shorts and purple bedroom slippers.

"Boy. Your family thought of everything," Willie said. "My grandma would be in a panic by now."

"Don't worry," I said. "Mom's in the kitchen pacing up and down, trying to think if she forgot anything."

Willie waved good-bye. "Have fun," he shouted as he pedaled away. I sat down to rest near our tent.

Some of the relatives weren't coming until Saturday, but a few were staying for the entire weekend. Even though Mom was still worried, I thought we were ready for them. The house was scrubbed from top to bottom, and the refrigerator and cupboards were stocked with more food than I'd ever seen anywhere except in the grocery store.

Tim got a bag of chips from the kitchen and hid it in the tent along with an extra flashlight and some games. Tim, Caroline, and I were sleeping in the tent so Grandma and Grandpa and Great-Grandpa Snodgrass could stay in the house.

They were the first to arrive. After lunch, Dad had driven to the airport and picked them up. Grandma and Grandpa Snodgrass live in Florida, so we don't see them very often. Grandpa's hair is still mostly red. He doesn't hear very well, so he talks pretty loud, mainly about golf. The first thing he did was measure us to see how much we'd all grown. "You children are certainly growing fast," he said. "Next thing you know, you will all be grown-up." He winked at Grandma. "We must be getting old to have grandchildren this big."

Grandma sniffed. "Maybe you are, but I'm not,"

she said. She pushed her blond curls back in place after hugging Aunt Henrietta.

Great-Grandpa didn't say much. He just sat in Dad's favorite chair.

Robbie patted his face. "Why is your face so bumpy?" he asked.

Great-Grandpa chuckled. "Those are wrinkles. I have them because I'm so smart."

Robbie patted his own face. "I wish I had wrinkles," he said.

"Who are you?" Great-Grandpa asked Tim.

"This is Tim and Caroline and Martin," Aunt Henrietta told him. "They are your great-grandchildren."

"Grandpa is getting a little forgetful," Grandma said.

"I have a present for you," Great-Grandpa told Tim. He reached in his pocket and handed him a pen.

"Thanks," Tim said. "I really don't need it, though."

"No, no," Great-Grandpa insisted. "It's a present."

Tim looked a little uncomfortable still, but he put the pen in his shirt pocket and sat down.

Robbie seemed fascinated with Great-Grandpa's wrinkles. He leaned over the chair studying Great-Grandpa's face.

"Who is this boy?" Great-Grandpa asked.

"This is Robbie," Grandma told him.

Great-Grandpa held Robbie on his lap and admired

Robbie's cars. Suddenly he looked up at Tim. "Say, that's a nice pen I see sticking out of your pocket. Would you mind if I borrowed it?"

Tim handed it back. Great-Grandpa looked at it and then stuck it back in his pocket.

Other relatives were arriving. Aunt Jane and Uncle Dave had brought their own tent and pitched it next to ours. "It sure is hot," Uncle Dave said, pausing to wipe his forehead.

"The weatherman says this is the hottest spring Ohio has had for fifty years," Tim said.

Our Ohio cousins, Matt, Tabitha, and Corey, grinned at us. We knew them pretty well. With their red hair and freckles, they looked enough like us to be brothers and sisters.

"This is going to be fun," Matt said. He was the closest to my age.

"Tomorrow, when everyone is here, we'll play baseball," Tim said, with a look at me. He knows I'm not very good at sports.

"Just be sure to do it in the backyard," Dad said. "That way any stray balls will go in the field and not in someone's lap."

"You are lucky to have such a big yard," Corey said. "If the reunion had been at our house, no one would have been able to move."

"What shall we do?" Tabitha asked.

"I've got an idea," Matt said. He reached in his bag

with a mischievous look and pulled out a bag of balloons. "How about a water balloon fight?"

While we were talking, a car pulled in the driveway. I recognized two cousins from California from the pictures Aunt Henrietta had showed me. I had never met them before. Their family was staying at one of the motels in town. They were teenagers and had great suntans and weird clothes. They sort of sneered at us when we ran over and asked if they wanted to join us.

"Get real," the girl said in a bored voice.

We snuck around to the spigot at the back of the house to fill up the balloons.

The grown-ups were all gathered around the picnic tables, talking. We looked for our unfriendly cousins, but they had disappeared.

We stood around with our full balloons. Caroline seemed to know what I was thinking. "If we dump these balloons on them, we'll get in trouble," she warned.

"Not if it is an accident." Matt grinned. "They might walk right into where we are playing."

I was the one who spotted them. They were hiding behind the garage.

"They're smoking!" Caroline exclaimed.

Tim grinned. "We'd better put out the fire before they hurt themselves."

Running around the corner of the garage, we

yelled, "Catch!" and threw the balloons.

"You rotten little jerks," the girl screamed. Water streamed down her face, and her carefully combed hair hung in wet straggles.

After the first angry look, the boy laughed, but our other cousin was still unhappy. "I'm going to tell," she said, sounding exactly like Caroline.

"Oh, come on, Andrea, they were just playing," the boy said.

"You'll probably want to explain about the cigarettes, too," Tabitha said.

Andrea glared. "You little dweebs. I knew I'd hate this family reunion."

Laughing, we ran back to the picnic tables. Some of the uncles were playing horseshoes, and Mrs. Albright was bringing out a big platter of lunch meats and rolls to make sandwiches. Grandma, Mom, and Dad followed with chips and a plate of vegetables for dipping. It was cooling off a little, and it was almost dark.

Great-Grandpa came out of the house. "You look like a nice young man," he said to Uncle Dave. "I've got something for you." He reached in his pocket and handed the pen to Uncle Dave.

The two teens filled their plates. The boy winked as he passed, and I decided he wasn't so bad after all. The girl stood next to a woman who was an older version of herself. The woman looked bored and picked at her food when her husband brought her a plate.

"I hope we don't have very many relatives like them," I told Tim.

Robbie was playing trucks with a little boy named Tommie. Mom and Tommie's mother took them into the house to wash their hands. Both of the boys were screaming at the top of their lungs, not wanting to stop playing.

Caroline shook her head. "What's it going to be like tomorrow when the rest of the relatives arrive?"

Great-Grandpa took his plate and wobbled over to Uncle Dave. "Say," he said, "that's a nice pen. I used to have one just like it."

"Would you like it?" Uncle Dave asked, handing it to him.

Great-Grandpa smiled broadly. Then he tucked the pen in his pocket and sat back down with his meal.

17

Even More Relatives

ON SATURDAY WE were up early. I hadn't slept very well crowded in the tent with Tim and Caroline, and it was already sticky and hot.

Caroline glanced at the thermometer that hung by the back door. "It's already eighty degrees outside. I've never seen it this hot in April."

"Mom was worried about snow, remember?" Tim remarked.

We stumbled into the house and found a line waiting for the bathrooms. Grandpa was in Mom and Dad's bathroom taking a shower, and Aunt Jane and Uncle Dave were in the main bathroom.

"Oh, great," Caroline said sourly. "We get to wait in line for our own bathroom."

"It's only for one day," Mom said. "And I'm sure it will only be for a few minutes."

The few minutes turned into nearly an hour, and by the time I got my turn there wasn't any hot water left. Everyone was in a pretty good mood, though. Caroline cheered up when she finally got her turn, and after breakfast she even offered to help me color the eggs for the Easter egg hunt. Mom helped us boil six dozen eggs. When they had boiled for ten minutes, we let them sit for a few minutes in cold water.

We covered the table with newspapers and dropped little tablets of color into cupfuls of water. Matt, Tabitha, and Corey arrived to help.

Dad left to go to the hospital to check on his patients. Even though he had arranged not to have any appointments all weekend, he had to visit the patients who were already sick. Mom went to the motels to pick up people who hadn't rented cars. Several more families who lived close enough to drive were arriving today.

We took turns using the dye until all the eggs were colored. "How are we going to mark the prize eggs?" I asked. We had a few prizes for the winner and runners-up.

"How about numbers?" Caroline suggested. She took a marker, drew a star, and put a number 1 inside.

"My mom hid eggs in the house last Easter because it was raining. We didn't find one of them for three weeks." Corey held his nose. "Phew!"

"We'd better hurry if we are going to have these hidden before everyone gets here," Tim said. He drew the number 2 on another egg.

We put the eggs back in the egg boxes to dry and dumped the cups in the sink. Caroline rolled up the newspapers and put them in the trash.

We fanned out to hide the eggs. Since everyone was gathering in the front yard we hid the eggs around the back of the house. We put some in easy sight for the really little kids. Others we hid in bushes and trees. Uncle George was pounding in stakes for a horseshoe game off to one side of the backyard, and Grandpa and Aunt Judith were putting up the volleyball net. "Don't let anyone over here," Caroline said with a sweeping gesture. "They might step on some eggs."

Mom was just returning with the first load of relatives when we finished.

The kitchen was rapidly filling up with food. All the relatives who lived nearby had brought covered dishes for lunch. The refrigerator was filled with interesting and good-smelling things to eat.

"Did you get the eggs all hidden?" Mom asked as she tucked still another casserole in the refrigerator.

"All done," I answered.

Mom looked out the window with a worried glance. "We had better do it soon. The Weather Channel is predicting thunderstorms late this afternoon."

"What will we do with all these people if it storms?" Caroline asked.

"Crowd them in the house, I guess," Mom said. "Let's hope the storm will be a quick one." Ohio often has ferocious thunderstorms during periods of unusually hot weather. But they usually last only ten or fifteen minutes.

I wandered around the yard. Everyone was kissing and hugging. I knew most of them, but it was the first time I had seen so many members of my family all together. It was amazing to think I was related to all these people. Everyone seemed especially glad to see Aunt Henrietta, and she was floating with happiness. All morning she walked around hugging and smiling and mixing up everyone's names. I was kind of glad the tape hadn't driven her away and made her miss this day.

Mom announced the egg hunt, and everyone moved to the backyard to watch. Grandpa stood on a chair. "Let's give the youngest children a few seconds' head start," he said. There were about ten kids under five lined up at the house. "On your mark, get set, go!" he shouted.

The older kids lined up, too, but Grandpa made them wait. Some of the little children didn't know what to do, and their moms and dads were pointing to the eggs. After a minute, Grandpa let the rest of the kids go. They swarmed across the yard. In less than a minute it was all over.

Caroline shook her head. "It took us two hours to do all those eggs."

I got to pass out the prizes. First prize was a big stuffed bunny. A little girl with bright red curls won it. Her name was Lisa, and she was a second cousin from New York I'd never met before. She sat right down on the grass and hugged and petted the bunny as though it were alive.

Aunt Henrietta stood by beaming at me. She had on a big straw hat to keep out the sun. "Isn't this wonderful," she exclaimed. "You are part of all this."

I thought about the family tree Miss Lawson had given me. I wouldn't even know where to put everyone. Maybe instead of branches they'd have to be little leaves. It made me smile, thinking of turning each person into a leaf. Maybe all the young ones would be buds, just starting to open. And Great-Grandpa would be an old leaf, curled and wrinkled, blowing in the wind.

I kept picturing everyone that way as I wandered around, listening to the conversations. Great-Grandpa was making his way through the crowd, passing out his pen and collecting it back again.

I saw Andrea. She was sitting under a tree polishing her fingernails bright red. She glared at me as I walked by. I thought about her being a little fungus growing on that family tree and it made me smile.

At noon the picnic tables were filled with every kind of food you could imagine. Even though I only took a tiny bit of each thing, my plate was heaping. I took my plate and sat down under a tree. Caroline joined me.

"Amazing, isn't it?" she said, waving her arms at the crowd.

"I can't even remember half their names," I admitted.

"I did meet one girl I liked. We figured out she's a second cousin. She's just like me. She's going to a special school for gifted kids. We're going to be pen pals."

After lunch, Tim organized a softball game. A lot of people wandered to the backyard to watch.

Mom walked by holding a tired-looking Robbie. "I'm going to see if I can get him to take a nap," she said.

"No nap," Robbie whispered in a sleepy voice.

Several other parents took the youngest children inside the house to rest. I let Sam out of the garage for some exercise.

"Is that your dog?" Andrea was leaning against a tree watching.

I nodded.

"He's cute," Andrea said, bending down to pat Sam.

"He knows how to shake hands," I bragged. "Shake, Sam." I held out my hand.

Sam put his paw in my hand.

"Can he do anything else?" asked Andrea.

"Not yet," I said. "I haven't had him very long."

"My mom wouldn't let me have a dog. She doesn't like animals."

Sam rolled over and let her scratch his tummy. "I didn't want to come here," Andrea said. She smiled a little. "I guess you could tell, huh?" She sighed. "All my friends wanted me to do stuff with them on Easter vacation. And here I am with a bunch of people I don't even know. I mean, who cares? We will probably never see each other again, right?"

I nodded. "Where is your brother?"

"Jason? Oh, he's playing softball. He's having a good time. He likes your brother Tim."

Aunt Henrietta came outside wearing her running shoes. "I ate too much lunch," she confided. "I think I'll take a little run. Do you feel like escaping the crowds for a while, or are you enjoying yourself?"

"It's pretty warm," I said.

"I'm not going to go very far—or very fast," she added. "My toe is a little sore."

Sam jumped eagerly around us. I knew he would like to have a chance to explore. I snapped on his leash, and we set off down the road at a leisurely pace.

Aunt Henrietta was running awkwardly, keeping her foot with the injured toe flat. We passed the corn-field and turned down a gravel road. The air was still and heavy, and sweat made my back itch.

"I guess you were right," Aunt Henrietta admitted. "It *is* too hot to run. Let's rest a minute."

We sat on a large boulder by the side of the road. Sam plopped beside us, his tongue hanging out as he panted.

Aunt Henrietta looked up at the sky. "It seems a funny color, don't you think?"

"Mom said she heard there might be thunder-storms this afternoon," I said.

"Maybe we'd just better head back," Aunt Henrietta said. She stood up, then suddenly grabbed my arm. "What's that?"

I listened. From the direction of town I could hear the wail of a siren. "That's the tornado siren," I yelled. "Come on!"

We sprinted toward home. The sky was getting a purplish tint and growing darker. "Come on," urged Aunt Henrietta. "That siren is so far away that they may not have heard it, especially with everyone talk-ing. Let's cut across the field."

We left the road and started across the field. To save time we ran diagonally, but it was harder to run across the freshly plowed furrows. Aunt Henrietta was running slightly ahead of me, but suddenly Sam bounded right in front of her feet and she went sprawling.

I tried to help her up. "Are you all right?" I shouted anxiously.

She grabbed her ankle. "I may have sprained it."

"See if you can run," I said. I cast a nervous look at the sky. It was an unfriendly shade of purple.

Aunt Henrietta took a few wobbly steps. "You'd better leave me here. You can send back help."

"No, I can't do that," I said with a worried look at the sky. A flash of lightning zigzagged to the ground not far away. "Lean on me," I said. "We'll make it." She steadied herself against me. I could tell she was in pain, but she kept on going. If I hadn't been so scared, it might have looked funny. We probably looked like runners in a three-legged race.

Aunt Henrietta's face was pale. "Come on," I encouraged her. "We're almost there."

The wind was getting stronger now. I could see the baseball players through the trees that separated our yard from the field. Some people who had been sitting and watching the game were standing up, looking around with growing alarm.

"Help!" I screamed. The wind seemed to blow my words away before I was heard.

At last people seemed to notice. They were pointing at us, and Uncle Dave and Dad were running to help.

"Go back," Aunt Henrietta shouted.

Suddenly I was aware of a sound. A roaring noise, far away but coming closer. I looked behind me just as the men reached us. Far away I saw a huge black cloud that grew smaller closer to the ground. The cloud was angry, swirling, coming closer even as I watched.

"Tornado!" I screamed. "It's heading right for us."

18

Tornado

IT SEEMED AS if things were happening in slow motion, although everyone was moving fast. Dad and Uncle Dave reached us just as I thought my legs would give out. "Run for the house!" Dad yelled as he reached out a hand to steady me. He and Uncle Dave almost carried Aunt Henrietta. The wind was blowing harder now, bending the trees with its force.

I reached the yard. Mom was at the door. "Everyone get inside," she screamed.

The wind was swirling little pieces of dirt and twigs that stung when they hit your skin. Uncle George and Grandpa were leading Great-Grandpa into the house. I saw Lisa, the little girl with her prize rabbit. She was standing by the garage staring at the rapidly approaching funnel as though she was too frightened to move. I scooped her up as I raced for the door.

The roar was louder now. People were crowding down the stairs to the basement. The little girl's mother was there, holding a small baby. "Oh, thank you, thank you," she cried. With the little girl in one arm and the baby in the other, she started down the stairs.

"Sam," I yelled. "I forgot Sam."

Andrea burst through the door carrying Sam like a baby. "I've got him."

Dad and Uncle Dave reached the house, and willing hands helped Aunt Henrietta down the stairs. "We need to open a couple of windows," Dad shouted to Uncle Dave. I remembered that I'd heard that in school. Opening windows relieved some of the air pressure in the house. I ran to help Dad open the dining room window. Uncle Dave opened a window on the other side of the house.

"Get downstairs," Dad yelled at me over the roar.

"Is everyone in?" Uncle Dave was yelling, too.

"Yes." Through the window Dad had just opened I could see the funnel. It was ugly and black, but it skipped along like a ballerina lightly tiptoeing across a stage. When it touched the earth, whole trees were wrenched from the ground and thrown down as though they were twigs. It was like looking inside some sort of giant vacuum cleaner gone crazy. I was nearly paralyzed with fear.

Dad grabbed my arm and almost dragged me to

the basement door just as the last few people made it down the narrow stairs. I saw Andrea just ahead of me. She was still holding on to Sam. Dad and Uncle Dave came right after me, closing the door behind them.

The roar was slightly less. Everyone was crowded into the unfinished room that Dad had been trying to turn into an extra family room for years. Several men had taken pieces of paneling and were nailing them over the windows.

Some of the children were crying, and their mothers were trying to calm them down.

"We're going to be all right," came Aunt Henrietta's calm voice. "This is one family reunion no one will forget."

"That's for sure," Uncle George said with a chuckle.

Suddenly the lights went out. Someone screamed. "I'm scared, Martin," Robbie said.

"We'll be okay," I called out. But I wasn't feeling too confident. The house seemed to creak and moan, and sometimes we could hear a loud bang as though something had crashed against the wall. I was frozen in terror. I heard a soft whine, and a furry body wriggled next to me. I put my arms around Sam. He was trembling, but he licked my nose to comfort me.

Aunt Henrietta's voice rose over the storm. "She'll be coming round the mountain," she sang. Her voice was clear and strong. After a minute other voices joined in.

There was a crash and a tinkle of glass from the laundry room as a window blew in. Now we could hear the storm again in all its fury. My ears felt funny.

"I don't like this dark," I heard a little girl say from across the room.

"There's an emergency flashlight plugged in along the wall," Dad said.

"Found it," Matt shouted, and the room was suddenly lit with enough light for us to see one another's frightened faces.

"It sounds as if the storm is moving off," Dad said. "But we'd better stay here a few more minutes to make sure it doesn't change direction. Is everybody all right?"

"I skinned my knee," Tim said.

"You did that playing baseball," Caroline said.

"It sounds better to say it was the tornado," Tim said.

"I'll go up and look around," Dad said at last.

He and Uncle Dave disappeared up the steps. A few minutes later, Uncle Dave called back down, "It's still storming, but the worst seems to be over."

People lined up to climb the stairs. I was surprised to find that the kitchen looked almost normal. But the living room was a disaster. A large tree branch had crashed through the picture window. Glass, leaves, and dirt had blown everywhere.

Uncle George had stepped outside. "Wow"—he tried to joke—"it looks like a tornado came through here."

The storm had done strange things as it skipped along. The picnic tables were still in place, but I could see one of the benches across the street. A car in the driveway was tipped over on its side, and the mailbox was gone. The whole top of a maple tree was gone, or maybe that was what had come through the front window. The yard was littered with little squares of something. "Roofing tiles," Dad said.

The new outdoor grill seemed to have disappeared along with all the baseballs, bats, and gloves dropped in the panic.

But the storm had not just taken things. It had left us some presents, too. The yard was full of papers, pieces of boards, and even an old lawn chair I'd never seen before.

Mrs. Albright pushed anxiously by me. "I've got to check on Harold," she called. But just then Mr. DeWitt's door opened. He stepped out on his porch and waved. Mrs. Albright ran over and they hugged.

Dad went back in to check the phones, but they were dead. "I'd better drive to town and see if anyone was hurt," Dad said.

Mom was still holding Robbie. She looked pale and stricken as she stared at the mess in the living room.

Aunt Henrietta put her arm around Mom's shoulders. "I think we were pretty lucky," Aunt Henrietta remarked. "No one was hurt, and with all these people here we will have this mess cleaned up in no time. It takes more than a little tornado to wipe out the Snodgrass family."

Almost like magic, work was divided. Andrea and several of the older girls took charge of the small children. Some of us scoured the yard, picking up the trash and small branches. Several of the aunts swept up the glass from the front room while the uncles got out chain saws to cut up the fallen trees. By the time the electricity came on that evening, the house, except for the missing window, looked almost normal.

Dad returned and reported that the storm had bypassed the town. "It knocked down two barns and demolished a trailer, but no one was hurt except for a man who was hit by a tree branch flying through the air," he said. "He just needed a couple of stitches on his head."

The man from the glass shop arrived. He covered the window with plastic and promised to replace the glass the next day. The garage came and towed away the overturned car.

"I'm hungry," Grandpa announced.

"Pizza," someone suggested.

"I'd like to see the pizza guy's face when we call

up and order enough pizza for seventy people," Tim whispered.

In the end Dad ordered pizza from three different pizza shops. The delivery boys did look amazed when they saw the crowd that was waiting for them. Everyone seemed different somehow, as though the afternoon had bound us together. A family, I suddenly realized. As the stars came out, people drifted away. Some were heading back to the motels and would return on Sunday, but a few were heading home. I was sorry to see each one go—even Andrea and her brother.

"Thanks for saving Sam," I said.

Andrea shrugged. "I like dogs." She smiled. "I thought I would hate it here, but it was kind of nice. And I doubt if any of my friends can say they lived through a tornado."

"If you come to California someday, we'll show you around," her brother said.

"Maybe we can arrange an earthquake if you get bored," Andrea joked.

Great-Grandpa walked by. "I've got something for you," he said, handing me the pen.

"Thank you," I said. "It's very nice."

I waved good-bye to several more departing relatives and then went to hunt up Great-Grandpa. He was sitting on the lawn chair the tornado had given us.

"Here's your pen, Grandpa," I said, holding it out to him.

Great-Grandpa winked slowly and patted my hand. "Oh no, son. I gave it to you."

19

Martin the Hero

"DAD, WILL YOU tell Robbie he can flush again?" Caroline said at breakfast a few days later. "It's embarrassing. What if one of my friends should use the bathroom after Robbie?"

I looked at Robbie, who was running a piece of French toast over his high-chair tray like a car.

"Maybe when he's twenty I'll let him flush again," Dad said from behind the morning paper.

Caroline sighed, but she didn't grouch anymore. Maybe she was happy because Mom had finally allowed her to wear lipstick to school. It was not very dark and you could hardly see it, but Caroline kept touching her lips as though she wanted to make sure it was still there.

"I've been invited to computer camp at the college this summer," she announced. "My teacher said we will stay in the dorms. There were only two kids picked in the whole town."

Dad put down the paper. "That's wonderful."

"I think I'll be going somewhere this summer, too," Tim bragged. "My coach said he thinks I'll be picked for the Baseball All-Stars. That means I'll get to travel around playing other state teams."

"I'm really proud of you children," Mom said.

"I'm not doing anything special," I mumbled.

"But you are our hero," Mom said.

I paused with a forkful of French toast halfway to my mouth. "What do you mean?"

"You saved Aunt Henrietta and that little girl, dummy," Tim said. "And maybe the rest of us, too. If we'd noticed just a minute later, someone might have been hurt."

I grinned. "I never thought about it. I guess I was a hero."

"Don't let it go to your head," Caroline teased. "You're still a dweeb."

"Lisa and her mother were staying for a week with friends in New Albany," Mom said. "One of them is a reporter for the *New Albany Sentinel*. He wants to do an article about you in the paper tomorrow. As a matter of fact, he wants to come and take a picture of you this afternoon."

Tim pounded me on the back. "Way to go!" he yelled. "My brother the hero."

Caroline laughed. "Remember last year when you were trying to think of some way to be famous?"

I felt my face getting red. I hadn't realized she knew about that. Once I had even chased a cat up a tree so I could rescue it and get my picture in the paper.

"I'm not sure I'm a hero," I admitted. "I was so scared my knees were shaking."

"That makes you all the braver," Aunt Henrietta said warmly. "You did it all in spite of your fear."

That afternoon Lisa and her mother came to the house. Lisa's mom was one of Dad's cousins. The reporter wanted us all there so he could take a picture of us together. Lisa was still holding the bunny, and she leaned over and gave me a kiss just as the photographer snapped a picture.

It was on the front page of the newspaper the next morning. The headline said: *A Kiss for a Hero,* and there was a big article that made me sound braver than I really was.

Dad went out and bought a whole stack of papers so he could send the article to all our relatives. The phone rang all night long with people calling to congratulate me.

When I got off the school bus the next morning, everyone clapped. Mr. Higgenbottom patted me on the back and told me he was proud of me.

"That was a really brave thing you did," Marcia said at recess.

"It really wasn't that much," I said. "I thought it would be really great to get all this attention, but it's kind of embarrassing."

"Well, I think you are very brave," she said. "And you are the nicest boy I know."

"He's the tornado kid," Willie said. "He comes swooping down, saving fair maidens in distress." He slouched against the school wall. "You're lucky. The storm didn't come close to my house."

"You're the one that's lucky," I said. "I never want to see a storm like that again."

"I would have been scared," Willie said.

"I was," I told him. "When we were all down in the basement, I was afraid our whole house was going to blow away. I've never been so scared in all my life."

Willie reached over and rubbed my head with his knuckles. "Of course you were," he said, in a perfect imitation of Aunt Henrietta.

I wiggled away from Willie's head rub and grinned at him. Willie was the type of friend you could tell anything to and he would understand.

"Someday I'm going to write a story about you," he said. "And then when I'm a famous actor, maybe they'll make it into a movie."

150

"Who would play me?" I asked.

Willie pretended to think. Then he gave me a knowing smile. "How about 'Cousin Agnes'?" he suggested slyly.

20

Another Surprise

MOM HAD ANOTHER surprise for me. "How would you like to go to Boston and watch the race?" she asked at breakfast. "Aunt Henrietta would like you to come."

"That would be great," I exclaimed. "But is she going to be able to run?"

"She's determined to try," Mom said. "Fortunately, it wasn't a bad sprain."

"I have an old friend living in Boston," Mrs. Albright said. She put a plate stacked high with golden brown pancakes on the table. "Her name is Deborah Sims. Since her children have grown and moved away she is all alone in her great big old house. She said she would love some company."

I speared three pancakes and reached for the syrup. "What about school?" I asked.

"I already talked to Miss Lawson," Mom said. "She thinks it will be a good educational experience."

"Do Tim and I get to go, too?" asked Caroline. She frowned at the five pancakes on Tim's plate and put one on her own.

"Not this time," Mom said. "Martin is the one who has gone running almost every time with Aunt Henrietta. Both of you have some exciting things coming up, and I think Martin has earned this trip. I'm going, too. The three of us will fly there early Sunday morning. Mrs. Albright's friend is picking us up at the airport."

"The race actually starts in a little town called Hopkinton," Aunt Henrietta said later. "We will run a little over twenty-six miles into Boston."

"That's a long ways," I said.

"At least the weather is a lot cooler," she said. After the tornado the temperature had dropped to a more normal sixty-five degrees. "And the television says it's about the same in Boston. I'm not sure I would have made it if it had remained hot."

After breakfast on Saturday morning, Aunt Henrietta put on her running shoes. Dad had showed her how to wrap her ankle for extra support. "This will be my last run before the big race," she announced. "Anyone want to join me?" Caroline hid behind the book on Greek history she was reading and pretended not to hear.

"I've got baseball practice in a few minutes," Tim said.

"I'll go," I said. I slipped into the running shoes Mom and Dad had bought me way back in February.

We did a few stretching exercises on the front porch. "Miss Lawson says the race is always on Patriots' Day," I told her. "That's the third Monday in April. She told us that last year there were nine thousand runners."

We started off at a smooth pace. "I won't be coming back after the race," she said. "I'm returning to my work."

I stopped running. "Why? I thought you liked it here."

Aunt Henrietta ran in place while she talked. "I do. It's been a wonderful visit. But it's good to go where I am really needed. The director of a refugee camp called last week. He's an old colleague of mine. He asked me to start a school for the children. It will be a real challenge because there isn't much money to use for schooling. Or anything else, for that matter."

"That sounds hard," I said.

"It is hard," Aunt Henrietta said. "It is also wonderful. I love what I do. I thought I wanted to retire a few months ago. But I really just needed a break, a time to get to know my family."

I wondered what Aunt Henrietta's new students would think of her. Would they see only a lady with bony knees and wild hair? I hoped it wouldn't take them as long as it had taken me to see the really great person underneath.

We started running again. I noticed a little limp and knew that her foot was still hurting. "Aunt Henrietta," I said, panting, "I never understood why this race is so important to you."

When she answered, her voice was steady and strong in spite of the distance we'd run. "When I was young, I was a pretty good athlete. In fact, I even dreamed of the Olympics. But there were no long-distance races for women back then, and I could never compete as a sprinter. Then I visited a friend who was working in an orphanage run by our church. Before I knew it, I was working there, too."

I nodded to show I understood. "So you never got a chance to do what you really wanted?"

"No, I didn't mean that. I did do what I wanted with my life. I did, however, always wonder if I could have made the Olympics, especially when women began to compete in longer races." She smiled. "I'm a little old for the Olympics now. Actually, I hadn't thought of running in the marathon until I read an article about it just before I flew home. I've kept in pretty good shape, and I just decided I wanted to try." Her voice was serious, as if she were talking to a grown-up.

"I think you'll make it," I said.

"Thank you." She glanced over at me. "I'm glad we had time to become friends. I know living with an old lady can be a pain sometimes."

I stopped for a minute to catch my breath. "I will be glad to get my room back. Sleeping in a room with Tim's sneakers—now, *that's* a pain."

We packed the car for the trip to the airport that night. Aunt Henrietta played with Robbie, chasing him around while they both barked like dogs.

"It will be nice to get back like we were. No more family stories, no more tales of starving kids," Caroline said as she watched Aunt Henrietta and Robbie. Then she smiled. "It's hard to believe, but I think I'm going to miss Aunt Henrietta."

"Me too," Tim said.

"How do you think she's going to do in the race?" Caroline asked.

Tim shook his head. "She's pretty stubborn. And she is a good runner, but I don't think she'll make it."

"She will," I said. I glared at Tim.

"She's sixty years old," Caroline said. "And I think her ankle still hurts. Tim's right. She won't make it. But it is kind of neat that she's trying."

21

Another Kind of Brave

THE PLANE TO Boston was packed. I had never flown before, so I was pretty excited. After we took off, the flight attendant came around and gave me some juice. By the time I drank it, the plane was starting to land. Only a little more than an hour ago we had been in Columbus.

Mrs. Albright's friend, Mrs. Sims, was at the Boston airport, holding a sign with our name. She whisked us away to her house, pointing out some of the sights along the way. "Too bad you are not going to be here longer," she said. "Boston is full of history. I could show you Paul Revere's house and the site of the Boston Massacre."

We pulled up in front of a brick house. It almost

touched the houses on either side of it. All the houses on the narrow street looked almost the same. Inside, it was cozy and comfortable, with big soft chairs and couches and a furry rug in front of a huge fireplace in the front room. Mrs. Sims led us up a narrow staircase and opened the first door. "This was my son's room," she said. "He's away at college."

It was small but nice. Several airplane models hung from wire hooked to the ceiling. "This will be great," I said.

Mrs. Sims fixed some fancy sandwiches and soup for lunch. The ladies stayed at the table talking after we ate. I excused myself and went outside to sit on the front steps. Some kids came by on skateboards. They looked at me curiously but didn't speak. A wind came up, enough to whisk some candy wrappers down the pavement. I glanced up at the sky. Since the tornado, wind made me nervous. Some hero I was. What would I do if I had to live where there were tornadoes all the time? Or wars?

There were two kinds of heroes, I decided. There were the ones like me, who got a fuss made over them because they'd had the chance to help save some people. Then there was another kind of hero, like Aunt Henrietta. No one ever wrote stories in the newspapers about her. She was the kind of person who spent her whole life thinking about other people first. I think she is the best kind of hero.

After a time, Aunt Henrietta came out and sat down beside me. "Did you ever notice how it can seem like forever when you are waiting for something?" she said. "Then all of a sudden it's here and you wish you had more time."

I nodded. "Like Christmas. You wait and wait. Then it's the day before, and it makes you a little sad because you know in just a few hours it will be over."

"Exactly." Aunt Henrietta nodded.

She touched my arm. "I hope you won't be disappointed in me. I might not make it. There are some pretty rough hills in the last part of the race."

"I'll still be proud of you," I said. "Even if you don't make it all the way."

The next morning, Mrs. Sims drove us to Hopkinton. It was a really small town. We arrived at eight o'clock, and even though the race didn't begin until noon, the streets were packed. Aunt Henrietta pushed through the crowds. "I have to register and get my number," she said.

Aunt Henrietta was limping slightly when she came back. "I'm not sure you should try this with that ankle," Mom said.

"I've waited my whole life for this," Aunt Henrietta said. "I'm not giving up now." She pinned her number on her shirt. We watched as the runners started lining up. These were the champion runners who were competing to win the prizes. The ones with the fastest qualifying times were in the first rows. Aunt Henrietta was a long way back from them.

"Some of those runners will be done in a little over two hours," Aunt Henrietta said. "But they give out medals until five o'clock."

"We'll drive a few miles down the course," Mrs. Sims said. "Then we can cheer you on."

"Good luck, Aunt Henrietta," I said.

We stood on the sidelines for a few minutes, but with the growing crowd of runners, Aunt Henrietta was soon lost from view. "It will get better as it goes along," said Mrs. Sims. "A lot of people will drop out as the race goes on."

There were already hundreds of people lined up all along the route. We finally found a place to park near a town called Framingham and lined up to wait. There were people stationed along the way with water and other drinks for the runners as they raced past.

It was a cool day. "This is perfect weather for a race," Mom said.

"I think I'd like to do this someday," I said.

Mom looked surprised. "I know I'm not very athletic, but I really kind of enjoyed running with Aunt Henrietta," I explained.

"Here come the first runners," Mrs. Sims shouted. People cheered as the champion runners raced by. Row after row passed us. It didn't seem as if very many had dropped out of the race yet.

"Do you see Aunt Henrietta?" I asked as I tried to peer through the crowd.

"I see her," Mom shouted.

We waved as she ran by. Her face was scrunched up as though she was in pain, but she managed a smile for us as she passed.

Mrs. Sims jumped up and down with excitement. "Let's go up a little farther. Maybe we'll see her again."

We ran back to the car and looked for another spot. Traffic was heavy, and by the time we got back to the sidelines, the first runners had already passed. A man standing by me said that this was about the fifteen-mile mark. "The runners will make it to Newton Hills soon," he said. "There are four hills in about two miles. They call the last one Heartbreak Hill."

The runners were coming more slowly now, and they were farther apart. Instead of grabbing a drink on the run, some were stopping to rest.

"It's three o'clock," Mrs. Sims said. "The big runners are already done. She has to come pretty soon or she won't make it by five."

Almost as though she'd heard, Aunt Henrietta came into sight. I grabbed a cup of water and ran out to meet her. Aunt Henrietta looked terrible. Her face was pale, and she was running with a limp. "Maybe you should rest," I said.

She shook her head. "I don't think I could get started again," she said. She drank the water in big gulps and handed back the cup as I ran a few paces beside her.

We climbed back in the car and headed for the finish line. The race ended in downtown Boston, and the traffic was so terrible that we didn't arrive until almost four-thirty. There was a place for family and friends to wait. Some of the crowd was already gone when we got there, but runners were still trickling in. Each one was given a medal. I glanced at Mom's watch. I could hardly stand the suspense. The minutes ticked on, closer and closer to the cutoff time.

Four-thirty passed and then four-forty-five. "She's not going to make it," I sighed. "All that work for nothing."

Mom put her arm around me and squeezed. "Aunt Henrietta did something she always wanted to do. So how could it be for nothing?"

Mrs. Sims looked at her watch. "She's only got five more minutes."

"Are you sure? Maybe your watch is fast," I said.

Mrs. Sims shook her head sympathetically.

I sat down on the side of the road.

"Wait, I see her!" Mom yelled. "I don't believe it. She's going to make it." Nearly a block down the road I saw Aunt Henrietta. She put on a little burst of speed as she saw us waving.

"Hurry!" I screamed. "It's almost time."

I saw her stumble and fall. "Oh no!" Mom cried.

The watching crowd moaned in sympathy. Aunt Henrietta struggled to her feet. Everyone cheered her on. "Come on, lady," someone called. "You can make it."

Aunt Henrietta's eyes were glued to the finish line. She seemed to make a superhuman effort as she crossed it. She jogged slowly to cool down as a woman put the medal around her neck.

"You made it, you made it!" I shouted.

Aunt Henrietta winked as she sagged against Mom and Mrs. Sims. "Of course I did," she said.

22

Home Again

WE STAYED ONLY one more day. Mom had a meeting with some engineers about the new highway on Wednesday afternoon, and she was worried that I would fall behind in school. Aunt Henrietta decided to stay a few days with Mrs. Sims to rest up before she headed to her new school. She promised to write as soon as she arrived.

Miss Lawson let me give a report about the race for extra credit. Even Steve and Lester, the biggest jocks in the room, seemed interested. "I'll bet I could do it," bragged Lester.

"Someday I really *am* going to run in the Boston Marathon," I told Willie and Marcia at lunch.

"I'll go with you," Willie said loyally.

I was glad to be back in my own bedroom, even though the house seemed empty without Aunt Henrietta. That night I took out the family tree Miss Lawson had given us back in January. Thanks to Aunt Henrietta I had most of the blanks filled in. I put a gold star next to Aunt Henrietta's name.

Dad noticed it on my desk when he came in to say good night. "A family is sort of like a tree," he said thoughtfully. "Like the leaves of a tree, we are all apart, and yet we are also connected."

"Aunt Henrietta gave us another family story, too," I said.

"Dad, can I flush?" Robbie called from the bathroom.

"No," we shouted together as we ran toward him.

Wired Youth

The Social World of Adolescence in the Information Age

Gustavo S. Mesch and Ilan Talmud

Routledge
Taylor & Francis Group

LONDON AND NEW YORK

Published in 2010 by Routledge
27 Church Road, Hove, East Sussex BN3 2FA

Simultaneously published in the USA and Canada
by Routledge
270 Madison Avenue, New York, NY 10016

*Routledge is an imprint of the Taylor & Francis Group, an Informa
business*

Typeset in Times by Garfield Morgan, Swansea, West Glamorgan
Printed and bound in Great Britain by TJ International Ltd, Padstow,
Cornwall
Cover design by Hybert Design

British Library Cataloguing in Publication Data
A catalogue record for this book is available from the British Library

Library of Congress Cataloging-in-Publication Data
Mesch, Gustavo, 1957-
    Wired youth : the social world of adolescence in the information age
/ Gustavo Mesch and Ilan Talmud.
        p. cm. – (Adolescence and society)
    Includes bibliographical references and index.
    ISBN 978-0-415-45993-8 (hbk.) – ISBN 978-0-415-45994-5 (soft
cover) 1. Internet and teenagers. 2. Technology and youth–Social
aspects. 3. Information society–Social aspects. 4. Information
technology–Social aspects. I. Talmud, Ilan. II. Title.
    HQ799.2.I5M47 2010
    302.23'10835–dc22

                                                        2009039113

ISBN: 978-0-415-45993-8 (hbk)
ISBN: 978-0-415-45994-5 (pbk)

Wired Youth

The debate on the social impact of information and communication technologies is particularly important for the study of adolescent life, because in their close association with friends and peers, adolescents develop life expectations, school aspirations, world views, and behaviours. *Wired Youth* investigates the driving forces of social interaction, such as shared interests and adolescents' need of diversification of their social circle, and shows how online activities are closely associated with offline social behaviour.

This book presents an up-to-date review of the literature on youth sociability, relationship formation, and online communication, examining the way young people use the internet to construct or maintain their interpersonal relationships. Using a social network perspective, the book systematically explores the various effects of internet access and use on adolescents' involvement in social, leisure and extra-curricular activities, evaluating the arguments that suggest the internet is displacing other forms of social ties. The core of the book investigates the motivations for online relationship formation and the use of online communication for relationship maintenance. The final part of the book focuses on the consequences, both positive and negative, of the use of online communication, such as increased social capital and online bullying.

Wired Youth is suitable for undergraduate and graduate students of adolescent psychology, youth studies, media studies and the psychology and sociology of interpersonal relationships.

Gustavo S. Mesch is an Associate Professor at the Department of Sociology and Anthropology, University of Haifa. He is currently the Chair of the Information and Communication Section of the

American Sociological Association. His main research interests include youth culture, technology and society, online communication and the interface of online and face-to-face social networks.

Ilan Talmud is a Senior Lecturer at the Department of Sociology and Anthropology, University of Haifa. His main research interests include social network analysis, the internet and society, economic sociology, organization and management theory and theories of social capital.

Adolescence and Society

Series editor: John C. Coleman

Department of Education, University of Oxford

This series has now been running for over 20 years, and during this time has published some of the key texts in the field of adolescent studies. The series has covered a very wide range of subjects, almost all of them being of central concern to students, researchers and practitioners. A mark of the success of the series is that a number of books have gone to second and third editions, illustrating the popularity and reputation of the series.

The primary aim of the series is to make accessible to the widest possible readership important and topical evidence relating to adolescent development. Much of this material is published in relatively inaccessible professional journals, and the objective of the books in this series has been to summarise, review and place in context current work in the field, so as to interest and engage both an undergraduate and a professional audience.

The intention of the authors has always been to raise the profile of adolescent studies among professionals and in institutions of higher education. By publishing relatively short, readable books on topics of current interest to do with youth and society, the series makes people more aware of the relevance of the subject of adolescence to a wide range of social concerns.

The books do not put forward any one theoretical viewpoint. The authors outline the most prominent theories in the field and include a balanced and critical assessment of each of these. Whilst some of the books may have a clinical or applied slant, the majority concentrate on normal development.

The readership rests primarily in two major areas: the undergraduate market, particularly in the fields of psychology, sociology and education; and the professional training market, with particular emphasis on social work, clinical and educational psychology, counselling, youth work, nursing and teacher training.

Also available in this series:

Adolescent Health
Patrick C.L. Heaven
The Adolescent in the Family
Patricia Noller and Victor Callan
Young People's Understanding of Society
Adrian Furnham and Barrie Stacey
Growing up with Unemployment
Anthony H. Winefield, Marika Tiggermann,
Helen R. Winefield and Robert D. Goldney
Young People's Leisure and Lifestyles
Leo B. Hendry, Janey Shucksmith,
John G. Love and Anthony Glendinning
Adolescent Gambling
Mark Griffiths
Youth, AIDS and Sexually Transmitted Diseases
Susan Moore, Doreen Rosenthal and Anne Mitchell
Fathers and Adolescents
Shmuel Shulman and Inge Seiffge Krenke

Young People's Involvement in Sport
Edited by John Kremer, Karen Trew and Shaun Ogle
The Nature of Adolescence (3rd edition)
John C. Coleman and Leo B. Hendry
Identity in Adolescence (3rd edition)
Jane Kroger
Sexuality in Adolescence
Susan Moore and Doreen Rosenthal
Social Networks in Youth and Adolescence (2nd edition)
John Cotterell
Adolescent Coping
Erica Frydenberg
Moving Out, Moving On
Shelley Mallett, Doreen Rosenthal, Deborah Keys and Roger Averill
Wired Youth: The Social World of Adolescence in the Information Age
Gustavo S. Mesch and Ilan Talmud

Contents

List of tables and figures   viii

1   The information age, youth and social networks   1

2   The internet at home   23

3   Sociability and internet use   45

4   Online relationship formation   63

5   ICT and existing social ties   80

6   The impact of ICT on social network structure   99

7   Online communication and negative social ties   119

8   Summary and discussion   136

References   150
Index   170

Tables and figures

Tables

1.1   Potential effects of information and communication
      technologies (ICT) on families with teenagers   13
1.2   Structural characteristics of social networks   18
1.3   Theories of ICT according to forms of embeddedness   22
2.1   Summary of internet effects on external family
      boundaries   28
2.2   Summary of internet effects on internal family
      boundaries   37
3.1   Prediction of the internet displacement principles   48
3.2   Examples of displacement and substitution effects   51
4.1   Perspectives on online relationship formation   76
5.1   Theories of computer-mediated communication   87
5.2   Structural processes affecting online relationship
      maintenance   96
6.1   Kinds of digital divide   101
6.2   Causes for social divide   103
6.3   Social consequences of digital divide   109
6.4   Theories of social capital   116
7.1   Summary of risk factors of online victimization   125

Figures

3.1   Time spent with family, friends and alone by internet
      users and non-users   57
6.1   Binding and bridging social capital   114

1 The information age, youth and social networks

This chapter describes the social implications for adolescents of the rapid penetration of information and communication technologies (ICT) into western societies. It is organized through a discussion of the place of ICT in the information society, the rise of the network society, and the parallel emergence of 'networked individualism', adolescence as a developmental life stage, and the association of technology and social relationships.

In most western countries the use of ICT in the workplace and home has become common. These technologies have been integrated into the daily activities of many individuals, not as a novel or extraordinary activity but to forge new paths for ordinary and not so ordinary activities to be accomplished. Many search for news, information, jobs and products; people communicate online and offline, diversifying their sources of information, communication and social support in their daily lives (Dutton *et al.*, 1987; Katz and Rice, 2002a; Wellman and Haythornthwaite, 2002). The integration of these technologies into everyday life seems to be an imperative of the information age, a historical period in which information and knowledge are produced and reproduced at a high rate. Information and communication technologies are the tools that facilitate access to opportunities, knowledge, resources and social capital which otherwise may be difficult to acquire. The internet is a global network that links computers, and through them governments, organizations and individuals support economic, social and information activity at a global level. Spanning geographic boundaries and converting the geography of locale in spaces of flows (Castells, 2000), the internet transfers information in copious volume and in real time, creating what some have described as a fluid society.

The information society and networked individualism

Social scientists have used different metaphors to describe the information age: post-industrial society, information society, network society, cyber-society, and more. Although we acknowledge the different conceptual views, we differentiate network society from the information age. Network society refers to a social organization in which individuals, groups, organizations and states show more flexibility in crossing boundaries, and individuals have greater awareness of the network configuration of their relationships (Castells, 1996; Wellman, 2001; Van Dijk, 2005). Information society denotes the growing tendency to involve computers in the maintenance of data records, information flows, knowledge systems and communication channels. Naturally, network society and information age are closely connected terms. Both concepts describe the economic, political and cultural changes and their consequent social organization in a society, resulting from the production of information. It is a shift from production-oriented to service-based occupations, the manipulation of symbols, and a decrease in the percentage of the labour force involved in the production of tangible products. Most importantly, society is characterized by the emergence of 'networked individualism' in which the likelihood of connectivity beyond the local group increases drastically (Wellman, 2001).

The notion of a network society rests on several social changes driven by technology. A central dimension of the change is the development of a new technological condition in which information technologies (including the internet and mobile phones) facilitate the formation of new forms of social organization and social interaction over electronically based networks. Information and communication technologies are not the cause of social change but they provide the infrastructure to make the change possible as they offer the means of communication necessary for the formation of new forms of production, management, organization and globalization of economic activities. A further important dimension of the network society is the shift of the culture to symbolic communication and to organization primarily around an integrated electronic system of communication and entertainment. Media are becoming more and more diverse, with specific audiences making different choices and causing fragmentation of the traditional means of mass communication. Hyperlinks entertainment and news sites are critical for human culture, and the internet is becoming the linchpin of the symbolic environment.

The result of the diverse changes is that the major functioning of society relies on networks. The concept of networks is elaborated later in this chapter. In the meantime we might look at networks as a form of social organization with certain qualities. They are flexible and adaptable, and electronic communications afford networks the capacity to decentralize and adapt the execution of tasks while coordinating purpose and decision making.

This concept of networked individualism was established by sociologist Barry Wellman (2001). He depicts society as having moved from a form of social organization in which we belonged to and interacted within small, densely knit, socially homogeneous social groups to a form in which we interact on an individual basis with individuals, regardless of membership of social groups. Individuals are born into families, live in neighbourhoods and have jobs at workplaces. In the past their social interaction was restricted to these social spheres, in which they tended to get together, become acquainted and establish closer or more distant social ties. Now, the information society is transforming this type of organization and interaction into one in which networks are built across distance, group boundaries are permeable, interaction is with diverse others, links shift from network to network, and hierarchies are becoming flatter and more complex.

As the use of instant messaging (IM) and social networking sites exemplify, rather than belonging to the same group, individuals in present-day society have their own personal networks through numerous applications. Although complex social networks have always existed, recent technological developments have yielded their emergence as a dominant form of social organization. Just as computer networks link machines, social networks link people. Often computer networks and social networks work conjointly, the former linking people in the latter, and people bring their offline situations to bear when they use computer networks to communicate (Wellman *et al.*, 1996).

The implication of networked individualism is that interpersonal relationships become more and more based on the specialized roles that people play. Such specialized relationships revolve around shared interests, common problems, short-time collaborations and the need for information. Specialized social networks consist of likeminded people, and the internet supports the development of groups and social connections based on shared interests and common lifestyles. Furthermore, people vary in the extent of involvement in different networks, participating actively in some, occasionally in others, and being silent lurkers in still others.

The capacity of the internet to support the production and consumption of information cannot be gainsaid. Since its first introduction into homes, in many countries its most frequent use has been for communication. It offers delayed (asynchronous) communication applications, such as email and forums, as well as real-time (or synchronous) applications such as instant messaging and social networking sites. Internet communication is used to keep in touch with known individuals, to support existing relationships with coworkers, family, and friends and to form new relationships. Youth are growing up in a multimedia and multicommunication environment. For many adolescents the internet is the main source of information and entertainment, and an important tool for communication. As youths tend to be the earliest adopters of this technology, their experience differs dramatically from that of their predecessors.

Public and academic discourse on the relationship between youth and ICT is ambivalent. Many commentators are enthusiastically utopian, maintaining that internet applications provide children with new opportunities for creativity and active learning (Tapscott, 1998; Prensky, 2001). Moreover, social policy emphasizes the development of skills such as computer literacy because these are believed to be needed for an increasing number of occupations. By this approach, which celebrates the emergence of the information age and the rise of network society, the electronic media are seen as means of empowerment, liberating children from social inequalities. At the same time the internet might have negative effects on teenagers. Because access can seldom be regulated effectively, youths risk exposure to inaccurate information and abusive content (Livingstone and Helsper, 2007). Moreover, the internet might be harmful to social and family life, as time spent on computer activity comes at the expense of participation in family, social, leisure and sports activities (Kayany and Yelsma, 2000).

The debate on the social impact of ICT is particularly important for the study of adolescent life, because adolescence is a period of speedy biological, psychological and social transformation, and of rapid expansion of social circles. In their peer group, in close association with friends and peers, adolescents develop life expectations, school aspirations, world views and behaviours.

Scholars from such diverse disciplines as cultural studies, psychology, sociology and communication have studied the communication aspects of the internet. In the early research we can identify the conceptual and methodological tensions that set the research agenda for subsequent years. In this chapter we refer briefly to only two of them, which are central to our conceptual argument: they are the interplay of technology and society with the online and with the offline world.

Technological and social views

Communication using the internet has been named computer-mediated communication (CMC, Rice, 1980). The term underscores two features that were influential in shaping research agendas. First, the word 'mediated' indicated a clear difference from interpersonal communication, in which individuals engage in symbolic interaction directly, without the use of technologies. Second, the features of the computer, the cultural artifact that is the mediator, were added to the concept and were assumed to shape the messages and interpersonal relations that it made possible. Technology, then, was assumed to constrain the options and meanings of the symbolic interaction between individuals. At the very start of the inquiry into the internet and sociability, tension arose between two major perspectives: technological determinism and social shaping of technologies. It partially overlapped the tension between virtuality and reality, between generative and reflective approaches.

We distinguish between studies that regard the internet as culture and those that regard the internet as a cultural artifact (Hine, 2005). To study the internet as a culture means to regard it as a social space in its own right, and to explore the forms of communication, sociability and identity produced in this social space and how they are sustained by the resources available in the online setting. From this perspective, the internet has been referred not as a communication channel but as a place for being or dwelling, capable of sustaining complex social spaces. One's online sociability is conceived as different and even separate from one's offline identity. It was viewed as having a life of its own, usually separate from real life, as a parallel reality of the participating individuals. In this view, the virtual space is a coherent social space that exists entirely within computer space, wherein new rules and ways of being could emerge. Individuals operating in an online community may be geographically dispersed, experiencing different hours of the day in different locales, but they share the same virtual space and rules and have a common history. They can therefore treat their online interactions as real. By this view online communication can exist in itself, completely separated from real life, and individuals can communicate at a distance, overcoming the fragmented character of offline life. Being online, individuals were not only released from the constraints of location but were also freed from the constraints of their offline personalities and social roles. Individuals could express online their real or inner selves, using the relative anonymity of the internet to be the person they wanted to be, the individual whom they described to others, experimenting with their identity and self (Bargh *et al.*, 2002).

By this view, the relative anonymity of life on the screen gives individuals a chance to express often unexplored aspects of the self and the creation of a virtual persona. Cyberspace becomes a place to 'act out' unresolved conflicts, to play and replay difficulties, to work on significant personal issues. Turkle (1996) summarizes this position: 'we can use the virtual to reflect constructively on the real. Cyberspace opens the possibility for identity play, but it is very serious play'. This approach has methodological implications. Conceiving the internet as an object of study means examining only the virtual persona, online communication and online social norms, rules and etiquettes, without even considering the other direction, namely how established social norms and values are reflected in the online world. In this case the internet has been hailed for the possibilities it is perceived to proffer its users to slough off the constraints of their material surroundings and bodies, enabling them to create and play with online identities. The human body is not only invisible online but is also deemed temporarily suspended, so that it becomes partially or completely irrelevant. Cyberspace was thus conceived as providing an escape from social inequalities such as racism or gender discrimination (Turkle, 1996). Similarly, from this perspective, internet communication creates new forms of social relationships, in which participants are no longer bound by the need to meet others face to face but can expand their social arena by meeting others, located anywhere in the online universe, mind to mind. Virtual relationships are more intimate, richer and liberating than offline relationships because they are based on genuine mutual interest rather than the coincidence of physical proximity. It is a zone of freedom, fluidity and experimentation, insulated from the mundane realities of the material world (Bargh *et al.*, 2002).

A completely different view obtains if one studies the internet as a cultural artifact, an object immersed in a social context, considering how the technology is incorporated in individuals' everyday lives, and how it is used as a means of communication in an offline social world (Howard *et al.*, 2002; Katz and Rice, 2002b). Researchers who take this position regard the virtual as inauthentic, a reflection of the real, and shaped by real-life social conditions and dispositions. The disembodied identities of the virtual world are seen as superficial, and online forms of communication as fleeting, individualized, one-dimensional exchanges, in contrast to the more permanent and complex nature of human engagements in the offline world (McLauglin *et al.*, 1995). ICT users are often characterized as so immersed in virtual interaction that they become detached from their offline social and physical surroundings, hence from their responsibilities in the real world (Kraut *et al.*, 1998; Nie *et al.*, 2002). Some commentators present a picture of children who are extremely absorbed in their online worlds as rejecting the real one and distancing themselves from offline social and familial relationships, withdrawing from the public outdoor space. This approach leads naturally to a probe of internet patterns of use and activity as a deviant form of social behaviour, a search for its pathological implications. This line of research developed such concepts as pervasive internet use, and compulsive internet use, to describe a small minority of individuals who spend long hours on the internet searching for information and communicating online.

The technological deterministic view presents the internet as an innovative force that exercises profound influence on children and youth. Technology generates new patterns of expression, communication and motivation. In describing this view, various terms have been used, ranging across 'the net-generation', 'the millennium generation' and 'digital natives' (Tapscott, 1998; Prensky, 2001). These labels attempt to identify a large group of young adolescents who grew up at the time of internet expansion and were exposed from early childhood to a media-rich environment. Immersed in these technologies they use computers with the greatest of ease, playing online games and constantly communicating and connecting to their friends by electronic devices. These youth create and use digital spaces for social interaction, identity expression and media production and consumption. Supporting this perspective, in the last decade scholars of media consumption have described adolescents' lives as characterized by media privatization in a multimedia environment (Livingstone and Bovill, 2001). The net-generation or digital natives are adolescents who, having grown up with the internet and its uses, express different values, attitudes and behaviours to those of their predecessors (Prensky, 2001). The net-generation is described as optimistic, team-oriented achievers who are talented in technology. Immersion in this technology-rich culture influences teenagers' skills and interests in important ways. According to this view, they think and process information differently from their predecessors, actively experiment, and depend on information technologies for searching for information and communicating with others. They are eager to acquire skills needed to develop creative multimedia presentations and to become multimedia producers, not merely consumers (Tapscott, 1998;

Prensky, 2001). Simply put, the internet has created a new generation of young people who possess sophisticated knowledge and skills with information technologies that express values that support learning by experience, the creation of a culture in a digital space and have particular learning and social preferences.

The notion of a net-generation is consistent with a deterministic view of the effect of technology on society. Technological determinism views technology as an independent force that drives social change (Bimber, 1994). Technology itself exercises a causal influence on social practices, and technological change induces changes in social organization and culture regardless of the change's social desirability.

This view is highly controversial, as it is difficult to assume that information and communication technologies are a force that homogenizes young people into a single entity with unique characteristics (Herring, 2007). Technology is an inherent part of society; it is created by social actors. Approaching technology as a social construction, it is important to note that social groups differ in the extent of access, skills and meanings they associate with technology. The same technology can have different meanings for different social groups of users. Technologies can and do have a social impact, but they are simultaneously social products that embody power relationships and social goals and structures (Smith, 1985). Technological changes are a process and do not have a single direction. Understanding the place of the internet in the life of young individuals requires avoiding a purely technological interpretation and recognizing the social embeddedness of the technology and variable outcomes (Sassen, 2002). The internet can be constitutive of new cultural features of young social life but these can also reproduce older conditions. A purely technological approach ignores material and cultural conditions within and through which these technologies operate. Digital spaces such as social networking sites, blogs and clip and photo sharing are owned by commercial companies that target youth and try to shape their consumption patterns. At the same time, by using these spaces youth become empowered, and they assume an important role in society as co-producers of internet content and reach out with their innovative presentations to large and global audiences.

A more accurate approach is to envisage the internet not as generating a new world but as reflecting some existing conditions of society. The internet is a space of activity, but its function is limited to supplementing existing means (face-to-face, cell phone, phone) and in some cases displacing them (Hampton and Wellman, 2001; Baym *et al.*, 2004). Rational considerations, such as the interaction of time, distance and cost are at the heart of decisions to use the internet instead of other channels. Existing characteristics of the relationships are instrumental and central in determining which channels to use and when. Strong ties make use of all the channels, weak ties only some of them (Haythornthwaite, 2002). The emphasis in this view is on the actor: the integration of the internet into existing relationships reflects the actor's rational choices in maintaining existing social ties.

The two perspectives differ as to whether the development of online worlds is a positive or negative occurrence, but they share the tendency to regard the real and the virtual as not only different but also discrete. This understanding of the relationship between online and offline has been increasingly subject to criticism. For example, the ability to access online spaces presupposes certain offline material resources – at least a computer and the electricity to run it. In additional, physical or material access are linked to digital and computer literacy, information skills and motivation (Van Dijk, 2005; Drori, 2006). In this book we attempt to see how online and offline worlds are connected, and we focus on adolescents, the group most involved in internet use, to show how online spaces are used and interpreted in the context of young people's everyday offline lives and the extent to which the internet as an arena of social interaction reflects, but can also modify, individuals' social involvement in personal relationships.

Adolescence and social ties

Adolescent attraction to friendship, its formation, and its quality have received much sociological attention (Kandel, 1978; Hallinan and Kubitschek, 1988; Crosnoe, 2000; Moody, 2001). Adolescence is a period characterized by rapid developmental changes. As children enter their teenage years they interact less with their parents, while peer relationships expand and assume greater importance (Giordano, 2003). Peers act as emotional confidants, provide advice and guidance, and serve as models of behaviour and attitudes (Crosnoe *et al.*, 2003). Studies show a significant relationship between the quality of one's friends and one's well-being. Adolescents who lack attachment to peers are more likely to report psychological distress and to harbour thoughts of suicide (Beraman and Moody, 2004). Although parents continue to influence behaviours and decisions, the time which adolescents spend with peers expands and peers become their most important reference group (Hartup, 1997).

The combination of societal change and expansion in the use of ICT challenges us to grasp whether the nature of adolescence has changed. In a review, Larson and Verma (1999) argued that adolescents face a world in which daily forms of social life are changing, with direct implications for their own lives. Daily interactions are likely to occur less and less in the context of stable, small scale, culturally homogeneous and tightly knit communities, and more and more in transitory, culturally heterogeneous, negotiated, and sometimes more impersonal relationships. There is a variety of social reasons for this process. Families are shrinking as the average number of children per woman has fallen in most western countries. In the short term, fewer children means that adolescents have fewer siblings; in the long term it implies fewer uncles and aunts, and far fewer cousins, nieces and nephews, that is, a much smaller extended family. Other contexts of interpersonal life are also affected by change, as schools, work and friendships tend to separate adolescents from adults. Adolescents tend to spend more time and more years in school and to engage in extracurricular activities than in the past. As families shrink in size, adolescents turn increasingly to peers for social support. These trends mean that peer relationships acquire greater importance in adolescents' preparation for adulthood. The internet further enlarges the adolescents' world of peer interactions and opens new communication paths with people outside their immediate community, across barriers of distance, ethnicity, age and gender, and with the advent of computerized translation programs even of language.

Youniss and Smollar (1985) studied extensively the meaning of friendship in adolescence and found that relationships with peers and parents usually do not compete but serve wholly different functions. Peers are generally more accepting than parents, who are necessarily more future oriented and concerned more with the potentially negative consequences of the children's behaviour. The elevated level of acceptance in the peer context and the tendency to focus on the present helps explain the higher levels of self-disclosure and mutual trust that often develop as a basic characteristic of adolescent peer ties. Adolescent friendships serve also as an academic resource. In one study adolescents whose friends liked school did well in school themselves and had fewer academic problems than did those whose friends were less academically oriented (Crosnoe et al., 2003).

Internet use by adolescents has increased enormously in recent years, and studies show that adolescents use the medium mainly for social purposes (Lenhart et al., 2001; Gross et al., 2002): they communicate after school, exchange gossip and information about homework, and obtain social support. Online relationships are already an integral part of adolescent culture and social life. Studies confirmed these relationships and reported that 14 per cent of US teenagers have formed close online friendships (Wolak *et al.*, 2003). Relationship formation and maintenance is one of the most appealing aspects of internet use for young people, given that forming relationships is a developmental imperative of adolescence and adolescents are closely involved with the technology.

Sociological studies on adolescent friendship (attraction, formation and quality) have relied mostly on the proximity–similarity hypothesis (Kandel, 1978; Shrum *et al.*, 1988). According to this perspective, homophily in social relationships results from the combination of proximity, which provides opportunities for frequent and mutual exposure and shared social status, which creates attraction between individuals who share the same social experience and context. People's daily activities are socially structured, creating an array of opportunities that tend to bring individuals into frequent contact. When people who share social status meet, social attraction and relationship formation are likely to occur because a given social status is associated with sharing similar life experiences and similar needs for information, communication, activities and support (Suitor *et al.*, 1995). Studies on adolescent friendships have typically relied on data from school samples, disregarding other contexts of friendship formation (see e.g. Kandel, 1978; Schrum *et al.*, 1988). This approach has several serious limitations. First, using the proximity–similarity hypothesis with school samples makes it impossible to disentangle the effects of proximity from those of similarity (Aboud and Mendelson, 1996). To ask respondents to name friends at school only (as most studies have done) is to ask for friends who are already in their proximity and therefore similar. This approach omits from the study friends who are not in proximity, do not attend the same school, and those who were met online. Second, the fundamental argument of the proximity–similarity hypothesis is that the quality of friendship between similar friends is higher than between less similar ones. Studies based on school samples cannot verify this hypothesis because they have not compared the quality of friendship in different social contexts of friendship formation.

Furthermore, recent studies have shown that adolescents make new friends not only in their neighbourhood and at school but also online. Occasionally, online friendships trigger face-to-face meetings (Gross *et al.*, 2002; Wolak *et al.*, 2003). There is some evidence that these relationships can become intimate and provide social support (Gross *et al.*, 2002; McKenna *et al.*, 2002). But most of these studies derive their data from samples of internet users, which precludes comparisons between the quality of online and face-to-face relationships.

Internet and family tensions

These developments have several implications for adolescents and their families. Families of adolescents need to adjust and adapt their relationships to accommodate the increasingly maturing adolescent. This is especially true in the information age, which breeds new areas of tension. Changes in parent–child relations are influenced by adolescents' growing desire to increase their sense of autonomy and individuation. As they grow up adolescents become less satisfied with their parents' authority over their personal lives and activities, and more willing to disagree openly with them, which can lead to heightened conflict (Youniss and Smollar, 1996). Many contentious exchanges concern parents' regulation of adolescents' everyday lives, such as curfew rules, friendship relations and personal activities such as use of internet, phone and television (Smetana, 1988; Collins and Russel, 1991). In the past, adolescents were exposed to friends at school and in the neighborhood, places where parents exerted great influence and control. Housing is determined by the parents' social standing; when they choose a residential environment they make a long-term decision on the composition of their young and adolescent children's peer group. The internet introduces an element of tension in this area, as adolescents can diversify their social networks beyond their school and neighbourhood, thereby weakening their parents' ability to control their associations.

Families are social systems characterized by a hierarchy of authority. The computer can change this hierarchy, as the adolescent, a frequent user, becomes the family expert upon whom other family members rely for technical advice and guidance (Watt and White, 1994; Kiesler *et al.*, 2000). Adolescents increase their resources vis-à-vis their parents and enhance their power within the family. Furthermore, as adolescents search for autonomy, parental controls over their activities steadily diminish. Studies have shown that although parents report supervising the sites their children visit, children usually report that their parents do not control their computer activities (Lenhart *et al.*, 2001; Livingstone and Bovill, 2001).

During adolescence children's and parents' expectations of each other change, and gaps in these expectations can cause family conflict (Steinberg and Silk, 2002). Children may expect adolescence to be a time of greater freedom, and parents may expect adolescents to self-

Table 1.1 Potential effects of information and communication
technologies (ICT) on families with teenagers

- Adolescents' diversification of social networks beyond their school and
  neighbourhood, thereby weakening their parents' ability to control their
  associations.
- Challenging the family hierarchy, as the adolescent, a frequent user,
  becomes the family expert upon whom other family members rely for
  technical advice and guidance.
- Parental supervision and monitoring of websites challenges adolescents'
  autonomy.
- Expectation gaps as parents expect computers are used to enhance
  academic performance and adolescents' expect computers to enhance their
  social lives.

---

regulate their behaviour so that social and leisure activities do not
interfere with school activities (Collins and Russel, 1991). Parents are
aware that computers can enhance academic performance. Studies
found that parents appreciated the new educational resources that the
internet provided for their children, but worried about the erosion of
standards (reading short articles instead of books) and the credibility
of online information (Subrahmanyam *et al.*, 2001), and expressed
concern that the internet may distract children from other activities.

Studies exploring family interaction about media issues report that
parents expect adolescents to self-regulate internet use and to make
efforts to restrict the time spent on computer-related activities so as
not to interfere with schoolwork and socializing (Livingstone and
Bovill, 2001; Pasquier, 2001). Parents may perceive frequent internet
use as a violation of their expectations, and it may become a source of
intergenerational conflict. We maintain therefore that the diffusion of
communication technologies can change the process of adolescent
social association and intergenerational relationships (see Table 1.1).

Social networks

Social networks are a theory and method for the study of patterns of
relationships and interactions among social actors. While other
perspectives focus on the actors' social characteristics, such as age,
gender, socio-economic status and personality, the focus of social
networks is on the properties of their interactions, such as their nature,
content, intensity and frequency (Haythornthwaite, 2005). Social network methods have been employed to study organizational behaviour,
inter-organizational relations, citation patterns, virtual communities
and other domains.

The social network perspective centres on the exchanges (or lack of exchanges) between two actors who form a pair. A social network relation denotes the type of exchange or interaction occurring in any pair in a system of actors. A pair who maintain an exchange or interaction are said to have a common tie that links them (Garton *et al.*, 1999). Across a set of actors, ties accumulate and create social networks. Such networks reveal the flow of resources (information, sociability, communication, goods, etc.) between actors and how sets of actors are connected to each other. The chief distinction between a network approach and other approaches is the focus on exchanges and interaction between actors, not on the individual characteristics of the actors engaged in the exchange of resources. Social network analysts seek to describe networks of social relations, their prominent patterns and the flow of information or resources through them, and to learn what affects the characteristics of social networks and what effect social networks have on people, organizations and communities. Social network analysis is used to describe the network and to explain how involvement in a particular network helps to explain the attitudes and behaviour of its members. Social network analysis is very helpful in describing how information and other resources flow through direct and indirect ties, how people acquire resources, and how individuals are associated with other network members.

Any study of social networks seeks out several of their central characteristics. Social networks differ in network size, that is, the number of social actors constituting the network. Large social networks provide more resources, as the individual can depend on more others to access social support, sociability and advice. Additionally, larger social networks tend to have more heterogeneity in their members' social characteristics and resources. The estimation of network size is often difficult, because it requires defining boundaries around individuals' networks, which can dynamically vary according to a person's everyday life. Recent studies suggest the existence of a cognitive constraint on the size of social networks, perhaps because the number or volume of neocortical neurons limits an organisms' information-processing capacity, and hence the number of social relationships which an individual can monitor simultaneously (Hill and Dunbar, 2003). Since the size of the human neocortex is known, the relationship between the group size and neocortex size can be used to predict the cognitive group size for humans. Dunbar (1993) used this approach to predict that humans should live in social groups of approximately 150 individuals. The same limitation seems to be working on the size of online social networks. Dunbar's findings created interest in the possibility that social networking sites might increase the size of human social groups. There is some evidence that the average number of friends in a Facebook network is 120, and that women tend to have somewhat more than men. But the range is large and some people have networks numbering more than 500. The number of people's active ties on an individual's friend list is smaller. An average man responds to the posting of only seven of those friends by leaving comments. An average woman is slightly more sociable, responding to ten (*Economist*, 2009). A recent study sample of 6000 adolescents' MySpace pages found that the median number of ties a teenager has in MySpace is 60. Girls have more listed ties than boys with a median of 103 ties (Pfeil *et al.*, 2009). These results suggest that network sizes both online and offline are lower but close to Dunbar's number of 150 ties. In the early stages of internet use there was concern that it was time consuming and might reduce the size of individuals' offline social networks, implying a social displacement effect (Kraut *et al.*, 1998). This issue is explored in Chapter 2.

Homophily is a well-established and central concept in social network analysis and describes the characteristics of the social network members. It indicates that contact and social interaction are more likely to occur with similar individuals. The notion implies a similarity attraction expectation: people are more likely to interact with others with whom they share similar traits, interests and life experiences (McPherson *et al.*, 2002).

Homophily seems to be the result of a structure of opportunities for interaction emerging from the social structuring of activities in society. Similar individuals tend to reside in the same neighbourhoods, to work in the same organizations and participate in the same activities (Feld, 1981). This aspect of homophily might be challenged, as individuals use information and communication technologies to maintain ties, but also to seek new ones, based on shared concerns, interests, hobbies and social support (Pearson *et al.*, 2006) and shared interests may bring into contact individuals who differ in their social background (Mesch and Talmud, 2007).

Another important concept concerned with the amount and type of network exchanges is multiplexity. The more numerous the exchanges in a tie, the more multiplex it is. Multiplex ties are not specific or limited to a single type of resource exchange but encompass the exchange of various kinds of social support, information and sociability. They are usually more intimate, voluntary, supportive and durable than unidimensional ties, and are maintained through more communication channels. Online social networks apparently tend to be less multiplex than offline social networks. Online communication fosters specialization as social ties are created around a shared specific interest or topic, and this specialization constrains the variation in the resources being exchanged.

A related issue is media multiplexity, a concept developed out of recognition that individuals communicate through a range of channels (Haythornthwaite, 2005). The social network approach can be used to see where relations and ties cross media lines: which kinds of groups maintain ties via multiple media, and which communicate only by means of a single medium. For example, an online community might coordinate a meeting by email, exchange information in the online community, and meet face to face. Individuals who belong to the same social network communicate using face-to-face meetings, phone and cell-phone conversations, short message service (SMS) and internet communication. With the introduction of new information technologies, communication with acquaintances, coworkers, family members and friends has undoubtedly become diversified, making the study of social networks difficult and complex. Today the study of social networks in our society requires us to ask ourselves who is talking to whom about what and via which media. The closer individuals are to each other, the more means of communication are seemingly used, indicating that studying networks online does not always reflect an individual's real network.

Centrality

Centrality refers to the identification of the users or individuals at the centre of the network, that is, the network members who have the most connections to others (degree centrality), or members who are tied to network segments not otherwise connected (betweenness centrality); in the latter case, the member whose departure might cause the collapse or disappearance of the network. The notion of centrality is important for many internet applications whose adoption and existence depend on network members who recruit to join the application. For example, instant messaging requires that individuals start using the application and invite others with whom they interact frequently to use it. If one member is at the centre and decides to move to another application, the entire network will very likely disappear from such an application. The cumulative effect is an application that was once highly used and is no longer in the market as it has lost its members; the network links people, but often people link networks.

Density

Density is a key structural dimension of social networks that measures the extent to which members of social networks know one another and their exchanges are reciprocal. More specifically, it measures the proportion of actual ties to all possible ties. Network density increases with transitivity in social relations. Given that member a knows member b and member b knows member c, if the conditional probability that member a also knows member c (or vice versa, assuming network symmetry) is high, then transitivity is prevalent (Wasserman and Faust, 1995). High density typically occurs in cohesive groups, and it is more likely to be pronounced in small communities.

Tie strength

Finally, an important concept is tie strength. A tie's strength is usually assessed by a combination of factors such as perceived closeness, intimacy and trust (Granovetter, 1973). Weaker ties are evinced in more casual relationships and in sparser exchanges; they typify relationships of those who enjoy fewer kinds of support. Weak ties are important in getting general information, accessing distant and non-similar contacts, and obtaining information that one's close ties do not possess. Strong ties exist in relationships on a high level of intimacy and trust, involving more self-disclosure, shared activities, emotional as well as instrumental exchanges, and long-term interaction (Marsden and Campbell, 1984). From this definition it can be argued that strong ties are the ones we develop with family, close friends and coworkers, that is, with people of the same social circle and similar in social terms. Their exchanges are frequent, the resources exchanged are of multiple types (emotional and instrumental), and they have a high level of intimacy, self-disclosure and reciprocity in exchanges. People with strong ties have powerful motivation to share their resources.

Weak ties are characteristics of acquaintances and casual or secondary contacts, and are deemed to develop between individuals who differ socially and belong to different social circles; their interaction is infrequent and primarily instrumental. They are organized around a common interest or need. One interesting aspect of weak ties is that because those who evince them belong to different social circles they can become a resource for information that is not known to the actor and his or her close social network (see Table 1.2).

Table 1.2 Structural characteristics of social networks

Network size	The number of social actors who constitute a network.
Homophily	The degree of social similarity within the network.
Resource multiplexity	The variety of resources types which are exchanged within the network.
Media multiplexity	Variation in the quantity of media used to maintain social ties in the network.
Centrality	Identification of individuals at the centre of the network.
Density	Measures the extent to which members of social networks know one another.
Tie strength	A tie's strength is usually assessed by a combination of factors such as perceived closeness, intimacy, duration, commitment and trust.
Reciprocity	The extent to which communication from one member to another is replied.

Social diversification

This approach attempts to link internet use, social interactions and the individual's social circles and resources. Theoretically, when used for communication purposes the internet seems to be a global communication device, bringing together individuals who share needs and interests in different locations without time limitations. Hardly any scholarly attention has been paid to the way in which the internet is associated with the geographic reach of personal ties, social heterogeneity and the ways in which ICT affects adolescents' mix of social interactions and social relationships.

From a more socio-structural perspective, social network analysts have also tended to see matters this way. They have argued that virtual communities can be viewed as social networks, linking individuals from different neighbourhoods, cities and countries (Wellman et al., 1996; Wellman, 2001). Systematic differences may be expected to exist between individuals who meet friends online and offline. The likelihood of online friendship formation will presumably be higher for adolescents who report low self-esteem and who also lack social closeness to face-to-face friends. Because people need intimacy and companionship, the internet provides a new space to meet others and create close relationships.

Information and communication technologies are conceived as agents of change in society because they support the rapid creation, diffusion and accessibility of information, the formation of social networks, and the accumulation of social capital. Their extensive use for communication purposes might lead to a change in the structure of the social networks, exposing people to non-similar others, overcoming the limitations of proximity, age and gender. This exposure to individuals with similar interests but different social background leads to a diversification of the social network, facilitating access to resources, information and knowledge, and is a potential means for the reduction of social inequalities.

At the centre of the diversification approach is a conceptualization of the internet and mobile devices as a space of activity and social interaction. The internet is not only about communication with existing ties. Certainly, many individuals and organizations use the internet as another channel of communication with existing ties, but the internet's innovation is precisely to provide opportunities for activities that induce social interaction, furnishing a space for exposure to new social ties. Here the social use represents more than a communication channel; often it is a space of social activity. People playing interactive games online do more than that: as in any game, the players form groups, interaction is recurrent, and names and phone numbers are exchanged. Forums are used for advice, social support and information search, creating opportunities for social interaction and involvement. It is not uncommon for users who are acquainted to introduce others to their social network.

Societies are characterized by varying levels of social segregation. In societies that reward individuals differentially according to income, prestige, ethnicity and power, stratification systems result in a differential ability of individuals to gain access to jobs and residential locations. As a result, individual social associations tend to be with people of similar social characteristics such as age, gender, marital status, ethnicity, religion and nationality. Studies on the formation, development, maintenance and dissolution of close social relationships have emphasized the importance of network homophily. Social similarity in the social network is the result of the opportunity structure for interaction, which emerges from the social structuring of activities in society. Feld (1981) used the concept of *foci of activity*, defining them as 'social, psychological, legal or physical objects around which joint activities are organized'. Whether they are formal (school) or informal (regular hangouts), large (neighbourhood) or small (household), foci of activity systematically constrain choices of friends. From this perspective, association with others is the result of a two-step process: foci of activity place individuals in proximity (for example, they provide opportunities for frequent meetings), which causes individuals to reveal themselves to each other. According to Feld (1981), whatever the basis of their initial association with a focus, it may be difficult, costly and time consuming not to associate with certain individuals who share the same foci. For all these reasons, individuals' association with particular foci of activity may have unintended social consequences for them. Specifically, people tend to choose their friends from the set of people available through these foci. The internet as a focus of activity becomes an institutional arrangement that brings individuals together in repeated interactions around the focal activities.

Consequently, an important motivation for individuals to form online relationships is to diversify their social network and identify other individuals who share their interests, concerns or problems, but who are not part of their social circle. Online social formation is thus not a general need, as not all individuals are involved in this activity; nor is it the result of insufficient relationships with family or friends but merely the need to find other individuals with similar interests, not available in the social network because of its deterministic similarity. Diversification of social ties, rather than a need for company and lack of social skills, motivates online relationship formation (Lin, 2005).

Network diversification can be linked to social capital; a concept that has been used to explain the actual and potential effects of online social interaction on society. Among several accepted definitions and operationalizations, social capital is generally understood as network ties that provide mutual support, shared language, shared norms, social trust, expansive reach of social ties and a sense of mutual obligation from which people can derive value (Huysman and Wulf, 2004). It is perceived as a by-product of social relations and as benefiting group members. Social capital has been linked to positive social outcomes such as low crime rates, better health, better educational achievement and higher income.

The definition emphasizes the central role of the size, structure, composition and trust in social networks (Wasserman and Faust, 1995; Monge and Contractor, 2003; Kadushin, 2004). According to these qualities, networks provide differential access to resources that include opportunities, skills, information, social support and sociability. Social capital – and one of its components, social networks – are structural concepts that refer not to dyadic interactions but to the characteristics of the groups in which people are embedded. Central to social capital is that it is made up of networks, norms of reciprocity and trust, which enable participants to act together more effectively to pursue shared objectives. The concept of trust refers to being able to rely on known individuals, but also on unknown individuals. So trust is a property of intimate relationships, but also refers to a generalized trust in other community members.

Putnam (2000) argued that active membership in community and in voluntary groups is decreasing, causing a decrease in social capital. Membership in voluntary associations and activities provides opportunities for gathering, social networking, developing networks and norms which deepen trust in society. This author cites the increased penetration of television into households as a central factor explaining the decrease in social capital. This reference to the negative effect of media impels scholars to investigate how involvement in online activities influences social networks, and ultimately social capital, in society.

An interesting issue is how a person's online and offline relationships affect social capital. This is important, if we think of the internet as supporting information exchange and interpersonal communication, linking individuals already involved in the same social circle, supporting past friendships and family ties that have become less active due to geographic mobility, and creating new acquaintances, thus expanding the social circle by bridging different social groups. The focus should be on social characteristics and media simultaneously, to understand which social groups benefit from online social ties, which do not, and how these benefits or deficits are translated into social life. A good place to start exploring these issues is the close social environment of young people, namely the family.

The effect of ICT on adolescents' social ties, as well as the impact of sociological and psychological factors on the uses and implications of ICT, can be summarized as shown in Table 1.3.

The two polar perspectives, technological determinism and social constructivism, are situated at the two extremes (presuming that only one effect of either social or technological factors is dominant). These extreme perspectives were quite common in the first studies of ICT. By contrast, most contemporary theories take into account both technological and social systems in shaping ICT structure and users' conduct. The theories in cells (1) and (2) assume high technological impact on the use of ICT, while the perspectives marked in cells (3) and (4) attribute a weak impact, if any, of technological impacts on the use and structure of online social ties (Wellman and Gulia, 1998; Katz and Rice, 2002b; Haythornthwaite, 2005).

Likewise, the theories in cells (1) and (3) attribute a strong impact of social factors on the use and implications of ICT. Media richness

Table 1.3 Theories of ICT according to forms of embeddedness

Dimension		Social context	
	Effect	*Strong*	*Weak*
Technological	Strong	1 Media richness; social affordance; net-generation; online diversification.	2 Technological determinism (i.e. lack of social cues).
	Weak	3 Social constructivism; social capital.	4 Networked individualism; relationship reconfiguration.

theory, for example, takes into account the technological characteristics in relaying complex information among users, while also accounting for the human capacity to discern complex social communication.

The theories in cell (1) implicitly assume a strong impact of social embeddedness on ICT as well as the undeniable qualities of ICT in fostering the expansion of adolescents' social relations. The last cell (4) does assume some impact of both technological and social factors on online social factors, yet these two factors are not considered very strong. Networked individualism and relationship reconfiguration (treated at length in Chapter 6) constitute key elements of the information age for people's choices of relational quality and communication, and for their construction of social networks. Certainly, sociological variables affect adolescents' choices, but they can choose communication and friendship ties with far fewer constraints than before the diffusion and domestication of ICT in classrooms, families and households. Young people's ability to choose among many ties to form, maintain and expand their social networks and to widen flows of communication with close friends has become possible only with the emergence and broad applicability of ICT.

2 The internet at home

In this chapter the impact of the adoption of the internet in families with adolescents is described. The discussion rests on the concept of family boundaries, one which accords well with the diversification approach we developed in the last chapter to capture the nature of changes in the family system and peer relations. Following the conceptual consideration we review research findings on the implications of the internet at home for parent–adolescent relationships. In the final part of the chapter we treat family adjustment, discussing the concept of family mediation and the different strategies that parents use to control family boundaries.

The rise in the use of the internet in society has stimulated research on how these new technologies are associated with everyday life. Scholars have studied the relationship of new information and communication technologies (ICT) and the extent of community involvement and participation (Hampton and Wellman, 2002; Kavanaugh and Patterson, 2002; Mesch and Levanon, 2003), interpersonal relations, sociability and social capital (Katz and Rice, 2002a; Nie *et al.*, 2002) and work (Haythornthwaite and Kazmer, 2002). Despite this large body of research on how communities, organizations and individuals adapt to new communication and information technologies, the existing research literature on the impact of computer technologies on the family is very limited (Watt and White, 1994; Hughes and Hans, 2001; Mesch 2006). This is surprising, as the incorporation of computer technologies into the home is a complex process in which the consumer plays an active role, involving making or not making them acceptable and familiar (Silverstone and Haddon, 1996). This so-called domestication process is one in which 'new technologies and services, by definition to a significant degree unfamiliar, and therefore both exciting but possibly also threatening and perplexing, are brought (or not) under control by and on behalf of domestic users'

(Silverstone and Haddon, 1996: 60). The idea of domestication implies a two-way process: the family needs to adjust to technologies, and this in turn affects family interaction patterns. In this chapter the focus is on the potential effects of ICT on the family and on how families cope with the new technology.

The family system and ICT

Here we draw on the conceptual framework developed by Watt and White (1994), who take a family development and human ecology approach to the study of the effects of ICT on the family. These effects are assumed to depend on the family's developmental stage (Watt and White, 1994), as the following examples show. The communication aspect of computers can support the process of mate selection, where individuals who have never met before can establish a close and intimate relationship; during pregnancy the couple can rely on online information and online forums to acquire health-related information and advice; at the stage of early preschool children, participation in a community bulletin board may provide the family with help in babysitting and finding activities for children (Mesch and Levanon, 2003); and in the post-parenting age, when adult children have left home, computers may facilitate family communication as they provide a new channel for family members to communicate and share experiences through email, instant messaging, or social networking sites (SNS).

Regarding the more specific influences of ICT in the family, Watt and White (1994) suggest turning to human ecology theory, which perceives human development as taking place within the context of relationships. By this perspective the family is a social system with permeable borders and technology is conceived as a major source of change. Technological innovations enter the family, creating changes in norms and social roles. A simple example is the need to accommodate the computer and to find space for the machine. While parents usually prefer to place media in the public spaces of the home, adolescents would rather locate it in their bedroom (Horst, 2008). The bedroom has a special meaning for adolescents as a place where they can conduct private activities. In that sense, arranging their room according to their needs, consuming media of their preference and decorating the room with symbols of youth culture are exercises in autonomy.

New information is converted into new functions, and one possible result is specialization as children sometimes acquire computer skills rapidly and take on the role of advisors and aides to other family members. This specialization involves changes in the nature of the relationships in the family subsystem, as knowledge is often reflected in doing tasks for the parents and at the same time monopolizing computer time.

According to the family developmental-ecological approach the family is a relatively closed social system and the internet is a technology that has 'opened a hole in the fence of the family' (Daly, 1996: 82). This conceptualization of the family emphasizes the importance of family boundaries as reflected in the need for privacy and family time as a functional requirement for the effective operation of the family system (Berardo, 1998). The boundaries between the family and the external world are important and necessary to preserve the parental role of socialization, and the nuclear family furnishes clear-cut, often rigid boundaries between public and private life and between children and adults (Elkind, 1994). Strong family relationships evolve through an awareness of boundaries between family members and the rest of the world. In their lives together, parents and children negotiate ideas about how and why they are similar to and different from each other, and from other families and people (Berardo, 1998).

Following the developmental-ecological approach rather than discussing the family in general, we now focus on one stage of the family life cycle: families with adolescents. In this stage, parents' and adolescents' relationships centre on issues of family boundaries, parental authority, adolescent autonomy and expansion of adolescents' social circles (Fuligni, 1998; Smetana, 1988).

The developmental-ecological approach is consistent with the diversification approach taken in this book. Information and communication technologies are conceived as an agent of change in society because they support the rapid creation, diffusion and access to information and the formation and maintenance of social networks (DiMaggio *et al.*, 2001; Lin, 2001). At the centre of the diversification approach is a conceptualization of the internet as a space of activity and social interaction. One innovative aspect of the internet is to provide opportunities for activities that induce social interaction. The internet provides a space for playing online games, presenting a public identity through the creation of a public profile in a social networking site, accessing information, connecting with new acquaintances and meeting new individuals. Through participation in interactive games groups are formed, interaction is recurrent and names and phone numbers are exchanged. Teenager forums are used for advice, social support and information search, creating opportunities for social interaction and involvement. It is not uncommon for teens who know each other to introduce friends or family members to other friends and family members, creating opportunities for social interaction with new acquaintances.

Family boundaries and information

The introduction of ICT to the home creates tensions in the perception of the family boundaries, both external and internal. As to the former, ICT holds the premise of moving many activities (such as working, learning and shopping) that were dispersed by industrial society back into the home (Tapscott, 1998: 251). The boundary between work and family has become blurred as people increasingly work from home (Silverstone and Haddon, 1996; Valcour and Hunter, 2005). While this allows the family more time together, there is a danger that work activities will interfere with family time (Chesley, 2005). The internet and cell phones provide the opportunity for continuous contact with work when one is at home, and with family when one is at work. This technological affordance has been linked to the blurring of boundaries between work and home which is assumed to increase the stress on family relations. A study in Australia tested the extent to which the use of ICT was perceived as affecting the work–family life balance. It found that the use of cell phones affected the perception of spillover of family life on to work time but not that of spillover of work activities on to family life (Wajcman, *et al.*, 2008).

An additional tension with implications for family boundaries is that ICT use exposes adolescents to larger amounts of information, covering any topic, anytime, anywhere. For the most part this information is very important as it supports schoolwork and homework. Yet, a central concern for parents is that adolescents are more exposed today to negative content as well, and the impact of this exposure might be serious for a number of reasons. First, adolescents are the most frequent users of the internet for both information search and communication purposes. Second, adolescence is a developmental period characterized by identity formation. In the creation of this identity youth search for answers to existential problems, and in doing so they might be exposed to wrongful information or information that is at odds with family values. Third, adolescence is a period of expansion of the peer group and high involvement in social relationships, which might expose the youth to other risks such as harassment and online bullying, a topic that is expanded in Chapter 7.

As for unwanted content, a major worry arising from the increase of internet access from home has become adolescents' exposure to pornographic content. The ease of access and the abundance of pornographic content on the internet tend to magnify anxiety about the harmful influence of internet pornography on minors. Pornography is perceived as more accessible to minors through the internet than in its traditional forms (Greenfield, 2004). Pornography is the term most often used for sexually explicit content that is primarily intended to arouse audiences sexually (Malamuth and Impett, 2001). The literature suggests a number of negative effects of frequent and long-term exposure to this material. First, it leads to more liberal sexual attitudes and greater belief that peers are sexually active, which increases the likelihood of first intercourse at an early age (Flood, 2007). Second, adolescents exposed to sexual behaviours outside cultural norms may develop a distorted view of sex as unrelated to love, affection and intimacy, and a desire for emotionally uncommitted sexual involvement (Byrne and Osland, 2000). Third, youth exposed to pornography may develop attitudes supportive of the 'rape myth', which ascribe responsibility for sexual assault to the female victim (Seto *et al.*, 2001; Flood, 2007). Studies on the extent of youth exposure to pornography have focused on 'chance' or unwanted internet exposure to pornographic material (Greenfield, 2004; Livingstone and Bober, 2004). Chance exposure is the receipt of pornographic material by email and pop-ups, and reaching sites with pornographic content fortuitously in the course of a search for material for homework. An implicit assumption is that the wide availability of X-rated material on the internet and through commercials results in involuntary exposure to this content (Greenfield, 2004). Results of these studies show that exposure by chance is frequent with between 10 to 30 per cent of youth reporting it (Wolack *et al.*, 2003).

Another risk is exposure to online hate content (websites), inciting to violence against, separation from, defamation of, deception about, or hostility towards others based on race, religion, ethnicity, gender or sexual orientation. The web is a unique medium that facilitates the dissemination of hate messages in a variety of forms, from cartoons and jokes to pseudo-educational narratives, and the use of multimedia. Frequent exposure to hate might result in the adoption of stereotypes, attitudes supporting racism, lack of empathy for minorities, aggressive behaviour and involvement in hate crimes. From the research literature it appears that despite the wide availability of hate sites, only 20 per cent of adolescents report having been exposed to content that advocates hatred of minorities. Of those exposed, more than a third (36 per cent) reacted by ignoring the site and its content. Another third informed a friend or an adult about the site (Mnet, 2005).

An additional concern for parents is that youngsters using the web might convey information about themselves and their families to marketers, enabling them to create detailed profiles of a family's lifestyle (Turow and Nir, 2000). Accurate or not, such portraits can influence how marketers treat family members; for example, what discounts to offer them, what materials to send them, how much to communicate with them and even whether to deal with them at all.

Parental concerns are reinforced when certain technological characteristics of the internet are considered. The internet has been portrayed as conducive to deviant behaviour because of its use in isolation from others, as opposed to consumption of other media, which is in the presence and even with the collaboration of others. The relative anonymity of the medium may promote activities that an individual does not usually engage in when he or she is part of a group, where members tend to conform to culturally accepted behaviour (Pardum *et al.*, 2005). See Table 2.1.

Table 2.1 Summary of internet effects on external family boundaries

Blurring of family's external boundaries	Weakening of parental control of information that family members have access to, and of access by external agencies to family information.	Blurring of the boundary between work and family life. Work interferes with family activities such as meals together, conversations and games. Family life interferes with work activities.
		Time displacement from family activities to individual-centred internet activities.
		Youth access to internet information including violent, hate and pornographic content.
		Providing information on family consumption patterns to commercial sites.

In sum, internet use for the search of information presents a challenge to family boundaries as it increases the unsupervised exposure of adolescents to a wide variety of content. Much of this content is important, for example, in supporting homework and searching for answers to existential issues. Yet this increased exposure might blur family boundaries, creating tensions. Families deal with these tensions and try to adjust to the new challenges that internet access poses by using technological and social devices to mediate adolescents' exposure. Later on in this chapter we present the strategies used by families to exert control over family borders and to restrict access to unwanted information by youth.

Internet and family time

Family cohesion is defined as the 'emotional bonding that family members have toward one another' (Olson *et al.*, 1983: 60). The meaning is a positive involvement of parents with their children, as reflected in shared activities, supportive behaviour and affection. The beneficial implications of family cohesion for children's behaviour and development enjoy strong support in the social sciences. Adolescents who report being close to their parents show higher achievements at school, fewer episodes of truancy and school dropout and fewer cases of seeking medical care for emotional or behavioural problems (Amato and Rivera, 1999).

Family time can be seen as a central dimension of both family cohesion and family boundary construction and preservation. If we think of families as social systems having a collective identity, that identity is the result of shared recollections of togetherness created as family members spend time together in shared meals, games and chatting (Daly, 1996). In western societies many families struggle with the concept of family time. In the dual career family, in which the boundaries of work and home are blurred, family time is sometimes the sharing of space and time that arises from the intersection of busy lives (Daly, 1996).

Although the ideal of private family time continues to be salient as a cultural ideal, a variety of forces impede the realization of this goal. With the proliferation of technology at home, families seem to be at the crossroads of two different tracks: one that provides them with many opportunities for shared activity within the home and another that easily distracts them into the solitary world of technology that demands their individual attention (Daly, 1996). Studies have shown that the time a family spends together in activities such as recreation are positively related to family cohesion (Orthner and Mancini, 1991). A recent large-scale study in the USA on internet use in families with adolescents found that members of all the families explicitly stated how much they valued spending time together. Many families scheduled time to watch television shows, movies and videos together. That is, parents and adolescents conceived the shared consumption of media as facilitating communication and bonding (Horst, 2008). A small but growing proportion of the families with adolescents increased family time, with parents engaging in the production of media together with their teenage children. In this way adolescents worked with the support of parents, learning new skills of multimedia production; parents described these activities as becoming involved in their childrens' interests and culture (Horst, 2008). Shared activities are described as forces contributing to clarifying and strengthening family boundaries because they create opportunities for interaction, communication and memories that contribute to the perception of the identity and uniqueness of one's family (Hofferth and Sandberg, 2001; Zabrieskie and McCormick, 2001).

A second explanation is time displacement, as it has been argued that internet use is negatively associated with family time. The main argument is that time spent on one activity cannot be spent on another (Nie *et al.*, 2002). Internet use is a time-consuming activity and in families that are connected to the internet high frequency of use might be negatively associated with family time and positively associated with family conflict. In fact, parents and adolescents have worried that internet use might have a negative effect on family communication and closeness (Turow and Nir, 2000; Jackson *et al.*, 2003). This concern received limited verification, mainly from studies conducted at the early stages of diffusion of the technology to the home. A study based on family time diaries found that internet use at home was negatively related to time spent with family. Furthermore, the reduction in family time was higher for the average internet user than for the average television watcher (Nie *et al.*, 2002). The perception that the amount of daily internet use might affect family time is expressed by both parents and adolescents. A study in the USA of a sample of youth and parents found that 29 per cent of parents believed that online time interfered with family time, while only 16 per cent of teens believed so (Rosen *et al.*, 2008). Another study conducted among a large sample of adolescents reported that internet use did not help them to improve their relationships with their parents, and that the internet consumed time they would have spent with their families (Lenhart *et al.*, 2001).

Still, before reaching a conclusion we should keep in mind that time spent with parents diminishes as the youngster becomes older. This is the result of social development: the older the adolescent the more likely he or she is to spend more time with peers than with parents. Therefore studies need to control for age. Such a study was conducted among a representative sample of Israeli adolescents, investigating how the amount of daily internet use by adolescents was related to family time and cohesion. The relation was found to be negative. This result was statistically signficant even after controlling for types of internet use, age, and number of siblings (Mesch, 2006).

While these studies provide evidence for a relationship between internet use and a reduction in family time, they treat the internet as a unified technology. Youth differ in the extent they use the internet for communication, information search and entertainment, and different uses probably have different effects on family time. A recent study on the association between different types of youth internet use and family time found evidence that internet use decreased the amount of time youth spent with their families. Notably, different youth activities had different effects. Playing online games decreased both the total time spent with the family and the time spent communicating with family members. Using the internet for communication with friends resulted in a small decrease in family time. However, using it for educational purposes such as searching for homework or doing homework did not affect family time (Lee and Chae, 2007).

Despite this evidence of a negative effect of youth internet use on family time, the overall picture has more complex generational effects. At the early stages of family ICT domestication, parents and children faced a generational divide, a gap in technology skills, where children were more likely to possess better skills than their parents. Today many more young parents have acquired the skills needed to use the internet in complex activities. This trend is reflected in a number of studies which suggest that rather than isolating children from their parents, the internet has become a shared household activity (Kaiser Family Foundation, 2003). However, as another study shows, the extent to which parents share time consuming and producing media with adolescents depends on parents' education and computer skills. Parents with less education and low computer skills are more likely to perceive the internet as a force that isolates them from their children (Horst, 2008).

In sum, most of the empirical evidence on the association between internet use and family time shows a reduction in the time parents and youth spend together (Lenhart *et al.*, 2001; Mesch, 2006; Rosen *et al.*,

2008). This evidence remains firm even when youth age is controlled, indicating the existence of an internet effect on family time. Recent studies indicate that internet use by youth for social and entertainment purposes has a more pronounced effect than its use for information search and homework (Lee and Chae, 2007).

ICT and parent–adolescent conflict

Family time is negatively associated with family conflict. Cross-sectional and longitudinal studies have shown that low levels of family time were associated with higher levels of conflict (Fallon and Bowles, 1997; Dubas and Gerris, 2002). Apparently, families that share time in common activities enjoy a higher quality of communication which facilitates discussion of disagreements before they become open conflicts.

There is some concern that internet access in the household may negatively affect patterns of interaction between parents and children, increasing intergenerational conflicts and weakening family cohesion (Watt and White, 1994; Lenhart *et al.*, 2001). Families are social systems characterized by a hierarchy of authority. The introduction of the computer has the potential to change that hierarchy as the adolescent becomes the family expert on whom other family members rely for technical advice and guidance (Watt and White, 1994). Under these conditions the adolescent increases his or her resources relative to the parents and also his or her ability to dominate the family sphere. A study of computer help-seeking among 93 US families found that teenagers were more likely than parents to help others in the family. Adolescents became the experts, and when parents needed help they had to rely on information and advice from them (Kiesler *et al.*, 2000). Similarly in the UK, traditional adult–child relations appear to be reversed in many households because children are more technologically competent than their parents (Holloway and Valentine, 2003). Thus, children, were able to define to a much greater degree than family members the meaning and uses of the computer in the home (Sutherland *et al.*, 2003). Through time it appears that parents, instead of increasing their skills and extending their power to control technology, have come to struggle with the situation. A recent large-scale survey of pre-adolescents and adolescents found that in many households the web had become work for the school-aged as parents assigned them 'cyberchores'. The study found that 38 per cent of youth helped parents to share photos and send emails to relatives online, and 36 per cent helped with parental information search.

Regarding the reasons, almost half of the teen respondents (47 per cent) said they performed 'cyberchores' because their parents lacked online skills; 29 per cent stated that they did so because their parents did not have time to do these jobs themselves.

Adolescence is a time when families need to adjust and adapt their relationships to accommodate the increasingly maturing adolescent. Many of their exchanges concern parents' regulation of adolescents' everyday lives, such as curfew rules, friendship relations and personal activities like phone and television use (Collins and Russel, 1991). Studies on adolescents show that as they become older they submit ever less to parental authority over aspects of their personal lives. At the same time they demand more and more autonomy and show greater readiness to disagree openly with their parents (Fuligni, 1998). Parents attempt to guide the use of the internet by creating rules on time and websites permitted. Communication and enforcement of the rules appear inconsistent. There is empirical evidence that parents and adolescents perceive the rules differently. A large-scale study of families and media showed that while parents were able to articulate the rules, children forgot to mention them or stated that their parents mentioned rules but these were open to negotiation. Parental discourse about rules very likely reflects their intentions more than actual deeds (Horst, 2008). A study of 1124 adolescents and their parents in Singapore found discrepancies between parents' and children's reports. For example, parents reported sitting with the adolescents while they were on the internet more often than the children did; and parents reported checking bookmarks or browser history more often than adolescents did. Parents tended to over-report the frequency of control and monitoring they exerted (Liau *et al.*, 2008). The pattern of communication existing in the family may be an explanation for the gaps found in the perception of rules regulating the use of the internet. In families in which parents and adolescents perceived their communication as open, empathetic, encouraging and trusting, their reports regarding family rules on the use of media were consistent (Cottrell *et al.*, 2007).

Of particular importance are the domains of parent–adolescent disagreement over authority and autonomy. In one study adolescents and parents were found to agree that parents had legitimate authority over moral issues (adolescent actions that could be harmful to others or violate mutual trust), prudential issues (smoking and drinking behaviour) and friendship issues (seeing friends that parents do not like). As for personal issues such as regulation of television time, regulation of phone calls and choosing clothes, adolescents regarded

these as less legitimately subject to parental jurisdiction, and obedi-
ence less obligatory, than other issues (Smetana and Asquith, 1994).
Furthermore, the frequency and intensity of parents' and adolescents'
conflicts over personal issues proved relatively high (Smetana and
Asquith, 1994).

During adolescence children's and parents' expectations of each
other change, and gaps in these expectations can cause family conflict.
Children may expect adolescence to be a time of greater freedom, and
parents may expect adolescents to self-regulate their behaviour so that
social and leisure activities do not interfere with school activities
(Collins and Russel, 1991). Parents are aware that computers can
serve as a tool to enhance academic performance. For example, word
processing programs that correct spelling and provide a thesaurus can
enhance language abilities. A study found that parents appreciated
the new educational resources that the internet provided to their
children, yet they worried about the erosion of standards (reading
short articles instead of books) and the credibility of online information (Subrahmanyam et al., 2000), and expressed concern that the
internet might distract children from other activities.

Studies exploring family interaction on media issues report that
parents expected adolescents to self-regulate internet use and to
make efforts to restrict the time spent on computer-related activities
so that they would not interfere with schoolwork and socializing
(Livingstone and Bovill, 2001; Pasquier, 2001). Parents may perceive
frequent internet use as a violation of their expectations, and it may
become a source of intergenerational conflicts.

The introduction of computers into the family has the potential to
create new conflicts over authority and autonomy. Parents' concerns
may impel them to formulate rules on the amount of internet use.
Adolescents perceive rules as interference in personal matters and an
attempt to reduce their aspirations for increased autonomy (Smetana,
1988). Computer use requires knowledge and skills, and children
acquire them before their parents. The balance of family power may
change as the adolescent becomes the person in the family to whom
others turn for technical help. Studies have shown that when this is
the case adolescents monopolize the machine and restrict the computer use of other family members (Watt and White, 1994; Kiesler
et al., 2000).

Another source of conflicts is the development of expectation gaps
between parents and youth. Parents seem to view the internet as a
positive new force in children's lives and surveys in different countries
report that the main reason families buy computers and connect their

children to the internet at home is for educational purposes (Turow and Nir, 2000; Lenhart *et al.*, 2001; Livingstone and Bober, 2004). Many parents believe that the internet can help their children to do better at school, do better research for homework and help them learn worthwhile things (Van Rompaey *et al.*, 2002; Livingstone and Bober, 2004). But not all teens use the internet in the same way. While some spend most of their internet time searching for information, acquiring skills and researching for homework, others mostly use it for social purposes (email, instant messaging and participation in chat rooms) and entertainment purposes (playing games online) (Livingstone and Bober, 2004; Lenhart, *et al.*, 2005). It is plausible to assume that when youth use the internet for social and entertainment purposes, parental expectations contradict the actual use, aggravating conflict between adolescents and parents. Conversely, using the internet for learning and education purposes, a usage highly valued by parents and consistent with parental expectations, will be negatively associated with family conflict (Mesch, 2003). Parents are concerned with the possibility that internet activities distract the children from school activities. Parents restrict the time they can play games and enter social network sites before schoolwork and household chores are completed (Horst, 2008).

Competition for scarce resources and computer location has been identified as another reason for parent–children conflict. In most households there is only one computer, and parents and children compete for its location and time using it (Lenhart *et al.*, 2001; Holloway and Valentine, 2003). Location is important as it is a reflection of the family's power structure and the type of relationships being developed. It has to do with several issues related to adolescence. First is the search for autonomy: as adolescence progresses, adolescents increasingly want a relaxation of control. Second is the power structure, as the adolescent becomes the expert in internet use and helping other family members becomes a source of increased power in the hierarchy. Finally, computer location has implications for the adolescent, as it has an effect on the amount and types of internet use.

Data from various surveys provide us with a sense that, unlike the television, the computer is still mainly located in open and public areas of the family such as the living room. A 2004 study gathered detailed information on internet access and use by British children and youth, with a representative sample of 1511 respondents aged 9 to 19 and their parents. It found that in 63 per cent of cases the television set was located in the children's room and in 37 per cent in a public space; the computer was located in a public space in 74 per cent of the cases (Livingstone and Bober, 2004). In the USA, the Pew Internet and American Life studies yielded similar values, indicating that, at the end of 2006, 74 per cent of youth indicated that the computer was located in a public area such as the living room and only in 25 per cent of the cases in the children's bedroom. The location of the computer varies according to age: the older the child, the more likely the computer is to be located in his or her bedroom. Generation M, a study on media lives of children aged eight to 18 years in the USA, found that only 23 per cent of children aged eight to ten reported having their computer located in their bedroom; this percentage rose to 37 per cent for the 15- to 18-year-old age group (Rideout *et al.*, 2005).

At this point the central question is to what extent do these conflicts exist, and how do they compare with other prevalent conflicts in adolescence. Mesch (2007), using a representative sample of the Israeli youth population, investigated perceptions of adolescents' conflicts with their parents. He aimed at conflicts over mundane issues such as household chores and homework, and the association of internet use with the frequency of the various types of argument. In particular, the study found that the frequency of perceived conflicts over the internet and computers was higher than that of conflicts over school-related issues and equal to that of disagreements over household chores. The most salient finding of the multivariate analysis was that computer and internet use exerted a generalized effect on perception of conflicts with parents. Adolescents with online friends reported a higher frequency of conflicts with parents over household chores than adolescents without online friends. The amount of internet use was positively associated with the perception of frequent arguments over school-related issues. Finally, perception of conflicts with parents proved associated with older age. Older adolescents reported conflicts over household chores, school-related issues and computer and internet use less frequently than did younger adolescents. After identifying the association between internet use and frequency of perceived adolescent–parent arguments, the final question of the study was whether these arguments had consequences for the young people's perception of family closeness (Table 2.2).

The most salient result of the multivariate analysis is that arguments over the internet and computer use have a statistically significant negative effect on family closeness. Arguments over household chores and school-related issues do not undermine the relations between parents and children, while computer and internet use do. As expected, family time is negatively related to family closeness. In sum,

Table 2.2 Summary of internet effects on internal family
boundaries

Internal border	Effects on parents' and children's expectations and family hierarchy.	Adolescents become technology experts and exercise control over computer time and location.
		Parents create media rules and adolescents tend to break them.
		Parents expect children to improve school performance and teens use the computer for social purposes.
		Parents expect self-regulation and adolescents expect more autonomy in the use of the internet.

this study indicated that only arguments over the internet have a negative effect on family cohesion.

Family adjustment and the internet

As we have shown in this chapter, the entry of the internet into the home affects various spheres of family functioning. The family becomes exposed to large amounts of information (both positive and negative) that circulate inside and outside the home. Youth become exposed to new acquaintances and parental control over their friends declines. Family time and cohesion might be reduced. At the same time the family as a system attempts to adjust to the technology. One way to adjust is to incorporate the internet as both a shared activity and a channel of communication. Is the internet used as a shared family activity in which children and parents use the technology together? A study conducted in a Toronto suburb investigated the extent that the internet was used together with the respondent's spouse and children. The numbers of hours per week that was used with spouse was found to depend on the average hours a week that the respondent used the internet. Heavy users spent 2.8 hours using the internet with their spouses and light users spent 1.2 hours doing so. As to using the internet with children, the results are similar, and for individuals using the internet more than 8 hours a week, on average 3.2 hours were spent using it together with the children (Kennedy and Wellman, 2007). In a recent study in the USA with a representative sample of the internet population, 54 per cent of the parents reported going online with another person a few times a week. Half of them (27 per cent) indicated that they go online with their children (Kennedy *et al.*, 2008).

An additional adjustment mechanism is the adoption of the internet for family communication. In Israel in 2007 we investigated the extent that the internet is used for communication between spouses and between parents and children, taking a representative sample of the country's population. We found that the cell phone had been rapidly adopted as an important channel of mediated communication between parents and between parents and children. Regarding spouses, 63 per cent of married respondents called their partner by cell phone every day; and 51 per cent of those with children aged between 12 and 18 called them every day. Email proved much less common: only 4 per cent of respondents sent an email to their spouse every day, and 1.7 per cent sent an email to their children every day. In Canada, mobile phone calls are also the leading channel of mediated communication between spouses and between parents and children (Kennedy and Wellman, 2007). In the USA, 47 per cent of couples with children and internet access communicate daily with their partner by cell phone, and only 8 per cent send an email daily. Regarding communication with children, 42 per cent of the couples with children aged seven to 17 years old communicate daily by cell phone and only 3 per cent send an email (Kennedy *et al.*, 2008). A study in the UK found that 13 per cent of cell phone text messages were sent to the spouse and 3 per cent to family members. Gender differences were found in the use of text messages. Messages between men were shorter than those between women, and text messages from men were longer to women. Women write longer messages on average than men (Yates and Lockley, 2008). In Australia, a recent study found that a third of all cell phone calls were made to family members. Cell phones were used for micro-coordination of family activities, the greatest number of calls being made to get information on the time of the children's arrival home (Wajcman *et al.*, 2008).

These studies in different countries yield a consistent picture and indicate that only a minority of families with children have managed to integrate the internet into their shared family activities, and far fewer use the internet for family communication. For the vast major-ity of families, mobile phones have been better integrated into family communication. As a shared activity the internet has been integrated by about a third of the families, indicating that this is certainly one form of adjusting family activities to internet. As a family channel of communication, the internet is well behind the cell phone, and it is difficult to say whether it will be integrated at all as a daily channel of mediated communication.

Parental mediation

Since the start of research on children's television watching, scholars have investigated the ways in which potential negative effects of the media can be reduced. One important approach has been to investigate how the family regulates and mediates these potential ill effects. Parental mediation means some form of effort by parents:

- to explain media content and guide children and teens in the interpretation of its content and its relationship to real world
- to reduce access and prevent exposure to unwanted content, and reduce interference of media consumption with educational, extracurricular or family activities.

Parental mediation is a concept that has been extensively studied in relation to children and youth exposure to television programmes. Bybee *et al.* (1982) studied parental media mediation and identified three dimensions: social co-viewing, restrictive mediation and strategic and non-strategic mediation.

Social co-viewing

Social co-viewing refers to the occasions when parents and children consume media content together, sharing the experience (Valkenburg *et al.*, 1999). Co-viewing may be an interactive activity, when parents and children discuss media content, or a passive activity, when all parties sit silently together in the same room, eyes focused on the screen. Through co-viewing, parents can monitor the content that youth are exposed to, and intervene if undesirable content is online. In this way co-viewing allows parents to discuss offensive content if they are so inclined. In the case of the internet, active co-viewing can be described as the extent to which youth and parents jointly use the internet for shared activities, including playing online games, searching for information and planning vacations. In a slightly different sense the concept describes family differences arising from the location of the computer. It is plausible to assume that when the computer is located in a family public area, its use by youngsters will be more controlled than when it is installed in a young person's room (Livingstone, 2007).

Restrictive mediation

Restrictive mediation is the formulation of rules for media consumption by young people. Families establish rules of computer time and/or the types of content, exerting control over what is watched. The use of rules to control viewing known as restrictive mediation can have important effects on children. A problem with investigation of rules is the extent of agreement on their existence. Various studies have reported that measures of restrictive parental mediation are not reliable because parents and children offer conflicting reports about computer and internet rules (Livingstone, 2007; Livingstone and Helsper, 2007). Parents tend to report their existence more than their children; parents' responses most probably reflect social desirability effects. In the specific case of the internet, two types of restrictive mediation have been used. One is the imposition of rules to limit the amount of time and the types of websites that parents allow. The other is installation in the computer of technological devices that restrict the web pages that can be accessed and software that informs parents of the web pages visited by their children (Eastin *et al.*, 2006).

Strategic and non-strategic mediation

Strategic and non-strategic mediation means making deliberate judgement about media content (strategic) or casual comments about media in general (non-strategic; Eastin *et al.*, 2006). In this case parents discuss with children different websites, show them techniques to check the reliability of the information given by a website, talk about the process involved in information creation and the relationship of the content to the real world, and are actively involved in their children's use of the internet.

Studies are starting to provide evidence on the extent that parental mediation is used to regulate children's and youngsters' exposure to the internet. Regarding co-viewing there is some empirical evidence that this is an effective technique. A study of youth in Korea found that parental recommendation of websites and co-viewing were positively related to educational online activities. That is, the more parents recommended websites for their children and the more they used the internet together, the more frequently children searched the internet for educational material for homework and played educational games (Lee and Chae, 2007). A recent study of teens who had profiles in social networking sites found that parenting style and mediation affected adolescent internet behaviour. Teenage children of parents who set limits and monitored online activities were less likely to disclose information in MySpace (Rosen, 2007).

There is a sense that parental mediation has intensified over time. A study of teens and parents in the USA found that most parents of teenagers who go online set time limits on their internet activities. While in 2000 only 41 per cent of parents had installed filtering software on home computers, in 2005 the figure was 54 per cent. In both years, 2000 and 2005, the same percentage of parents (62 per cent) reported checking the websites that their children visited. In 2006, 69 per cent of parents reported having rules about how much time the child can spend online, 85 per cent had rules on the kinds of personal information the child could share, and 85 per cent had rules on the kinds of websites that their children may or may not visit (Lenhart *et al.*, 2007). Similar findings are reported in a study in Canada. Comparing findings for 2001 and 2005, the survey found that in 2005 the percentage of parents reporting rules was higher for all rules, indicating an increase over time in parental awareness of the need to monitor and set rules on their youngsters' online behaviour. This study also investigated the effect of the rules, comparing online behaviour of youth from homes with and without rules. The findings indicate that teens from the former were less likely to visit non-permitted sites than youth from the latter. Furthermore, the amount of time spent by youth online depended on the existence of a rule. Children of grades 10 to 11 from families without any rules spent an average of 3.8 hours a day online; the figure for youth from families with rules was 2.5 hours (Media Awareness Networks, 2005).

The type of parental strategy used depends on the parenting style, of which four have been singled out: authoritarian, authoritative, permissive and neglectful. Authoritarian parents place a high level of demands on their children and a low level of warmth, and restrict autonomy. Authoritative parents monitor and impart clear rules for their children's behaviour, but provide a high level of warmth and allow for autonomy. Permissive parents are low in demands on their children, are responsive to their needs and provide high levels of autonomy. Permissive parents are non-traditional and lenient, and allow considerable self-regulation and avoid confrontation (Eastin *et al.*, 2006). Authoritative parents use evaluative and restrictive mediation techniques more than authoritarian and neglectful parents. Blocking of sites was practised by authoritarian, authoritative and permissive parents. Parental mediation was associated with age, and the older the child the less it was applied (Eastin *et al.*, 2006). More evidence of a link between parenting style and media use comes from a US study of parents and teens. The study focused on youth who participated in social networking sites, and investigated the influence of parental styles on their online behaviour. Authoritative parents proved the most likely to view their teens' social networking page, followed by authoritarian and permissive parents. Authoritative and authoritarian parents were more likely to set limits on computer behaviour (Rosen, 2007). Thus the link between parenting style and parents' rule setting and monitoring seems to be strong; but other factors are at work as well. Wang *et al.* (2005) investigated the correlates of parental rules. A multivariate analysis was conducted on internet rules, checking websites and monitoring software. Teen's age was found a highly significant predictor of internet rules and monitoring software. Parents subjected older teens less often to time limits on internet use, and were also less likely to place monitoring software on the computer. Parents' age and gender were associated with whether they checked the websites their teens visited. Older parents were less likely to check websites than younger ones, and fathers were more likely to check than mothers. Parents' education proved a significant predictor of monitoring software but not of rules. In sum, fathers, younger parents, parents who use the internet with their children and parents of younger teens engage in a higher level of parental monitoring (Wang *et al.*, 2005).

Conclusion

In this chapter the process of internet domestication has been described. We took a developmental-ecological approach, which conceptualizes the effect that children's and adolescents' exposure to internet content might have on family boundaries. The effect of integration of the internet is diverse: it increases young people's exposure to helpful content, but also to unwanted content. The latter includes non-reliable information, pornography and hate, which are expected to influence the youth's view of the world. Concern about content is particularly important because adolescence is a developmental stage when teens search for information that provides answers to mundane issues in which youth express interest.

After concluding that the internet influences the permeability of the family system, our discussion went on to inquire into the extent that the technology affects internal family borders. In the second part of the chapter we turned to the effects of the internet on parent–adolescent relations, focusing on three central dimensions: youth–parent conflict, family time and family cohesion.

Family time is important for the development of family cohesion. It tends to dwindle after children enter adolescence, as they spend less of it with parents and more with peers (Smetana, 1988). We presented evidence that even after controlling for age, daily internet use by youngsters has a moderately negative effect on family time. This association requires further investigation, as the results might represent a period effect. When technologies are innovative they need time to be learnt, and this learning time may temporarily be at the expense of time of social interaction. When the technology has become integrated, the time needed for its use decreases and its effect on family time might diminish.

The empirical evidence presented likewise seems to indicate that internet use is associated with an increase in conflict between parents and youngsters. This is indicated in studies on the effect of the internet alone, but it also features in studies on conflict associated with internet use as well as other developmental conflicts between parents and youth, for instance, over school grades and household chores. Still unclear from the studies are the sources of these conflicts. There is some evidence that they may be related to the relations created online: one study showed the level of conflict to be higher for youth who reported having online friends. Such friends constitute an additional challenge to family boundaries, as parents generally exert some control over the type of friends their children have. For teens who use the internet for relationship formation, this usage might be a source of conflict with their parents as it threatens family boundaries. Other sources of conflict have not enjoyed research attention and future studies on the subject are essential. The presence of rules and their violation and exposure to content forbidden by parents are areas that require more research.

The last part of the chapter was devoted to family adjustment to the internet, reviewing a new and growing area, namely the application to the internet of the concept of parental mediation, widely used in television studies. The concept seems relevant to the study of family efforts to adjust to and adopt the internet, but it seems more appropriate for the internet's informative aspect. Regarding the social network, that is, applications used for relationship formation and maintenance, more theoretical and empirical work is needed before it can be transferred from television to internet studies. This social use of the internet is the focus of the next chapter, wherein the question of whether the internet has an effect on youngsters' sociability is explored in detail.

3   Sociability and internet use

The purpose of this chapter is to investigate the association of internet use with adolescents' sociability. We take a multidimensional approach, examining how internet use is connected to various dimensions of sociability. In this chapter we delve into the different versions of the displacement hypothesis, so as to prepare the ground in the next chapter for scrutinizing the motivations for online friendship formation.

In the last decade scholars of media consumption have described adolescents' lives as being characterized by media privatization in a multimedia environment (Livingstone and Bovill, 2001). In western societies young people's cultural consumption includes a large number of media artifacts such as television sets, video cassette recorders (VCRs), landline and cell phones, play stations, compact disc players, MP3 players and computers. An important observation is that over time households tend to acquire more than one media item and privatize media consumption. Adolescents appropriate the media and more and more media tools move from the public spaces of the household to private places – from the living room to the bedrooms; they pile up in the teenagers' rooms. In various western countries children's and youngsters' bedrooms contain many of the devices listed above. This is privatization of media and it entails more and more indoor activity. These processes give rise to expectations and concerns.

The wide exposure of adolescents to these media seems to be a central cultural characteristic of a new generation, the 'net-generation', youths who have access to new information and communication technologies (ICT) and are eager to acquire skills needed to develop creative multimedia presentations and to become multimedia producers and not merely consumers (Tapscott, 1998; Prensky, 2001). Referring specifically to computers and internet access and use, scholars have indicated that children will master language and maths skills through them. For example, word processing software with automatic error correction and grammar structure suggestions can be construed as learning tools that with practice help children and adolescents to acquire better writing skills. Software can be used to improve mathematical skills by helping the teenager in a field in which it is necessary to practise a great deal.

However, the potential negative effects of media privatization and bedroom culture have sparked public concern. The rapid adoption by youth of numerous media artifacts raises the question of how teens manage their already busy social life. In the public and scholarly discourse the existence of a risk has been mooted: intensive use of new media leads to 'time displacement' and 'activity displacement' (Lee and Kuo, 2002; Lee and Leng, 2008). Put simply, it is argued that the use of computers and the internet requires time, which is passed at the expense of time adolescents spend with parents and peers (Kraut *et al.*, 1998; Nie *et al.*, 2002; Lee and Leng, 2008). Moreover, when adolescents immerse themselves in new multimedia environments they retreat from sports and other leisure and extracurricular activities (participation in games with peers and attending meetings), which are critical for the development of their physical and social skills (Sanders *et al.*, 2000). Public health concerns have been voiced that excessive computer use is conducive to internet addiction and weight gain (Subrahmanyam *et al.*, 2000; Kautiainen *et al.*, 2005).

Displacement argument has drawn two types of criticism (Robinson *et al.*, 2000; Gershuny, 2003). One is that internet use is not necessarily at the expense of other activities. This position rejects the idea that time is a given. The internet facilitates information search, communication, game playing, file downloading and other activities, and thus provides a technological infrastructure for a more efficient way of conducting these activities. It is not at the expense of other activities because technology can decrease the time required to coordinate social activities with peers and friends or for research activities for homework. According to this view, adolescents are using these communication tools primarily to reinforce existing relationships, both with friends and romantic partners. More and more they are integrating these tools into their 'offline' worlds, using, for example, social networking sites to get more information about new entrants into their offline world. Note that adolescents' online interactions with strangers, while not as common now as during the early years of the internet, may have benefits, such as relieving social anxiety. Electronic communication may also be reinforcing peer communication at the

expense of communication with parents, who may not be knowledge-
able enough about their children's online activities (Subrahmanyam
and Greenfield, 2008). The second criticism rejects the assumption that
internet use is a solitary activity, conducted alone and without the
involvement of others. In fact, according to this view most internet
use is social. Rather than isolating the user, the internet facilitates
interpersonal contact, so that users may actually be more socially
involved than others. The arguments presented in this chapter have
been explored partially among adult populations, and no conclusive
knowledge exists about how they apply to adolescents. Furthermore,
as adolescence is a crucial period in the development of social skills,
any isolating effects should be taken more seriously in respect of
youth. Finally, empirical findings on time and activity displacement
are considered in the context of multitasking, that is, the simultaneous
use of different communication channels and media.

After reviewing the most important arguments in the literature, this
chapter presents in detail available findings on the link between
internet use and sociability. The focus is on the association of internet
use with the consumption of other media, involvement in social
activities and time with peers.

The displacement hypothesis

The origin of the displacement hypothesis can be traced to the early
days of television. Once acquired, this medium seems to impose high
demand on children's already busy schedules, and the question arose
concerning how they find room for its active consumption. Regarding
the internet, at the early stages of its adoption by households it was
asked if the introduction of this new medium into users' busy schedules would cause a reduction in time spent on other activities, social
relations and community involvement (Kraut *et al.*, 1998; Kayany
and Yelsma, 2000; Nie *et al.*, 2002).

The notion of displacement is simple: it assumes that a new medium
such as the internet requires time, which is taken at the expense of
other activities important for adolescents' social and cognitive development. In this type of analysis a central assumption was a zero-sum
relationship among the various activities (Table 3.1). The view was
that youth and children are in a conflict situation and make decisions
that result in the displacement of other activities in order to free up
enough time to accommodate media consumption (Neuman, 1991).

Study of the displacement hypothesis calls for some methodological
considerations. Measures of time in each activity are usually gained

Table 3.1 Prediction of the internet displacement principles

Functional similarity	Internet use results in less newspaper reading, less listening to radio programmes and less time watching television.
Marginal fringe activities	Internet use reduces the time spent on organized activities such as participation in extra-curricular activities and sports.
Physical and social proximity	Internet use reduces the time spent in face-to-face and phone interpersonal communication. Replaces time used in family activities.
Transformation	Old media changes and adapts to internet competition.

through individual reports. Self-report is not always reliable because of difficulties recalling how much time has been invested in each activity per day. Second, as the number of media increases and some media become integrated in a single tool, not all media activities are measured; the risk arises of some being left out. Then it is hard to know if there is displacement of or an increase in time spent, and where the displaced time goes and where the extra time comes from.

Principles of displacement

Displacement hypothesis assumes that the type of media and activities likely to be displaced depend on several principles. According to the principle of functional similarity, youngsters will be more likely to desert media that appear to satisfy the same needs as the internet but less effectively. Television and internet serve an entertainment function, so by this principle internet use might reduce the time used to watch television, read newspapers and books, listen to the radio, etc.

A second principle concerns marginal fringe activities: more casual and unstructured activities are more likely to be displaced than organized and structured ones. Unstructured activities lack specific time boundaries and have an undefined character other than spending spare time. According to this principle, internet use may displace free play, going out with friends to hangouts, casual visiting and time spent relaxing.

The third principle is transformation, namely established media will come to be used in a more specialized way. With the entry of a new medium, the old medium will adapt by transforming and changing its content so as not to compete but to avoid competition. According to this principle, television will provide different content not found in the internet or not competing with it.

The last principle concerns physical and social proximity: activities will be displaced if they share the same physical space and provide less satisfaction than the internet. According to this principle home chores are done in the same space where the internet is located, but the latter provide less psychological satisfaction and will be displaced in favour of internet use. After presenting the definition of the principles we turn now to a more detailed account of them.

The study of the effect of internet use on media consumption is important. The internet is in itself a multimedia environment that provides access to a large variation of content. It differs from other media in that it provides access to information, news, diverse types of entertainment (music, movies, radio, games, etc.). Learning the internet's possible effect on the use of other media requires studies in which more than one internet use is compared with a large number of alternatives. But before we can reach any conclusions we must distinguish early studies from late ones. Early results might have been affected by the new medium's novelty and innovation, with increased attention to these, but as time passes and the media becomes increasingly incorporated into the daily life of youth, the displacement effects might come back to the point of departure. Another temporal consideration is the development of the internet itself. Not all its features were available at first, but they came into use over time.

Early studies found some indication of a media displacement effect. A study that compared adults and adolescents for self-reported use of internet on television viewing, newspaper reading, telephone use and family conversations found evidence of functional displacement. Time spent watching television was found less for internet users; also, scores of adults and children showed a significant difference. Children reported higher displacement effects than adults on television viewing and phone conversations. The extent of displacement in youth was related to their internet daily use: heavy users tended more to report displacement (Kayany and Yelsma, 2000). While this effect was also reported in other early studies (Nie *et al.*, 2002), the kind of displacement might be more pronounced when the relative importance of each medium for individuals is taken into account. Data on respondents' rating of the importance to them of watching television, reading newspapers and using online media in searching for information and entertainment will most likely show stronger effects among users who in the first place rated the use of traditional media low and the use of the internet high.

A serious limitation of the studies outlined above is their cross-sectional design. This design provides information on media use and infers displacement from comparison of group behaviour. Long-itudinal studies allow inference of differences in media use for the same individuals through time. In a well-designed longitudinal study, 1251 high school students were surveyed in 1999 and 2000 for the extent of their internet use and six other activities: television viewing, newspaper reading, radio listening, participation in sports and physical exercise, interaction with family, and socializing with friends. Increased internet use proved associated with decrease in television viewing only. Also, changes in how these respondents perceived the importance of internet use predicted changes in how they perceived the importance of television, newspaper and radio as information sources. As the youngsters' perception of the internet as an important medium increased, they reported a decrease in the importance they attached to television and newspapers but not to radio (Lee and Kuo, 2002). With the steadily greater integration of the internet in adolescents' daily life, and the addition of more options for activities online, we may be witnessing an effect other than displacement, namely substitution. Ever more news sources are becoming available online, from newspapers to web portals and blogs constantly updated, as well as music clips, radio stations and television channels. So youth might refrain from reading newspapers or watching television, preferring to conduct these same activities online rather than search for new ones. In that case the internet does not displace the other media but provides a new channel to media consumption online. This so-called substitution effect differs from displacement. Relatively few studies have expanded the displacement framework for the substitution one. A recent study that assessed displacement and substitution effects provides preliminary support for this claim. The more time users spent online for news and information, the less they were found to spend on reading newspapers; the more time they spent online for entertainment the less they spent watching television (Lee and Leng, 2008). These preliminary results indicate the need for more investigations of this possibility (see Table 3.2).

Regarding the principle of marginal fringe unstructured activities are more likely to be displaced than structured activities. Internet use is more likely to displace free play and going out with friends. One of the most persistent themes in the literature is the possibly narrower social world of adolescent internet users than that of non-users. We now take a close look at the adolescents' participation in peer, leisure and sports activities, asking whether adolescents who use the internet are more or less likely to be involved in leisure and sports activities. To the extent that the internet is an isolating activity, we expect to

Table 3.2 Examples of displacement and substitution effects

Displacement	Substitution
Internet use reduces the frequency of reading newspapers and books.	Newspapers and books are read online.
Internet use reduces the frequency of face-to-face meetings with friends.	Communication with friends after school hours is carried through instant messaging and social networking sites.
Internet use reduces the frequency of meeting friends for playing games.	Video games are played regularly with friends online.
Internet use reduces the use of encyclopedias and books for doing homework.	Homework is done conducting online search for relevant materials for school.

find differences between adolescents who do and do not use the medium in the type and amount of participation in social gatherings, sports and evening courses.

Finally, we relate the study of social involvement and association to a quantitative dimension of friendship, and ask if adolescents who do and do not use the internet differ in the size of their social network of close friends. After presenting the results we discuss again the extent of social participation/isolation, taking into account the contexts of adolescent involvement: peers and friends.

Participation in activities and the social development of adolescents

The development of a child from infancy to adulthood requires involvement in different social and leisure activities with others. These activities provide contexts for learning and opportunities for engagement with others (Larson and Verma, 1999; Hansen *et al.*, 2003). Each context engages participants in a set of behaviours and rules and result in learning social skills and a body of knowledge. Activities such as play and conversation provide opportunities for developing social and emotional skills. The quantity of time spent on these activities serves as an indication of the exposure to different social experiences, with more time leading to greater absorption of the skills and knowledge of that context (Hofferth and Sandberg, 2001).

Children learn not only in formal settings such as schools. For early adolescents, play is an integral part of learning social norms and behaviour as well as school material. During play children develop initiative, self-regulation and social skills (Larson and Verma, 1999). Some activities are structured, such as playing cards, board games and unspecified indoors and outdoor play including computer games. Others are structured activities, such as sports programmes and participation in youth groups and organizations (Pellegrini and Smith, 1998). Activities of this type are expected to promote children's academic achievement and social behaviour. Activities are a central component of friendships. Youniss and Smollar (1985) found that in their close relationships male and female adolescents enjoy activities that take them out of their homes and allow them to interact with each other independently of parental involvement or observation. These include going to movies, parties, concerts and sports events, or just driving around or hanging out together. The nature of the activity does not seem important; what matters is that friends are together and out of the home, implying distance from parents and association with peers. Some differences can be found between males and females. Males prefer doing things together, whereas females enjoy mostly talking together. When close friends talk, the topic is more likely to involve personal issues and problems if the friends are female than if they are male. This does not imply that friendships between adolescent males lack personal or intimate communication, but that this aspect is more characteristic of close friendships between females.

The developmental importance of participation in extracurricular and leisure activities with others for adolescents' social and academic development has been demonstrated, and the extent that internet use interferes with this development is a central issue to be explored, which we do in the next sections of the chapter.

Finally, there are issues of personality, as individuals who report low self-esteem may be more involved in internet use to compensate for their social anxiety (Kraut *et al.*, 1998; Nie *et al.*, 2002). In our study we explored this possibility. Respondents were asked to indicate how important it was for them to spend time with their friends, how important it was to have close friends, and how important it was to have friends always willing to listen to them. Reponses were given on a four-point Likert scale from 'Not important at all' to 'Very important'. Users and non-users showed no significant differences in the extent of pro-social attitudes, and the findings do not support the argument that internet users are less socially oriented than non-users. Youngsters without access to the internet in both 2001 and 2004 did not report having more or less interest in having friends than those who used the internet.

Internet and activity displacement

With the increase in internet use by adolescents, concerns exist that internet use may be at the expense of other social, sports and scholastic activities. Some studies have shown that adolescents who used computers were more overweight than non-users (Attewell and Battle, 1999; Hughes and Hans, 2001; Attewell *et al.*, 2003). Nie *et al.* (2002) formulated the hypothesis of activity displacement based on studies of the influence of media in the household and suggested that given time limitations, time used on the internet is at the expense of face-to-face interaction and social participation. This argument maintains that internet activity requires time and is conducted in solitude. Therefore, individuals connected to the internet, particularly frequent users, will presumably report a high degree of lack of involvement in sports, leisure and social activities conducted outside the household. The basic assumption of this model is that time spent on one activity cannot be spent on another (Nie *et al.*, 2002). The internet is time consuming and children who stay online for long spells are liable to be affected in their involvement in peer-related activities. The balance between the acquisition of internet skills for participating in the information society and more traditional activities is an important area of discourse among academics and practitioners who research adolescents and their parents.

In our study of Israeli adolescents we asked them to indicate the frequency of their participation in 13 activities. Answers were provided on a five-point scale: every day, two or three times a week, one to three times a month, several times a year, not at all. By means of a principal components factor analytic technique and varimax rotation, the 13 activities were found to represent three dimensions. One was *social activities*, that is, activities usually conducted in the presence of other friends. These included going to a party at a friend's house, to discotheques, to the movies, to arcades and to concerts, and cruising with other friends. The second dimension was *extracurricular and sports activities*, such as taking evening courses, participating in a youth movement, and participating in sports activities. These questions were asked in two separate studies for adolescents who report using and not using the internet, for the years 2001 and 2004. The findings were consistent, and showed that adolescents who used the internet were more, not less, involved in most activities social in nature and conducted in the presence of others than adolescents not connected to the internet. In both 2001 and 2004 this was the case regarding going to discotheques, going to the movies and walking about with friends in the neighbourhood; likewise in both years regarding extracurricular and sports activities.

But it is premature to conclude that internet use is associated with more, not less, participation in social activities as the differences between internet users and non-users may be due to other causes. For example, participation in some social activities, particularly extra-curricular, requires an outgoing personality or close involvement in a social network, but also the ability to pay the costs of consumption. We should explore the association of internet use with participation in social activities after controlling for family income and parental education as proxy measures of socio-economic status. This control is important to eliminate the possibility of self-selection, meaning that at this point in the history of internet access middle-class groups may be over-represented in its user population. Other important con-siderations are the closeness adolescents feel themselves to be to their parents. There are theoretical arguments that when adolescents do not feel close and do not receive sufficient parental support, they tend to go to their friends, spend time with them and substitute peer support for the lack of parental support.

Bearing all the above in mind, in our study of Israeli adolescents we conducted a multivariate analysis in which we tested three models for the association of internet use with the three dimensions of adolescent activities defined above. The multivariate analysis controls for other characteristics, beyond internet use, that might affect involvement in social and extracurricular activities and the consumption of other types of media. We found internet use positively associated with par-ticipation in social activities in both years. Participation in social activities was associated with other variables as well, and the effect of these was higher than that of internet use. Males were more likely to participate in socially organized activities than females. Socio-economic status also seemed an important factor, and participation in these activities was less frequent as mother's education was lower. As expected, in both years individuals who reported positive attitudes toward their friends showed more frequent participation in social activities. Adolescents who reported having had friends for years, and who felt close to their friends, were more involved in social activities. The same multivariate analysis was conducted regarding frequency of participation in extracurricular activities, which proved related to developmental factors as well. In both years frequency of participa-tion in these activities was higher among younger than among older adolescents, and again males tended to participate in extracurricular activities more than females. Taken together, the most consistent finding of the different models was the absence of any evidence for the time displacement hypothesis. Indeed, internet users formed a group of adolescents more likely to participate in social and extracurricular activities than non-users.

Similar results were obtained in two separate surveys in the USA. The Pew Internet and American Life project conducted two studies of teens and their parents (in 2004 and 2006) that afford us an additional opportunity to compare changes in teenage internet activity over time. In both surveys young internet users were asked to indicate the extent of their participation in four extracurricular activities: a school club such as drama or language, a school sports programme, other extracurricular activity like bands, and a club or sports programme not affiliated with school such as a church youth group. The two years 2004 and 2006 evinced much stability. For example, regarding a school club, 35 per cent of young internet users reported participating in both years; 50 per cent reported participating in a school sports programme; 41 per cent reported participating in other extracurricular activity; 56 per cent reported participating in a club or sports programme not affiliated with their school.

Time displacement

The 'activity displacement' hypothesis has a temporal component as well. An adolescent's involvement in social activities may not be affected merely by his or her being connected to the net; the amount of time he or she invests in each session may be detrimental to participation in normative adolescent activities. Accordingly, we tested for the effect of the frequency of internet use on young users' participation in all activities. Again, frequency of use was found not statistically significant, and results of the regression analysis supported the earlier descriptive findings: involvement in social activities and extracurricular activities was positively associated with internet use. Thus, even controlling for developmental factors such as age, socioeconomic status and closeness of family and friends, internet use is not an activity that isolates individuals but contributes to their engagement in social activities. As Gershuny (2003) argues, the internet has probably become an efficient coordination tool, resulting not in isolation but in expanded relations with others as it facilitates the coordination of mutual activities and reduces the cost of arranging meetings. Moreover, internet use had no effect on the use of the old media, and internet users did not differ from non-users in their use of radio, television, and books.

Internet and time with peers

Another concern of parents, teachers and the public is that the internet may distract children from other developmentally important
activities, such as spending time with friends, and that computers
may have an isolating effect on children (Lenhart *et al.*, 2001;
Subrahmanyam *et al.*, 2001). Consideration of the presumed anti-
social or asocial nature of computers has led some to conclude that,
regardless of the instrumental benefits, excessive preoccupation with
computers may pose a risk especially to children's social relationships.

Adolescence is a period characterized by developmental changes in
the social and physical realms. As children enter their teenage years
they interact less with their parents and peer relationships take on
greater importance (Steinberg and Silk, 2002; Giordano, 2003). Peers
act as emotional confidants, provide advice and guidance to others
and serve as models of behaviour and attitudes. But evidence suggests
that parents continue to influence their children's behaviours and
decisions well into their teens in important ways (Collins *et al.*, 2000).
But whereas in childhood parents were the main source of social
relationship, during adolescence parents represent only one circle, and
peers form another important component (Crosnoe, 2000; Crosnoe *et
al.*, 2003; Giordano, 2003). Furthermore, early adolescents attach
greater importance to acceptance by peers than by parents, and
increasingly turn to their peers for advice and comfort, distancing
themselves from their parents.

In our research conducted in Israel, we asked adolescents three
questions to ascertain their subjective perception of time spent with
peers and alone. The questions probed a typical week in the school
year and asked how many evenings adolescents spent with their
family, friends and alone. Responses ranged from 0 to 7 and are
summarized in Figure 3.1.

The results show that in both 2001 and 2004 internet users reported
spending fewer evenings with their parents than non-users. In 2001
non-users spent on average of 4.46 evenings a week talking and
playing with parents, whereas internet users spent only 3.42 evenings
a week doing so. The results for 2004 were similar, as non-users
spent on average 4.24 evenings with their parents and internet users
spent only 3.8 evenings with them. Internet users, however, reported
spending more evenings with their friends than non-users in both 2001
and in 2004. In 2001 internet users reported spending more evenings
alone (2.48) than non-users (1.80). All the differences are statistically
significant.

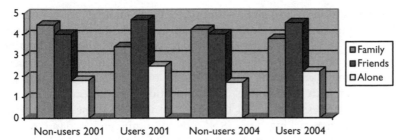

Figure 3.1 Time spent with family, friends and alone by internet users and
    non-users

Figure 3.1 shows that internet users spent less time with their parents
but more with their friends and alone than non-users. Spending less
time with parents and more time with friends may be associated not
only with internet use but also with a developmental process that is
common in adolescence. We expected gender differences as well, as
females may spend more time with their parents and less with friends
and alone than males. We tested this possibility but found that the
differences in evenings spent with parents, friends and alone did not
differ by gender. We also checked each age category separately and
found internet users of all ages tended to spend less time with parents
and more time with friends and alone than non-users.

The results presented in Figure 3.1 may reflect the effects of other
factors as well. To control these, we conducted a multivariate analysis
and explored the extent to which internet use in general was associated with the amount of time spent with family, friends and alone. As
to time spent with friends, in this area of sociability internet users and
non-users evinced no statistically significant difference in either year.
Positive attitudes toward friendship and participation in social activities were the most important predictors of time spent with friends.
Regarding the number of evenings spent alone, internet users reported
spending more time alone than non-users, but only in 2001.

The results suggest that overall internet use has a minor association
with the time that adolescents spend with their friends and alone. On
the positive side, internet users are not isolated from their friends, as
internet use has no effect on time spent with friends. Internet use
slightly decreases the time spent with family and slightly increases the
time being spent alone. We conducted the same analysis for internet
users alone to find out whether frequency of daily use was associated
with time spent with friends and time spent alone. Frequency of daily
use was found not to affect in any way time spent with friends and

time spent alone. Consistent with our previous findings, we concluded that having an internet connection and frequency of its use were not related to time spent with friends and time spent alone, indicating again the absence of evidence for an internet isolation hypothesis. This finding is consistent with the results of a recent study in the US that concluded that online communication has become a central aspect of adolescents' social life. The use of instant messaging (IM) and social networking sites (SNS) to maintain and expand school relationships is widespread among youth. The internet and cell phones are friendship driven technologies that provide continuous contact with friends, social support and the coordination of dyadic and group activities conducted both online and face to face (Boyd, 2008).

Internet use and network size

A final consideration in respect of potential isolation through internet use is the size of the network of friends. The number of close friends is only a quantitative measure of social support, not of its content or of the adolescent's ability to mobilize these ties for companionship, support and resources; but it is nevertheless an additional dimension of the social circle. Individuals may differ in the size of their social circle, and even if a reduced size can provide companionship and social support, the smaller the size of their circle, the higher the likelihood that individuals will perceive themselves as less able to mobilize friends for companionship and support. Assuming that individuals have multiple responsibilities, simple arithmetic suggests that a teenager who has only two close friends will face the possibility of these friends being busy more frequently than a teenager who has three friends.

We investigated the association of internet use with number of close friends. Adolescents were asked to name up to six close friends and provide information about their age, gender, place of residence, place where they met and length of time they had known each other as friends. On average each adolescent reported having five friends (SD 1.472). Of the sample, 6.3 per cent reported having two friends or fewer, and 77 per cent reported having between four and six close friends. Comparison of adolescent internet users and non-users for the average number of their friends elicited no statistically significant difference.

Network size does vary with age (the older the adolescent, the larger the number of friends reported), but again the results point to the importance and relevance of developmental factors. Age proved related to frequency of internet use, and also to the size of the social network. But age was not related to differences in each age category in the number of friends as reported by internet users and non-users. Nor were any gender differences found.

We did find an important difference by nationality. When we inspected separately the size of the social network of Israeli Arabs and Jews we found that only among the Jewish population were there differences in the number of friends based on internet use. On average, Jewish adolescents who did not access the internet reported 4.7 friends (SD 1.49), and adolescents who did access it reported on average 5.1 friends (SD 1.40). The difference is not substantial but it is statistically significant and indicates that among the Jewish population internet use is associated with more social involvement, not less.

One explanation for this finding has to do with the higher rate of technological penetration among Jewish adolescents in Israel, which means that is very likely that being connected to the internet is important for being socially involved. Adolescents connected to the internet used it mainly for social purposes, to facilitate the maintenance of friendship even after school hours. The high rate of internet penetration among Jewish adolescents may make it mandatory to be connected in order to be 'in' and maintain good relationships at school. In Arab society the rate of penetration is relatively low, and being connected to the internet does not increase the size of the circle of friends because friendships are maintained primarily face to face or by traditional channels of communication.

Displacement or multitasking?

The idea of displacement is simple, yet as we have shown in this chapter there is little empirical evidence for its very existence or for the existence of real negative effects on adolescents' social involvement. Alternative explanations for this state of affairs are possible, and a natural candidate is multitasking. With the extensive use of computers, multitasking has become part of the way teens manage a busy life. Media multitasking can be defined as engaging in more than one media activity at a time, by switching constantly back and forth between such diverse activities as email, IM, web search and text messaging friends (Foehr, 2006). In a comprehensive study on multitasking in the USA, teenagers were asked how often when principally using any one of four media (reading newspapers, watching television, using computers and video games) did they concurrently use other media. About a quarter replied that they multitasked most of the time, about half said they did so from time to time, and only 20 per cent said they never did. A central finding of that study was that multitasking was not common when the primary medium being used was television. Not surprisingly, multitasking was very common when the computer was primarily in use, as the other activities were computer related. When using email, 83 per cent of the respondents reported conducting other media activity simultaneously. When using instant messaging or searching websites, 75 per cent reported doing so simultaneously with consumption of other media. When used for computer games, the computer was very likely also used for instant messaging and phone conversations. Its use for instant messaging was probably concomitant with searching websites, emailing and watching television. When used for sending emails, the popular secondary activities were found to be eating, watching television and other computer activities. Finally, when searching for websites the most popular secondary activity was conducting instant messenger conversations.

This preliminary study provides some important insights that can serve for the future exploration of the displacement hypothesis. First, it renders evidence of the primary role of television and of teenagers' reluctance to conduct other activities when watching television pro-grammes. It also attests that computer use is associated with conduct-ing other computer-related activities at the same time. A web search was often combined with instant messaging, chatting and emailing. This finding indicates that using the internet does not displace other activities such as homework, entertainment and social involvement. The difference is that these activities are conducted simultaneously, sometimes providing content for friends' exchanges.

Future studies on the effects of the internet or other new media on media use and social involvement should include measures of dis-placement, but also of multitasking.

Early studies on the effect of the internet in adolescence focused on both the potential costs and potential benefits of internet use. Some studies exposed the potentially positive effects of the internet and of computers based on the ability of these technologies to foster young people's academic and intellectual development, increasing their lan-guage and analytical skills (Tapscott, 1998), and to furnish the tools which adolescents need to shift from being passive consumers of the media to active producers of multimedia presentations, blogging and musical composition. Others were more concerned with the potential effects on a central aspect of adolescence, namely participation in social activities and social networks. They expressed concern that internet use may lead to social isolation or a decrease in individuals' involvement in social activities and social networks.

The major argument for potentially negative effects was the dis-placement hypothesis, which suggests that internet use is at the expense of other areas of social involvement. In this chapter we disaggregated the different components of the argument and tested them one by one. We showed that the displacement argument has been formulated differently by different authors. Some have argued for a displacement of activities, suggesting that the internet is an activity which requires time and therefore may reduce time left for participating in social and leisure activities. Testing this argument we found that adolescents who used the internet were more, not less, involved in most activities that are social in nature and conducted in the presence of others. For example, in both 2001 and 2004 internet users reported on average a higher frequency of participation in social activities such as going to discotheques and movies, and strolling with friends through the neighbourhood. In both years too, internet users reported a higher frequency of participation in evening classes outside school and in sports activities. Our findings accordingly disprove the argument that internet use is detrimental to participation in extra-school activities and show that internet users are more active in these activities than non-users.

Another explanation for the displacement hypothesis suggests that time used for internet activities reduces time spent with parents and friends, and as the use of computers and the internet is suspected of being a solitary activity conducted in isolation from others, it might be time spent alone. This argument is important because the sig-nificant others during adolescence are parents and friends. We put this argument to the test, using our surveys of adolescents in Israel. Initi-ally we found mixed support. Without controlling for other relevant variables, the descriptive findings show a decrease in internet users' time spent with parents and an increase in time spent with friends. But we suspected that this shift in emphasis may be the result of a devel-opmental process unassociated with internet use, so we conducted a multivariate analysis, again on data for 2001 and 2004. The results suggest a minor effect of internet use and that only in 2001, when a relatively small percentage of the adolescent population had access to the medium. By 2004 more than two thirds of adolescents had access to the internet and this effect had disappeared. The effect of age, a measure of maturation during adolescence, was consistent and larger, indicating its greater importance. There was also clear evidence that spending time with friends is related to structural opportunities for this. Adolescents who reported participating in social activities and extracurricular activities also reported spending more time with friends. Therefore our analysis does not support the time displacement hypothesis.

Lack of evidence of any isolating effect of the internet is important to our central argument. The main concern of this book is the motivation for online relationship formation and the structure of adolescents' social networks in the information age. In Chapter 1 we put forward the argument that online friendship formation may not be associated with social isolation and lack of social skills, but with a need for diversification and expansion of social networks. As adolescents are characterized by high similarity with their friends and the lack of geographic mobility to meet others, we suggest that the need to diversify and expand social networks, not isolation, drives online friendship formation, and we have shown that internet users do not represent a socially isolated group of the adolescent population.

Our argument is that the internet is being incorporated into adolescents' everyday life and is becoming part of the web of their responsibilities and social involvements. From this perspective, internet use is not at the expense of other activities or of time spent with family and peers, but is incorporated into them and represents an additional space of activity. Indeed, this incorporation diversifies their activities, their sources of information and guidance, and their social relationships.

4 Online relationship formation

As stated in the last chapter, online sociability is an integral part of young people's digital literacy and cultural consumption of techno-logical artifacts. The ability of the internet to facilitate online contact, especially with geographically remote people, has caught the popular imagination and the empirical attention of researchers studying online relationship formation.

Prior to the information age, adolescents' social choices were severely restricted by time and place. Their lack of geographical mobility and their belonging to an age group expected to go to school structurally reduced their social circle to friends who were met in the neighbourhood, at school and at extracurricular activities. Proximity was a central social constraint for relationship formation. Living in the same neighbourhood and attending the same school transpires in a high level of social similarity.

As mentioned, studies have shown that in western countries, teen-agers have evinced a very high percentage of adoption and use of the internet (Mesch, 2001; Lenhart et al., 2001, 2005; Livingstone and Bober, 2004). These studies apprise us of the active role that youth play, and that the parents' and the adolescents' views regarding information and communication technologies (ICT) do not always converge. Parents indicate that the computer is bought and connected to the internet, reflecting their willingness to provide a tool to improve their children's academic performance, to provide access to infor-mation needed for schoolwork, to adapt to the school requirement of typed assignments and to link the teens to the information society. By contrast, teens experience the internet as a tool for social purpose and play (Lenhart et al., 2001; Livingstone and Bober, 2004; Cohen et al., 2008). Boase and Wellman (2006) argue that in contrast to the popular image of the internet as a trigger and facilitator of new relationships, 'only a relatively small proportion of internet users have ever met someone new online'. Indeed, studies performed on the early adopters of the internet before the year 2000 had indicated that only negligible proportion of the population have met a new friend online (Katz and Rice, 2002b). But as we will show later, the magnitude of meeting new contacts online has sharply risen.

Adolescents play an active role in their communicative conduct. Consequently, their primary uses of the internet do not always match their parents' expectations and wishes. Adolescents are most likely to use the internet to communicate with others for social and gaming purposes, and in some cases to reach out and communicate with others not of their proximate or immediate social circle at school or in their neighbourhood. Moreover, adolescents learn to utilize computer-mediated communication as an additional form of social environment, developing digital literacy and making new contacts over the internet. Online relationships nowadays appear to be an integral part of youth culture (Helsper, 2008a). The technological features of ICT smooth barriers of communication, yet they cannot completely abolish the effects of social constraints on social interaction. The odds of forming new relations are higher among the socially similar, geographically close, and having at least one friend in common ('transitive relations', Kadushin, 2004). A US study has reported that 14 per cent of US teenagers have formed close online friendships (Wolak *et al.*, 2003). A study in the UK found that 11 per cent of the adolescents reported meeting new acquaintances online (Livingstone and Bovill, 2001). In Israel we found in our study that 12 per cent reported having at least one close tie that was met online (Mesch and Talmud, 2006a). Forming online relationships might be one of the most appealing aspects of internet use to young people, given that forming relationships is an important developmental task of adolescence, and in this task youth are limited in their choices by geographical constraint.

Understanding the process involves studying motivations impelling youth to form relationships online, their choice of communication channels and content, the effect of online ties on young people's existing ties and social life, and the quality of online associations. In this chapter we tackle these topics.

The very meaning of internet social use requires elaboration. Studies usually highlight the widespread use of electronic mail, instant messaging (IM), chat rooms and bulletin boards in identical terms, regardless of the specific application in question (Gross *et al.*, 2002; Livingstone *et al.*, 2005). Research has been focused on various kinds of use such as social connection, shared identities, content, social investigation, social network surfing and status updating (see Joinson, 2008).

The notion of online relationship formation requires conceptual clarification. Most research has not clearly defined what is meant by online ties. It was largely conducted to elucidate the effects of channel characteristics on interpersonal communication, emphasizing the lack of social presence, lack of richness and lack of clues in internet communication (Sproull and Kiesler, 1986), and it sought the conditions under which this communication is non-personal or becomes hyperpersonal (Walther, 1996; McKenna *et al.*, 2002). Another direction has been research to understand channel choice across distances and to inquire whether one online communication supplements or substitutes the use of other channels of communication among kin, friends and coworkers. These studies show that internet use is associated with more and not less communication, and that the more individuals contact by phone and face to face the more they contact using email (Chen and Wellman, 2003); it is suggested that connectivity increases local and long-distance communication (Hampton and Wellman, 2002). Most of this research reflects the conduct of online communication but makes no major effort to define the nature of the online relationship. Lack of conceptual clarity may lead to contradictory findings. In our view the definition of online and face-to-face ties has to do with the origin of the relationship and not with the mode of communication. Youth communicate with close schoolfriends using instant messaging, electronic mail, social networking sites (SNS) and school forums (Boneva *et al.*, 2001). In this case, one can have friends that meet everyday at school yet conduct most of their communication online. Our interest is in the differences between online and face-to-face ties, so that our definition is that online ties refer to individuals who first met online by means of applications such as electronic email, instant messaging, social networking sites, chat rooms or online game groups. A face-to-face friend is one who was met in person, in a setting such as school, the neighbourhood or other extracurricular activity (Mesch and Talmud, 2006b; Buote *et al.*, 2009).

This definition is associated with the view that we adopted of the internet as a space of activity and social interaction. Usually studies focus on the use for communication but surveys from different countries show that a very frequent use of the internet by young people is also for online games (Lenhart *et al.*, 2005). For us, the internet is not only about communication with existing ties. True, many adolescents use it as another channel of communication with existing relationships; but the internet's innovative aspect is the opportunities it renders for social interactivity by means of the space provided for meeting new individuals. This social use represents more than a communication channel – it is often a space for social activity. People playing interactive games online do more than that: as in any game, the players form groups, interaction is recurrent and names and phone numbers are exchanged. Teenager forums are used for advice (including health problems), social support and information search, creating opportunities for social interaction and involvement. It is not uncommon that teens who know each other introduce friends or family members to other friends and family members, thereby creating opportunities for social interaction with new acquaintances.

Motivations for online relationship formation

Studies aiming to explain motivation for online relationship formation have mainly relied on the effect of existing personality characteristics and the social needs perspective. This holds that forming and maintaining strong interpersonal bonds is a fundamental need (Baumeister and Leary, 1995), critical for healthy development (e.g. Sullivan, 1953). Young people form relationships to meet compelling needs for intimacy, self-validation and companionship (Baumeister and Leary, 1995). This requirement is particularly intense for adolescents, whose social circle at this developmental stage is expanding from the family to the peer group. This need for affiliation is universal, but some people undoubtedly lack the skills and ability to create and sustain intimate relationships face to face. This is due to certain personal characteristics such as social anxiety or shyness, which reduce their ability to form face-to-face social ties (Mesch, 2001; McKenna et al., 2002). According to this view, frequent internet use for social purposes is especially attractive to individuals who feel socially insecure, express social anxiety, have a low self-concept and are introverts (Hamburger and Ben-Artzi, 2000). For these individuals, online communication has some features that make the creation of relationships online easier than face to face. The perceived anonymity of the medium is taken to facilitate the disclosure of intimate information, and the anxious and shy adolescent assumes that anonymity serves as a shield against the embarrassment felt when personal and intimate information is released to known others (McKenna et al., 2002). In addition, at the early stages of online communication, electronic space allows communication without the disclosure of physical appearance, thus allowing individuals who feel that they are less physically attractive or socially skilled to communicate and develop relationships in a more secure environment (McKenna *et al.*, 2002). The global nature of online communication also makes it easier to find others who share common interests, hobbies and concerns. In such cases social relationships and intimate disclosure develop on the basis of shared interests and not physical attraction.

Studies present some interesting evidence on the association of personality characteristics and online relationship formation. The first HomeNet study was a longitudinal investigation of 93 nonrepresentative families in the Pittsburg area. They were provided with computers and an internet connection free of charge for three years. The study found extroversion was negatively related to frequency of internet use; introverts were more likely to be frequent internet users (Kraut *et al.*, 1998). Internet effects proved to differ according to personality characteristics, in particular extroversion/introversion. The authors found support for the 'richer get richer hypothesis': extroverts reported more internet use and creating more online relationships. Introverts who used the internet extensively reported less social involvement. In sum, internet use was associated with better outcomes for extroverts and worse outcomes for introverts. In particular, extroverts who used the internet more reported increased well-being, including low levels of loneliness. In contrast, introverts who were heavy internet users showed a decline in their well-being (Kraut *et al.*, 2002). The HomeNet study was based on the dystopian assumption that the internet exerts negative effects on the individual's well-being, partly because of another assumption that time invested in the internet is non-social time, diverted from other sources of sociability.

Others who subscribe to these perspectives have investigated the link between personal attributes and online activities, such as sensation seeking and internet dependence (Lin and Tsai, 2002). The social needs outlook has found much corroboration in social psychology. A study in the Netherlands with a sample of 687 adolescents investigated personality characteristics and the perception of online communication. Socially anxious and lonely adolescents were found to value online communication more strongly. Youngsters with these personality characteristics perceived the internet as providing them with more opportunities to reflect and control the messages they sent, and they regarded online communication as deeper and more reciprocal than face-to-face communication (Valkenburg *et al.*, 2006). Similarly, Wolfradt and Doll (2001) investigated in Germany the relation between extraversion/introversion and three internet uses (information, entertainment and interpersonal communication) among 122 adolescent internet users. The social needs hypothesis was supported in that specific personality traits such as neuroticism proved positively associated with the entertainment motive and with the interpersonal communication motive; extroversion was positively associated with the communication motive only. Accordingly, Wolfradt and Doll (2001) argued that personality traits predict corresponding types of internet activities. All in all, existing knowledge indicates that personality characteristics are influential in the use and choice of this medium for relationship formation. Online communication is an important means for socially anxious, introverted and lonely adolescents to overcome their inhibitions in face-to-face settings. The internet not only offers such young people a new venue to fulfill the need for association and involvement in a social circle, but it also compensates for their lack of social skills and ultimately may help them to gain self-confidence, to be enjoyed later in face-to-face interactions.

The association between online communication and relational closeness is particularly interesting. Using a large sample of Dutch youth aged 12 to 17 years, Valkenburg and Peter (2007a) investigated whether online communication stimulated or reduced closeness to friends, and whether intimate disclosure of personal information online affected their closeness to online ties. These authors found that only 30 per cent of the adolescents perceived online communication as effective in disclosing personal information. Furthermore online communication with others who were met online proved to have a negative effect on the perceived closeness to friends (Valkenburg and Peter, 2007a). One possible explanation for the perception of less degrees of relational closeness of online ties is provided by an Israeli study with a large representative sample of adolescents in which this perception was found to result from length of communication. Online ties are acquainted for less time than face-to-face ties, so they are still at the phase of relationship development and therefore perceived to be of lesser depth and breadth (Mesch and Talmud, 2006a). Yet as time goes by, and as the topics of conversation expand from a small number of shared interests to a wide range, the perceived connection is assumed to grow closer.

Virtual interactions and online spaces are seen as further sites of interaction in which youth can explore their identities and sense of themselves (Stern, 2004). As they get older, their internet literacy as well as their tendency to share personal information seems to grow, though with limited understanding of the risks involved (Livingstone, 2008). Still, perceptions regarding the risk involved in online relations have been modified: while in 2003 distrust in online ties was associated with geographical proximity between persons, the link between mistrust of the internet to geographical proximity had disappeared between 2003 to 2006 (Dutton and Shepherd, 2003; Helsper, 2008b). Additionally, young people report a growing dependency on the internet for activities ranging from managing their daily lives to building and maintaining online social interaction. The embeddedness of ICT in social structure creates a dual nature of communicative space, where both adolescents' offline and online domains serve as facilitators of communicative action in key life experiences (McMillan and Morrison, 2006). Over time, enthusiasm for meeting strangers on the internet wanes and reports of boredom surface even among children (Livingstone and Bober, 2004).

In our Israeli study we found qualitative evidence that adolescents seem to be cautious in their connections with unknown others. We found that after the young people became acquainted online and discovered common interests and topics of discussion, sometimes they would exchange emails, often using IM, then they would communicate by phone, and finally in few cases they arranged to meet face to face in public spaces. This is cautious progress, moving from online meeting as strangers, followed by a rise in the frequency of communication and in the number of its channels. The goal of these successive moves is the establishment of trust, resulting from progressive disclosure of personal information (Mesch and Talmud, 2007).

Furthermore, the concept of stranger is not always adequate to describe relationship formation online. Frequently, instant messaging and email are ways to introduce mutual friends to each other (Wolak *et al.*, 2003). This happens when a new friend is introduced to an existing group or when an adolescent suggests to another friend that he or she meet a new person who has the same interests or the same personal problems. In other cases adolescents get to meet new friends when they participate in chat rooms, often general ones in which adolescents discuss hobbies, musical preferences or personal problems. Sometimes they are more specialized rooms in which they find individuals who share their hobbies, musical tastes or other political or social interests (Wolak *et al.*, 2003).

Interpersonal lives and computer activities of early adolescents reflexively amplify each other. Contemporary moral development is less about mastering distinctly right and wrong answers, and more about negotiating different social contexts. Additionally, even in a computer-mediated communication (CMC) environment, interpersonal and even intimate clues can be possible (Walther, 1996). There is evidence that the number of personal relationships occurring via the internet is increasing as more people gain access to it (Underwood and Findlay, 2004; Lawson and Leck, 2006). What adolescents do after school hours, through the windows of their computer screens, has become an integral and important part of their individual and social identity formation and of their moral development (Bradley, 2005).

Valentine and Holloway (2002) found a rich variety of adolescents' strategies to reconfigure their personal activities between offline and online spaces. The study found four ways in which adolescents aged 11 to 16 incorporated their offline worlds and their online spaces: by direct (re)presentations of their offline identities and activities; by the production of alternative identities also contingent on their offline identities; by the reproduction online of offline class and gender divides; and by reducing the ways in which everyday material realities limit the scope of their online activities. These authors also identified different processes whereby adolescents incorporate online space into their offline worlds: online activities maintain and develop both distant and local offline relationships; information gathered online is incorporated into offline activities; and online friendships are incorporated into or reconfigure offline social networks and position within networks (Valentine and Holloway, 2002).[1]

ICT facilitates powerful relations and interactions that positively benefit adolescents. Virtual interactions and online spaces are seen as additional sites of interaction, where youth can explore their identities and sense of themselves, also experiencing a sense of freedom, enthusiasm and power (Maczewski, 2002; Leander and McKim, 2003). An interesting example is inter-racial contact in chat rooms. An early argument was that in the space of electronic communication youth tend to be more egalitarian in their communication with members of minority groups than they are face to face (Tapscott, 1998). Another study that compared general discussions in moderated and unmoderated chat room interactions found differences in the likelihood of exposure to negative remarks about a racial group. Youth in moderated chat rooms had a lower likelihood of such exposure than youth in unmoderated chat rooms. Still, an important finding of the study is that race is openly discussed, so that children from different racial groups get the opportunity to encounter each other, and most of the discussions use a neutral and accepting language (Tynes *et al.*, 2004).

---

1 For a general theory considering reconfiguration of ICT communication, see Walther (1996).

Participation in chat rooms enlarges the number of contacts, diversifies them to other groups that youngsters might not meet at school, and provides opportunities to explore racial identity in a relatively positive environment.

Online support seems to serve both as expansion of face-to-face social support and well-being and a compensatory device for the lack of it. Tichon and Shapiro (2003a, 2003b) revealed that in comparison with their adult counterparts, youth with chronic health needs are offered online more social companionship and emotional aid, rather than tangible assistance or instrumental support. Gross *et al.* (2002) studied 130 seventh graders from a middle-class public school in California for the relation between their internet use and their daily well-being. Time spent online was not associated with dispositional or daily well-being. However, as suggested by intimacy theory, the closeness of instant message communication partners was inversely associated with daily social anxiety and loneliness at school, above and beyond the contribution of dispositional measures. Youth who felt relatively socially anxious and/or lonely at school on a daily basis were more likely to communicate by IM with people with whom they did not have a close affiliation.

Adolescents' conduct offline seems similar to their conduct online. Their ways of social coping online and offline are markedly associated. Seepersad (2004) found a strong relationship between avoidant coping strategies offline and internet use for entertainment. Moreover, adolescents who considered communication the most important use of the internet also contended with loneliness through expression of emotion and social coping. Results suggest that online and offline coping behaviours are strongly related, especially if they are avoidant (Seepersad, 2004). Many positive and negative developmental behaviours, such as dating, smoking, formation of musical tastes and frictional violence, are transferred via adolescents' peer social networks (Neal, 2007).

But we mostly argue that this perspective emphasizes personality attributes, while ignoring the social context in which online friendship formation occurs. We suggest an alternative social structural approach to online adolescents' communication.

Adolescent friendships, networked individuals and information society

For some young users, the internet is becoming another location to meet and socialize, and relations created there also tend to migrate to other settings (Mesch and Levanon, 2003; Wolak *et al.*, 2003). As young people become less controlled by traditional social authorities, they can overstep their geographical limits and their local groups' boundaries, using electronic communication technologies (Wellman, 2001). As the internet provides the informational space and collective organization for social interaction, with time ties created online become new social ties that are integrated into the adolescent's social life (Parks and Floyd, 1996; McKenna *et al.*, 2002).

This increase in adolescents' new relationships started online creates concern among scholars, parents, the public and legislators for the young people's safety. Through the internet they can meet online unknown individuals and develop non-geographically based social networks. Parents and practitioners have expressed concern that this indiscrimate exposure to individuals across age and gender lines might result in harassment, bullying and victimization (Mitchell *et al.*, 2003). As Holloway and Valentine (2003) have noted, this concern is rooted in the social construction of adolescents, as individuals in need of guidance, supervision and protection from adults to fully develop their potential.

The internet is typically used by adolescents as an additional space of activity and social interaction, which often complements rather than replaces offline spaces of social communication, activity and gathering. There is evidence that adolescents' technical and social understanding of the internet improves with age and duration of internet use (Yan, 2006). Networked publics provide an additional virtual context for youth to develop social norms in negotiation with their peers, forming social ties, maintaining friendship networks and accruing information and entertainment items and devices from remote environments. The adolescent is a sophisticated 'networked individual', who negotiates a wider range of messages and identities using a multiplex means of computer-mediated, mobile and face-to-face channels of communication.

Adolescents' online activity and subculture are unique. This distinctiveness stems from both an age effect and a generational effect. The age effect refers to the influence of life-stage characteristics on adolescents' social conduct and network structure. The generational (or cohort) effect refers to the cultural change to which adolescents are exposed to in their formative years. Nowadays they skilfully master computer and internet literacy, online communication, smart cellular phone and hypertextual literacy. Message boards, instant messaging and web-blogs – all are unique artifacts that allow early adolescents to share and discuss ideas and feelings, ask and answer each other's questions, or showcase projects, all of which promote a pro-social attitude. Storytelling and dialogue have always been a part of educating and entertaining youth. The use of digital technologies may actually encourage different types of literacy, including verbal and visual skills, as well as what is often referred to as digital fluency (Huffaker, 2004). If in the past the formation of the youth culture was limited to neigh-bourhood hangouts, now spaces and channels of interaction are expanded, allowing individuals to find peers to share interests, hobbies and feelings conditional upon having access and skills.

Expansion of weak ties via online social networks compensates, in particular, youth with deprived life outcomes. A study of social net-works sites has suggested a close association between the use of Facebook and social capital, the firmest relationship being with 'bridging social capital'. In addition, Facebook usage was found to interact with measures of psychological well-being, suggesting that it might provide greater benefits for users experiencing low self-esteem and low life satisfaction (Ellison *et al.*, 2007).

Typically, adolescents' offline networks are denser and much more age and sex homogeneous than adults'. Typically adults also have more options to form new social ties drawn from more diversified social foci of activity than adolescents. Peer-group pressure on ado-lescents is more likely to encourage homophilious, dense social ties, comprising of closely knit, transitive relations (in which a person's friends know his or her third party as well), which tend to be geo-graphically proximate.

Social affordance and dual embeddedness of friendship ties

The key question is whether adolescents' online social ties are sig-nificantly distinct from their offline social networks. Two scholarly perspectives are relevant here: technological determinism and social construction of technologies, partially overlapping the tension between virtuality and reality, generative and reflective approaches.

While technological determinism holds that ICT completely changes sociability, as it moulds the social character of communica-tion, social construction of technology argues that technological use is entirely determined by social factors. Similarly, we distinguish studies that regard ICT as culture from those that regard ICT as a cultural artifact, embedded in social structure (Hine, 2005). To study ICT as a culture means to regard it as a social space in its own right, and to explore the forms of communication, sociability and identity pro-duced in this social space and the ways they are sustained by the resources available in the online setting. The internet has been referred not as a communication channel but as a space for being or dwelling, capable of sustaining complex social spaces. In this sense, online sociability was conceived as different and even separate from one's offline identity.

In this view, the virtual space is a coherent social space that exists entirely within a computer space, and in which new rules and ways of being could emerge. Online communication can exist in itself, completely separated from offline, 'real' life; individuals can communicate at a distance, overcoming the fragmented character of offline life. Being online not only afforded relief from the constraints imposed by location or identity, but freed people from the bonds associated with their 'offline personalities' and social roles. The sharp opposition between offline and online spaces, or between the 'real' and 'virtual', especially regarding friendship formation, maintenance, learning and adolescents' subcultural coalescence, display, identity and even resistance, derives mainly from the utopian perspective of digital space (Wilson and Atkinson, 2005).

In our view, the ICT space reflects social structure, and access and use are dependent on a social stratification process. Individuals bring to their online participation the diverse social status that they occupy and their social norms of behaviour. Yet, at the same time online conduct exerts some transformative effects on adolescents' behaviour and friendship formation. Conceptualizing the internet as foci of activity, we argue that ICT is embedded in social structure. The internet is yet another sphere of social interaction and action, where social agents play digital games and exchange information, social support and other instrumental and expressive resources. The internet is conceived as a social arena of shared activities. Hence the social context moulds relationship formation, not merely individual motivations and preferences. Social relationships are human interactions in digital environments, and can no more be taken for granted than they can in face-to-face settings. Technological features impact the use of ICT as well, by reducing costs, proximity considerations and scope of choice among various channels of synchronous and asynchronous communication devices. Digital social interaction embeds certain properties from adolescents' offline social networks as well as from the digital environment; these act as social contextual facilitators, relevant to online sociability. These properties are in fact social affordance devices, bringing individuals together for purposes that create opportunities for social interaction, and exposing individuals to one another. Individuals can express in virtual communicative space their real or inner selves, using the relative anonymity of the internet to be the person they want to be, the individual they describe to others, experimenting with their identity and self (Bargh *et al.*, 2002). In other words, the effect of technological factors on online communication is indirect. It is mediated by adolescents' self-perception of the medium's attributes (Schouten *et al.*, 2007).

A comprehensive survey of 1303 adolescents in Seoul, Singapore and Taipei found that the internet users among them differed in their internet connectedness patterns in the nature of their social environments, in their family social status and in other environmental factors (Jung *et al.*, 2005). Most notably, the rate of internet adoption by peers was an important factor explaining internet use. As the proportion of friends using the internet increased, the more likely was the user to find technical support and to broaden and intensify online communication, thus increasing the likelihood of connecting to the internet. Considering that online activities are more likely to be shared among peers, the high rate of participation in these activities suggests a strong effect of peer groups in the likelihood of connecting to the internet (Jung *et al.*, 2005). Similarly, the emotional support that some Dutch adolescents received online (and offline) was affected by whether they were residents of urban or rural area (Dooris *et al.*, 2008). See Table 4.1.

Effects of online relationship formation on social networks

Nowadays online relationship formation is a part of adolescents' social activities. True not all young people make contacts online, but from the studies reviewed in this chapter and from our own we can conclude that close to 20 per cent of adolescents making contacts online is not uncommon. The last part of this chapter is dedicated to understanding some of the potential effects of this behaviour on young people's social circles.

An important dimension of social networks, and one at the centre of many studies, is the extent that creating online social ties reduces, enlarges or does not change the number of friends. Studies have warned that excessive internet use may isolate adolescents from their friends. As we saw in Chapter 3, available data indicate that the size of a social network is not negatively affected by online relationship formation. A temporary decrease may be expected as more energy and time are invested in the creation of online ties, but over time, as online associations become integrated, the size of the network even slightly increases as new associations are added and old ones kept

Table 4.1 Perspectives on online relationship formation

Disciplinary origin	Perspective	Implications
Psychology	Motivation theory	Correlation between personality traits and communication needs and gratification.
	Social needs	Either the expansion of social ties, or the compensation for face-to-face relationship scarcity.
	Sensation seeking; intimacy theory	Compensation for anxiety, isolation, or stimuli.
Social structural	Dual embeddedness	Reconfiguration of communication strategies; coping in virtual space is similar to offline life.
	Social affordance	Information spreads rapidly in CMC, but neither universally nor homogeneously.
	Social network analysis	Homophily and transitivity drives relationships formation, but online relations are larger in size, weaker and more sparse.

(Mesch and Talmud, 2006a; Valkenburg and Peter, 2007b). In that sense the effect of online relationship formation seems not to differ from the effect of cell phones. Igarashi *et al.* (2005), analysing text messages over cellular phones in Japan, found general support for the claim that mobile phones can change social networks among young people by increasing the number of possible contacts and promoting selective relationship formation. Mobile phones increase the frequency of communication and allow opportunities for expanding interpersonal relationships.

The effect of expansion of social networks seems more pronounced on extroverts than on introverts and varies according to attachment style, but overall online relationship formation enlarges the social network for the majority of adolescents who choose to become involved in this activity (Hamburger and Ben Artzi, 2000; Buote *et al.*, 2009).

Associating with similar people is another social network dimension influenced by online relationship formation. One of the most significant and consistent findings reported in the literature is that social relationships are characterized by social similarity or homophily. Studies of the formation of close social relationships have emphasized the importance of social similarity in friendship and attraction in intimate social relationships. Similarity moulds network ties and results in homogeneous social networks in terms of socio-demographic, behavioural and interpersonal characteristics. This tendency of individuals to associate with others who are similar to them has important social consequences. For example, similar individuals exchange information that suits their personal characteristics and social style. By mutual influence or by association, they reject social links and information coming from others who differ from them in social attributes, attitudes or values. Contact with similar individuals limits personal social horizons, restricting the exposure to different others.

In our Israeli study we found that adolescents who created online social ties also reported a higher heterogeneity of their social network by age, gender and location. We compared youngsters with online friends and with face-to-face friends for the respective average age difference between those friends and themselves. The former reported that their online friends were on average older than themselves; the latter did not report this. The difference was small, online friends being on average a year and a half older. We also found that female adolescents who reported online ties had more heterogeneous networks than their male counterparts, but this is consistent with female adolescents' offline ties as well. So to some extent online friendship formation breaks through the barriers of age–grade segregation imposed by the social structure of schools.

An important consideration is the perceived closeness of youth to their online ties and their possible effect on their perceived closeness to their face-to-face ties. Online relationship formation is a dynamic process, and accordingly calls for longitudinal studies. Unfortunately, such studies are not to be found; existing studies mostly rely on cross-sectional, static analysis. Adolescents perceived their online ties as less close than face-to-face ties (Mesch and Talmud, 2006b; Valkenburg and Peter, 2007a; Buote *et al.*, 2009). The perception of being less close to online friends seems to depend on the developmental stage of the relationship. Online ties are relatively newer than face-to-face ties and based on narrow shared interests. Relationships take time to develop and the process of moving from being perceived as less close requires more investigation. Regarding their effect on existing ties, there is no evidence that youth are exchanging close friendships for distant and narrow ones. Online ties, then, seem not to replace but to supplement face-to-face connections.

A highly consistent finding in the literature is that school years are characterized by gender-based segregation. There is evidence that the extent of segregation decreases over the years, in particular from middle school to high school, but it remains relatively high even at the end of high school (Shrum *et al.*, 1988). Studies have shown that in adolescence there is a 'sex cleavage' in friendship relations (Cotterell, 1996). In our study we compared the percentage of friends of the opposite sex as reported by youth with and without online friends. We found less sex segregation for the former than for the latter (Mesch and Talmud, 2006a). Adolescents whose friends were similar in age, ethnic background and place of residence were more likely to report forming friendships online (Mesch and Talmud, 2006a).

Another component of the shared opportunity for mutual exposure is residential proximity. Proximity facilitates the likelihood of friendship formation and communication by increasing the probability that individuals will meet and interact (Monge and Contractor, 2003). Proximity is of particular importance for adolescents limited in their geographic mobility as they must rely on public transportation, which is not always reliable. The new media have been described as substituting face-to-face and local friendships, and as expanding and reconfiguring friendship formation. For adolescents who are restricted in their physical mobility, and for whom the main arenas of social interaction are the school, the neighbourhood and extracurricular activities, the internet represents a new focus of common activities. Adolescents connect to the internet, chat, and exchange email with friends, with friends of friends and with unknown individuals. In these activities they encounter a new space that facilitates joint activities and social interaction. For adults, as well as for a large majority of adolescents, the internet is an innovative place for social interaction, different from the phone and television.

Conclusion

In this chapter we have discussed how online spaces are used in the context of relationship formation and the creation of friendship ties by means of ICT. We have emphasized the role of online communication as providing an alternative and also a complementary space for relationship formation, given the specific restrictions that youth face. These are mainly geographic, constituting a contextual barrier that motivates some adolescents to turn to the internet to seek others who share their specific interests or differ in their racial/ethnic background and social characteristics. Beyond the structural constraints, we found that individuals with certain personality characteristics, among them introversion, self-concept and attachment style, were more drawn to forming relationships online.

Heterogeneity in adolescents' social networks, occurring more often when the origin of the friendship is online, has developmental implications that require further investigation. For example, Stanton-Salazar and Spina (2005) found that non-romantic, cross-gender online relationships between adolescents proved an important source of social support. They afforded emotional support, particularly for the males. If the internet reduces friendship gender segregation for young adolescents, in the future this may have an impact on the process of dating and first-time sexual relationships. Another potential effect is in the early exposure to individuals of diverse ethnic and racial groups and of varying political views. If this is confirmed in future research, the internet is very likely to become a central agent of socialization, which has to be integrated into our understanding of youth socialization.

The division in research of the virtual from the real does not of course accurately capture the lived social experiences and identity negotiations of adolescents in their socialization process or in their belonging to peer groups. Nor does it encompass the complexity in which offline and online spaces are mutually embedded.

The emergence of ICT into adolescents' identity management, personal communities and friendship formation seems to have changed the character of 'private' and 'public' spaces, constituted by adolescents' activities on and around the screen. In the next chapter we connect elements of offline and online interactions regarding the maintenance and expansion of social ties, and the diversification of social networks through ICT.

5　ICT and existing social ties

Online communication can be intimate, personal or non-personal. In the previous chapter we explored online sociability patterns, inquiring into the motivation for online friendship formation through exploration of relational patterns such as homophily and proximity. We also saw that adolescents create relationships not only in traditional settings such as school and neighbourhood, but also online. In this chapter we take a closer look at the use of online communication to maintain existing relationships.

In doing so, we ask how characteristics of social ties affect the likelihood of using online communication to sustain friendship networks, and if relational patterns of social networks affect the use of online communication with friends.

Friendship is a special type of relationship, characterized by closeness and intimacy, trust and commitment, deemed reflected in the communication channels used. Close friends are individuals with whom we share personal information, concerns and grievances. True, we also discuss with our friends everyday experiences such as the movies we have seen, our views on political issues, our feelings about music clips and different experiences at school. But none of these topics requires real closeness, and all can be discussed equally with other schoolmates or neighbours. Sharing intimate information, such as our romantic feelings and our problems and misunderstandings with parents, requires a higher level of closeness that admits intimacy and trust without fear that this information will be disclosed in public and embarrass us. Attraction to friendship, its formation, and its quality in adolescence are topics that have received much sociological attention (Kandel, 1978; Crosnoe, 2000; Moody, 2001). This period in life is characterized by rapid developmental changes, and as children enter their teenage years they interact less with their parents. Peer relationships expand and assume greater importance (Youniss and

Smollar, 1996; Giordano, 2003). Peers act as emotional confidants, provide each other with advice and guidance, and serve as models of behaviour and attitudes (Berndt *et al.*, 1989; Hartup, 1997; Crosnoe *et al.*, 2003). Studies found a significant relationship between the quality of an individual's friends and well-being (Hartup, 1997; Collins *et al.*, 2000). Adolescents who lack attachment to peers are more likely to report psychological distress and low psychological well-being (Beraman and Moody, 2004). Although parents continue to influence behaviours and decisions, the time that adolescents spend with their peers expands and they become their most important reference group (Hartup, 1997).

Sociological studies on adolescent friendship attraction, formation and quality have mostly relied on the proximity–similarity hypothesis (Kandel, 1978; Shrum *et al.*, 1988). According to this perspective, homophily in social relationships is a two-step process. It results from the combination of social, geographical and institutional proximities that provide joint opportunities for frequent and mutual exposure and shared social status, which in turn create attraction among similar individuals who share the same social experience and context. Activities in which people participate in their daily lives are socially structured, creating an array of opportunities that tend to bring them into frequent contact (Suitor *et al.*, 1995).

Studies of close social relationships have emphasized the importance of homophily (Hartup, 1997; McPherson *et al.*, 2002), as we indicated in the last chapter. Homophily is frequent because it provides important rewards. Similar individuals are likely to participate in enjoyable joint activities with others who have similar interests, and in that way to receive validation of their attitudes and beliefs (Aboud and Mendelson, 1996). Joining in the same activities increases the frequency of social interaction and provides social support across a wide variety of aspects of social life. Not surprisingly, similarity has been associated with stable and strong ties (Hallinan and Kubitschek, 1988). When dissimilarity exists at the beginning of relationships, or ascribed social statuses are mismatched, relationships tend to be unstable and are more likely to terminate as individuals move on to other relationships in which there is greater similarity (Hallinan and Kubitschek, 1988).

Among adolescents, proximity is also important for friendship, as it establishes the boundaries within which the individual adolescent's choice of friendship is constrained by social or geographic location. A major location for meeting and making friends is school: there adolescents spend a large part of their waking hours. But other settings might be important as well. Adolescents spend their free time in neighbourhood hangouts that they frequent after school. In shopping malls, video arcades and movie theatres usually located in the neighbourhood or nearby, groups of adolescents spend leisure time, getting to know others who might live in the same neighbourhood or locality but do not attend the same school (Cotterell, 1996). In sum, homophily in social relationships can be explained as originating from a combination of opportunities for mutual disclosure and shared life experiences. Activities in which individuals participate in their daily lives are socially structured, creating an array of opportunities that tend to bring similar people into frequent contact. School, workplace and neighbourhood haunts are places where social activities are organized (learning, work, leisure). The social structuring of these activities tends to bring similar individuals into frequent contact, encouraging the development of social relationships. These different foci of activities are the structural constraints in which individual choices are made (Feld, 1981). Foci of activity, a measure of proximity, might differ in how close they bring similar individuals. Some social contexts are more homogeneous in terms of age, gender and place of residence, such as the school, but the assumption made by school sample studies that friendships are created only at school may be criticized. Friendships can be created in other social settings. Friends, even if attending school, meet in different social contexts and their friendships outside school have migrated there. Our knowledge of adolescents' friendships may benefit also from consideration of the context of acquaintance, and how this context is related to the quality of social relationships.

Furthermore, adolescents are a segment of the population whose information and communication technologies (ICT) use has dramatically increased in recent years. Theories of computer-mediated communication (CMC) are sceptical about its potential use to maintain and reinforce existing relationships.

Theoretical perspectives on online communication

A review of CMC theories reveals a number of perspectives. The first, usually referred as the *lack of contextual clues* approach, is based on the conception that different channels of communication transmit different amounts of information (Daft and Lengel, 1984; Sproull and Kiesler, 1991; Bargh and McKenna, 2004). Information, in communication terms, refers not only to words but also to the social context or socially implicit knowledge in that communicated bundle. From this perspective, scholars argue that CMC provides a *limited social presence* as compared with face-to-face communication, and that the lack of communicators' social and contextual cues affects the perception of the messages, the perception of the individuals sending the messages, and eventually the social connections between communicators (Sproull and Kiesler, 1991; Tidwell and Walther, 2002). Several theories take this approach. For example, the basic assumption of media richness theory (Daft and Lengel, 1984) is that media differ in their ability to handle rich information, embedded with socially tacit knowledge and complex meanings. The richness of a medium refers to its capacity to transfer non-verbal and verbal cues and allow immediate feedback, to its language variety, and to its use of diverse channels. Based on the assumption that face-to-face communication is a rich medium, whereas CMC is a leaner one, the theory expects rich media to be used for complex and equivocal messages and leaner media for less equivocal exchanges. According to Kahai and Cooper (2003), media richness theory emphasizes that media differ in their ability to facilitate changes in the understanding of messages. Face-to-face communication is richer than written communication because it facilitates changes in the understanding of messages between communicators. To facilitate communication and task performance, rich media include multiple cues in addition to words, such as voice inflection, body gestures, non-verbal messages, immediacy of feedback and bi-directional communication. Multiple cues allow rapid message reinterpretation, clarification and personalization. Personal feelings and emotions are infused and messages are tailored to the receiver's current needs. Language variety is the range of meanings that can be conveyed by the available pool of symbols in a language. The critical elements are multiplicity of cues and immediacy of feedback, which enable communicators to clarify the message.

The *social presence theory* belongs to this family and refers to the extent to which a medium is perceived as conveying the communicators' actual physical presence. Social presence depends not only on the communication of words, but also on a variety of non-verbal cues such as physical distance, postures, facial expressions and the like. According to this theory, different types of media vary in their capacity to transmit information about facial expression, direction of looking, posture, dress and non-verbal and vocal cues. Low social presence media are used when intimate and personal communication is minimal. From the perspective of social presence theory, computer-mediated communication is unable to convey the message of emotions. For a message to be effective, two conditions must be met –

multiplicity of cues and immediacy of feedback – both of which promote the clarity of the message. This theory predicts that media facilitating multiple cues and immediacy of feedback yield more frequent socio-emotional communication, communication with a *personal content*, and the formation of *meaningful personal associations*. Media that lack social presence result in communication with low personal content.

The *cues-filtered-out theory* (Sproull and Kiesler, 1986) similarly posits that social presence declines with the move from face-to-face to computer-mediated communication; messages become more impersonal. Sproull and Kiesler (1986) state that CMC reduces social context cues, aspects of the physical environment and non-verbal hierarchical status cues, the absence of which is said to reduce interpersonal impressions.

According to Sproull and Kiesler (1986), without non-verbal tools a sender cannot easily alter the mood of a message, communicate a sense of individuality, or exercise dominance or charisma. Moreover, communicators feel a greater sense of anonymity and detect less individuality in others. Scholars of this outlook, which evolved from early work on CMC, argue that the bandwidth is insufficient to carry all the communication signals needed to convey social, emotional and contextual content. In text-only systems, for example, both task information and social information are carried in the same single verbal/linguistic channel, which may be adequate for most task information but cannot transmit non-verbal information such as body motions, voice tone, and so on (Sproull and Kiesler, 1986). Filtering out social, emotional and contextual information can obviously entail important consequences for the interaction, especially when the main focus is on the development of an interpersonal relationship.

These early theories were highly deterministic technologically, assuming that limitations inherent in the text-based communication prevent the support of strong (supportive and intimate) ties but can support weak ones (that supply information). The theories do not account for the socio-structural context of existing relationships, and the emphasis is on communication features. Furthermore, only the *lack-of-social-clues* theory considers the social context, which they assert is not clear, so the communicators experience a lack of social control. This results in an inability to create communication with real personal content, but also in negative communication such as flaming and verbal aggression (Sproull and Kiesler, 1986).

An alternative perspective has emerged to account for the evidence that under certain circumstances individuals communicating online are able to maintain personal and intimate relationships just as in face-to-face settings. This is usually referred to as the socio-emotional perspective (Kahai and Cooper, 2003). Walther (1996) developed the hyper-personal interaction model, arguing that in certain cases CMC, rather than producing impersonal communication, can lead to hyper-personal or intimate communication. The model, based on principles of social psychology, argues that CMC can support more intimate communication than face-to-face communication. According to this approach, the absence of non-verbal cues, identity cues and temporal characteristics may prompt online users to engage in selective self-presentation and partner idealization, enacting exchanges more intimate than those that occur in face-to-face interactions (Tidwell and Walther, 2002). The hyper-personal model acknowledges the problem that CMC lacks reliable information about the communicators, but it also implies that the development of a close and personal relationship requires primarily frequent communication and time. If individuals communicate frequently, intensely and for a long period of time, they are highly likely to develop a shared system of symbols. Online communication can reach intimacy, be personal and support close relationships.

Spears and Lea (1992) likewise developed the *social identity and deindividuation* (SIDE) model, arguing that the lack of non-verbal cues in online communication is not detrimental to personal communication. According to this approach, the communicators' personal goals and needs are the sole determinants of its effects, and people engage in interpersonal and mediated communication for purposes that are individual in nature. Different individuals are motivated in various ways to participate in the communication process, and each has a distinctive motivation, determining the communicators' willingness (or lack thereof) to disclose their offline, real selves. The specific individual purposes determine the communication outcome, regardless of particular features of the communication channel in which the interaction takes place.

Bargh and McKenna (2004) maintain that some of the characteristics of ICT can under certain circumstances be conducive to the development of personal and intimate communication. According to these scholars, several qualities of the internet, such as anonymity, lack of gating features and the availability in cyberspace of individuals who have the same specialized and shared interests can paradoxically stimulate personal communication. Regarding anonymity, these authors argue that intimate relationships require self-disclosure, which increases the experience of intimacy in social interactions. Disclosure of intimate information occurs after trust and liking have been established between partners, and intimacy is difficult to reach when one is concerned that personal and intimate information may be embarrassing should it become known to members of one's close social circle. The relative anonymity of internet interactions greatly reduces the risk of such disclosure, particularly of intimate aspects of oneself, because here one can share inner beliefs and emotional reactions with less fear of disapproval and sanction. Such anonymity can be relevant to all people, but especially to adolescents, who under anonymous conditions can avoid the embarrassment of exposing their feelings and ideas to others, all the more if they are members of an 'invisible minority' such as homosexuals. A second reason for greater self-disclosure online is the invisibility of the usual features that obstruct the establishment of a close relationship. Easily discernable features such as physical appearance (attractiveness), evident shyness, or social anxiety are barriers in everyday life to relationship formation. These gates often prevent people who are less attractive physically or less skilled socially from developing relationships to the point where disclosure of intimate information can begin. On the internet such features are not initially in evidence, hence they do not stop potential relationships from getting off the ground. Finally, the unique features of the internet enable individuals easily to find others who share their specialized interests. The implications according to Bargh and McKenna (2004) are that online communication can support closeness and intimacy. See Table 5.1.

Youth social network effects in the adoption of media

In the last ten years the communication environment of western youth has changed as they are increasingly using the internet for communication and social purposes. A recent study in the USA found that 89 per cent have access to the internet. Most of the use is for social purposes, as 93 per cent send and receive emails, 68 per cent send and receive instant messages, 55 per cent have a profile in a social networking site (SNS), 28 per cent have created or work in an online journal (blog) and 18 per cent visit chat rooms (Lenhart *et al.*, 2007). In Canada, a recent study showed that 77 per cent send and receive instant messages, 74 per cent send and receive email, 24 per cent visit chat rooms and 19 per cent have created or work in an online journal (Media Awareness Networks, 2005). In Europe figures vary according to country, but the trend in the use of social applications is similar. For example, in the UK 81 per cent send and

Table 5.1 Theories of computer-mediated communication

Technologically deterministic

Theory	Postulate	Implication
Lack of contextual clues, limited social presence.	CMC provides a limited social presence as compared with face-to-face communication.	A lack of social and contextual communicators' cues affects the perception and quality of social connections between communicators.
Media richness theory.	Media differ in their capacity to convey rich information, embedded with socially tacit knowledge and complex meanings.	
Cues-filtered-out theory.	Impersonality reduces interpersonal impressions.	Inability to create communication with real personal content, but also in negative communication such as flaming and verbal aggression.

Conditional models (indeterministic)

Hyper-personal theory.	Computer-mediated communication can support more intimate communication than face-to-face communication.	Frequency, duration and commitment create intimate relations online.
Social identity and deindividuation (SIDE) model.	Lack of non-verbal cues in online communication is not detrimental to personal communication.	Anonymity, lack of gating features and availability in cyberspace of individuals who have the same specialized and shared interests, can even stimulate personal communication.

receive email, 78 per cent send and receive instant messages and 20 per cent participate in chat rooms. In Italy the percentages are lower: 59 per cent of the youth send and receive email, 49 per cent send and receive instant messages and 33 per cent participate in chat rooms (Media Awareness Networks, 2005). Adolescents' online interactions with strangers are not as common now as during the early years of the internet (Subrahmanyam and Greenfield, 2008). Most online interactions are with close friends: to keep in touch after school hours, exchange gossip, share information about homework, coordinate gatherings and activities and ask for social support.

Online communication has become an integral part of the youth culture; the high diffusion is associated with the 'network effect', the phenomenon whereby a service becomes more valuable as more people use it, thereby encouraging ever-increasing numbers of adopters. The network effect becomes significant after the number of users has reached a certain figure, usually referred to as the critical mass. The network effect often results from dissemination by word of mouth. Later on, known others play a more significant role. So while some individuals adopt the system initially because someone has told them about it, later they may adopt a service because everyone they know uses it. Then, as the number of users increases the system becomes even more valuable and is able to attract a wider user base.

The network effect has two kinds of value. One kind is for the user, namely the benefit that accrues from the plain fact that he or she is using the product. The other is the value of the network itself, namely the benefits to the user resulting from others using the same product. The network effect indicates that the extensive use of email, instant messaging (IM) and social networking sites by teens is the result of its diffusion through social networks, mostly face to face. Evidence can also be found that people who socially interact eventually use multiple types of communication channels concurrently. In other words, not only is the adoption of specific applications (IM, SNS) social, but their use may depend on the nature of existing social networks. Close friends have a higher likelihood of communicating through a diversity of communication channels: face-to-face meetings, phone and cell phone conversations, online communication, and more (Haythornthwaite, 2002; Baym *et al.*, 2004; Mesch and Talmud, 2006b).

It is interesting to note that both short message service (SMS) and IM are used to support an important developmental task of adolescence: the creation of a sense of autonomy. SMS messages allow teenagers to work within the constraints imposed on them, such as their not driving, hence their reliance on public or parental transport, and the need to balance school and parental requirements with their social desires. SMS allows teenagers to stay in touch and communicate when doing homework and when at extracurricular activities (Ito, 2005). For teenagers in traditional groups that constrain cross-sex meetings without adult control, IM serves to communicate with friends of the opposite sex without the knowledge and control of parents and siblings. In a study of Arab and Jewish Israelis, Mesch and Talmud (2007) found that Arab youngsters blended their IM use with other computer work. If a parent or sibling approached, IM use was rendered temporarily invisible through window management, namely by minimizing or hiding the chat window.

Studies on adolescents' internet use consistently present the idea that instant messaging is used as an additional communication tool rather than displacing the telephone (Lenhart *et al.*, 2001; Gross *et al.*, 2002; Gross, 2004; Lenhart *et al.*, 2005). Most instant messaging partners are friends or best friends from school. Their online interactions occur in a private setting, with friends who are part of their daily offline lives, covering ordinary yet intimate topics. Moreover, teens' communication of intimate topics may strengthen their closeness with friends, as shown in Valkenburg and Peter's findings that adolescents with a high frequency, intensity and rate of chatting felt closer to their friends (Valkenburg and Peter, 2007a).

Instant messaging and social networking sites differ from other online communication channels in a variety of characteristics. As we have already mentioned, the adoption of the technology is social, as it results from a group of friends settling on a particular IM or social networking system. IM is adopted because of peer pressure, which helps to create a critical mass of users in a social group. Today, for adolescents to be part of a peer group they must engage in perpetual communication online after school hours. Those who do not cannot be part of the peer group. Not being online or not having an IM user name means exclusion from most of the daily social interaction. Using IM requires having an active list of buddies and being on a friends list by the authorization of peers. In that sense, the use of IM with strangers is uncommon as its appeal is mainly to existing friends.

While chat rooms and online forums are technologies which link individuals around a shared topic of interest and concern, instant messenger, text messaging and social networking sites are technologies typically linking teens who have some knowledge of one another, belonging to the same social circle or to the social circle of their friends.

Compared with other communication channels such as email, online forums and chat rooms, IM has unique features. It is synchronous communication, mostly one to one or one to many. IM chatters enjoy real-time conversations and have a short spell to think before replying. Users are aware of other users' online presence and can choose to communicate to others and signal their status (online, offline, away or busy). The application allows multitasking, namely to perform other tasks and chat at the same time. A blocking mechanism allows users to remove themselves from another user's list or to remove a friend from the list. At the same time, users are not able to communicate with others who are not enrolled with the same provider.

Young people's use of instant and text messaging might be motivated by the need to belong to, maintain and develop an existing social circle. In recent years a number of studies have confirmed this argument. In a study of late adolescents' motivations for IM use, participants named mainly four. One was social entertainment, in which the user conducted IM communication to spend spare time and to stay in touch with friends. Next was task accomplishment, namely to learn from others how to do things, generate ideas and make decisions. The third motivation was social attention, in particular mitigation of loneliness and getting support and affection from peers. The least frequent motivation named by the participants was meeting new people (Flanagin, 2005).

When used to connect with members of the peer group, IM promotes rather than hinders intimacy, with frequent IM conversations encouraging the desire to meet face to face with friends (Hu *et al.*, 2004). The main uses of IM are for socializing, event planning, task accomplishment and meeting people (Grinter *et al.*, 2002; Flanagin, 2005), such that IM has a positive effect when used with known friends. Conversely, visiting chat rooms expands the size of young people's networks and provides complementary social support; but this apparently is at the expense of intimacy with known friends and results in a perception of increased alienation and conflict, and decreased intimacy and companionship with face-to-face friends. These two different activities clearly serve different functions.

In a recent study in the USA by the Pew Internet and American Life Project, 91 per cent of all social networking teen respondents said they used the sites to stay in touch with friends they saw frequently; 82 per cent used them to stay in touch with friends they rarely saw in person; and 72 per cent used the sites to make plans with their friends. Only 49 per cent used them to make new friends (Lenhart *et al.*, 2007). In the

UK, findings were similar in that although users reported massive numbers of individuals as 'friends', the actual number of close friends was approximately the same as that of face-to-face friends (Smith, 2007). The research found that although the sites allowed contact with hundreds of acquaintances, people tended to have around five close friends and 90 per cent of the contacts were people they had met face to face. Only 10 per cent were contacts made with total strangers (Smith, 2007). The comparative Ofcom study found that on average only 17 per cent of respondents with a profile in social networking sites used the site to talk with people they did not know (Ofcom, 2008).

Another study, investigating a sample of pre-adolescents, examined whether online communication reduced or increased perceived closeness to existing friends. Online communication using IM proved to exert a positive effect on perceived closeness to friends. This effect came about mainly because IM communication is conducted with friends who are known and represent an additional channel of communication that reinforces existing ties (Valkenburg and Peter, 2007b). Yet another study of pre-adolescents (seventh graders) probed the role of IM in their social lives. Participants reported using the application for more frequent social interaction with their friends, for gossip and for romantic communication. The most frequent motive, stated by 92 per cent of the respondents, was hanging out with a friend after school hours. Participants described their IM partners as long-standing friends and peers, first met at school. The study investigated the association between IM use and psychological well-being. Participants who reported feeling lonely at school on a daily basis were found more likely to have chat room sessions with individuals they met online and did not know face to face. Teens who felt well connected with their school friends tended to use IM to seek out additional opportunities for social interaction with them after school hours, mostly as a continuation of conversations that had started during school hours (Gross *et al.*, 2002). In a longitudinal study of 812 Dutch adolescents, Valkenburg and Peter (2009) found that the positive effect of instant messaging on relational quality was entirely attributable, or could be 'explained' by, the tendency to increase intimate disclosure and personal information to close friends through this medium. Although self-disclosure could be risky, with potential for detrimental usages such as flaming and harassment, over time users learn to develop precautionary devices in their internet use (McCowan *et al.*, 2001), and the differences in relational quality between online and offline channels diminish as the relationships develop (Chan and Cheng, 2004).

Communication channel choice

Other factors are also involved in the choice of communication channel. Communication is an integral part of social relationships and takes place in a social context that includes geographic location, origin and intensity of the relationship, and the information that is being communicated (Sproull and Kiesler, 1986). In that sense, whether already existing characteristics of a relationship and its social context affect the choice of an online or offline channel of communication is an important question. Geographic location serves as a social context that provides opportunities for channel choice. People in proximity are more likely to participate in joint activities and to be physically exposed to each other; and to communicate face to face, people must be in geographic proximity or have easy physical access to each other. For example, among adolescents, proximity is important for friendship formation as it establishes the boundaries within which they choose friends. A major location for meeting and making friends is school, where adolescents spend many of their waking hours. Yet other settings might be important as well. Adolescents spend their free time in neighbourhood haunts that they frequent after school. These may be shopping malls, video arcades and movie theatres, usually located in the neighbourhood or nearby, where groups of adolescents get to know others who might live in the same neighbourhood or locality but do not attend the same school. While geographical proximity or access is a necessary condition for face-to-face communication, it does not restrict the ability to use other channels of communication. In other words, when individuals are in physical proximity due to place of residence or activity, they are more likely to use face-to-face communication. The costs involved in such communication (travelling and available time) rise with physical distance.

Strength of tie is important as well, as face-to-face meetings to socialize and spend time together are more likely with ties one feels close to. Face-to-face meetings with distant ties are more likely to be conducted in formal settings and for formal purposes. Interestingly, although computer-mediated communication facilitates global communication, it mostly serves for locally based ties (Hampton and Wellman, 2001; Livingstone, 2007).

Another factor influencing the choice of communication channel is relationship origin. The use of the internet has diversified and expanded the sources of relationship formation to the online space. Individuals make new friends in the neighbourhood, school and workplace, but also online; and often the last-named connection moves to face-to-face meetings. Relationships created online are likely to be maintained through online communication, certainly during the first steps of relationship formation; but even after the communicators have met in person they tend to continue relying mostly on online communication for small talk and coordination of shared activities. In addition, little overlap is apparent between offline and online friendships, and individuals are very likely to create two different sets of social networks, one with individuals they have met online and the other with people with whom the relationship began offline, without much overlap between them (Mesch, 2009a). This argument implies that some relationship antecedents (such as geographical proximity and relationship origin) are instrumental in the choice of communication channel.

An important component of communication choice is multiplexity, or multiple dimensions of relational flows. It is high when individuals are connected in multiple activities and discussions. Unlike formal relationships, in which social interaction is partial and based on social status, friendship is more holistic. A friend differs from a coworker or a relative in not being restricted to a few topics of conversation or a few shared activities. To be friends is to be together and to talk about anything. Multiplexity exists where a tie between two or more people encompasses multiple activities or topics of conversation, rather than a single activity or a shared topic. Studies show that multiplexity increases ties' strength (Boissevain, 1974; Knoke and Kuklinski, 1982; Kadushin, 2004). Additionally, multiplexity is statistically associated with social similarity (homophily) and is reported among friends of similar social background such as age, gender, ethnicity, school, academic performance and social status (Stoller *et al.*, 2001). Background similarity or homophily increases the likelihood of contact multiplexity.

Multiplexity is divided into activity multiplexity (shared social actions) and content multiplexity (the number of issues shared by a pair of friends). Multiplexity is a typical indicator of village community life and is an important indicator of intimacy and trust (Wasserman and Faust, 1995; Kadushin, 2004).

Another important element is relationship strength. Social ties differ in terms of the intensity of the relationship. Friendship, for example, is distinct from other types of social relationships because contact with friends is more intense. It seems reasonable then that strong ties will tend to communicate by a variety of communication channels. Their social interaction is more frequent and includes intimate and non-intimate conversations, and is not restricted to specific topics or activities. This holistic characteristic implies the use of a wide variety of channels, from face-to-face, through phone and cell phone, to online communication (Haythornthwaite, 2002; Baym et al., 2004).

In our Israeli studies of adolescents' online and offline friendship ties, we investigated the extent to which social relationships originating online and offline differ. We compared these relationships on several central dimensions, in particular duration and communication content. Multiple communication channels are a central component of any association because they indicate 'thick communicative action', shared multiple interests, intimacy and closeness. We also asked whether relations migrate from setting to setting, blurring the boundaries between offline and online. Finally, we showed how interpersonal trust differs according to the origin of the relationship.

We found that closeness to a friend is a function of social similarity, content and activity multiplexity, and duration of the relationships. Friendships that originated on the internet are perceived as less close and less supportive because they are relatively new, and online friends are involved in fewer joint activities and topics of discussion. Furthermore, strength of ties seems to be a developmental process, becoming firmer with age; also, it is greater for boys than for girls (Mesch and Talmud, 2006a).

Our results, based on two representative samples of the Israeli adolescent population, consistently show that the diverse social contexts in which individuals reveal themselves to each other are important. The highest degree of similarity in friends was found in schools. Apparently, age-graded segregation and the fact that schools mainly depend on local enrolment combine to create a high degree of friends' similarity in age and place of residence. Friends met in the neighbourhood were less similar to the respondents, and friends met online were the least similar to them. These results indicate that the higher levels of homophily reported in previous studies, which were based on school samples alone, might overestimate the extent of friends' homophily.

Our Israeli results also indicate that adolescents' developmental factors also affect the tendency to relational similarity. Of all three indicators of similarity (gender, age, proximity), age was found to have a negative relationship to the likelihood of similarity. In other words, over and above the effect of proximity, the older the adolescent the less likely was friendship similarity to occur. Another indication of a developmental process was the effect of length of acquaintance. The longer the time a friend was known, the more likely was social similarity to exist. Keeping friends from the past seems to reinforce the effect of proximity in the development of social similarity in adolescence; the past has an effect on the present state of friendship (Mesch and Talmud, 2006a, 2007).

The question of maintaining online relational quality over time is particularly relevant for close, salient and intimate friendship ties. Valkenburg and Peter (2007a) found that adolescents who communicated more often with their friends online felt closer to their existing friends than those who communicated less often online. Similarly, Blais *et al.* (2008) examined to what extent using the internet for different activities affected the quality of close adolescent relationships (i.e. best friendships and romantic relationships). In a one-year longitudinal study of 884 adolescents, they tested whether visiting chat rooms, using instant messaging (ICQ), using the internet for general entertainment, or participating in online gaming predicted changes in the quality of best friendships and romantic relationships. Blais *et al.* (2008) found that internet activity choice influenced later relationship quality in both kinds of relationship. More specifically, using ICQ was positively associated with most aspects of romantic relationship and best-friendship quality. In contrast, visiting chat rooms was negatively related to best-friendship quality. Using the internet to play games and for general entertainment predicted a decrease in the quality of the relationship with best friend and with romantic partner. These findings reflect the important and complex functions of online activity and virtual socialization for the development and maintenance of relationships in adolescence in the information age. Similarly, Lee (2007) found that adolescents' overall social offline relational quality determined the likelihood of online communication, and resulted in cohesive friendship ties, which in turn even led to higher school connectedness. See Table 5.2.

Online and face-to-face convergence

In many contexts, information and communication technologies supplement, interweave with, or replace traditional routes of communication (Hardey, 2004; Subrahmanyam and Greenfield, 2008; Maidden, 2009). While adults tend to judge online communication against an idealized image of face-to-face conversation, young people evaluate a wide range of options – face to face, email, instant messaging, chat rooms, phones, SMS – according to their communicative needs. The evidence presented in this chapter shows that adolescents may in fact improve their social relationships through online communication

Table 5.2 Structural processes affecting online relationship
          maintenance

Process	Feature	Outcome
Network effects on diffusion.	Transitivity and homophily drive the adoption of ICT by adolescents.	Rapid adoption of ICT by adolescents via peer 'word-of-mouth' influence.
Media choice and content choice.	Multiplexity: spillover between face-to-face interaction and ICT.	Multiple channels intensify relational strength and tie maintenance.
More choice between media channels (IM, chat rooms, social networking site, mobile phones).	Users' versatility.	More communication autonomy for the adolescent user; choice is associated with relational strength.
Transitivity, homophily and proximity govern relational patterns.	Online communication is mainly for maintaining existing social ties among socially similar people.	Social closure and structural diversification of online networks.
Convergence of face-to-face and online worlds.	The divide between offline and online spaces is growing blurred and fading away.	Reciprocal effects of online and offline spheres.

activities, but also by utilizing the internet as a source of shared
activities and common culture among peer groups. Some ethnographic studies suggest that children use online games together with
their friends, and information and ideas gathered online are used as
common topics for offline interaction (Valentine and Holloway, 2002;
Lee, 2007; Lenhart, 2009). The conversational content among adolescent users is often mundane; being readily in touch with their
friends is what counts for them (Gross, 2004).

Online communication seems to foster offline links. Online communication is rarely an escape from offline context; rather, durable
online and offline ties are mutually embedded and reinforcing. The
technological affordance of online relations, as well as the fact that
online relational patterns are embedded in the general social structure,
cause ICT to promote rather than undermine existing social contacts

with friends from school, connecting adolescents into local rather than global networks (Mesch and Talmud, 2006a; Lee, 2007).

Another tension in the potential outcomes of the use of online communication that needs to be addressed is between social diversification and social bonding. Certain technologies might support expansion of social relationships, including access to information, knowledge and skills that teens cannot access due to residential segregation. Diversification is very likely to take place together with social bonding. The use of technologies that require previous knowledge, and even membership of the same social circle, can be applied to coordinate group activities, to continue conversations which started at school, to express personal and intimate concerns, and to provide social support. In that sense, these technologies can support the development of peer group cohesion and the formation of a sense of solidarity and togetherness for those who are part of the social circle. Additionally, many issues typical of the adolescent developmental stage have partially become transformed from face-to-face to online interactions, or have been affected by virtual space. Both online and offline spheres involve issues of adolescents' intimacy, identity formation, peer pressure and individual autonomy, as well as bullying, harassment and racism (Subrahmanyam and Greenfield, 2008).[1]

Leskovec and Horvitz (2008) found that people tend to communicate more online when they have similar age, language and location, and that cross-gender conversations are both more frequent and longer than conversations with the same gender. Transitivity and homophily, which drive the formation of social networks, may exclude others who lack access to the technologies and those who are not accepted by the group (Kadushin, 2004; Leskovec and Horvitz, 2008). The transitivity of adolescents' social networks contains an additional benefit: it can facilitate overcoming or minimizing the possibility of deceit. Mutual contacts can vouch for the offline identities of online friends. Additionally, local social networks can provide more contacts to verify online identities (Wolak *et al.*, 2003).

Still, the social affordance of the ICT makes remote communication easier, and is a benefit for those who have no friends with common interests in their geographically close environment. For these, the internet serves as a compensatory device for the lack of sufficient support in the own group.

---

1 On negative social ties see Chapter 7.

A marginal adolescent can construct a virtual identity, thus compensating for his or her lack of support in offline ties. Adolescents were found to experiment more than adults with their identity in the virtual environment (Šmahel and Machovcova, 2006). Moreover, the internet can facilitate like-minded strangers to become more supportive of one another by maintaining frequent virtual interactions. A recent study on offline 'strangers' in tightly integrated online communities who explore their passion with like-minded people showed that the integration of offline and online life supports 'passion-centric' activities such as shared hobbies or lifestyles (Ploderer et al., 2008).

Nevertheless, for adolescents propinquity governs their relational patterns (Kadushin, 2004). That is, most of their online ties are situated in their school, their neighbourhood and same place of residence, although this regularity is higher in face-to-face relations (Mesch and Talmud, 2006b). The intricate interaction of motivations for the use of different technologies with the particular type of social circle involved has to be made clear for an understanding of the effects of information and communication technologies on the size, composition and nature of the social relationships which characterize adolescence in the information age.

With the passage of time, the online/offline comparison is apparently becoming a faded and even false dichotomy. Many ties operate in both cyberspace and the physical realm. They do not exist only online. Instead, adolescents use online contact to fill the spells between face-to-face meetings and to coordinate joint activities and work. Computer-mediated communication supplements, arranges and amplifies in-person and telephone communications rather than replaces them. The internet offers ease and flexibility regarding whom one communicates with, what medium to choose, when to communicate and the communication duration. In reality, online relationships often substitute empty spots in people's lives, a process deemed important, especially where residential dispersal and dual careers reduce the availability of leisure and family times.

In the next chapter we address directly the implications of the integration of face-to-face and online social ties for the creation, maintenance and modification of social capital.

6 The impact of ICT on social network structure

In this chapter we examine three central questions. First, how hetero-geneous is the composition of adolescents' social ties becoming, and how much is this change linked to social and technological factors? Second, does this change affect the strength of adolescents' social ties? Third, what is the effect of information and communication tech-nologies (ICT) on social capital, specifically whether ICT supports *bonding* or *bridging* social capital? We also examine the impact of network density and internet use on the quality of social relations among contemporary adolescents, and the impact of ICT on their ability to reconfigure their social networks and relational pattern. To put these important questions in context, we start with a discussion of the digital divide and its implications.

Digital divide

From stratification to normalization

'Digital divide' means the uneven distribution of access to, and the asymmetric utilization of the internet (Anderson *et al.*, 1995; Fong *et al.*, 2001). It is important analytically to differentiate ICT access from ICT use. Access is the right to use a computer that is connected to the internet in a private space, such as the home, or at a public point of access such as a library. Use can be of different types. In an infor-mation society, using the internet for computer games has different implications and outcomes from using it to gather information rele-vant for schoolwork. The former use is expected to help the develop-ment of motor skills, the latter school-related skills.

Many conceive the internet as an agent of change in society because it allows rapid diffusion of information, the creation of social net-works and the accumulation of social capital (DiMaggio *et al.*, 2001;

Lin, 2001; Van Dijk, 2005). The internet can also reduce social inequalities by lowering the cost of information and enhancing the ability of socially marginal groups to gain human capital, compete for good jobs and otherwise improve their life chances (Anderson *et al.*, 1995). At the same time, many scholars are concerned that the internet is creating a post-industrial society of information haves and have-nots that enlarges rather than reduces existing inequalities (DiMaggio *et al.*, 2001). Narrowing the digital divide has become a concern of social activists, non-profit organizations, political activists and governments.

Exploring the digital divide, we must distinguish aspects of access (owning a computer, having access to the internet and a broadband connection) from dimensions of use (general cultural literacy, degree of computer literacy and differences in type of use). Recent studies have suggested that the definition of the digital divide should cover, in addition to gaps in access, inequalities in the extent of use, types of internet use, quality of technical connections and ability to evaluate the quality of information (DiMaggio *et al.*, 2001; Van Dijk, 2005). Geographers and economists tend to emphasize uneven access to the internet; sociologists and psychologists underscore the size of gaps in internet use.

The categories of internet access and use may be collapsed into a multidimensional concept of internet connectedness (Jung *et al.*, 2001; Loges and Jung, 2001). But the utility of this multidimensional approach is doubtful, as it may hide the sources of inequality. For example, lack of any kind of access to the internet is not the same as lack of significant usage opportunities (Van Dijk and Hacker, 2003). For the adult population, access may be defined as a continuum (Loges and Jung, 2001), but this definition seems unsuitable for the adolescent population. Most adolescents who have internet access in the developed world have already acquired some basic computer and internet skills and literacy. As digital access and opportunity to use the web involve the realization of social, economic and cognitive resources, there is a strong association between internet access and social inequality (Van Dijk, 2005).

Studies have exposed several disparities between those who do and do not use the internet (Katz *et al.*, 2001), structured primarily along ethnic, gender, socio-economic, age and urban–rural lines (DiMaggio *et al.*, 2001; Livingstone, 2003; Chen and Wellman, 2004; Van Dijk, 2005; Drori, 2006). Usually, the ethnic majority reports greater access to the internet than minorities (Hoffman and Novak, 1998; Fong *et al.*, 2001; Chen and Wellman, 2004). It is possible that various forms

Table 6.1 Kinds of digital divide

Kinds of digital divide	Description
Access	The degree to which a person has access to ICT at home, at work, or in a public place.
Use	Kinds of use, frequency and duration of usage.
Digital literacy	The degree to which a person is competent in ICT, computers and hypertextuality.
Multidimensional	A combination of all three, usually applies to the adult population.

of disadvantage multiply the likelihood to sustain or increase the inequality in certain populations because they are excluded from the computer revolution that is shaping our society (DiMaggio *et al.*, 2001; Attewell *et al.*, 2003). The results of the Pew Internet and American Life Project (Lenhart *et al.*, 2003) indicated that 'having a college degree, being a student, being white, being employed, and having a comfortable income each independently predicts Internet use' (p. 41).

Despite evidence that the globalization process is dominated by the values, culture and power of the dominant western countries in the developed world, the emergence of expansive cyber-networks utilizing relatively low-cost computer devices suggests the possibility of a bottom-up globalization process as well (Lin, 2001; Chen and Wellman, 2004). Moreover, the rise of ICT implies a 'new era of democratic and entrepreneur networks and relations where resources flow and are shared by a large number of participants with new rules and practices' (Lin, 2001: 28–29). Lin argues further, 'with the increasing availability of inexpensive computers and ever-increasing web capabilities which transcend space and time, we are facing a new era of social networks in the form of global villages' (Lin, 2001: 50). See Table 6.1.

Access and use

Amplification or normalization?

The ability to maintain digital exchange with close friends and to form new virtual relations with new contacts is closely connected to ICT access and literacy. It can be argued that while physical access to computers and to the internet and mobile phones is becoming increasingly universal, at least in western countries, the types of use differ along social stratification lines, creating a new type of digital divide with profound consequences for the future. Use diversity is notably important because internet network skills and digital literacy are acquired mainly through informal training (Van Dijk, 2005). The complex relation of sociological categories of stratification to informal training in internet skills led Van Dijk (2005) to predict that over time the internet access and use divide would grow wider (Drori, 2006). Because internet skills and kinds of use are 'soft', being structurally associated mainly with material wealth, income disparity and the household's cultural capital, Van Dijk (2005) foresees that the rate of information and online literacy skills will continue to accelerate differentially for those who have skills and those who do not. By contrast, the diffusion, contagion and adoption perspectives argue that over time the gaps between social categories will shrink relatively, and the digital divide in access and in use will become greatly normalized (Van Dijk, 2005). For this reason the study of ICT (especially the internet) needs to scrutinize skill disparities and use diversification, in addition to the divide in access. Furthermore, the knowledge-acquisition process, especially by means of digital information, is a self-reinforcing cycle (Parayil, 2005). Therefore, the effect of differential acquisition of computer skills, online use and internet experience can produce a chiasmic digital divide in the future. At the same time, extensive adoption of the internet may narrow digital gaps to a minimum, as was the case with phone use.

We follow Van Dijk (2005) to further clarify the distinction between factors associated with various types of digital divide. The *categorical divide* is a digital divide in access or use predicted by sociological categories associated with a general social inequality in the distribution of resources, such as age, gender, ethnicity, class, race and education. *Material access* refers to the actual physical or economic ability to be connected to the internet, either at home or at school. *Skills access* refers to the possession of digital skills, including information retrieval and processing (Hargittai, 2002). *Usage access* refers to the dissimilar division of use and usage time. *Motivational access* refers to avid motivation to use the internet, which in turn may influence categorical inequality, the networks to which individuals belong, or their characteristic manner of conversing via computer-mediated communication (CMC).

If the digital divide persists or deepens, it may also affect other social aspects, as computer-mediated communication is associated with the configuration of online and offline friendships and with individuals' self-image (Di Gennaro and Dutton, 2006). Enlarging the

Table 6.2 Causes for social divide

Causes and barriers for digital divide	Deprived category
Gender	Girls (dissipating)
Education, ethnicity, class, socio-economic background	Low educated, lower socio-economic households, minorities
Technological infrastructure	Low-income countries
Language barriers	Non-English speakers (dissipating)
Regional differences in development	Peripheral regions

digital divide may amplify the class division in individuals' self-image and diversification into distinct social networks (see Table 6.2).

Factors associated with inequalities in access

Research has identified several factors associated with gaps in internet access and use (see Table 6.3). In general, the higher one's socio-economic status and education level, the higher one's rate of access to the internet (Leigh and Atkinson, 2001). Income is related to internet access, as middle- and upper-class households are more likely to be able to afford computer ownership and internet connection. But despite the focus of early reports on income differences, the effect of educational attainment on internet use is twice that of income, even after the introduction of controls in multivariate analysis (Robinson *et al.*, 2000). One possible reason for this educational effect is the positive relation of number of years of education to holding service industry jobs where the use of computers is common; examples are finance, banking, marketing, mass communication, legal services and the civil service. Employment in the service industry increases exposure to computers and people who are exposed develop both the positive attitude and skills that facilitate internet use at home as well. Family background is an important determinant of adolescents' ICT literacy and usage. An American study with young students found that those with access to a computer at home when they were younger than ten years old showed significantly higher levels of full-spectrum ICT technology use than other demographic groups. Students' age on first encounter with computers at school had no significant impact on their full-spectrum technology use (Ching *et al.*, 2005).

Disparities in internet use may also have to do with the language of the internet. This is predominantly English, which may be a barrier to access by groups that are not fluent in that language. In most western societies these are usually the minorities. Although less than one in ten people in the world speak English, over 80 per cent of websites are in that language, which LaVoie and O'Neill (2003) see as a form of cultural imperialism. Even in the USA, English is not the dominant language in ethnic minorities. Greenspan (2002) shows that Hispanic-American internet users tend to spend their online time using more Spanish than English. Furthermore, the dominant position of languages such as English, French and German does not help small countries. The infiltration of the internet into Greek society remains lower than in other European countries (Vryzas and Tsitouridou, 2002).

According to various reports (e.g. Spooner *et al.*, 2001), internet use is lowest among minorities. In the USA, for example, Hispanic and African Americans are less likely to go online than whites. A Meta-morphosis Project conducted in seven areas across Los Angeles (Jung *et al.*, 2001) found that more than 70 per cent of the Chinese American and Caucasian respondents had computers at home, as against 52 per cent of African Americans, 50 per cent of respondents of Korean origin, 23 per cent of Mexican origin, and 16 per cent of Central American origin.[1] An early examination of internet access yielded a similar pattern: internet connection varies across ethnic lines. It was reported by 63 per cent of Caucasian respondents, as against 52 per cent of Chinese origin, 44 per cent of African Americans, 38 per cent of Korean origin, and less than 20 per cent of Latino origin. Ethnic minorities are more likely to belong to economically disadvantaged social groups that cannot afford a computer or the necessary internet connection hardware. Evidence also suggests that in some cases less affluent individuals who are users are more likely to become non-users later on (Katz and Rice, 2002b).

New information technologies can improve school achievement. For the minority of disabled people who do have access to the inter-net, however, its use can lead to significantly improved frequency and quality of social interaction. A study on disabled Chinese people found that the internet significantly reduced existing social barriers in their physical and social environment (Guo *et al.*, 2005). The intro-duction of learning software in schools is deemed an important pedagogical development because it facilitates individualized learning;

---

1 The study inferred ethnicity based on neighbourhood, and therefore overestimated its effect on internet access by the ecological fallacy.

a step-by-step approach is taken in exposing students to school material, completing exercises and receiving online interactive feedback. This type of learning is conceived as superior because it involves a personalized approach to student needs. Structured socialization to ICT, as at school, where individuals have assured access, seems to offset many of the traditional ways in which the digital divide is thought of. Clearly, aspects of the digital divide are minimized in this environment (Cotton and Jelenewicz, 2006). ICT socialization can improve other kinds of literacy. Writing a term paper using word processing software that includes automatic spellchecking, thesaurus and a dictionary may improve students' writing skills as misspellings are corrected automatically and students assimilate the rules of writing word by word. The internet can be used to search for information, encouraging students to explore and integrate numerous, diverse and global sources of information. Schools utilize adolescents' rapid learning of computer skills and their multimedia capabilities to encourage their creativity as they work collectively on projects that combine text, colour, music, picture and video clips.

The internet exposes adolescents early to ideas and attitudes that create in them greater emotional and intellectual openness. Through this medium they can observe the world in a global context and enter a space where even those from disadvantaged groups in society feel included. With knowledge resources at their fingertips, children and adolescents of the net-generation consider access to and active search for information and the expression of opinion a fundamental right. Innovation follows, as more and more children and adolescents use the ICT to create their own world. The pace of the internet makes adolescents aware of a virtual world as an extension of their own face-to-face cosmos, so that they internalize demands for fast processing and communication in real time.

In fact, there is public concern that young people who lack access to home computing may become disadvantaged because they cannot acquire skills needed for the adult job market. The absence of home computers can translate into lower educational achievement. The concern is broader, as most studies have focused only on lack of access as a barrier that can exacerbate current social inequality. But an additional concern is that even if low-income children gain access to home computing, children from poorer homes may not gain as much from it as affluent children do (Attewell and Battle, 1999). In a study in the USA, an important finding is that minority adolescents tend to use the computer for games rather than developing cognitive skills relevant to school performance (Attewell *et al.*, 2003; Van Dijk,

2005), thereby widening the existing gap in ethnic stratification. According to Attewell *et al.*'s study, home computing, which held out great promise that poorer children could catch up educationally with their more affluent peers, in fact widens the educational gap between them. One important reason for this educational gap may be the differential use of the internet by different groups of adolescents. Some adapt ICT to their needs and may use it for purposes unrelated to school, such as games, music and videos.

Many studies inquire into gender inequalities in the frequency of internet use. Men appear more likely than women to use it (Chen and Wellman, 2004). This inequality starts early in life: boys are connected to the internet more often than girls (Bimber, 2000; Terlecki and Newcombe, 2005). But multivariate analyses have shown that the gap in access to the internet reflects male/female differences in income and other resources (Bimber, 2000). Still, this access gap is becoming significantly narrower. In the USA, moreover, the gender gap in access to the internet has practically closed (OECD, 2001; Pew Internet and American Life, 2003) and some claim that gender and income differences in aggregate internet use (hours spent using ICT) reflect the social composition of the population rather than a true digital divide (Van Dijk and Hacker, 2003). Yet as regards internet use, a gender gap clearly remains, at least in user's type of activity, if not in use duration (Van Dijk, 2005; Cotton and Jelenewicz, 2006).

Structural and cultural factors, rooted in a patriarchal society, are seen to prevent women from gaining equal access to the internet (Van Zoonen, 2002). Several studies found gaps between men and women in internet use (DiMaggio *et al.*, 2001) and claimed that male dominance in the quantity and quality of usage reflects cultural stereotypes in western society, with male control embedded in access to technology and its structure. In recent years, however, the feminist approach has claimed that the internet is a 'women's world' (Van Zoonen, 2002). Chen and Wellman (2004) show that in the USA 51 per cent of internet users are female and in Mexico 42 per cent; in Germany and Italy the number of female users is lower than that of male users but is on the rise. Studies reveal a direct relation between gender and internet access and use. Three North American national surveys (Kennedy *et al.*, 2003) found significant differences between female and male participants in frequency of use (Horrigan and Rainie, 2002), type of use (Chen and Wellman, 2004), and internet knowledge acquisition (Wilson *et al.*, 2003). Additionally, women are more likely to use the internet to stay in touch with remote relatives (Boneva *et al.*, 2001). Gender differences are especially marked in high school, and are consistent across samples (Whitley, 1997). In Israel more high school boys used ICT than girls; by contrast, age differences were found to apply to complex applications, not to the extent of ICT use (Nachmias *et al.*, 2001). Beyond these quantitative dimensions, research found that interaction patterns in computer-mediated communication were gendered (Soukup, 1999).

The digital divide is often investigated as an aspect of the 'diffusion of innovation'. As a fairly recent innovation, personal computer (PC) penetration and internet access are generally lower for older than for younger people (Rogers, 1995). The pace of adoption is also faster in younger age groups across OECD countries (OECD, 2001). Scholars have found that use declines with age, but they have failed to distinguish age effects from cohort effects of the digital divide. By contrast, gender differences in the use of new technologies appear quite small, and tend to disappear. In the USA and Iceland the gender gap is statistically insignificant (OECD, 2001), but female users tend to be in younger age groups than male users. Diffusion rate is associated with family background, as the adoption rate of high income households is faster than that of lower income households (Martin and Robinson, 2007). Nevertheless, in several countries such as Sweden and Japan the gender difference in the use of new technologies is prominent.

The notion of digital divide is also applicable to children and adolescents. Using the National Educational Longitudinal Survey (NELS88), Attewell and Battle (1999) found that computer ownership did not predict closure of the digital gap. Eighth-grade teenagers from more affluent and educated families scored higher on maths and reading tests than their poorer and less educated peers who had computers at home (Attewell *et al.*, 2003).

We found in our Israeli studies that in 2001 the digital divide in Israel was a function of the level of parental education, nationality, gender and age. By contrast, by 2004 the observed differences were only partially related to socio-economic standing. Apparently, cultural factors, a propensity for social networks and gender expectations explain the digital gap in the types and magnitude of use. Analysts of social stratification and cultural capital predict that the digital gap grows wider over time (Van Dijk, 2005), but we do not find evidence of a widening digital divide. Instead, we find a more subtle diversification of internet use according to the adolescent user's type of interest and social location. Internet gaps in access and in use, we conclude, are embedded in social structure.

Age differences are clearly evident as well. This is mostly a cohort effect, reflecting a similar historical experience with the web, and not merely a life course or cognitive effect. Studies have reported a negative relationship between age and internet use (Kraut *et al.*, 1998): as with other technologies, younger individuals are more likely to adopt it. Computer literacy, degree of software competence and ability to use the web are clearly conversely related to age. This finding is consistent across all age groups (Hargittai, 2002).

Macro variables affect the permeability of the digital divide. OECD statistics consistently show how firm characteristics, especially firm size, rate of ICT penetration into the country and the urban–rural divide, affect access and frequency of internet use (OECD, 2001). The aggregate statistics of access and use are affected by macro-level variations, but also by individual-level variations. Wilson *et al.* (2003) have shown that community resources and infrastructure interact with personal resources, skills and attitudes to facilitate or delay the adoption of new technologies.

Aspects of a digital divide also exist in terms of whether one uses the internet for specific purposes. However, once individuals begin using the internet, few racial differences exist. Internet experience and gender affect particular types of internet usage, suggesting that the digital divide is a complex, multilayered phenomenon (Barzilai-Nahon, 2006; Cotton and Jelenewicz 2006; Vehovar *et al.*, 2006). Social location in the stratification system is closely associated with internet skills and computer literacy. Competent internet users can employ the new media strategically as an alternative to existing communication channels, and to expand or maintain their social networks. Thus, ICT users may choose to replace or complement the communication channels they use to connect with close friends (Cho *et al.*, 2003).[2] We have reported elsewhere (Mesch, 2001; Mesch and Talmud, 2006a) that online friendships are formed to expand existing social networks or to compensate for their deficiencies. The motivation to use the internet varies according to the type of social activity one is engaged in or the type of social network to which one belongs (Steinfeld *et al.*, 2008). Adolescents have the time, flexibility and know-how to cope with new media (Katz and Rice, 2002a). But their patterns of internet access and use may also have to do with their cultural frameworks, their communicative styles, their peer group's norms and particularly their socio-psychological needs. Like any

---

2 In addition to connection and interaction, people may use the internet for learning, acquisition and consumption, but it is beyond the scope of this study to discuss these patterns of use and needs.

Table 6.3 Social consequences of digital divide

Theory	Prediction
Amplification	The rich get richer; digital divide augments other forms of social inequality, especially education and skills.
Normalization	Low-cost ICT can diminish other kinds of social inequality.

other social activity, the internet can be classified into distinct network clusters. So social engagement in the net and peer-group climate of individuals probably affect their internet access and use above and beyond cultural and social dimensions of stratification.

The various positions on the social impact of the internet derive from arguments about social affordability, which are dominated by two contrasting views: technological determinism and social constructivism. Earlier in the book we showed that these two perspectives are at two polar extremes regarding the relative impact of technological versus social factors in the use of ICT for the formation and maintenance of online social ties. Assuming the technological determinism of ICT, early conceptualizations described the weakness of electronic media in supporting social ties. This early perspective was sceptical of the ability of CMC to support strong ties. Because CMC provides access to a wider audience of individuals who may share interests and hobbies, it has been suggested that the environment of reduced social cues on which CMC is based is better suited to supporting weak ties by reducing the risks associated with contacting unknown individuals (Sproull and Kiesler, 1986; Rice and Love, 1987).

Social constructivists, by contrast, argue that aspects of online communication, such as anonymity, isolation and the absence of 'gating features', facilitate finding others with the same interests, making it easier for individuals to form strong ties (McKenna *et al.*, 2002; Joinson, 2008). The relative anonymity of the internet reduces the risks of such disclosure, especially of intimate information (McKenna *et al.*, 2002).

From divide to diversification

Differential use of social capital

The rapid diffusion of ICT, especially in the form of internet technology of Web 2.0 applications and cellular phones, makes the convergence between ICT media more possible and more comprehensive.

Content originating from one medium can be directly linked to other digital media (Katz and Rice, 2002b). As digital information becomes more available, inequalities in access appear to narrow down (Van Dijk, 2005).

A great deal of scholarly attention has been devoted recently to the impact of the internet on quality of life. There are two contradictory outlooks: a *dystopian school*, which regards individualization, urbanization and globalization, combined with the rapid incorporation of ICT in households, as destructive of the social fabric, and a *utopian perspective*, depicting the ICT as significantly contributing to the emancipation of individuals and of identity groups from constraints of time and space, and even from critical elements of the social structure such as gender, race, geographic boundaries and class background (Wellman *et al.*, 2003; Boase and Wellman, 2006). Yet even proponents of the dystopian view, such as Cummings *et al.* (2002), admit that '[though] online relationships are less valuable than offline ones, indeed, their net benefit depends on whether they supplement or substitute for offline social relationships' (p. 103).

An effective way to examine these schools is to scrutinize how ICT in general, and the digital divide in particular, is linked to adolescents' social capital. An important element in assessing the quality of life in modern society is the nature of social relations. This has been a central tradition in sociology and related disciplines. Since the seminal work of Emile Durkheim, all theories of social relations, but most specifically network models of social structure, have been concerned with structural measures of relational quality and the effects of relational quality on significant outcomes. In his classic study Durkheim (1952) shows that social cohesion has a curvilinear association with social pathologies. Too dense social ties or too sparse a social system result in elevated societal rates of suicide. By contrast, moderate social cohesion is a necessary condition for a healthy social fabric.

Social scientists have been intrigued by the possible effect of dense networks on social processes (Monge and Contractor, 2003). But social network and community theorists differ over the presumed effect of social ties on relational quality. The theory of structural holes, derived from Georg Simmel's image of the modern city (Simmel, 1990), posits that individuals' degrees of freedom intensify insofar as they have many 'non-redundant' ties (Burt, 1992). In other words, to the extent that individuals are connected to others, who in turn are not connected to one another, they enjoy 'structural autonomy'. In this sense, the very disconnection from one's peers is one's social capital. To the extent that individuals have many unconnected others, they can manipulate contacts, information flow, gossip, timing, control and social differentiation, and gain rewards from social interactions. According to this view, being positioned among 'structural holes' provides leverage power.

The structural holes perspective claims that sparse networks can be social capital: individuals can accumulate it and profit from it. Studies have found that even individuals' psychological well-being is associated with the number of strangers in one's networks (Burt, 1992). At the community level, Granovetter (1973) claimed that societal integration was possible precisely because of the existence of weak ties. Tocqueville's notion of the 'art of association' as a condition for individual freedom is also relevant here. In this view, a 'healthy individual' is engaged in a social group, which saves one from selfishness. At the same time, the plurality of social groups ensures that no strict control is exercised over the individual (Tocqueville, 1954).

The 'art of association', learned by adolescents of the net-generation and enacted through their social relations, is a basic element in promoting an adult life of civic engagement (Putnam, 2000). At the psychological level, scholars celebrate the emancipation of the individual, particularly members of minority groups, by means of internet access. These scholars echo the idea that low density, that is, the segmentation of social ties, is a necessary condition for individual autonomy and freedom from social constraints, which is particularly relevant for hidden or invisible minorities (McKenna *et al.*, 2002). Individuals who have many non-overlapping social ties occupy a position that enables them to experience relative autonomy in their actions (Burt, 1992). Density is considered a conventional measure of group cohesion, but many scholars have used density as an over-simplified measure of the degree centrality index (Wasserman and Faust, 1995: 181–182).

At the other theoretical pole, students of social and community integration emphasize the effect of dense social networks on the viability of individuals' moral, occupational and political behaviour. An individual who is locked into a cohesive group and possesses many dense, transitive ties experiences a high level of confidence, coherence and social control. Coleman (1988) underscores the contribution of 'social closure' to children's educational attainments. Robert Putnam (1995) emphasizes the importance of dense social networks for public morality and civic engagement. Rafaeli and colleagues demonstrate how social density benefits the community of internet users (Rafaeli *et al.*, 2003), and Woolcock (1998), among many others, shows the value of *binding social capital* on the collective production of national wealth. This perspective also echoes the 'community lost' notion, which holds that the introduction of ICT accelerates the segmentation of social ties (White and Guest, 2003).

These two perspectives could not be more diametrically opposed. The theory of 'structural holes' asserts that the individual profits from *bridging social capital* across social disconnection in sparse networks. By contrast, the perspective of 'network integration' maintains that individuals, groups and communities gain collective and individual rewards from their *binding social capital*, typically through their social interconnection throughout dense networks.

Bonding social capital and relational strength are associated (Ellison *et al.*, 2007). Granovetter (1973) argued that most bridging ties are weak (although most weak ties are not necessarily bridges). Bridging social capital consists mainly of weak ties because these are not transitive, hence go beyond the individual's immediate network clusters. By contrast, strong ties tend to be more cohesive and closely knit. They are more prevalent in close-knit clusters of cohesive peer groups. Still, there is little doubt that global virtual social connections, transcending the confines of time and space, contribute to the emergence of a 'networked individual' who has a much greater capacity to increase his or her bridging social capital (Wellman *et al.*, 2003; Kennedy and Wellman, 2007). As Nan Lin (2001) claims:

> There is little doubt that the hypothesis that social capital is declining can be refuted if one goes beyond the traditional interpersonal networks and analyzes the cyber-networks. . . . We need to compile basic data and information on the extent to which individuals are spending time and effort engaging others over cyber-networks, as compared to the use of time and effort for interpersonal communications, other leisure activities (television watching, travel, eating out, movie- and theater-going). . . . We need to estimate the amount of useful information gathered through cyber-networks as compared to traditional media.
>
> (Lin, 2001: 233)

We have already shown in previous chapters that peers act as emotional confidants, providing each other with advice and guidance, and serving as models of behaviour and attitudes. In adolescence individuals are inclined to spend more time with their peers, treating one another as their most important reference group (Hartup, 1997).

There is evidence, especially in health matters, that online communication promotes social support and expansive social interactions

(Kavanaugh and Patterson, 2002; Robinson *et al.*, 2000) rather than isolation and depression as previously had been argued (e.g. Kraut *et al.*, 1998; Nie *et al.*, 2002). Additionally, Ito (2005) argues that adolescents are substituting poorer quality social relationships (i.e. weak ties) for strong ties that provide better relational quality.

Chan and Cheng (2004) found significant differences between relationships formed through CMC and offline. Online relationships proved shallower than offline relationships, although the difference diminished as the relationships continued to develop (Chan and Cheng, 2004). We have also shown in previous chapters that social similarity and residential proximity serve as important factors in the formation and maintenance of social ties among adolescents. These structural conditions – conformity, homophily, proximity – foster the emergence of social cliques among adolescents' networks.

Adolescents' online social networks slightly increase social heterogeneity and enlarge relations across geographic location (Mesch and Talmud, 2007). Social networks websites are used predominantly to enlarge bridging social capital. Ellison and colleagues (2007) found that young adults used social networking sites (SNS, such as Facebook) to maintain large and heterogeneous networks of friends. Similarly, Steinfeld *et al.* (2008) found a relatively high number of contacts for Facebook users (mean of 223 in 2006 and 339 in 2007). They concluded that 'emerging adults are using Facebook to maintain large, diffuse networks of friends, with a positive impact on their accumulation of bridging social capital' (Steinfeld *et al.*, 2008: 444). Because they performed a longitudinal study, they could assert that the technology facilitates the expansion of bridging social capital. Moreover, they found that online social networking sites provide the technological affordances to expand network size, deemed especially beneficial for those with lower self-esteem who otherwise are hard pressed to form and maintain large and heterogeneous social networks. In other words, social network sites provide an avenue for enlarging bridging social capital, serving also as a compensatory device for youngsters who lack offline social networks. Accordingly, digital differentiation can be observed in the virtual world, contrary to offline ties. Online social networks are more permeable, diversified, fragmented and fluid.

ICT is used also to maintain existing relations with closed ties. Adolescents' closed friendships are more prevalent in cohesive social circles. To what extent do social cohesion and transitive ties affect adolescents' relational quality? What are the effects of dense networks around individual adolescents on their social capital?

Social network density

Density is a key structural dimension of social networks, measuring the extent to which members of social networks know one another. More specifically, it measures the proportion of actual ties to all possible ties. Network density increases with transitivity in social relations. Given that member *a* knows member *b* and member *b* knows member *c*, if the conditional probability of member *a* also knowing member *c* (or vice versa, assuming network symmetry) is high, then transitivity is prevalent (Wasserman and Faust, 1995). High density typically occurs in cohesive groups, and it is more likely to be pronounced in small communities. Figure 6.1 shows that the

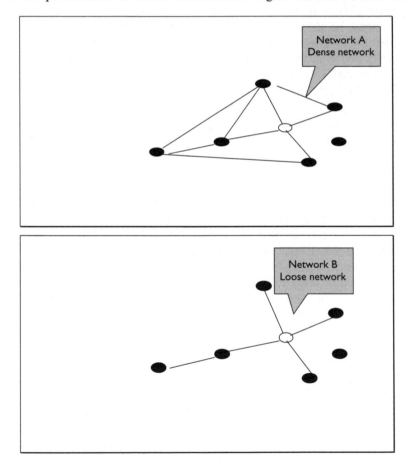

Figure 6.1 Binding and bridging social capital

number of links (lines) between actors (points) is higher in Network A, which is consequently denser than Network B.

In terms of social capital, the white node (actor) in Network B enjoys actual or potential benefits, accruing to her through her position in structural holes (Burt, 1992). These benefits include access to non-redundant information (Burt, 1992), control over information flows, quicker communication timing and the ability to manipulate information flows (Burt, 2005).

By contrast, actors in Network A are situated in a dense social network, hence are deemed to enjoy actual or potential 'profits' typical of binding social capital: interpersonal trust, shared norms and a tendency to closeness, tie stability, reciprocity and a joint capacity to seek help from one another (Lin, 2001; Kadushin, 2004).

The relational quality of adolescents in the information age

We propose that there has been a gradual shift from the digital divide to a more complex phenomenon of digital social network diversification, amplified by both technological applications of ICT and by adolescents' tendency to create ties – even among strangers – with similar others, due either to social similarity or to shared interest in a topic.

Narrowing the physical digital divide in accessing ICT technology leads to widening heterogeneity in adolescents' digital social networks. As inequalities in access to CMC fade, and ICT becomes more widespread, more individual adolescents bear fewer social constraints and fewer costs in forming new social relations via ICT. As the basic social propensity is to form contacts with similar others, the structural end result is more heterogeneous social networks, or diversification of online space (see Table 6.4).

Bridging social capital and *bonding social capital* are both nested in the human propensity for homophily. But there are significant differences. Certainly, network ties consisting of bridging social capital have less relational strength, social homophily and geographic proximity than ties consisting of binding social capital. Yet even bridging social capital is more likely to occur among adolescents with the same kinds of interests and tastes. Another important feature of the ICT is the complementary use of online social networks to extend offline social networks; through ICT even isolated individuals can compensate for a dearth of offline ties, while central individuals can deepen their everyday contacts with their close peers and expand their communicative devices by means of multiple communication media such

Table 6.4 Theories of social capital

Theory	Bridging social capital	Bonding social capital
Social morphology	Broad range, a variety of kinds of friends, many weak ties, connecting network clusters.	Homogeneous networks, closely knit, dense social ties; stable, durable, transitive social ties.
Presumed benefits	Information broker, cognitive flexibility, broad reach of tastes, fashion, and innovation, weak ties, individual autonomy.	Trustful strong relations, mutually committed, social and emotional support.
Presumed costs	Shallow relations, lack of emotional support.	Social control, peer pressure.

as face to face, internet or mobile phone (Cohen *et al.*, 2008), while at the same time expanding their social ties, mainly through their internet access. Put differently, the use of social capital depends on the individual's position in their networks. ICT has a great potential for recombining adolescents' online and offline social networks, where they operate according to net-generational 'networked individualism' (Wellman *et al.*, 2003).

Online and offline social networks tend to expand as the young people grow older (Mesch and Talmud, 2007). Their groups seem more cohesive than those of typical modal adults. To what extent can they trust and share secrets with one another in a cohesive group, where peers' social control over the individual is tighter?

In our study of Israeli adolescents, we found that adolescents' relational strength was inversely associated with network density. In other words, social closure diminishes adolescents' relational quality. Paradoxically, even among adolescents membership of too dense a social cluster apparently reduces their emotional affiliation and attachment to their peer group. Conversely, individuals situated in a sparse social network have more intense ties with the group. This evidence corroborates the predictions of the structural holes perspective that individuals' autonomy will be directly connected to their well-being (Burt, 1988, 1992). We found internet use inversely related to relational strength and social capital, a result consistent with our previous findings showing that internet use increased heterogeneity of ties and proximity among peers. It furnishes moderate and partial support for the dystopian perspective of the effects of ICT on relational quality.

The effect of the internet on social capital is conditioned by social structural variables as well as personal attributes. Youths' structural position determines the resources they exchange over the internet as well as in face-to-face relations, creating through joint social activity shared sentiments and a sense of mutual support. Transitive ties are a robust indication of both social support and social control. In the adolescents' society, their relational quality is therefore associated with the structural condition of personal autonomy.

Being connected to different network clusters elevates adolescents' relational quality. This finding also corroborates Burt's argument that structural autonomy is positively associated with well-being and personal welfare (Burt, 1990). It could also be connected to the arguments raised by prominent psychologists that sometimes online relations with strangers contribute to adolescents' development (Subrahmanyam and Greenfield, 2008). Future studies should also inquire into the associations of network density, social support, popularity and rejection. These relations may be contingent on larger social contexts and should therefore be examined in different cultures.

ICT is often used by adolescents as a compensatory device. Social ties that solely exist through the internet probably have less relational strength and communicative depth. Ties accessible only on the internet are perceived as 'external' to the participants' already existing social networks. Adolescents who use the internet to create bigger networks do so at the cost of weaker relationships. Although strong ties are a common source of emotional support and intimacy, they are also a mechanism of social control, making the individual subject to the pressures exerted by their peer group. This is especially true of transitive ties, which are the foundation of adolescents' social networks. Transitive social ties amplify imitation, social influence and social selection (Pearson *et al.*, 2006). So to safeguard their well-being many adolescents choose non-redundant ties, where their online and offline friends are not attached. In network analytic terms, having non-redundant ties enhances the individual's 'structural autonomy' (Simmel, 1990; Burt, 1992) and minimizes the social constraints and social control of their conduct exercised by their peers.

There is some evidence that those who occupy positions containing bridging social capital tend to have certain personality traits, especially higher degrees of extraversion and a capacity for self-monitoring (Burt *et al.*, 1998; Kalish and Robins, 2006). More research is needed to examine the relations of personality traits, network position and social resources acquisition and exchange.

In this chapter, we have shown the shift from a binary digital divide in access to social network diversification through ICT. As the latter is both a technological and a social device (Katz and Rice, 2002a), using CMC assists adolescents to reshape their relationship configuration across ICT platforms and face-to-face interactions.

We also raised a key outcome of ICT, considered highly pertinent to adolescents' new capacity for relational configuration: the adolescent's ability to mould his network is less costly and more flexible. This novel ability has positive outcomes: Valkenburg and colleagues (2006) found that the more people used social network sites, the greater the frequency of interaction with friends, to the benefit of users' self-esteem and life satisfaction. Often, using ICT increases social support and self-esteem. Valkenburg and Peter (2007a) found that unlike non-socially anxious adolescent respondents, socially anxious respondents perceived the internet as more valuable for intimate self-disclosure, which led to more online communication. Using ICT technology, a teenager can nowadays expand his network size by forming contacts with strangers. This ability is not restricted to bridging social capital. Adolescents can compartmentalize their communication with close peers with very little difficulty, under the aegis of computer-mediated communication.

As network size of internet users grows larger, future studies should investigate how the social bridging and bonding kinds of social capital are negatively associated with relational quality in other settings, using comprehensive research instruments for ICT (Cohen *et al.*, 2008). More specifically, such studies should examine how the co-evolution of online and offline network construction, selection and peer influence affect adolescents' network reconfiguration and how existing attitudes to technology and the net generation's new literacy work on the relational quality of contemporary youth.

7 Online communication and negative social ties

The social network perspective focuses on exchanges (or the lack of) between pairs of actors. A social network relation denotes the type of exchange or interaction between any pair of actors in a system of actors. The network approach differs from other approaches mainly in its focus on exchanges and interactions between actors, not on the individual characteristics of the actors engaged in the exchange of resources. Social network analysis is used to describe the network and to explain how involvement in a particular network helps to explain its members' attitudes and behaviour. As most social networks reflect exchanges that provide companionship, social support, information and social identity, most analysis has naturally centred on the positive or socially accepted resources which are available through them.

However, social network analysis has also been used to study networks of deviant behaviour, such as drug use, criminal involvement and bullying. Most of this book has taken a social network perspective to understand the changes in social structure of young adolescents' social networks. From the perspective of social diversification we have discussed how online networks affect the size, composition, social similarity and range of contact of young adolescents. At the same time, we should note that since the use of information and communication technologies (ICT) began to expand there has been social concern with the potential negative effects of these networks, particularly regarding youth. In one famous case in the USA, the use of identity deception to harass a young female through a social networking site (SNS) resulted in the tragedy of suicide. Meigan Meier had been instant messaging (IM) with a 'cute' boy she had met over the social networking site MySpace. She struck up a friendship with 'Josh' and the pair exchanged dozens of messages. Josh was the fake name used by an adult female neighbour who lived in the same street. When 'Josh' told her 'he' didn't want to be her friend and called her a 'liar and slut' she became depressed. She committed suicide a few days later after her online friendship ended. In another case Ryan Patrick Halligan was bullied for months online. Classmates sent the 13-year-old boy instant messages calling him gay. He was threatened, taunted and insulted incessantly online. Eventually, in 2003, Ryan killed himself. These of course are extreme cases; online harassment for the most part has consequences, but not so radical. In this chapter we address this issue, the main task being to sort out what is new about cyberbullying from what is not and belongs to more traditional forms of peer harassment known before the advent of information society. The aims are to identify incidents of cyberbullying and harassment, to identify personal and family characteristics of youth who are the victims of such experiences, and to identify some consequences of such victimization.

Cyberbullying from a social network perspective

In our understanding of the role of youth social networks it is positive outcomes that are almost always emphasized. From a normative social perspective, social networks have an important role on the individual and social levels. On the individual level, the existence of social ties is linked to the development of a positive social bond to social institutions. Having friends means developing social skills, as through social interaction we internalize social norms, expectations and social values. On the aggregate level, social ties link individuals to society and support the development of a common identity and social solidarity. Through social interaction, namely exposure to each other, individuals develop mutual obligations, trust and commitment. The existence of social ties affords the individual access to companionship, information and romantic involvement. In the literature on youth, social bonds with other peers have indeed been associated with compliance with social values and social norms, but with avoidance of deviant behaviour as well. Supportive and mutual ties have been linked to keeping clear of engagement in deviant and non-normative behaviour both offline and online, to avoid the negative consequences of suffering social sanctions at the hands of significant others.

At the same time we should recognize that social ties can carry negative outcomes, commonly thought to be the result of lack of social ties alone. Not belonging to a large network, not experiencing closeness to existing ties, or belonging to a low density network are all assumed conducive to deterioration in mental health (Beraman and Moody, 2004). Note, however, that negative outcomes may result from being involved in negative social ties – negative in the sense of hostile, aggressive and humiliating interactions (Beran and Li, 1995; Berson *et al.*, 2002). In this chapter we address these adverse aspects and focus on their prevalence, sources and consequences.

From bullying to cyberbullying

Bullying is a serious social issue as it is a vicious threat to a welcoming and supportive educational environment. Grave consequences have been identified in victimized people, including suicide attempts, eating disorders, running away from home, depression, dropping out of school and aggressive behaviour in adulthood (Borg, 1998; Kaltiala-Heino *et al.*, 1999; Olweus, 1999; Hawker and Boulton, 2000).

Historically, bullying is a common form of youth violence that affects children and teenagers, mostly when engaged in age-related activities such as going to school and travelling to or from school or when in public places such as hangouts (Patchin and Hinduja, 2006). Accordingly, in the past bullying has been extensively studied as a behaviour enacted in children's and adolescents' natural habitats such as the neighbourhood and school and at social gathering places. As to the prevalence of bullying, the data show that 10 to 15 per cent of students aged 12 to 18 years had been bullied in the previous 30 days (Devoe *et al.*, 2002; Galinsky and Salmond, 2002).

Bullying is conceived as an act of aggression with the attempt to exert domination through inducing fear. According to dominance theory (Hawley, 1999), students use aggression against weaker fellows to gain access to resources, including high sociometric status among peers. Bullies will therefore occupy more central network positions and hold more physical and social power, while victims will probably not be at the centre but more peripheral on the network than their classmates. Mouttapa *et al.* (2004) found that victims received fewer friendship nominations and occupied less central positions in the friendship network than other members. Socially, for different reasons, they were less integrated in the school groups and of an inferior social status in the school network.

An issue more relevant to our argument is the major importance of the youth network as a protective factor. During adolescence an attempt is made to attain social status in the peer network. Achieving good grades, participating in extracurricular activities, socializing and displaying cultural symbols are in part tools for adolescents striving to achieve social status. Targets of bullying at school tend to be children who are not well integrated in their social networks and known to be lonely or isolated. Well-integrated children are not targeted, as their friends are more likely to be in their company and to intervene in threatening situations (Mesch *et al.*, 2003). Network analysis has been used to investigate whether school sociometric status is associated with bullying victimization. Centrality, an index of popularity, is linked to both pro-social and anti-social behaviors. In their study of fourth and sixth grade males, Rodkin *et al.* (2000) found that boys perceived as non-aggressive, cooperative and leaders, and boys perceived as aggressive, equally occupied a central position in their classmates' social network. Some studies have specifically examined bullies' and victims' sociometric characteristics. Victims were often found to be rejected by their peers and lonelier than other students (Graham and Juvonen, 1998). There is evidence that a display of reciprocal friendships (e.g. students nominate a friend and receive a friendship nomination from that friend) protects students against victimization (Boulton *et al.*, 1999). Thus many young people are able to avoid the experience of bullying at school mainly due to peer or parental support (Farrington, 1993; Nansel *et al.*, 2001; Mesch *et al.*, 2003). Peers represent a support system, and studies on social networks and bullying have shown that victims are more likely to have friends who are non-aggressive, and offenders have ties to others who are aggressors (Mouttapa *et al.*, 2004). Another notable result of these studies is the importance of closeness of children to parents. When children inform their parents of bullying experiences, they are able to intervene and inform the school authorities (Farrington, 1993; Mesch *et al.*, 2003). These findings indicate the relevance of studying social networks for the understanding of bullying.

Concomitant with increased use of the internet has been increased reporting on cyber-harassment, sexual solicitation and cyberbullying (Berson *et al.*, 2002; Li, 2006; Patchin and Hinduja, 2006). Online bullying is an overt, intentional act of aggression against another person; it is wilful, intentional and repeated harm-doing, making rude or nasty comments about others online, spreading rumours and distributing short video clips that are offensive or embarrassing to the victim (Ybarra and Mitchell, 2004). Cyberbullying involves the use of information and communication technologies such as email, cell phone, text messages, instant messaging (IM), defamatory personal websites and defamatory online personal polling of websites to support deliberate, repeated and hostile behaviour by an individual or group – all intended to harm others (Rosen, 2007).

By utilizing information and communication technologies, bullying enjoys the advantage of several characteristics of the medium that transform the essence of the phenomenon as we know it. First, online communication in its very nature might induce bullying behaviour (Giuseppe and Galimberti, 2001). Communication that lacks non-verbal cues, status symbols and proximity to the victim may produce a behaviour that is self-oriented and not concerned with the feelings and opinions of others. Self-orientation may lead to lack of inhibition and negative perceptions of others, resulting in an increase in online bullying. Second, offenders exploit the internet's relative anonymity, through the use of screens or nicknames, to hide their true identity. An overall feeling of fear is generated in the victim, not knowing the perpetrator's identity; he or she does not know whether the perpetrator is or is not a classmate or a person met online (Li, 2007). Fear of unknown cyberbullies harms the educational and accepting environment essential to the classroom. The school is perceived as a hostile environment where victims feel unsafe, and such a child might avoid this by not attending classes. Third, the online environment provides a potentially large audience for the aggressive actions. This might appeal to perpetrators and furnish them positive feedback for their actions. Fourth, the large audience may amplify the negative effects of online bullying on the victim, as the harassment is being watched by all known acquaintances even beyond the school and neighbourhood. In sum, we may conclude that a salient difference between school and cyberspace is that in the latter a large number of perpetrators can be involved in the abuse, and classmates who eschew bullying at school will engage in it in cyberspace, hiding behind anonymity.

Past studies on real-life bullying have shown the importance of the audience, as 30 per cent of bystanders were found to express attitudes supporting the aggressors rather than the victims. The longer the bullying persists, the more bystanders join, and the more the bystanders join the worst are the consequences (Boulton *et al.*, 1999).

Prevalence and consequences of cyberbullying

An early survey in Canada showed that one quarter of young internet users reported they had experienced receiving messages containing hateful things about others (Mnet, 2005). Ybarra and Mitchell (2004) conducted a large study of young internet users in the USA and found that 19 per cent of the adolescents reported being bullied. Victims of online bullying were more likely than non-victims to be the target of offline bullying as well, but the correlation was far from perfect. A more recent online study of young internet users found that 29 per cent were victims of online bullying (Patchin and Hinduja, 2006). Online bullying seems to be increasing over the years. A study by the Crimes Against Children research centre that compared the results from two US national youth internet surveys in 2000 and 2005 found that self-reported online victimization of bullying increased from 6 to 9 per cent. Also, the percentage of children reporting cyberbullying others online increased from 14 to 28 per cent. In that study, being cyberbullied was defined as receiving mean, nasty messages, being threatened with bodily harm, being called names and having others tell lies about the victim on the internet. Inspecting in more detail the types of online bullying to which youth are exposed online, a study in the USA found that 13 per cent had experienced a situation of others spreading a rumour online about them, 6 per cent a situation in which someone posted an embarrassing picture of them online without their permission, and 13 per cent had received a threatening or aggressive email or text message (Pew Internet and American Life, 2006).

As to risk factors, studies have indicated that the higher the frequency of internet use, the higher the risk of cyberbullying (Patchin and Hinduja, 2006; Mitchell *et al.*, 2007; Rosen, 2007). Victimization occurs more often in internet spaces used for communication with unknown individuals such as chat rooms and social networking sites than through email and IM (Hinduja and Patchin, 2008). Recently a secondary analysis was conducted of the Pew Internet and American Life study of parents and teens (2006) on the link between teenagers' internet activities and victimization. When types of internet activities were divided into searching for information, entertainment (playing games online) and communication, it was found that only using the internet for communication was associated with the likelihood of cyberbullying. In particular, youth who had a profile in a social networking site or a clip-sharing site (such as YouTube) and participated in non-moderated chat rooms were at higher risk than youth who did not participate in these activities. Online games were not found associated with the risk of online bullying (Mesch, 2009b). An online profile in social networking and clip-sharing sites provides personal characteristics, disseminates contact information and exposes the adolescent to potential contact with motivated offenders, probably unknown. This private information is the raw material that might be used by potential offenders to call youngsters names, threaten them and ridicule them. Consistent with this approach, the same study showed that attitudes supporting disclosure of personal information predicted the likelihood of cyberbullying victimization. Youths who reported greater willingness to disclose personal infor-

Table 7.1 Summary of risk factors of online victimization

Online bullying	• An act of aggression, wilful and repeated harm, including making nasty comments, spreading rumours, sending offensive text messages and posting embarrassing clips or photographs.
Individual risk factor	• Victim of bullying at school. • Lack of supportive social ties.
Exposure factors	• High frequency of internet use. • Willingness to share personal and intimate information online.
Online activities	• Participation in chat rooms. • Participation on forums. • Having a profile in a social networking site.
Technology-induced	• Internet anonymity. • Reduced inhibition in making aggressive comments. • Large internet audience.

mation to other individuals when meeting for the first time were more likely to report being victims of cyberbullying (Mesch, 2009b).

On entering online space some adolescents are more willing than others to disclose personal information without being asked to. A recent study of young people's public profiles in MySpace showed that these contained personal information such as pictures of themselves with friends or family. A number of youth inserted pictures of themselves posing in swimsuits and underwear. Information on habits such as smoking and alcohol use could be found. Some even included their contact information such as the school they attended and phone numbers. Public disclosure of such information increases the risk of cyberbullying (Hinduja and Patchin, 2008). Not surprisingly, participation in chat rooms heightens the risk of cyberbullying still more, as participants are likely to engage in conversations with strangers, some of whom may be offenders. Studies have already found that online conversations tend to develop intimacy, and individuals are more likely to share private and personal information online because of the relative anonymity of the medium. Interestingly, playing online games was not found to be associated with risk of cyberbullying. Individuals engaged in this activity are most probably oriented to a less expressive and more instrumental form of communication, focused not on personal characteristics but on characteristics of the game (Mesch, 2009b). See Table 7.1.

The findings direct our attention to the role of online social networks, as online victimization is associated with the use of social media. This means internet applications that are used for communication, in particular those which expose youth to networks of individuals who are unknown or who are known but may use a false identity, facilitates their aggression.

Outcomes

For several reasons the effects of cyberbullying might be more pronounced than those of traditional bullying. An important characteristic of bullying is that when moving from physical to virtual space its intensity increases. In traditional bullying the possibility exists of physical separation between the aggressor and the victim, but in cyberbullying physical separation does not guarantee cessation of acts such as sending text messages and emails to the victim. Second, with the internet the abuser has a sense of anonymity and often believes that there is only a slim chance of detection of the misconduct. Third, when bullying is technologically supported, the aggressor is not aware of the consequences of the aggression. The screen does not allow a view of the victim's emotional expression. Anonymity and absence of interaction may make the aggressor still less inhibited and increase the frequency and power of cyberbullying (Heirman and Walrave, 2008).

Being a victim of online bullying has negative effects on adolescents' well-being. Victims are more likely to engage in high risk behaviours such as low school commitment, neglect of grades and alcohol and cigarette consumption (Finkelhor *et al.*, 2000). An emotional aspect also exists. After a bullying event the victim reports feeling angry and upset, and has difficulty concentrating on schoolwork. Online bullying has proven to have a negative effect on parent–child relationships and on relations with friends (Patchin and Hinduja, 2006). Regarding actions taken by victims, most respondents said they took none, 20 per cent decided to stay offline and only 19 per cent went to their parents and told them about the incident (Patchin and Hinduja, 2006). As these data show, the aggressors' perception that their acts incur no consequences seems to reflect the low likelihood that victims will take any action and report such incidents to teachers and parents. Thus, aggressors continue with their misdeeds because they do not face any negative social reaction.

Recently the danger has increased with the establishment of social network sites that provide platforms for publishing hate and cyberbullying. Examples are Enemybook, Snubster and Hatebook. These utilities describe themselves as antisocial; subscribers may add to the Friend feature, adopted from the basic idea of Facebook, an additional feature of enemies, the reasons for choosing them as enemies and spreading their secrets, and can invite others to join them in their bullying (Hammond, 2007).

Explaining cyberbullying

The explanation of online victimization requires a socio-technical framework incorporating patterns of internet use, the nature of computer-mediated communication, and individual characteristics that affect the quality of ties. The pivotal element is the existence of opportunities for an aggressor. These are likely to arise as young people conduct their regular activities online: cyberbullying is possible only for adolescents who have access to the internet. That said, even for internet users the likelihood of being victims of cyberbullying varies according to the amount of daily time use, types of internet use and extent of disclosure of information. The concept of diversification is useful. We have shown in previous chapters that internet use for communication purposes is an important element in youngsters' social life. Participation in online communication is an important component in the explanation of cyberbullying. Consistent with our argument, frequent internet use and high level of internet skills increase the risk of being bullied online (Ybarra and Mitchell, 2004).

Participation through social media (email, instant messaging, social networking sites, forums and chat rooms) have an effect on the size, composition and quality of social ties, increasing exposure of youth to them. The effect varies according to each application, and the risk of exposure to victimization varies accordingly. Participation in chat rooms and forums and exchange of emails expose youth to new ties with unknown others. With some of them the exposure can have positive consequences as youth are able to meet others who share their interests and concerns and are able to exchange resources that are not located in the existing network. At the same time, internet activity enlarges the youth network; hence the risk to exposure to others with whom negative relationships may develop. The more unknown individuals become part of the social network, the greater the likelihood of meeting some who might become aggressors. The risk may also intensify due to the heterogeneity of the expanding network's composition. This raises the likelihood of the adolescent meeting others who are socially different (in age, race, ethnicity) from him or her, and social heterogeneity might be a further source of aggression. Some older individuals might express interest in associating with teens to harass them or solicit them sexually. Also, the addition of online ties to the youth network might temporarily decrease the strength of existing ties, reducing the sources of social support available to the individual. The extent that cyberbullying is carried out by strangers remains to be assessed as existing evidence is more anecdotal than based on large-scale studies. Due to the anonymity of the medium it is difficult to establish perpetrators' identities or if they belong to the victims' social network or not. As most of the adolescents' use the internet to connect with schoolmates and members of the peer group, it is plausible that the offenders are more likely to belong to the immediate social circle and less to be unknown strangers.

The use of social media such as IM to maintain existing ties and keeping a profile and communicating with friends through social networking sites expose youth to the risk of online victimization, but by a different mechanism. The incorporation of IM and social networking sites into adolescents' lives transforms their relationship with peers. When teens arrive home every day, rather than disconnecting from their friends they enter a state of perpetual connection as IM is on all the time, text messages arrive and conversations continue. In this case online bullying becomes an extension of school bullying, conducted after school hours through electronic communication. Now the possibility of after-school disconnection from or avoidance of contact with aggressors decreases. Cyberbullying often starts at the school or in the neighbourhood and it continues online, as affirmed by adolescents themselves. In one study, US teens were asked where they thought someone of their age was more likely to be bullied or harassed. It is interesting that while 29 per cent replied that it was more likely to happen online, the vast majority of these young internet users, 67 per cent, thought that it happened more often offline. Only 3 per cent thought that it happened equally online and offline (Pew Internet and American Life, 2006). For teenagers, online bullying can be emotionally debilitating, particularly because it is mainly a continuation at home of the aggression in the playground by known others from their social network. With traditional bullying, on arriving home the youngster felt safe and there was a respite from the aggression; now the aggression follows the adolescent home and can go on 24 hours a day. There is no place for the youngster to hide, even at home, from the persistent aggression (Rosen, 2007). A study in Canada (Li, 2007) investigated different forms of electronic bullying and found that the most frequently reported were email (20 per cent), chat rooms (33 per cent) and mobile phone texting (13 per cent). In the UK a study of the different channels of cyberbullying in greater depth found similar results. Phone calls, text messages and email bullying were the most common forms. Distributing a picture/video on websites and instant messaging were reported to a lesser degree (Smith *et al.*, 2006). The study also investigated the impact of each cyberbullying type and found that the picture/video clip was considered the most harmful by youth, followed by phone calls, text messages and website. Bullying by email, instant messaging and chat rooms was perceived as not very harmful (Smith *et al.*, 2006).

Important too is that online bullying requires some knowledge of the victim. When conducting online activities, individuals differ in their readiness to share personal information. Some are less willing to provide contact and personal information than others. Providing personal information can be considered a risk factor for victimization, particularly when it is given to strangers (Mesch, 2009b).

Another significant element is the way in which the internet is perceived; this affects the user's behaviour. In many ways the effect of the added value of communication technologies to face-to-face bullying is the well known disinhibition effect, often associated with the use of these technologies. Suler (2004) noted that cyberspace can be conducive to behaviours that may not be revealed in the offline world. Various factors contribute to creating a subjective perception that fosters the disinhibition effect. Among the most salient characteristics are anonymity, asynchronicity and dissociative imagination. Anonymity means the individual's subjective perception that the use of a nickname online separates him or her from the real world and his or her real identity is not known to others. This sense of anonymity might give rise to actions for which the actor does not feel responsible, at least not in the way he or she feels responsible for actions performed in a social circle in which his or her identity is known to friends, teachers and parents. Asynchronicity means that often individuals interact online not in real time, especially when communicating through email, forums and social networking sites. Not interacting in real time means that individuals do not experience in real time the reactions of others, or get immediate negative feedback for their actions. This lack of interactivity might multiply aggressive acts against others as their reactions and feelings are not revealed immediately or as part of the social interaction between the teens.

Dissociative imagination means a situation in which some individuals evaluate online events differently and separately from face-to-face events. Certainly anonymity may reinforce this feeling that online norms of behaviour unacceptable in a face-to-face situation are acceptable online. This is sensed as a different sphere, less real, or with fewer real consequences, for the victims. Disinhibition can be linked to the 'lack of social cues' perspective, which holds that the deficit of online communication lies in the lack of social cues, of non-verbal signals that denote social status, and of the emotions of the participants in interpersonal communication. Accordingly, in the case of cyberbullying the victim's emotional reactions are not present. The aggressor is unaware of the victim's distress, fear, tears and other emotional reactions. He or she is thus likely to increase the aggression attempts without setting limits on it that would otherwise derive from interpersonal contact and interactivity. These perceived charac-teristics cannot be taken as the sole factors responsible for all online bullying activity. They work in combination with the aggressor's personality and family characteristics, which they interact with to amplify their effect.

Linking traditional bullying and cyberbullying

Is cyberbullying independent of bullying at school and in the neigh-bourhood? Some observers have advanced the idea that cyberbullying is a new phenomenon, largely the result of children and adolescents coming into contact with strangers and unknown individuals in open chat rooms online. In these spaces of conversation and social interaction strangers hold conversations with young people, making derogatory ethnic and sexual comments, or deriding their contribu-tions. However, recent studies point more and more to a link between school bullying and cyberbullying. A study in Canada found that the most important predictor of cyberbullying victimization was victims being bullied at school (Li, 2007).

Bullying and cyberbullying are closely related, and in many cases the bullying possibly started at school and/or in the neighbourhood and then spread to cyberspace. In fact, cyberspace serves bullies as yet another venue in which to harass others, as they take advantage of the high rate of internet use among youth. Another possibility is that bullying starts online, and later the perpetrators take it into the real world, converting it into face-to-face bullying.

In trying to resolve this issue we face the problem of identifying the aggressor. As the internet often provides anonymity, victims do not always know who the perpetrator of the aggressive behaviour is. A study reported that 25.6 per cent of the respondents said that they were cyberbullied by schoolmates, 12.8 per cent by people outside school. The most surprising finding was that 46.6 per cent did not know who cyberbullied them (Li, 2006).

Over time, online bullying seems to be on the rise. The percentage of victims of cyberbullying has increased despite the decrease in participation in open chat rooms and forums and an increase in the participation in IM and social networking sites. These results provide an additional indication that cyberbullying is aggression by known others, such as schoolmates, taking advantage of social networking media (e.g. Instant Messenger, social network sites, SMS). As noted earlier, a study by the Crimes against Children research centre compared the results of two national youth internet safety surveys in 2000 and 2005 and found that the amount of cyberbullying had increased. In Rosen's study (2007), although only 11 per cent of the teens reported being harassed, 57 per cent of parents and 34 per cent of teens reported that they were concerned about harassment on MySpace. Clearly, the use of communication channels that link youth with friends and friends of friends is associated with an increase of cyberbullying; this supports the argument of a link between this and offline bullying. Rather than being new, cyberbullying seems to be a supplement to school aggression.

Online harassment

We have already argued that the internet is a space of social activity. Youth activities include participating in online games, online discussions, online social support and social networks. Participation in this social space might expose youth to the risk of online harassment. This notion refers to unwelcome and uninvited comments or attention. The comments provoke negative emotions and are insulting because of their gender or ethnic content. This can take the form of offensive sexual or racist messages, jokes and remarks purposely initiated by the harasser to humiliate the victim. Youth are victims of this type of online harassment. A study in the USA reported that 62 per cent of youth participating in a representative national survey reported receiving unwanted sex-related emails (Mitchell *et al.*, 2007).

A form of harassment that creates public concern is online sexual solicitation. Several large-scale studies have been conducted to assess the prevalence of online sexual solicitation. Regarding the frequency of harassment, a US study found that 13 per cent of youths aged 10 to17 years reported experiencing an unwanted sexual solicitation on the internet in the previous year (Wolak *et al.*, 2003). In the UK, 9 per cent of children and youth aged 9 to 17 reported having received unsolicited sexual material online and 7 per cent reported receiving sexual comments online (Livingstone and Bober, 2004). In Canada, a study asked about the frequency and place of sexual harassment in the previous year, providing us with a rare opportunity to compare the frequency of sexual harassment in different social contexts. According to the data, overall 12 per cent of adolescents in grades 7 to 11 reported having experienced sexual harassment in the previous year. There was a significant gender difference. Nine per cent of the boys and 14 per cent of the girls reported sexual harassment. When asked about the space in which the harassment occurred, 8 per cent said on the internet, 6 per cent at school, 2 per cent on the phone and 2 per cent on the cell phone. The study also asked about the relationship with the offender and found that 52 per cent reported that the harasser was known from the real world while 48 per cent did not know who the harasser was (Wing, 2005). The results are consistent in other countries as well. A study conducted in Australia asked 502 young children aged 8 to 13 years about the extent they were exposed to different experiences; it found that 5 per cent were exposed to obscene language (Kidsonline@home, 2005).

The few studies that investigated online sexual solicitation indicate that the likelihood of being a victim of this aggression depends on the application that teenagers use. One study found that the locations where youth most frequently reported online sexual solicitation were email, social networking sites and chat rooms (Ybarra and Mitchell, 2008). But blogging in general was not related to sexual solicitation. Bloggers who customarily interacted with unknown others were the only ones found to be at risk of sexual solicitation (Ybarra and Mitchell, 2008). Adolescents who blogged proved more likely than youth who did not blog to post personal information online, including their real names, age and pictures of themselves, as well as disclosing personal experiences. Yet as the study shows, blogging in itself is not related to increased risk of online sexual solicitation. The risk of sexual solicitation becomes high only when the teen interacts with people met online. Furthermore, most of the youths who write a blog do not interact with people they meet online and do not respond to their messages (Ybarra and Mitchell, 2008).

Adolescents' choice of internet applications probably reflects a selectivity effect. Youngsters who have unsatisfactory ties with parents and friends choose to use chat rooms to compensate for this by engaging in communication with unknown others. Such activity is a risk factor for online sexual solicitation. For example, a study that compared adolescents who used chat rooms with those who did not found that chat room users were more likely to have low self-esteem, to not feel safe at school and to have been physically abused in the past. Thus, the study reported that for boys and girls alike chat room use was significantly associated with adverse psychological characteristics. In contrast, other internet activities did not show a consistent pattern of positive associations with these factors (Beebe *et al.*, 2004).

Racial and ethnic online harassment has been reported in studies conducted in chat rooms in which adolescents participate. The anonymity of online interactions may lower control of racist remarks. A study that compared moderated and non-moderated adolescents' chat rooms reported that in the latter an individual had a 59 per cent chance of being exposed to racial and ethnic harassment remarks, and in the former a 19 per cent chance (Subrahmanyam and Greenfield, 2008).

The aggressor in this type of online harassment is usually an unknown other online user who was met briefly in a forum or chat room; he or she identified the intended victim's social status characteristics and set about harassing them. A follow-up study that investigated risk factors of online harassment found that the likelihood of exposure to sexual solicitation and sexual harassment was associated with exposure variables: high frequency of internet use and high frequency of participation in risky sites. Age was also related, as young adolescents were more likely than older ones to undergo this experience (Fleming *et al.*, 2006).

In sum, bullying and harassment have not just moved from physical to virtual space, their intensity has magnified as well. Physical separation of aggressor and victim does not guarantee disengagement and cessation of acts of bullying – not in terms of frequency, scope, or severity of the inflicted harm. With the advent of Web 2.0, cyberbullying includes the use of email, chat, instant messaging, clips and blogs, which serve to embarrass and threaten, to make rude or vicious comments, and to spread rumours or clips and photographs of the victim in embarrassing situations. Cyberbullying, a serious form of cyber-harassment, has a number of important components:

1   Cyberbullies are aggressors who seek implicit or explicit pleasure through the mistreatment of other individuals.
2   Cyberbullying (like bullying) involves repetitious harmful behaviour.
3   A power differential between bullies and victims should be expected, and in the case of the electronic environment this differential might also be observed in computer literacy.

Internet users often believe that there is only a slim chance of misconduct being detected online, so threats and harassment have become prevalent among young users (Lanning, 1998).

Inquiry into young people's social networks today requires study of the patterns of internet adoption and of online and face-to-face networks. Adolescents' adoption and use of the internet are related to the social network to which each of them belongs. The choice of internet social applications such as forums, chat rooms, email, instant messaging and social networking sites depends on which online activities are carried out by others who belong to the peer group. A member's engagement in online communication requires that the other members have adopted the internet for communication purposes.

Internet adoption and integration into routine communication with others has an effect on a youth's access to positive and supportive ties, but also on the extent of his or her exposure to negative encounters and persistent harassment, with all its negative consequences to his or her well-being. From the studies reviewed, it is clear that some adolescents become exposed to repetitive aggression and harassment. Such exposure depends upon the online activities being conducted. The motivation to use forums and chat rooms is undoubtedly different from the motivation to use instant messaging and social networking sites. From the psychology literature we learn that shy individuals with higher levels of social anxiety are more likely to use forums and chat rooms. From the sociological literature we learn that individuals wishing to expand their networks and access to others who share their interests and concerns are more likely to do so. Through these applications youth are better able to establish social ties with others who share their interests and hobbies; but at the same time they become exposed to strangers who may belong to a socially different group, hence to some risk of harassment by strangers.

The motivations to use instant messaging and social networking sites are apparently different, having more to do with an attempt to maintain and reinforce existing social ties with present friends met at school and in the neighbourhood. The greatest danger of cyberbullying thus seems to be less from strangers than from known others; and as noted, cyberbullying is less likely to be a new behaviour than aggression which has acquired an additional medium – cyberspace. The use of the internet accordingly amplifies negative behaviour, allowing it to be conducted at school and after school hours as well.

These conclusions should be qualified, as bullying is a relatively new and developing behaviour that has to be monitored over time. As new applications are being developed, including social networking sites which openly instigate calling friends names and identifying them as enemies, we must follow the progress of cyberbullying and its connection with face-to-face and online behaviours. What is new about cyberbullying seems to be diversification of sources of risk (online activities) and diversification of kinds of bullying (using a new medium to bully).

8   Summary and discussion

Since the expansion of the use of information and communication technologies (ICT), and especially following the increasing integration of the internet and mobile phones, academic discourse on the implications of computer-mediated communication (CMC) for social interaction has risen dramatically. A large group of scholars, mainly studying the internet as a novel cultural artifact, suggested that ICT represents a social sphere in itself, a space for dwelling, capable of generating and sustaining new and complex forms of social interaction and activity. Youth have been given various appellations, from the 'net-generation' through the 'millennium generation' to 'digital natives' (Tapscott, 1998; Prensky, 2001). These labels attempt to identify young adolescents as a unique cohort who have grown up during the expansion of the internet and have been exposed since early childhood to a media-rich environment. They use computers, play online games and constantly communicate with and are connected to their friends by electronic devices. They are immersed in these technologies, using digital spaces for social interaction, identity expression and media production and consumption. Simply put, the argument is that the internet has created a new generation of young people who possess sophisticated knowledge and skills in information technologies that express values which support learning by experience and the creation of a culture in a digital space, and they have particular learning and social preferences.

Another stream of scholars argued that ICT has not affected any basic social patterns and has not created a new youth culture (Herring, 2007). Proponents of this view see ICT as a cultural artifact, an object immersed in a social context. They consider how the technology is incorporated into people's everyday lives and how it is used as a means of communication within an offline social world (Howard *et al.*, 2002; Katz and Rice, 2002b). By this approach, the information and communication technologies have not generated novel and different experiences, but are principally a new venue to conduct old things. For these researchers, the social uses of ICT are mostly restricted and similar to the use of other communication technologies, such as landline and cell phones. Their purpose is merely to connect individuals already known to one another. Youth who use the internet are not a unique generation; the fundamental developmental issues they have to cope with, such as identity formation, autonomy, social participation and socialization, are the same as those of all young people. They are handled in the same traditional ways and technology supports the accomplishment of these developmental tasks (Herring, 2007).

So while the transformative view focuses on online ties only, the 'no change' view focuses on how people who have face-to-face contact use the ICT to sustain these relationships over time and space.

We expanded and modified both the above views of ICT, using the concept of social diversification, that is, maintenance but more especially expansion of the size and composition of the social network beyond the structural factors that limit adolescents' associations. At the centre of the diversification approach is a conceptualization of ICT as a space for activity and social interaction.

We presented ICT as an object around which joint activities are organized, no different from the neighbourhood or the school. Our approach sees the ICT as an arena that reflects existing social ties, but which can also modify individuals' social involvement in personal relationships. More specifically, the objective of this book was to explore how the use of the ICT and online relationships affect the structure, content and closure of adolescents' social circles. We asked what are the social motivations to form online social relationships, and whether online ties diversify the social circle and provide access to resources and social capital. The concept of diversification implies that the innovative aspect of the internet is to provide opportunities for activities which induce social interaction resulting in a space for meeting new individuals.

Societies are characterized by varying levels of social segregation. Social stratification processes and social norms segregate youth from other age groups and from youth of a different ethnic and social class group. As a result, adolescents tend to associate socially with individuals of similar social characteristics such as age, gender, marital status, ethnicity, religion and nationality. This similarity may replicate existing social inequalities and block access to information and skills not available in the restricted social circle. Among adolescents, proximity is important for friendship formation because it establishes the boundaries within which they choose friends. Every individual occupies several separate but overlapping social worlds, each a potential sphere for association. A key location for meeting and making friends is school, where adolescents spend a large part of their waking hours. But other settings may be important as well. Adolescents spend their free time in neighbourhood hangouts that they frequent after school. In shopping malls, video arcades and movie theatres, usually in the neighbourhood or nearby, groups of adolescents get to know others who live in the same neighbourhood but do not attend the same school (Cotterell, 1996). Unlike groups that are geographically more mobile and exposed to more diverse foci of activity, adolescents lack geographic mobility and are trapped in social relationships that involve individuals similar to themselves.

Diversification is a concept that can be linked to social capital. Although there are several accepted definitions and operationalizations of this concept, it is agreed that social capital refers to network ties that provide mutual support, shared language, shared norms, social trust and a sense of mutual obligation from which people can derive value (Huysman and Wulf, 2004). The definition emphasizes the central role of the size, structure, composition and trust in social networks. Based on these qualities, networks provide differential access to resources that include opportunities, skills, information, social support and sociability. In the diversification perspective, the internet is conceived as a social arena of shared activities that provides an opportunity for maintenance of bonds in existing friendships, but also for expansion of the social circle to others who provide linkage to resources not available in the socially segregated and similar peer group. Unlike earlier researchers, who sought a general effect of ICT use on people's social involvement, we focused on a comparative analysis of adolescents' associations based in the origin of their settings: online or face to face.

ICT reflects social structure and at the same time exerts significant transformative effects on relational patterns. Conceptualizing ICT as foci of activity, we were able to produce a review illustrating that ICT is embedded in social structure. It is yet another sphere of social interaction and action, where adolescents play games, exchange information, offer social support and share other instrumental and expressive resources. Like the more realistic syntopian perspective put forward by Katz and Rice (2002b), we argued that online activities are therefore closely associated with offline social behaviour, where the driving forces of social interaction are shared interests and adolescents' need of diversification of their social circle. Online friendship formation is associated with the social similarity of existing ties, indicating that the motivation to expand an adolescent's network is to diversify her or his social circle. This trend carries important implications for the changing nature of adolescence in the information society. First, using information and communication technologies, adolescents incorporate into their social circles friends who are more likely to be socially different from themselves, in contrast to their more homogeneous offline relations. A speculative question is how different from current patterns future social mechanisms of friendship formation and sociability via ICT will be. Second, contemporary online friendship formation is not a deviant case but is becoming increasingly common. It potentially exposes young individuals to new sources of information, social support, acquaintance and friendship ties, expanding their social capital. Third, study of the organization of adolescent peer groups requires a novel approach, one that should integrate social networks ties made at school, in the neighbourhood and through ICT. Such integration might produce research results different from those that have mounted up over the years in respect of societies in which young people's friendships were geographically bounded. Fourth, the internet is a challenge to parent–adolescent relationships. The search for autonomy, as a developmental task, continues to be salient, but the internet changes parents' ability to control the adolescent's exposure to values, activities and social connections. In low income households, adolescents become technology experts and parents must rely on their skills. The sources of teens' information become diversified and might challenge parental values. Online activities are difficult to control and monitor and access to individuals belonging to a different social circle expose youth to alternative viewpoints and experiences.

The use of different social media to stay perpetually in contact with peers raises the question of how youth accommodate online participation in their full schedules. With the extensive use of computers, multitasking has become part of the way teens manage a busy life. Media multitasking can be defined as engaging in more than one media activity at a time, switching constantly between such activities as email, instant messaging (IM), web search and sending text messages to friends (Foehr, 2006). True, some multitasking existed in the past, with adolescents doing homework and listening to music at the same time. But now it has been expanded from media to social multitasking, namely conducting various conversations simultaneously with different members of the peer group and using different channels: doing homework while participating in online chats and contacting friends by short message service (SMS). In that sense, the involvement of youth in peer groups and social networks has become more intensive and intermittent, most likely strengthening the bond of young people to their social networks and intensifying their mutual expectations. One question that will need to be addressed in the near future is how media multitasking and perpetual contact with peers affect family time and family communication, which are the building blocks of the family socialization process.

Certainly, online social engagement is still associated with general traditional sociological variables such as ethnicity, gender, age, family background and residential location. That is, diversification is limited by existing material conditions and in that sense it raises important questions of social marginality. In earlier chapters we indicated that access to and use of information and communication technologies is a source of youth empowerment. Social media are adopted through networks, as peers make a decision to adopt a specific instant messenger provider, a specific game site or a specific social networking site. In that way a central component of peers' interaction moves online and escapes parental and school control. Youth thereby obtain spaces of interaction that support the development of existing ties, the making of new ties and access to diverse and novel sources of information. Furthermore, youth have the opportunity to go from passive consumption of media to active engagement in the co-production of information in the information society. One important development in the internet culture is a change in the connection of youth and media. Today youth are active participants in the creation of media content. The advent of Web 2.0 has increased youngsters' ability to become active creators of and contributors to information and content online, as well as passive consumers. The lower costs of coordinating creative efforts and distributing materials allow individuals to generate their own content and to collaborate with others in social, economic and political activities. Social media platforms facilitate various ad hoc and formal online communities, small as well as large-scale. There user-generated-content (UGC) flourishes: bloggers post news and analysis, independent musicians distribute their music (MySpace), and amateur photographers post their photos (Flickr) or distribute their videos (YouTube). Youth today are actively involved in web production and tend to appropriate portions of it and to convert them into youth zones. Teens also produce unique, stand-alone content for the web, like blogs, which allow a more interactive dialogue. Weblogs are a kind of diary shared with a larger audience; they present details of people's everyday lives, daily concerns, thoughts and emotions, consumer talk and television and movie critiques. As such weblogs are a popular way of building identity, socialization in the information-based society and social interaction. All these considerations produce the need to develop an understanding of some youths' marginalization in the information society. Access and use are not universal; by cultural choice or due to socio-economic circumstances a portion of adolescents are disadvantaged. Their lack of access to communication and information technologies might result in disconnection from mainstream society. While the consequences of access and use have been studied extensively, the social and developmental consequences of 'disconnection' require the development of research programmes (Katz and Rice, 2002a; Van Dijk, 2005). In particular, there is a need to address the psychological and sociological consequence that not having access, or not having fast access to the internet might result in social isolation from peer-group members who coordinate their activities through internet social applications.

Lack of access or restricted access to the internet also has implications for the acquisition of skills in the information society. The use of social media is becoming a regular requirement for new employees. Social networking sites are more and more instrumental in the job-hunting process and applicants are more and more recruited through social networking sites. Employers no longer rely completely on word of mouth or print ads to display the jobs they post. Information on job openings is becoming more and more available through social networking sites and micro-blogging. Social networking skills were always important in finding a job. The significant change is that social networking is now conducted online, diversifying the number and type of employees and employers who can be approached. As stated, social media skills are becoming required in many jobs. Firms are realizing that customers are expressing their views on products online and need to have a picture of customers' views of their products and for marketing their products. Social media skills can in the near future become an additional literacy required of employees. Lack of access or restricted access to the internet might be a limitation in an applicant's skills and reduce the chances of being offered a job.

Cyberspace is a distinct focus of activity, where specific rules and norms of behaviour are applied and where different kinds of communication occur. Although ICT is a distinct sphere of action, it cannot be wholly reduced to communication. And although ICT is socially embedded, it cannot be wholly reduced to components of social structure. At the same time, we have specified the transformative role that the ICT plays in social interaction. The supporters of the 'no change' perspective have attempted to evaluate how online and offline relationships affect one another. Informed by earlier research on media effects such as television, their studies focused on how the ICT affected the size of social circles, the extent of involvement in social, family and community activities, and the use of other communication devices. That research was guided by the assumption of displacement, meaning that time invested in media was at the expense of time devoted to social activities such as school learning, extracurricular activities and family time (Nie *et al.*, 2002). But that approach fails when one considers that the central use of ICT is interpersonal communication, linking individuals who are already in the same social circle, supporting previous friendships, creating new acquaintances and moving from online to multi-channel communication. Accordingly, we searched for transformative effects, namely how ICT use and online friendship formation affect the social composition and structure of adolescent friendships, finding evidence for diversification in the network structure of adolescent social ties. Furthermore, scholars have assumed – without empirical evidence – that online ties are inevitably weak. But we reviewed studies showing that online ties over time often become face-to-face ties, and therefore bear a remarkable resemblance in terms of the trust and social support they proffer.

At the current stage of ICT diffusion, online relationships are weaker because they lack certain characteristics. First, they are recently created social ties and they need time to build up a joint history, common identity and collective memory; previous studies have found these to be associated with the strength of ties. Second, they are created around specific and shared interests, and in some cases start slowly, moving to more generalized topics of discussion and joint activities. Thus, online ties are temporarily weaker, representing an early historical period of development; but as time goes by they provide more generalized activities and topics of interest (Mesch and Talmud, 2006a). Our argument and findings imply that online social ties are incorporated into an individual's life, but not at the expense of close and intimate relationships. Thus, online relationships expand the size of the social networks, supporting the diversification approach.

Early approaches to computer-mediated communication (CMC) were technological determinism and social constructivism. The former assumes that CMC has an intrinsic effect of its own, reshaping social relations inside and outside cyberspace; the latter ignores the unique nature of media, depicting offline relations as primarily more relevant.

Similarly, technological determinism attributes either dystopian or utopian content, either liberating or alienating characteristics, to ICT, while social constructivism overlooks ICT's technological ingredient entirely, assigning it unlimited interpretative flexibility, which can be infinitely moulded by social forces (Katz and Rice, 2002a).

In contrast to these two perspectives, we have presented a socio-logical approach to digital social ties, asserting that online social interaction is embedded in the larger social structure, and that indi-vidual social resources are associated with offline and online relations. More specifically, we cited some research inquiring into the social aetiology of ICT activity and virtual relations, as well as the impli-cations of virtual social capital for individual social resources and for relational quality.

As 'new adopters', adolescents have dramatically increased their ICT use. Furthermore, adolescents have a fresh outlook or novel 'cohort effect' in that their digital skills and cultural surroundings take for granted the very existence of digital means and a multimedia environment, and they use these media mainly for social purposes (Lenhart *et al.*, 2001; Gross *et al.*, 2002). ICT is highly important also for accessing and transferring information and knowledge. Theories of the digital divide distinguish inequality in access, mainly attributed to inequality in material and physical well-being, from inequality in use, mainly ascribed to the cultural, motivational and skill gaps in the ability to appropriate ICTs. Over time, the existence of the digital divide has become associated not only with differential access by social groups to technology but also with greater general social inequality. ICT use is regarded as connected to the accumulation of cultural capital, knowledge resources and social capital (Van Dijk, 2005). The social stratification or amplification perspective argues that unequal distribution of social and economic resources is associated with uneven access to ICT, and in turn may in the future amplify disparity in skills, education, social literacy and civic participation between those who have and who do not have access (Van Dijk, 2005). By contrast, the normalization hypothesis argues that the rapid diffusion of ICT may in time narrow the digital divide as more and more population segments and social categories possess and have access to it, as has been observed in other media such as television and phone, including mobile phone (Katz and Rice, 2002a). Yet ICT use is also socially embedded: the intrinsic technological and dynamic characteristics of ICT may be used differently by various social categories. The erosion of the digital divide among youth is good news, as it may minimize prospective gaps in important processes such as status attainment and civic participation in the future mature population. But the unrelenting diversification in ICT use also raises questions regarding prospective significant personal differences in social capital and social standing of the current adolescent generation. A literature review suggests the conversion of the traditional digital divide into a more subtle diversification of ICT use and online sociability according to kind of interest and friendship similarity of adolescent users. In other words, users are adopting ICT in different spheres and ways according to their cultural predispositions. Future research should focus on the extent to which diversification in ICT adoption and use will affect life chances.

Adolescents use ICT mainly for social purposes. Undergoing a critical and troublesome developmental stage, adolescents need support outside of their family households. As their relations with other family members change, as they seek separation and indivi-duation, family authority and rules are repeatedly challenged and reconfigured, and social support and social interaction with peers are vital for the adolescent's adjustment and well-being. Significant num-bers of parents regard ICT as a potential risk, exposing their children to hazards involved in contact with unknown individuals (Cohen *et al.*, 2008). Beyond these legitimate concerns, ICT is not just another arena of family conflict over entertainment resources, time allocation and wherewithal, but also a space of social interaction where ado-lescents can increase their social capital through access to knowledge and the construction of new social ties. Ongoing negotiation within families over ICT use is closely linked to existing family boundaries and family conflicts in other spheres of life, affecting, in turn, ado-lescents' online network conduct and structure. In other words, family mediation of ICT use is relevant to the differences in the extent that ICT supports adolescents' diversification of social networks.

Young people nowadays utilize multiple channels of communica-tion for social relations, from face-to-face meetings, SMS and instant messaging to social networking sites, to maintain and create new social ties. Adolescents' trust in online friends is still less than in face-to-face relations, but it seems to be increasing. Adolescent internet users' ability to reconfigure the personal network is less costly, more flexible and much more feasible than is that of non-internet users. This novel capacity has mostly positive outcomes. Some adolescents amplify their spread of contacts, expanding their bridging social capital by forming new ties in ICT platforms, while others use ICT to compensate for a fragile social position. Additionally, ICT is pri-marily used to solidify close friends' ties by multiplex communication, and to extend binding social capital among adolescents. Especially during adolescence, network closure and cohesive social ties are necessary 'building blocks' for the construction of 'binding social capital', enjoying the benefits of trust, social support, mutual commitment, identity maintenance and fortification, and reciprocal resource exchange.

ICT is a sphere of social activity but with specific autonomous technological features. ICT ties tend to be age-homogeneous, but a significant portion of them are quite heterogeneous in terms of residence location and gender. Adolescents' social networks can be predictive of deviant behaviour and school dropping out (Cairns *et al.*, 1989). The relatively influential contagion effect and imitation conduct by an ego's alters could be constitutive. During adolescence a stable network of social support and peer influence is functionally necessary.

Still, the ICT may add new acquaintances to an ego's network, but this is correlated with lower network density. More importantly, ICT use reduces relational quality, but it gains in expanding social ties. Social resources are positively associated with adolescents' network heterogeneity (see Lin, 2001: 207). The steady application of the principle of social similarity shows that network expansion does not occur at random: adolescents are more likely to form social ties with others who share their interests, but at the same time are exposed to strangers who may belong to a socially different group. Thus they would be exposed to some risk of bullying (even from schoolmates), stranger harassment and verbal violence. As ICT's technological features lower costs, some adolescents become exposed to recurrent aggression and harassment. The likelihood of being exposed to negative online conduct depends on the kinds of online activities pursued and the ICT channel chosen. The risk of a negative tie depends on motivation, personality and kind of use. Isolated and timid individuals who mainly aim at compensating their lower stock of offline social capital by expanding their networks are more likely to be exposed to negative ties.

Katz and Rice (2002a) claim that ICT use in itself is an indication of social capital, as it enables networked individuals (Wellman *et al.*, 2003) to activate social relations by utilizing digital technology and linking various spheres of life (Katz and Rice, 2002a: 337–339). ICT compensates for sparse social capital, and increases sociability, because its network is less costly, more elastic and fluid, and can be a kind of peer-to-peer or group-based formation (Monge and Contractor, 2003: 318–321).

ICT ties and telephone ties may be conceived as similar, but they are quite different in some important respects (Cohen *et al.*, 2008). ICT operation is affected by social categories, the unique nature of information technology, and the individual's social networks (Katz and Rice, 2002a: 345–346). People make different use of it according to their various social locations and according to nationality, gender and religion. Moreover, though virtual relations are cost free and can be formed in principle almost at random, like offline social ties they are not. In both media – internet and telephone – social structure governs the formation and reconfiguration of relational patterns. Moreover, technology adoption itself is socially embedded. Over and above cost and barriers to physical access, digital complexity is a continuing source of digital divide and network diversification (Katz and Rice, 2002a). The blending of technological complexity and network diversification intensifies the variety and richness of adolescents' online social networks. The integration of information technology with everyday social life has created a complex phenomenon, where social contexts, information channels and network properties interact (Katz and Rice, 2002a). The virtual arena is at the same time socially embedded, but operates under autonomous technical rules. The hypertextual nature of this medium, the modularity of its components, its tendency to reduce hidden social cues and the unique literacy of its users are bound to raise important questions about the scope of ICT use in future generations. It cannot therefore be understood without close attention to processes of social affordance.

Concluding remarks

Emergence of a new kind of literacy

The spread of ICT in the household, school and interpersonal relations, as well as the partial integration of the internet with mobile phones, have led to a dramatic rise in adolescents' computer literacy. The integration of internet and mobile phone has yielded an extraordinary increase in adolescents' personal autonomy in choice of media channel as well as choice of online friends.

As the net-generation, adolescents' digital and mobile orientation is more 'embodied' in their taken-for-granted reality. ICT technological features per se cannot affect communication patterns; instead, people's perception of the technology creates their tendency to activate these technical characteristics (Valkenburg and Peter, 2009). For contemporary adolescents of the 'information age', their positive ICT orientation enables them to manoeuvre their relational management in 'real' and virtual space, and to develop their social skills online and offline. In fact, the net-generation's conduct seems to epitomize the modal 'networked individual' (Wellman *et al.*, 2003).

Network size and relational depth

Adolescents' who participate in online networks increase their overall network size. Though the ability to reach a physically remote person online is virtually boundless technologically, the ability to make new online acquaintances is hampered by social constraints: physical proximity, social similarity and transitivity are still the overarching principles of adolescents' online social networks. Consequently, most adolescents' frequent communication links are with their peers, close friends, of the same age, same gender and same residential area.

Although most online ties are shallower than close and meaningful offline relationships, ICT amplifies relational quality with close friends, and to a lesser extent with remote ties with shared interests. For some adolescents, online relations serve as a compensatory outlet for their relative lack of face-to-face emotional support from their peer group – support deemed essential for their vulnerable and confusing developmental stage.

Diversification versus closure

The combination of social and technological attributes of ICT – highlighted by the theory of social affordance – enables similar friends (demographically or sharing similar interest) to be connected in homogeneous networks. The facilitation of expanding ties to similar others is augmented by the social networking sites, where a friend of one's friend tends to become one's friend as well. The combination of homophily and transitivity dramatically diversifies ICT networks into homogeneous clusters. In fact, face-to-face networks tend to be less homogeneous than social networking sites.

Digital divide

We denoted two possible outlooks on the digital divide. The first states that the diffusion of the ICT is far from evenly distributed or uniform. Moreover, gaps in ICT access, use and literacy are parallel to many other sources of social and economic inequalities. As a result, digital divides lead to the amplification of other inequalities, as social and academic skills will depend closely on digital access, use and literacy (Van Dijk, 2005). By contrast, the normalization scenario puts forward the view that in the foreseeable future inexpensive diffusion of the ICT will make it available for all social strata and places, albeit not in the same proportion. As a result, many digital divides will decrease in scope, intensity and quality (Katz and Rice, 2002a).

Negative and positive effects over time

Like dark streets at night, virtual dark alleys can be full of detrimental effects and potential hazards for the adolescent users. Still, over time ICT users learn to develop precautionary devices, especially regarding disclosure of intimate and personal information and conduct with strangers. As most new contacts are made according to principles of transitivity, mutual friends can vouch for a contact's trustworthiness or attest to her or his abusive behaviour. Additionally, many websites develop the institution of new users' social norms and technological devices for misconduct (reporting abuse, users' blocking, etc.), which minimize the detrimental effects of online networks. It seems to us that future generations will learn safe surfing, as in their other walks of life. Prospective digital literacy and higher awareness of ICT uses and misuses will go hand in hand in the future.

Social integration of ICT in everyday life

Though ICT has unique communicative characteristics, many of its key features cannot totally abolish the effect of social structure on adolescents' relational capacity. Though ICT ties are generally weaker, sparse and shallower, to the extent that a medium is richer, relational quality is more similar to face-to-face interaction. Additionally, to the extent that an online relation is frequent and durable, its pattern is more akin to a face-to-face relationship.

ICT is mostly positive for sociability, for resources exchange, for acquiring heterogeneous contacts and for social support. ICT use is both social and technological. It contains both a positive potential and a negative threat to the quality of adolescents' social lives. Online spaces are used as a continuation of everyday communication, to reflect on events at school and to plan joint activities. At the same time, online experience of conducting multiple activities and conversations with others is incorporated into youngsters' approach to daily life. As a result, the binary depiction of the boundaries between offline and online are deemed less relevant and meaningful. Demarcating the boundaries of virtuality and reality has become ever more difficult and vague, as ICT and social structure mutually affect each other in various ways. These reciprocal effects will continue to be at the centre of social and technological policies, public discourse and scientific investigation.

References

Aboud, F.E. and Mendelson, M.J. (1996) Determinants of friendship selection and quality: developmental perspectives. In W.M. Bukowski, A. Newcomb and W.W. Hartup *The Company They Keep: Friendship in Childhood and Adolescence*. New York: Cambridge University Press.

Amato, P.R. and Rivera, F. (1999) Paternal involvement and children's behavior. *Journal of Marriage and Family*, 61(2), 375–384.

Anderson, R., Bikxon, T., Law, S.A. and Mitchell, B. (1995) *Universal Access to E-mail: Feasibility and Social Implications*. Santa Monica, CA: Rand Foundation.

Attewell, P. and Battle, J. (1999) Home computers and school performance. *The Information Society*, 15, 1–10.

Attewell, P., Suazo-Garcia, B. and Battle, J. (2003) Computers and young children: social benefit or social problem? *Social Forces*, 82, 277–296.

Bargh, J.A. and McKenna, K.Y.A. (2004) The internet and social life. *Annual Review of Psychology*, 55, 573–590.

Bargh, J.A., McKenna, K.Y.A. and Fitzsimons, G.M. (2002) Can you see the real me? Activation and expression of the 'true self' on the internet. *Journal of Social Issues*, 58, 33–48.

Barzilai-Nahon, K. (2006) Gaps and bits: conceptualizing measurements for digital divide/s. *The Information Society*, 22, 269–278.

Baumeister, R. and Leary, M.R. (1995) The need to belong: desire for interpersonal attachments as a fundamental human motivation. *Psychological Bulletin*, 117, 497–529.

Baym, N.K., Zhang, Y.B. and Lin, M.C. (2004) Social interactions across media: interpersonal communication on the internet, telephone and face-to-face. *New Media and Society*, 6, 299–318.

Beebe, T.J., Asche, S.E., Harrison, P.A. and Quinlan, K.B. (2004) Heightened vulnerability and increased risk taking among adolescent chat rooms users: results from a statewide school survey. *Journal of Adolescent Health*, 35, 116–123.

Beraman, P.S. and Moody, J. (2004) Adolescents' suicidability. *American Journal of Public Health*, 94, 89–95.

Beran, K.M. and Li, A. (1995) Bully and victim problems in elementary schools and students beliefs about aggression. *Canadian Journal of School Psychology*, 11, 153–165.

Berardo, F. (1998) Family privacy: issues and concepts. *Journal of Family Issues*, 118(19), 4–10.

Berndt, T.J., Miller, K. and Park, K. (1989) Adolescents' perceptions of friends' and parents' influence in other aspects of their school adjustment. *Journal of Early Adolescence*, 9, 419–435.

Berson, I.R., Berson, M.J. and Ferron, J.M. (2002) Emerging risks of violence in the digital age. *Journal of School Violence*, 2, 51–71.

Bimber, B. (1994) Three faces of technological determinism. In M.R. Smith and L. Marx (eds) *Does Technology Drive History*. Cambridge, MA: MIT Press.

Bimber, B. (2000) Measuring the gender gap in the internet. *Social Science Quarterly*, 81, 868–876.

Blais, J.J., Craig, W.M., Pepler, D. and Connolly, J. (2008) Adolescents online: the importance of internet activity choices to salient relationships. *Journal of Youth Adolescence*, 37, 522–536.

Boase, J. and Wellman, B. (2006) Personal relationships: on and off the internet. In D. Perlman and A.L. Vangelisti (eds) *Handbook of Personal Relations*. Cambridge: Cambridge University Press.

Boissevain, J. (1974) *Friends of Friends: Networks, Manipulators and Coalitions*. Oxford: Blackwell.

Boneva, B., Kraut, R. and Frohlich, D. (2001) Using e-mail for personal relationships: the difference gender makes. *American Behavioral Scientist*, 45(3), 530–549.

Borg, M.G. (1998) The emotional reaction of school bullies and their victims. *Educational Psychology*, 18, 433–444.

Boulton, M.J., Trueman, M., Chau, C., Whitehand, C. and Amatya, K. (1999) Concurrent and longitudinal links between friendship and peer victimisation: implications for befriending interventions. *Journal of Adolescence*, 22, 461–466.

Boyd, D. (2008) Friends. In I. Mizuko, H. Horst, M. Bitanti, D. Boyd, S. Herr, P.G. Lange *et al. Hanging Out, Messing Around, Geeking Out: Living and Learning with New Media*. Boston: MIT Press.

Bradley, K. (2005) Internet lives: social context and moral domain in adolescent development. *New Directions for Youth Development*, 108, 57–76.

Buote, V.M., Wood, E. and Pratt, M. (2009) Exploring similarities and differences between online and offline friendships: the role of attachment style. *Computers in Human Behavior*, 25, 560–567.

Burt, R.S. (1988) A note on strangers, friends and happiness. *Social Networks*, 9(4), 311–332.

Burt, R.S. (1990) Kinds of relations in American discussion networks. In C. Calhoun, M.W. Meyer and W.R. Scott (eds) *Structures of Power and*

Constraint: Papers in Honor of Peter M. Blau. New York: Cambridge University Press.

Burt, R.S. (1992) *Structural Holes: The Social Structure of Competition.* Cambridge, MA: Harvard University Press.

Burt, R.S. (2005) *Brookerage and Closure: An Introduction to Social Capital.* New York: Oxford University Press.

Burt, S.R., Jannotta, E.J. and Mahoney, T.J. (1998) Personality correlates of structural holes. *Social Networks*, 20(1), 63–87.

Bybee, C., Robinson, D. and Turow, J. (1982) Determinants of parental guidance of children's TV viewing for a special subgroup: mass media scholars. *Journal of Broadcasting*, 26(3), 697–711.

Byrne, D. and Osland, J.A. (2000) Sexual fantasy and erotica/pornography: internal and external imagery. In L.T. Szuchman and F. Muscarela (eds) *Psychological Perspectives on Human Sexuality.* New York: Wiley.

Cairns, R.B., Neckerman, H.J. and Cairns, R.B. (1989) Social networks and the shadows of synchrony. In G.R. Adams, T.P. Gullota and R. Montemayor (eds) *Biology of Adolescent Behavior and Development.* Newbury Park, CA: Sage.

Castells, M. (1996) *The Rise of the Network Society.* Oxford: Blackwell.

Castells, M. (2000) Materials for an exploratory theory of network society. *British Journal of Sociology*, 51, 5–24.

Chan, D. and Cheng, L. (2004) Stages of relationship development: a comparison of offline and online friendship qualities. *Journal of Social and Personal Relationships*, 21, 305–320.

Chen, W. and Wellman, B. (2003) *Charting and Bridging Digital Divides: Comparing Socio-economic, Gender, Life Stage and Rural–Urban Internet Access and Use in Eight Countries.* http://www.amd.com/usen/Assets/content_type/ DownloadableAssets/FINAL_REPORT_CHARTING_DIGI_DIVIDES. pdf (accessed 26 June 2009).

Chen, W. and Wellman, B. (2004) The global digital divide within and between countries. *IT and Society*, 1(7), 39–45.

Chesley, N. (2005) Blurring boundaries? Linking technology use, spillover, individual distress, and family satisfaction. *Journal of Marriage and Family*, 67(5), 1237–1248.

Ching, C.C., Basham, J.D. and Jang, E. (2005) The legacy of the digital divide. *Urban Education*, 40(4), 394–411.

Cho, J., De Zuniga, H.G., Rojas, H. and Shah, D. (2003) Beyond access: the digital divide and internet uses and gratifications. *IT and Society*, 1(4), 46–72.

Cohen, A.A., Lamish, D. and Schejter, A.M. (2008) The wonder phone in the land of miracles: mobile telephony in Israel. In R.E. Rice (ed.) *New Media: Policy and Social Research Issues.* Cresskill, NJ: Hampton Press.

Coleman, J. (1988) Social capital and the creation of human capital. *American Journal of Sociology*, 94, 95–120.

Collins, W.A. and Russel, G.J. (1991) Mother–child and father–child relationships in middle childhood and adolescence: a developmental analysis. *Developmental Review*, 11, 99–136.

Collins, W.A., Maccoby, E.E., Steinberg, L., Hetherington E.M. and Bornstein, M.H. (2000) Contemporary research on parenting: the case for nature and nurture. Annual progress in child psychiatry and child development. *American Psychologist*, 55, 125–154.

Cotterell, J. (1996) *Social Networks and Social Influences in Adolescence.* London: Routledge.

Cotton, S.R. and Jelenewicz, J.M. (2006) A disappearing digital divide among college students? Peeling away the layers of the digital divide. *Social Science Computer Review*, 24, 497.

Cottrell, L., Branstetter, S., Cottrell, S., Rishel, C. and Stanton, B.F. (2007) Comparing adolescent and parent perceptions of current and future disapproved internet use. *Journal of Children and New Media*, 1, 210–226.

Crosnoe, R. (2000) Friendships in childhood and adolescence: the life course and new directions. *Social Psychology Quarterly*, 63(4), 377–391.

Crosnoe, R., Cavanagh, S. and Elder, G.H. (2003) Adolescent friendships as academic resources: the intersection of friendship, race, and school disadvantage. *Sociological Perspectives*, 46(3), 331–352.

Cummings, J.N., Butler, B. and Kraut, R. (2002) The quality of online social relationships. *Communications of the ACM*, 45(7), 103–108.

Daft, R.L. and Lengel, R.H. (1984) Information richness: a new approach to managerial behaviour and organizational design. In L.L. Cummings and B.M. Staw (eds) *Research in Organizational Behavior*. Greenwich, CT: JAI.

Daly, K.J. (1996) *Families and Time: Keeping Pace in a Hurried Culture.* Thousand Oaks, CA: Sage.

Devoe, J.F., Rudy, S.A., Miller, A.K., Planty, M., Peter, K., Kaufman, P. *et al.* (2002) *Indicators of Schooled Crime and Safety*. Washington, DC: US Department of Education.

Di Gennaro, C. and Dutton, W.H. (2006) The internet and the public: online and offline political participation in the United Kingdom. *Parliamentary Affairs*, 59, 299–313.

DiMaggio, P., Hargitai, H., Neuman, W.R. and Robinson, J.P. (2001) Social implications of the internet. *Annual Review of Sociology*, 27, 307–336.

Dooris, J., Sotireli, T. and Van Hoof, S. (2008) Distant friends online? Rural and urban adolescents' communication on the internet. *Tijdschrift Voor Economische En Sociale Geografie*, 99(3), 293–302.

Drori, G. (2006) *Global E-Litism: Digital Technology, Social Inequality, and Transnationality*. New York: Worth Publishers.

Dubas, J.S. and Gerris, J.R.M. (2002) Longitudinal changes in the time parents spend in activities with their adolescent children as a function of child age, pubertal status, and gender. *Journal of Family Psychology*, 16(4), 415–427.

Dunbar, R.I.M. (1993) Co-evolution of neocortical size, group size and language in humans. *Behavioral and Brain Sciences*, 16, 681–735.

Durkheim, E. (1952) *Suicide: A Study in Sociology*, trans. J.A. Spaulding, ed. G. Simpson. London: Routledge and Kegan Paul.

Dutton, W.H. and Shepherd, A. (2003) *Trust in the Internet: The Social Dynamics of an Experience Technology*. Research Report no. 3. Oxford Internet Institute. http://www.oii.ox.ac.uk/resources/publications/RR3.pdf (accessed 26 June 2009).

Dutton, W.H., Blumler, J.G. and Kraemer, K.L. (1987) *Wired Cities: Shaping the Future of Communications*. Boston, MA: GK Hall.

Eastin, M., Greenbers B.S. and Hofschire, L. (2006) Parenting the internet. *Journal of Communication*, 56, 486–504.

Economist (2009) Primates on Facebook: even online, the neo cortex is the limit. http://www.economist.com/sciencetechnology/displaystory.cfm?story_id=13176775 (accessed 26 June 2009).

Elkind, D. (1994) *Ties that Stress: The New Family Imbalance*. Cambridge, MA: Harvard University Press.

Ellison, N.B., Steinfeld, C. and Lampe, C. (2007) The benefits of Facebook 'friends:' social capital and college students' use of online social network sites. *Journal of Computer Mediated Communication*, 12, 1143–1168.

Fallon, B.J. and Bowles, T.V. (1997) The effect of family structure and family functioning on adolescents' perceptions of intimate time spent with parents, siblings and peers. *Journal of Youth and Adolescence*, 26, 25–43.

Farrington, D. (1993) Understanding and preventing bullying. In M. Tony *Crime and Justice: A Review of Research*. Chicago: University of Chicago Press.

Feld, S.L. (1981) The focused organization of social ties. *American Journal of Sociology*, 86(5), 1015–1035.

Finkelhor, D., Mitchell, K. and Wollak, J. (2000) *Online Victimization: A Report on the Nation's Youth*. Alexandria, VA: National Center for Missing and Exploited Children.

Flanagin, A.J. (2005) IM online: instant messaging use among college students. *Communication Research Reports*, 22(3), 175–187.

Fleming, M.J., Greentree, S., Cocotti-Muller, S., Elias, K.A. and Morrison, S. (2006) Safety in cyberspace: adolescent safety and exposure online. *Youth and Society*, 38, 135–154.

Flood, M. (2007) Exposure to pornography among youth in Australia. *Journal of Sociology*, 43, 45–60.

Foehr, U. (2006) *Media Multitasking among American Youth: Prevalence, Predictors and Pairings*. Washington, DC: Henry J. Kaiser Family Foundation.

Fong, E., Wellman, B., Kew, M. and Wilkes, R. (2001) *Correlates of the Digital Divide: Individual, Household and Spatial Variation*. Toronto: Office of Learning Technologies, Human Resources Development Canada.

Fuligni, A.J. (1998) Authority, autonomy, parent–adolescent conflict and cohesion. *Developmental Psychology*, 4, 782–792.

Galinsky, E. and Salmond, K. (2002) *Youth and Violence: Students Speak Out for a More Civil Society*. New York: Families and Work Institute.

Garton, L., Haythornwaite, C. and Wellman, B. (1999) Studying online social networks. In S. Jones *Doing Internet Research*. Thousand Oaks, CA: Sage.

Gershuny, J. (2003) Web use and net nerds: a neo-functionalist analysis of the impact of information technology in the home. *Social Forces*, 82, 141–168.

Giordano, P.C. (2003) Relationships in adolescence. *Annual Review of Sociology*, 29, 257–281.

Giuseppe, R. and Galimberti, C. (2001) *Towards Cyber-Psychology: Mind, Cognitions and Society in the Internet Age*. Amsterdam: IOS Press.

Graham, S. and Juvonen, J. (1998) Social-cognitive perspective on peer aggression and victimization. *Annals of Child Development*, 13, 23–70.

Granovetter M. (1973) The strength of weak ties. *American Journal of Sociology*, 78, 1360–1380.

Greenfield, P.M. (2004) Inadvertent exposure to pornography on the internet: implications for peer-to-peer file sharing networks for child development and families. *Applied Developmental Psychology*, 25, 741–750.

Greenspan, R. (2002) American surfers keep it simple. http://www.internet news.com/stats/article.php/1466661 (accessed 4 October 2009).

Grinter, R., Palen, L. and Eldridge, M. (2002) Instant messaging in teen life. Paper presented at CSCWO2 New Orleans, 16–20 November.

Gross, E.F. (2004) Adolescent internet use: what we expect, what teens report. *Applied Developmental Psychology*, 25, 633–649.

Gross, E.F., Juvonen, J. and Gable, S.L. (2002) Internet use and well-being in adolescence. *Journal of Social Issues*, 58(1), 75–90.

Guo, B., Bricout, J.C. and Huang, J. (2005) A common open space or a digital divide? A social model perspective on the online disability community in China. *Disability and Society*, 20(1), 49–66.

Hallinan, M. and Kubitschek, W.K. (1988) The effects of individual and structural characteristics on intransitivity in social networks. *Social Psychology Quarterly*, 51, 81–92.

Hamburger, Y.A. and Ben-Artzi, E. (2000) The relationship between extraversion and neuroticism and the different uses of the internet. *Computers in Human Behavior*, 16, 441–449.

Hammond, E. (2007) No place to hide. *Financial Times*, 5 November. http://www.davidbyrne.com/journal/misc/11_03_07_FinancialTimes.php (accessed 2 February 2009).

Hampton, K. and Wellman, B. (2001) Long distance community in the network society: contact and support beyond Netville. *American Behavioral Scientist*, 3, 476–495.

Hampton, K. and Wellman, B. (2002) The not so global village of Netville. In B. Wellman and C. Haythornthwaite *The Internet in Everyday Life*. Oxford: Blackwell.

Hansen, D.M., Larson, R.W. and Dworkin, J.B. (2003) What adolescents learn in organized youth activities: a survey of self-reported developmental experiences. *Journal of Research on Adolescence*, 13(1), 25–55.

Hardey, M. (2004) Mediated relationships: authenticity and the possibility of romance information. *Communication and Society*, 7(2), 207–222.

Hargittai, E. (2002) Second-level digital divide: differences in people's online skills. *First Monday*, 7(4). http://firstmonday.org/issues/issue7_4/hargittai.

Hartup, W.W. (1997) The company they keep: friendships and their developmental significance. In A. Slater and D. Muir (eds) *Blackwell Reader in Developmental Psychology*. Oxford: Blackwell.

Hawker, D.S.J. and Boulton, M.J. (2000) Twenty years of research on peer victimization and psychological maladjustment: a meta analysis. *Journal of Child Psychology and Psychiatry*, 41, 441–445.

Hawley, P.H. (1999) The ontogenesis of social dominance: a strategy-based evolutionary perspective. *Developmental Review*, 19, 97–132.

Haythornthwaite, C. (2002) Strong, weak, and latent ties and the impact of new media. *Information Society*, 18, 385–402.

Haythornthwaite, C. (2005) Social networks and internet connectivity effects. *Information, Communication and Society*, 8, 125–147.

Haythornthwaite, C. and Kazmer, M. (2002) Bringing the internet home: adult distance learners and their internet, home and work worlds. In B. Wellman and C. Haythornthwaite *The Internet in Everyday Life*. Oxford: Blackwell.

Heirman, W. and Walrave, M. (2008) Assessing concerns and issues about the mediation of technology in cyberbullying. *Cyberpsychology: Journal of Psychosocial Research on Cyberspace*, 2(2), 1–12.

Helsper, E.J. (2008a) Gendered internet use across generations and life stages in the UK. Paper presented at the AOIR Conference, Copenhagen, October. http://www.oii.ox.ac.uk/microsites/oxis/presentations/Gender_and _Lifestage_EH_AOIR_2008.pdf (accessed 26 June 2009).

Helsper, E.J. (2008b) Perceptions of security and risks on the internet: experience and learned levels of trust. Presentation slides from IT Security in Practice Conference, Aarhus University, 24 January. http://www. oii.ox.ac.uk/microsites/oxis/events/20080124_EH_Aarhus_Conference.pdf (accessed 26 June 2009).

Herring, S.C. (2007) Questioning the generational divide: technological exoticism and adult constructions of online youth identity. In D. Buckingham *Youth, Identity and Digital Media*. Cambridge, MA: MIT Press.

Hill, R.A. and Dunbar, R.I.M. (2003) Social network size in humans. *Human Nature*, 14(1), 53–72.

Hinduja, S. and Patchin, J.W. (2008) Personal information of adolescents on the internet: a quantitative content analysis of MySpace. *Journal of Adolescence*, 31, 125–146.

Hine, C. (2005) Internet research and the sociology of cyber social scientific knowledge. *The Information Society*, 21, 239–248.

Hofferth, S.L. and Sandberg, J.F. (2001) How American children spend their time. *Journal of Marriage and Family*, 63, 295–308.

Hoffman, D. and Novak, T.P. (1998) Bridging the racial divide on the internet. *Science*, 280, 390–391.

Holloway, S. and Valentine, G. (2003) *Cyber-Kids: Youth Identities and Communities in an On-Line World*. London: Routledge.

Horrigan, J.B. and Rainie, L. (2002) Emails that matter: changing patterns of internet use over a year's time. *IT and Society*, 1, 135–150.

Horst, H. (2008) Families. In I. Mizuko, H. Horst, M. Bitanti, D. Boyd, S. Herr, P.G. Lange *et al. Hanging Out, Messing Around, Geeking Out: Living and Learning with New Media*. Boston: MIT Press.

Howard, P.E.N., Rainie, L. and Jones, S. (2002) Days and nights on the internet. In B. Wellman and C. Haythornwaite *The Internet in Everyday Life*. Oxford: Blackwell.

Hu, Y., Fowler-Wood, J., Smith, V. and Westbrook, N. (2004) Friendship through IM: examining the relationship between instant messaging and intimacy. *Journal of Computer Mediated Communication*, 10(1). http://Jcmc.indiana.edu/vol10/issue1/hu.html (accessed 26 June 2009).

Huffaker, D. (2004) Spinning yarns around the digital fire: storytelling and dialogue among youth on the internet information technology. *First Monday*, 9(1). http://firstmonday.org/issue9_1/huffaker/index.html.

Hughes, T.R. and Hans, J.G. (2001) Computers, the internet and families. *Journal of Family Issues*, 22, 776–790.

Huysman, M. and Wulf, W. (2004) *Social Capital and Information Technology*. Cambridge, MA: MIT Press.

Igarashi, T., Takai, J. and Yoshida, T. (2005) Gender differences in social network development via mobile phone text messages: a longitudinal study. *Journal of Social and Personal Relationships*, 22(5), 691–713.

Ito, M. (2005) Mobile phones, Japanese youth and re-placement of social context. In R. Ling and P. Pederson (eds) *Mobile Communications: Re-Negotiation of the Social Sphere*. London: Springer-Verlag.

Jackson, L.A., Von Eye, A., Barbatsis, G., Biocca, F., Zhao, Y. and Fitzgerald, H.E. (2003) Internet attitudes and internet use: some surprising findings from the HomeNetTOO project. *International Journal of Human Computer Studies*, 59, 355–382.

Joinson, A.N. (2008) 'Looking at', 'looking up' or 'keeping up with' people? Motives and uses of Facebook. Proceedings of CHI Conference, Online Social Networks, Florence, Italy, 5–10 April.

Jung, J.Y., Kim, Y.C., Lin, W.Y. and Cheong, P.H. (2005) The influence of social environment on internet connectedness of adolescents in Seoul, Singapore and Taipei. *New Media and Society*, 7(1), 64–88.

Jung, J.Y., Qiu, J.L. and Kim Y.C. (2001) Internet connectedness and inequality: beyond the divide. *Communication Research*, 28(4), 507–535.

Kadushin, C. (2002) The motivational foundation of social networks. *Social Networks*, 24(1), 77–91.

Kadushin, C. (2004) Introduction to social network theory. Some basic network concepts and propositions. Chapter 2: Unpublished manuscript. http://stat.gamma.rug.nl/snijders/Kadushin_Concepts.pdf (accessed 26 June 2009).

Kahai, S.S. and Cooper, R.B. (2003) Exploring the core concepts of media richness theory: the impact of cue multiplicity and feedback immediacy on decision quality. *Journal of Management Information Systems*, 20, 263–299.

Kaiser Family Foundation (2003) *Growing Up Wired: Survey of Youth and the Internet in the Silicon Valley*. Washington, DC: Henry J. Kaiser Family Foundation.

Kalish, Y. and Robins, G. (2006) Psychological predispositions and network structure: the relationship between individual predispositions, structural holes and network closure. *Social Networks*, 28(1), 56–84.

Kaltiala-Heino, R., Rimpela, M., Martunen, M., Rimpela, A. and Rantanen, P. (1999) Bullying, depression, and suicidal ideation in Finnish adolescents. *British Medical Journal*, 319, 348–351.

Kandel, D.B. (1978) Homophile, selection, and socialization in adolescent friendships. *American Journal of Sociology*, 84, 427–436.

Katz, J.E. and Rice, R.E. (2002a) *Social Consequences of Internet Use, Access Involvement and Interaction*. Cambridge, MA: MIT Press.

Katz, J.E. and Rice, R.E. (2002b) Syntopia: access, civic involvement, and social interaction on the net. In B. Wellman and C. Haythornthwaite *The Internet in Everyday Life*. Oxford: Blackwell.

Katz, J.E., Rice, R.E. and Aspden, P. (2001) The internet 1995–2000: access, civic involvement and social interaction. *American Behavioral Scientist*, 45, 405–419.

Kautiainen, S., Koivusilta, L.K., Lintonen, T., Virtanen, S.M. and Rimpela, A.H. (2005) Use of information and communication technology and the prevalence of overweight and obesity among adolescents. *International Journal of Obesity*, 29, 925–933.

Kavanaugh, A. and Patterson, S.J. (2002) The impact of community computer networks on social capital and community involvement in Blacksburg. In B. Wellman and C. Haythornthwaite *The Internet in Everyday Life*. Oxford: Blackwell.

Kayany, J.M. and Yelsma, P. (2000) Displacement effects of online media in the socio-technical contexts of households. *Journal of Broadcasting and Electronic Media*, 44(2), 215–230.

Kennedy, T.L.M. and Wellman, B. (2007) The networked household. *Information, Communication and Society*, 10(5), 645–670.

Kennedy, T., Wellman, B. and Klement, K. (2003) Gendering the digital divide. *IT and Society*, 1, 72–96

Kennedy, T.L.M., Smith, A., Wells, A.T. and Wellman, B. (2008) *Networked Families*. Washington, DC: Pew Internet and American Life Project.

Kidsonline@home (2005) Internet use in Australian homes. Sydney: Australian Broadcasting Authority.

Kiesler, S., Zdaniuk, B., Lundmark, V. and Kraut, R. (2000) Troubles with the internet: the dynamics of help at home. *Human–Computer Interaction*, 15, 322–351.

Knoke, D. and Kuklinski, J. (1982) *Network Analysis*. Beverly Hills, CA: Sage.

Kraut, R., Patterson, M., Lundmark, V., Kiesler, S., Mukopadhyay, T. and Scherlis, W. (1998) Internet paradox: a social technology that reduces social involvement and psychological well-being? *American Psychologist*, 53, 1011–1031.

Kraut, R., Kiesler, S. Boneva, B., Cummings, J.N. Helgeson, V. and Crawford, A.M. (2002) Internet paradox revisited. *Journal of Social Issues*, 58(1), 49–74.

Lanning, K.V. (1998) Cyber 'pedophiles': a behavioral perspective. *The APSAC Advisor*, 11(4), 12–18.

Larson, R.W. and Verma, S. (1999) How children and adolescents spend time across the world: work, play, and developmental opportunities. *Psychological Bulletin*, 125, 701–736.

LaVoie, D. and O'Neill, H. (2003) Trends in the evolution of the public web: 1998–2002. *D-Lib Magazine*, 9(4).

Lawson, H.M. and Leck, K. (2006) Dynamics of internet dating. *Social Science Computer Review*, 24(2), 189–208.

Leander, K.M. and McKim, K.K. (2003) Tracing the everyday 'sitings' of adolescents on the internet: a strategic adaptation of ethnography across online and offline spaces. *Education, Communication and Information*, 3(2), 211–238.

Lee, P.S.N. and Leng, L. (2008) Assessing displacement effects of the internet. *Telemetric and Informatics*, 25, 145–155.

Lee, S.J. (2007) The internet and adolescent social capital: who benefits more from internet use. PhD dissertation, University of Texas at Austin.

Lee, S.J. and Chae, Y.G. (2007) Children's internet use in a family context: influence on family relationships and parental mediation. *Cyber Psychology and Behavior*, 10(2), 640–644.

Lee, W. and Kuo, E.C. (2002) Internet and displacement effect: children's media use and activities in Singapore. *Journal of Computer Mediated Communication*, 7(2).

Leigh, A. and Atkinson, R.D. (2001) Clear thinking on the digital divide. *Policy Report*, 1–20.

Lenhart, A. (2009) It's personal: similarities and differences in online social network use between teens and adults. Paper presented at International Communications Association Annual Meeting, Chichago, May. http://www.pewinternet.org/Presentations/2009/19-Similarities-and-Differences-in-Online-Social-Network-Use.aspx (accessed 30 September 2009).

Lenhart, A., Lewis, O. and Rainie, L. (2001) *Teenage Life Online: The Rise of the Instant-Message Generation and the Internet's Impact on Friendships and*

Family Relationships. Washington, DC: Pew Internet and American Life Project.

Lenhart, A., Horrigan, J., Rainie, L., Allen, K., Boyce, A. and Madden, M. (2003) *The Ever-Shifting Internet Population: A New Look at Internet Access and the Digital Divide*. Washington, DC: Pew Internet and American Life Project.

Lenhart, A., Madden, M. and Hitlin, P. (2005) *Teens and Technology: Youth are Leading the Transition to a Fully Wired and Mobile Nation*. Washington, DC: Pew Internet and American Life Project.

Lenhart, A., Madden, M., Rankin, A. and Smith, M.A. (2007) *Teens and Social Media*. Washington, DC: Pew Internet and American Life Project.

Leskovec, J. and Horvitz, V. (2008) Planetary-scale views on an instant-messaging network. *Physics and Society* [physics.soc-ph] [arXiv:0803.0939v1]

Li, Q. (2006) Cyber bullying in schools: a research of gender differences. *School Psychology International*, 27, 157–170.

Li, Q. (2007) Bullying in the new playground: research into cyber-bullying and cyber-victimization. *Australasian Journal of Educational Technology*, 23(3), 435–454.

Liau, A.K., Khoo, A. and Ang, P.H. (2008) Parental awareness and monitoring of adolescent internet use. *Current Psychology*, 27, 217–233.

Lin, N. (2001) *Social Capital: A Theory of Social Structure and Action*. Cambridge: Cambridge University Press.

Lin, N. (2005) Social capital. In J. Beckert and M. Zagiroski (eds) *Encyclopedia of Economic Sociology*. London: Routledge.

Lin, S.S.J and Tsai, C.C. (2002) Sensation seeking and internet dependence of Taiwanese high school adolescents. *Computers in Human Behavior*, 18(4), 411–426.

Livingstone, S. (2003) Children's use of the internet: reflections on the emerging research agenda. *New Media and Society*, 2, 147–166.

Livingstone, S. (2007) Strategies of parental regulation in the media-rich home. *Computers in Human Behavior*, 23, 920–941.

Livingstone, S. (2008) Taking risky opportunities in youthful content creation: teenagers' use of social networking sites for intimacy, privacy and self expression. *New Media and Society*, 10(3), 393–411.

Livingstone, S. and Bovill, M. (2001) *Children and their Changing Media Environment: A European Comparative Study*. Hove, UK: Lawrence Erlbaum Associates Ltd.

Livingstone, S. and Bober, M. (2004) *UK Children Go Online*. London: London School of Economics, Dept of Media and Communication.

Livingstone, S. and Helsper, E. (2007) Taking risks when communicating on the internet. *Information, Communication and Society*, 5, 619–644.

Livingstone, S., Bober, M. and Helsper, E. (2005) Active participation or just more information? Young people's take-up of opportunities to act and interact on the internet. *Information, Communication and Society*, 8(3), 287–314.

Loges, W.E. and Jung, J.Y. (2001) Exploring the digital divide: internet connectedness and age. *Communication Research*, 28, 536–562.

McCowan, J. Fisher, D., Page, R. and Homant, M. (2001) Internet relationships: people meet people. *Cyberpsychology and Behavior*, 4(5), 593–596.

McKenna, K.Y.A., Green, A. and Gleason, M. (2002) Relationship formation on the internet: what's the big attraction? *Journal of Social Issues*, 58, 9–31.

McLauglin, M., Osborne, K.K. and Smith, C.M. (1995) Standards of conduction usenet. In S.G. Jones *Cyber-society*. Thousand Oaks, CA: Sage.

McMillan, S.J. and Morrison, M. (2006) Coming of age with the internet: a qualitative exploration of how the internet has become an integral part of young people's lives. *New Media and Society*, 8(1), 73–95.

McPherson, M., Smith-Lovin, L. and Cook, J.M. (2002) Birds of a feather: homophile in social networks. *Annual Review of Sociology*, 27, 415–444.

Maczewski, M. (2002) Exploring identities through the internet: youth experiences online. *Child and Youth Care Forum*, 31(2), 111–120.

Maidden, M. (2009), Eating, thinking and staying active with new media. Paper presented at National Institute of Child Health and Human Development Conference, 2 June. http://www.pewinternet.org/Presentations/2009/15-Eating-Thinking-and-Staying-Active-with-New-Media.aspx (accessed 30 September 2009).

Malamuth, N.M. and Impett, E.A. (2001) Research on sex and media: what do we know of the effects on children and adolescents? In D.G. Singer and J.L. Singer (eds) *Handbook of Children and Media*. Thousand Oaks, CA: Sage.

Marsden, P.V. and Campbell, K.E. (1984) Measuring tie strength. *Social Forces*, 63, 482–501.

Martin, S.P. and Robinson, J.P. (2007) The income digital divide: trends and predictions for levels of internet use. *Social Problems*, 54(1), 1–22.

Media Awareness Networks (Mnet) (2005) *Young Canadians in a Wired World*. http://www.media-awareness.ca/english/research/YCWW/phaseII (accessed 26 June 2009).

Mesch, G.S. (2001) Social relationships and internet use among adolescents in Israel. *Social Science Quarterly*, 82(2), 329–340.

Mesch, G.S. (2003) The family and the internet: the Israeli case. *Social Science Quarterly*, 84, 1038–1050.

Mesch, G.S. (2006) The family and the internet: exploring a social boundaries approach. *Journal of Family Communication*, 6(2), 119–138.

Mesch, G.S. (2007) Internet use, family boundaries and the perception of parent adolescent conflicts. Unpublished manuscript. University of Haifa, Israel.

Mesch, G.S. (2009a) Social context and adolescents' choice of communication channels. *Computers in Human Behavior*, 25(1), 244–251.

Mesch, G.S. (2009b) Parental mediation, online activities and cyberbullying. *Cyberpsychology and Behavior*, 12(4), 387–393.

Mesch, G.S. and Levanon, Y. (2003) Community networking and locally based social ties in two suburban localities. *City and Community*, 2, 335–351.

Mesch, G.S. and Talmud, I. (2006a) Online friendship formation, communication channels, and social closeness. *International Journal of Internet Sciences*, 1(1), 29–44. Available at http://www.ijis.net/

Mesch, G.S. and Talmud, I. (2006b) The quality of online and offline relationships, the role of multiplexity and duration. *The Information Society*, 22(3), 137–148.

Mesch, G.S. and Talmud, I. (2007) Similarity and the quality of online and offline social relationships among adolescents in Israel. *Journal of Research in Adolescence*, 17(2), 455–465.

Mesch, G.S., Fishman G. and Eisikovits, Z. (2003) Attitudes supporting violence and aggressive behavior among adolescents in Israel: the role of family and peers. *Journal of Interpersonal Violence*, 18, 1132–1148.

Mitchell, K., Finkelhor, D. and Wolak, J. (2003) The exposure of youth to unwanted sexual material on the internet: a national survey of risk, impact, and prevention. *Youth and Society*, 34(3), 330–358.

Mitchell, K.J., Ybarra, M. and Finkelhor, D. (2007) The relative importance of online victimization in understanding depression, delinquency, and substance use. *Child Maltreatreatment*, 12(4), 314–324.

Monge, P.R. and Contractor, N.S. (2003) *Theories of Communication Networks*. Oxford: Oxford University Press.

Moody, J. (2001) Race, school integration, and friendship segregation in America. *American Journal of Sociology*, 107(3), 679–716.

Mouttapa, M., Valente, T., Gallaher, P., Rohrbach, L.A. and Unger, J.B. (2004) Social network predictors of bullying and victimization. *Adolescence*, 39(154), 315–335.

Nachmias, R., Mioduser, D. and Shemla, A. (2001) Information and communication technologies usage by students in an Israeli high school: equity, gender, and inside/outside school learning issues. *Education and Information Technologies*, 6(1), 43–53.

Nansel, T.R., Ovepeck, M., Pilla, R.S., Ruan, W.J., Simons-Morton, B. and Chedit, P. (2001) Bullying behaviors among US youth: prevalence and association with psychological adjustment. *Journal of the American Medical Association*, 285, 2094–2100.

Neal, J.W. (2007) Why social networks matter: a structural approach to the study of relational aggression in middle childhood and adolescence. *Child and Youth Care Forum*, 36, 195–211.

Neuman, S. (1991) *Literacy in the Television Age*. Norwood, NJ: Ablex.

Nie, N.H., Hillygus, D.S. and Erbring, L. (2002) Internet use, interpersonal relations and sociability: a time diary study. In B. Wellman and C. Haythornthwaite *Internet in Everyday Life*. Oxford: Blackwell.

OECD (2001) *Understanding the Digital Divide*. Paris: OECD.

Ofcom (2008) Social networking: a quantitative and qualitative research report. www.ofcom.org.uk (accessed 1 October 2008).

Olson, D.H., Russel, C.S. and Sprenkle, D.H. (1983) Circumflex model of marital and family systems. *Family Processes*, 22, 69–83.

Olweus, D. (1999) *Bullying at School: Long-Term Outcomes for Victims and an Effective School-Based Intervention Program*. New York: Plenum.

Orthner, D.K. and Mancini, J.A. (1991) Benefits of leisure experiences for family bonding. In B.L. Driver, P.J. Brown and G.L. Peterson *Benefits of Leisure*. New York: Vantage.

Parayil, G. (2005) The digital divide and increasing returns: contradictions of informational capitalism. *The Information Society*, 21, 41–51.

Pardum, C.J., L'Engle, K.L. and Brown, J.D. (2005) Linking exposure to outcomes: early adolescents' consumption of sexual content in six media. *Mass Communication and Society*, 8(2), 75–91.

Parks, M.R. and Floyd, K. (1996) Making friends in cyberspace. *Journal of Communication*, 46, 80–97.

Pasquier, D. (2001) Media at home: domestic interactions and regulation. In S. Livingstone and M. Bovill (eds) *Children and their Changing Media Environment. A European Comparative Study*. Mahwah, NJ: Lawrence Erlbaum Associates, Inc.

Patchin, J. and Hinduja, S. (2006) Bullies move beyond the schoolyard. *Youth Violence and Juvenile Justice*, 4(2), 148–169.

Pearson, M., Steglich, C. and Snijders, T. (2006) Homophily and assimilation among sport-active adolescent substance users. *Connections*, 27(1), 47–63.

Pellegrini, A.D. and Smith, P.K. (1998) Physical activity play: the nature and function of a neglected aspect of play. *Annual Progress in Child Psychiatry and Child Development*, 69, 5–36.

Pew Internet and American Life Project (2003) *The Ever-shifting Internet Population*. Washington, DC: Pew Internet and American Life Project.

Pew Internet and American Life Project (2006) Parents and teens. http://www.authoring.pewinternet.org/Shared-Content/Data-Sets/2006/November-2006–Parents-and-Teens.aspx (accessed 1 January 2009).

Pfeil, U., Arjan, R. and Panayiotis, Z. (2009) Differences in online social networking – a study of users' profiles and the social capital divide among teenagers and older users in Myspace. *Computers in Human Behavior*, 25, 643–654.

Ploderer, B., Howard, S. and Thomas, P. (2008) Being online, living offline: the influence of social ties over the appropriation of social network sites. *CSCW*, 8, 8–12.

Prensky, M. (2001) Digital natives, digital immigants. *On the Horizon*, 9, 1–6.

Putnam, R. (1995) Tuning in, tuning out: the strange disappearance of social capital in America. *Political Science*, 28, 664–683.

Putnam, R. (2000) *Bowling Alone: The Collapse and Revival of American Community*. New York: Simon and Schuster.

Rafaeli, S., Barak, M., Dan-Gur, Y. and Toch, E. (2003) Knowledge sharing and online assessment. Paper presented at E-Society Proceedings of the 2003 IADIS Conference. IADIS e-Society.

Rice, R.E. (1980) The impacts of computer-mediated organizational and interpersonal communication. *Annual Review of Information Science and Technology*, 15, 221–250.

Rice, R.E. and Love, G. (1987) Electronic emotion: socio-emotional content in a computer mediated communication network. *Communication Research*, 14, 85–108.

Rideout, V., Roberts, D. and Foehr, U. (2005) *Generation M: Media in the Lives of 8–18 year olds*. Menlo Park, CA: Henry Kaiser Foundation.

Robinson, J.P., Kestnbaum, M., Neustadtl, A. and Alvarez, A. (2000) The internet and other uses of time. In B. Wellman and C. Haythornthwaite *The Internet in Everyday Life*. Oxford: Blackwell.

Rodkin, P.C., Farmer, T.W., Pearl, R. and Van Acker, R. (2000) Heterogeneity of popular boys: antisocial and prosocial configurations. *Developmental Psychology*, 36, 14–24.

Rogers, E.M. (1995) *The Diffusion of Innovations*, 2nd edn. New York: Free Press.

Rosen, L.D. (2007) *Me, MySpace, and I: Parenting the Net Generation*. London: Palgrave Macmillan.

Rosen, L.D., Cheever, N.A. and Carrier, L.M. (2008) The association of parenting style and child age with parental limit setting and adolescent MySpace behavior. *Journal of Applied Developmental Psychology*, 29, 459–471.

Sanders, C.E., Field, T.M., Miguel, D. and Kaplan, M. (2000) The relationship of internet use to depression and social isolation among adolescents. *Adolescence*, 35, 237–242.

Sassen, S. (2002) Toward a sociology of information technology. *Current Sociology*, 50, 365–388.

Schouten, A.P., Valkenburg, P.M. and Peter, J. (2007) Precursors and underlying processes of adolescents' online self-disclosure: developing and testing an 'internet attribute-perception' model. *Media Psychology*, 10, 292–315.

Seepersad, S. (2004) Coping with loneliness: adolescent online and offline behavior. *Cyber-Psychology and Behavior*, 7(1), 35–40.

Seto, M.C., Maric, A. and Barbaree, H.E. (2001) The role of pornography in the etiologic of sexual aggression. *Aggression and Violent Behaviour*, 6, 35–53.

Shrum, W., Neil, C. and Hunter, S. (1988) Friendship in school: gender and racial homophile. *Sociology of Education*, 61, 227–239.

Silverstone, R. and Haddon, L. (1996) Design and the domestication of information and communication technologies: technical change and everyday life. In R. Silverstone and R. Mansell *Communication by Design, The*

Politics of Information and Communication Technologies. Oxford: Oxford University Press.

Simmel, G. (1990) *The Philosophy of Money*, edited by D. Frisby, trans. T. Bottomore and D. Frisby from a first draft by K. Mengelberg. London: Routledge.

Šmahel, D. and Machovcova, K. (2006) Internet use in the Czech republic: gender and age differences. In F. Sudweeks and H. Hrachovec (eds) *Cultural Attitudes towards Technology and Communication*. Murdoch, Australia: School of Information Technology, Murdoch University.

Smetana, J.G. (1988) Adolescents' and parents' conceptions of parental authority. *Child Development*, 59, 321–335.

Smetana, J.G. and Asquith, P. (1994) Adolescents' and parents' conceptions of parental authority and personal autonomy. *Child Development*, 65, 1147–1162.

Smith, L. (2007) Online networkers who click to 1000 friends. *The Times*. http://www.thetimes.co.uk/tol/news/science/article2416229 (accessed 20 September 2009).

Smith, M.R. (1985) *Military Enterprise and Technological Change: Perspectives on the American Experience*. Boston, MA: MIT Press.

Smith, P., Mahdavi, J., Carvalho, M. and Tippet, N. (2006) *An Investigation into Cyberbullying, its Forms, Awareness, and Impact, and the Relationship between Age and Gender in Cyberbullying*. London: Goldsmith College, University of London, Unit for School and Family Studies.

Soukup, C. (1999) The gendered interactional patterns of computer-mediated chat rooms: a critical ethnographic study. *The Information Society*, 15(3), 169–176.

Spears, R. and Lea, M. (1992) Social influence and the influence of the 'social' in computer-mediated communication. In M. Lea (ed.) *Contexts of Computer-mediated Communication*. Hemel Hempstead: Harvester Wheatsheaf.

Spooner, T.H., Rainie, L. and Meredith, P. (2001) *Asian-Americans and the Internet: The Young and the Connected*. Washington, DC: Pew Internet and American Life Project.

Sproull, L. and Kiesler, S. (1986) Reducing social context cues: electronic email in organizational communications. *Management Science*, 32, 1492–1512.

Sproull, L. and Kiesler, S. (1991) *Connections*. Cambridge, MA: MIT Press.

Stanton-Salazar, R.D. and Spina, S.U. (2005) Adolescent peer networks as a context for social and emotional support. *Youth and Society*, 36(4), 379–417.

Steinberg, L. and Silk, J. (2002) Parenting adolescents. In M. Bornstein (ed.) *Handbook of Parenting. Volume 1: Children and Parenting*, 2nd edn. Mahwah, NJ: Lawrence Erlbaum Associates, Inc.

Steinfeld, C., Ellison, N.E. and Lampe, C. (2008) Social capital, self esteem and use of online social network sites. *Journal of Applied Developmental Psychology*, 29, 434–445.

Stern, S. (2004) Expressions of identity online: prominent and gender differences in adolescents' WWW home pages. *Journal of Broadcasting and Electronic Media*, 48(2), 218–233.

Stoller, E.P., Miller, B. and Guo, S. (2001) Shared ethnicity and relationship multiplexity within the informal networks of retired European-American sunbelt migrants. *Research on Aging*, 23, 304–335.

Subrahmanyam, K. and Greenfield, P. (2008) Online communication and adolescent relationships. *The Future of Children*, 18(1), 119–146.

Subrahmanyam, K., Kraut, R.E., Greenfield, P. and Gross, E.F. (2000) The impact of home computer use on children's activities and development. *The Future of Children*, 10, 123–144.

Subrahmanyam, K., Kraut, R.E., Greenfield, P. and Gross, E.G. (2001) The impact of computer use on children's and adolescents' development. *Journal of Applied Developmental Psychology*, 22(1), 7–30.

Suitor, J.J., Pillemer, K. and Keeton, S. (1995) When experience counts: the effects of experiential and structural similarity on patterns of support and interpersonal stress. *Social Forces*, 73, 1573–1588.

Suler, J. (2004) The online disinheriting effect. *Cyber-Psychology and Behavior*, 7, 321–326.

Sutherland, R., Furlong, R. and Facer, K. (2003) *Screenplay: Children and Computing in the Home*. London: Routledge-Falmer.

Tapscott, D. (1998) *Growing Up Digital: The Rise of The Net Generation*. New York: McGraw-Hill.

Terlecki, M. and Newcombe, N. (2005) How important is the digital divide? The relation of computer and videogame usage to gender differences in mental rotation ability. *Sex Roles*, 53(5–6), 433–441.

Tichon, J.G. and Shapiro, M. (2003a) The process of sharing social support in cyberspace. *Cyberpsychology and Behavior*, 6(2), 161–170.

Tichon, J.G. and Shapiro, M. (2003b) With a little help from my friends: children, the internet and social support. *Journal of Technology in Human Services*, 21(4), 73–92.

Tidwell, L.C. and Walther, J.B. (2002) Computer-mediated communication effects on disclosure, impressions, and interpersonal evaluations: getting to know one another a bit at a time. *Human Communication Research*, 28, 317–348.

Tocqueville, A. de. (1954) *Democracy in America*. New York: Schocken.

Turkle, S. (1996) Parallel lives: working on identity in virtual spaces. In D. Grodin and T.R. Lindlof *Constructing the Self in a Mediated World: Inquiries in Social Construction*. Thousand Oaks, CA: Sage.

Turow, J. and Nir, L. (2000) *The Internet and the Family 2000: The View from the Parents, the View from the Kids*. Philadelphia, PA: Annenberg Public Policy Center at the University of Pennsylvania.

Tynes, B., Reynolds, L. and Greenfield, P. (2004) Adolescence, race and ethnicity on the internet: a comparison of discourse in monitored vs unmonitored chat rooms. *Applied Developmental Psychology*, 25, 667–684.

Underwood, H. and Findlay, B. (2004) Internet relationships and their impact on primary relationships. *Behaviour Change*, 21(2), 127–140.

Valcour, P.M. and Hunter, L.W. (2005) Technology, organizations, and work–life integration. In E.E. Kossek and S.J. Lambert *Managing Work–Life Integration in Organizations: Future Directions for Research and Practice*. Mahwah, NJ: Lawrence Erlbaum Associates, Inc.

Valentine, G. and Holloway, S.L. (2002) Cyberkids? Exploring children's identities and social networks in on-line and off-line worlds. *Annals of The Association of American Geographers*, 92(2), 302–319.

Valkenburg, P.M. and Peter, J. (2007a) Preadolescents' and adolescents' online communication and their closeness to friends. *Developmental Psychology*, 43(2), 267–277.

Valkenburg, P.M. and Peter, J. (2007b) Online communication and adolescent well-being: testing the stimulation versus the displacement hypothesis. *Journal of Computer-Mediated Communication*, 12, 1169–1182.

Valkenburg, P.M. and Peter, J. (2009) The effects of instant messaging on the quality of adolescents' existing friendships: a longitudinal study. *Journal Of Communication*, 59, 79–97.

Valkenburg, P.M., Krcmar, M., Peeters, A.L. and Marseille, N.M. (1999) Developing a scale to assess three styles of television mediation: 'instructive mediation', 'restrictive mediation' and 'social coviewing'. *Journal of Broadcasting and Electronic Media*, 43, 52–66.

Valkenburg, P.M., Peter, J. and Schouten, A.P. (2006) Friend networking sites and their relationship to adolescents' well-being and social self-esteem. *Cyber-psychology and Behavior*, 9(5), 584–590.

Van Dijk, J. (2005) *The Deepening Divide: Inequality in the Information Society*. London: Sage.

Van Dijk, J. and Hacker, K. (2003) The digital divide as a complex and dynamic phenomenon. Special issue: remapping the digital divide. *The Information Society*, 19, 315–326.

Van Rompaey, V., Roe, K. and Struys, K. (2002) Children's influence on internet access at home: adoption and use in the family context. *Information, Communication, and Society*, 5(2), 189–206.

Van Zoonen, L. (2002) Gendering the internet: claims, controversies and cultures. *European Journal of Communication*, 17(1), 5–23.

Vehovar, V., Sicherl, P., Husing, T. and Dolnicar, V. (2006) Methodological challenges of digital divide measurements. *The Information Society*, 22(5), 279–290.

Vryzas, K. and Tsitouridou, M. (2002) The home computer in children's everyday life: the case of Greece. *Learning, Media and Technology*, 27(1), 9–17.

Wajcman, J., Bittman, M. and Brown, J.E. (2008) Families without borders:

mobile phones, connectedness and work–home divisions. *Sociology*, 42, 635–652.

Walther, J.B. (1996) Computer-mediated communication: impersonal, interpersonal and hyperpersonal interaction. *Communication Research*, 23(1), 3–43.

Wang, R., Bianchi, S. and Raley, S. (2005) Teenager's internet use and family rules: a research note. *Journal of Marriage and Family*, 67, 1249–1258.

Wasserman, S. and Faust, K. (1995) *Social Network Analysis*. Cambridge: Cambridge University Press.

Watt, D. and White, J.M. (1994) Computers and the family life: a family developmental perspective. *Journal of Comparative Family Studies*.

Wellman, B. (2001) Computer networks as social networks. *Science*, 293, 2031–2034.

Wellman, B. and Gulia, M. (1998) Net surfers don't ride alone: virtual communities as communities. In P. Kollok and M. Smith (eds) *Communities in Cyberspace*. London: Routledge.

Wellman, B. and Haythornthwaite, C. (2002) *The Internet in Everyday Life*. Oxford: Blackwell.

Wellman, B., Salaff, J., Dimitrova, D., Garton, L., Gulia, M. and Haythornthwaite, C. (1996) Computer networks as social networks. *Annual Review of Sociology*, 22, 213–238.

Wellman, B., Quan-Haase, A., Boase, J. and Chen, W. (2003) The social affordances of the internet for networked individualism. *Journal of Computer Mediated Communication*, 8(3). http://jcmc.indiana.edu/vol8/issue3/index.html (accessed 26 June 2009).

White, C.J. and Guest, A.M. (2003) Community lost or transformed? Urbanization and social ties. *City and Community*, 2, 239–259.

Whitley, B.E. (1997) Gender differences in computer-related attitudes and behavior: a metaanalysis. *Computers and Behavior*, 13(1), 1–22.

Wilson, B. and Atkinson, M. (2005) Rave and straightedge, the virtual and the real, exploring online and offline experiences in Canadian youth subcultures. *Youth and Society*, 36(3), 276–311.

Wilson, K.R., Wallin, J.S. and Reiser, C. (2003) Social stratification and the digital divide. *Social Science Computer Review*, 21(2), 133–143.

Wing, C. (2005) *Young Canadians in a Wired World*. Erin: Media Awareness Network.

Wolak, J., Mitchell, K.J. and Finkelhor, D. (2003) Escaping or connecting? Characteristics of youth who form close online relationships. *Journal of Adolescence*, 26, 105–119.

Wolfradt, U. and Doll, J. (2001) Motives of adolescents to use the internet as a function of personality traits, personal and social factors. *Educational Computing Research*, 24(1), 13–27.

Woolcock, M. (1998) Social capital and economic development: toward a theoretical synthesis and policy framework. *Theory and Society*, 27(2), 151–208.

Yan, Z. (2006) What influences children's and adolescents' understanding of the complexity of the internet? *Developmental Psychology*, 42(3), 418–428.

Yates, S.J. and Lockley, E. (2008) Moments of separation: gender, (not so remote) relationships, and the cell phone. In S. Holland *Remote Relationships in a Small World*. New York: Peter Lang.

Ybarra, M.L. and Mitchell, K.J. (2004) Online aggressor/targets, aggressors and targets: a comparison of associated youth characteristics. *Journal of Child Psychology and Psychiatry*, 45(7), 1308–1316.

Ybarra, M.L. and Mitchell, K. (2008) How risky are social networking sites? A comparison of places online where youth sexual solicitation and harassment occurs. *Pediatrics*, 693, 351–357.

Youniss, J. and Smollar, J. (1985) *Adolescent Relations with Mothers, Fathers and Friends*. Chicago: University of Chicago Press.

Youniss, J. and Smollar, J. (1996) Adolescents' interpersonal relationships in social context. In T. Berndt and G.W. Ladd *Peer Relationships in Child Development*. New York: Wiley.

Zabrieskie, R.B. and McCormick, B.P. (2001) The influences of family leisure patterns on perceptions of family functioning. *Family Relations*, 50(3), 281–289.

Index

Aboud, F.E. 81
academic performance 13, 34–5
activities 51–2, 53–5
adolescence and social ties 9–12,
    115–18, 147; *see also* peer
    relationships; social networks
age 94, 107–8
Amato, P.R. 28
Anderson, R. *et al.* 99, 100
anonymity 6, 66, 84, 85–6, 109;
    negative consequences 28, 123, 125,
    126, 128, 129–30
art of association 111
Asquith, P. 34
Atkinson, M. 74
Atkinson, R.D. 103
Attewell, P. *et al.* 105–6, 107
Australia 26, 132
autonomy 24, 33, 35, 52, 88–9, 110,
    116, 117

Bargh, J.A. *et al.* 75, 85–6
Battle, J. 105, 107
Baumeister, R. 66
Ben-Artzi, E. 66, 76
Beraman, P.S. 81, 120
Berardo, F. 25
Bimber, B. 106
Blais, J.J. *et al.* 95
blogging 86, 132, 140–1
Boase, J. 63–4
Bober, M. 35–6, 69, 132
Boneva, B. *et al.* 65, 106
Boulton, M.J. *et al.* 122
Bovill, M. 34, 45, 64

bullying 27, 121–2; *see also*
    cyberbullying
Buote, V.M. *et al.* 76, 77
Burt, R.S. 110, 111, 115, 116, 117
Bybee, C. *et al.* 39
Byrne, D. 27

Campbell, K.E. 17
Canada 37–8, 41, 86, 123, 128–9, 130,
    132
cell phones 38, 58, 76
centrality 122
Chae, Y.G. 31, 32, 41
Chan, D. 91, 113
chat rooms 64; bullying 124, 125, 127,
    129; friendships 69, 91, 95; inter-
    racial contact 70–1; motivation for
    use 90, 132, 134; negative effects
    132–3; use 86, 88
Chen, W. 65, 106
Cheng, L. 91, 113
China 104
Ching, C.C. *et al.* 104
Cho, J. *et al.* 108
Coleman, J. 111
Collins, W.A. 33, 34
communication channel choice 92–5;
    duration of relationship 94–5;
    geographic location 92; homophily
    94; multiplexity 93; quality over
    time 95; relationship origin 92–3,
    94; relationship strength 93–4
computer location 24, 35–6, 39–40
computer-mediated communication
    (CMC) 5, 64, 82; anonymity 85–6;
    cues-filtered-out theory 84, 87*t*;

hyperpersonal interaction model 85, 87*t*; lack of contextual clues 82–4, 87*t*; limited social presence 83–4, 87*t*; media richness theory 83, 87*t*; risk 109, 144; social identity and deindividualtion (SIDE) model 85, 87*t*; socio-emotional perspective 85
Cooper, R.B. 83, 85
Cotterell, J. 78, 82
Cottrell, L. *et al.* 33
Crimes Against Children 124, 131
Crosnoe, R. *et al.* 10
cues-filtered-out theory 84, 87*t*
Cummings, J.N. *et al.* 110
cyberbullying 122–31, 133–4; audience 123; disinhibition effect 129–30; explanations 127–30; hate sites 126–7; outcomes 126–7; prevalence 123–4; risk factors 124–5, 125*t*, 145; social network perspective 120–1; and traditional bullying 130–1
cyberspace 6

Daft, R.L. 83
Daly, K.J. 25, 29
deviancy 28
digital divide 99–109, 101*t*, 143–4, 147–8; access and use 99–103; categorical divide 102; diffusion of innovation 107; inequalities in access 103–9; material access 102, 103–4; motivational access 102, 108; skills access 102, 105, 141; social divide 102–3, 103*t*, 108–9, 109*t*; usage access 102
digital literacy 72–3, 102, 146–7
DiMaggio, P. *et al.* 100, 106
disabled people 71, 78, 104
displacement hypothesis 46–51, 61–2; displacement or multitasking? 59–60; functional similarity 48, 48*t*, 49–50; marginal fringe activities 48, 48*t*, 50; physical and social proximity 48*t*, 49; principles of displacement 48–51, 48*t*; and substitution effects 50, 51*t*; transformation 48, 48*t*
dissociative imagination 129–30

Doll, J. 67–8
Dooris, J. *et al.* 75
Drori, G. 102
Dunbar, R.I.M. 14–15
Durkheim, E. 110
dystopian perspective 110, 116

Eastin, M. *et al.* 40, 41–2
Economist 15
education: computer use 45–6, 63, 103–1, 105–6; internet access 103; internet use 13, 31, 34–5, 40–1, 45–6, 103; personalised learning 104–5
Elkind, D. 25
Ellison, N.B. *et al.* 73, 112, 113
email 64; bullying 128–9; communication with family 38; communication with friends 65; cyberbullying 127; multitasking 60; negative effects 132; relationship formation 69; use 38, 65, 69, 86, 88
employment 141
ethnicity *see* race and ethnicity

Facebook 15, 73, 113
family: adjustment and the internet 37–9; cohesion 29–30, 36–7, 37*t*, 43; computer location 24, 35–6, 39–40; cyberchores 32–3; impact of ICT 23–6, 28*t*, 37*t*; internet and tensions 12–13, 13*t*; internet for family communication 38–9; parent–adolescent conflict 32–7, 43, 64, 144; parental mediation 39–42, 43; size and social support 10; time 29–32, 36, 43, 46, 56–7, 57*f*
family boundaries 23, 26–9, 28*t*, 37*t*, 144
Faust, K. 111, 114
Feld, S.L. 15, 19–20
Finkelhor, D. *et al.* 126
Fleming, M.J. *et al.* 133
Flood, M. 27
foci of activity 19–20, 74, 82, 138–9
Fong, E. *et al.* 99
freedom 110
Fuligni, A.J. 33

Galimberti, C. 123
Garton, L. *et al.* 14
gender 52, 54, 77, 78, 79, 94, 97, 106–7
Generation M 36
geographic location 11, 78, 81–2, 92, 113
Germany 67–8, 106
Gershuny, J. 46, 55
Giuseppe, R. 123
globalization 101
Graham, S. 122
Granovetter, M. 17, 111, 112
Greece 104
Greenfield, P.M. 27, 47, 88, 97, 117, 133
Greenspan, R. 104
Gross, E.F. *et al.* 71, 91
Guest, A.M. 112
Guo, B. *et al.* 104

Hacker, K. 100, 106
Hallinan, M. 81
Hamburger, Y.A. 66, 76
Hampton, K. 65
Hargittai, E. 102, 108
Hartup, W.W. 81
hate 27–8, 126–7
Hawley, P.H. 121
Haythornthwaite, C. 13, 16
health and well-being 9, 46, 73, 81, 117
Heirman, W. 126
Hill , R.A. 14
Hinduja, S. 121, 124, 125, 126
Hofferth, S.L. 51
Holloway, S. 32, 35, 70, 72
homophily 11, 15, 19, 77, 81–2, 94, 97, 115
Horst, H. 24, 30, 31, 33, 35
Horvitz, V. 97
Huffaker, D. 73
human ecology theory 24–5
Huysman, M. 20
hyperpersonal interaction model 85, 87*t*

Iceland 107
ICT (information and communication technologies) 1, 2;

digital literacy 72–3, 102, 146–7;
domestication process 23–44, 31;
social embeddedness 21–2, 22*t*, 148–9; social impact 4, 18–19, 25, 136–7; *see also* digital divide
identity: in cyberbullying 123;
formation 26, 70; online 5–6, 68, 70, 74–5, 98; online deception 119–20
Igarashi, T. *et al.* 76
Impett, E.A. 27
information age 1, 2
information society 2–4
instant messaging (IM):
characteristics 89–90; closeness to friends 58, 65, 71, 91, 95;
motivations for use 90, 134;
multitasking 60; negative effects 119, 128; use 3, 64, 69, 86, 88
internet 2, 6; access 99–103;
communication 3–4, 5, 19, 31, 38–9; compulsive use 7; as cultural artifact 6–7, 73; as culture 5–6, 73–4; digital literacy 102;
educational use 13, 31, 34–5, 40–1, 45–6, 103; effects on family boundaries 28; as foci of activity 19–20, 74; information 1, 4;
language 104; pervasive use 7;
social view 8–9; technological view 7–8, 9; use by adolescents 10–12, 86, 99–103; *see also* digital divide
Israel: autonomy 89; digital divide 107; family 36, 38; internet and time 56–9, 61–2; internet use and activities 53–5; relational quality 68, 69, 94, 116; social networks 77
Italy 88, 106
Ito Daisuke 05 113
Ito, M. 89

Japan 76, 107
Jung, J.Y. *et al.* 75, 100, 104
Juvonen, J. 122

Kadushin, C. 64, 115
Kahai, S.S. 83, 85
Kaiser Family Foundation 31
Kandel, D.B. 11, 81
Katz, J.E. 64, 104, 108, 138, 145

Kautiainen, S. *et al.* 46
Kayany, J.M. 49
Kennedy, T.L.M. *et al.* 38, 106, 112
Kidsonline@home 132
Kiesler, S. *et al.* 32, 34, 65, 84
Korea 40–1
Kraut, R. *et al.* 15, 52, 67, 108
Kubitschek, W.K. 81
Kuo, E.C. 46, 50

Lanning, K.V. 134
Larson, R.W. 10, 52
LaVoie, D. 104
Lea, M. 85
Leary, M.R. 66
Lee, P.S.N. 46, 47
Lee, S.J. 31, 32, 41, 95
Lee, W. 46, 50
Leigh, A. 103
Leng, L. 46, 47
Lengel, R.H. 83
Lenhart, A. *et al.* 30, 35, 41, 65, 86,
    90, 101
Leskovec, J. 97
Levanon, Y. 24, 72
Li, Q. 123, 128–9, 130–1
Liau, A.K. *et al.* 33
Lin, N. 101, 112, 115
Lin, S.S.J. 67
literacy 72–3, 102, 105, 146–7
Livingstone, S. 34, 35–6, 40, 45, 64,
    69, 132
Lockley, E. 38
Loges, W.E. 100
loneliness 67, 71, 90, 91

McCowan, J. *et al.* 91
Machovcova, K. 98
McKenna, K.Y.A. *et al.* 66–7, 108,
    111
McMillan, S.J. 69
McPherson, M. *et al.* 15
Malamuth, N.M. 27
Mancini, J.A. 30
marketing 28
Marsden, P.V. 17
McKenna, K.Y.A. *et al.* 85–6
media 2; communication channel
    choice 92–3; content creation
    140–1; influences 21; multiplexity

16; network effects in adoption 86,
    88–91; privatization 45, 46
Media Awareness Network 41, 86, 88
media richness theory 21–2, 83, 87*t*
Mendelson, M.J. 81
Mesch, G.S. 24, 31, 35, 36, 38, 64, 65,
    66, 68, 69, 72, 77, 78, 89, 94–5, 108,
    113, 116, 122, 124, 125, 129
Mexico 106
Mitchell, K.J. *et al.* 72, 123, 127, 131,
    132
Mnet 01 28, 123
mobile phones *see* cell phones
Moody, J. 81, 120
moral development 69–70
Morrison, M. 69
Mouttapa, M. *et al.* 121, 122
multiplexity 15–16, 93, 144–5
multitasking 59–60, 90, 139–40
MySpace 15, 41, 119, 125, 131

Nachmias, R. *et al.* 107
Neal, J.W. 71
negative social ties 119–35, 145, 148;
    bullying 121–2; cyberbullying
    120–1, 122–31; identity deception
    119–20; online harassment 119–20,
    131–5
net-generation 7–8, 45–6
Netherlands 67, 68, 75, 91
'network effect' 88
'network integration' 112
network size 14–15, 58–9, 147
network society 2
networked individualism 2, 3–4, 22,
    116, 147
networks 2–3
Neuman, S. 47
Newcombe, N. 106
Nie, N.H. *et al.* 30, 49, 52, 53
Nir, L. 28

Ofcom 91
Olson, D.H. *et al.* 29
O'Neill, H. 104
online communication:
    asynchronicity 129;
    communication channel choice
    92–5; disinhibition effect 129–39;
    existing friends 88–91; and face-to-

face convergence 95, 96–8; and family time 31; social diversification and social bonding 97; social network effects in adoption of media 86, 88–91; theoretical perspectives 82–6, 87*t*; *see also* negative social ties
online forums 89, 127, 134
online gaming 31, 60, 65, 66, 95, 96, 124
online harassment 119–20, 131–5
online identity 5–6, 68, 70, 74–5, 98
online relationships 10–12, 63–79, 76*t*, 142; adolescent friendships 71–3; concept 65–6; effects on social networks 75–8, 93; moral development 69–70; motivations 66–71, 76*t*; new relationships 63–4, 65–6, 71–2; and personality characteristics 66–8; relational quality 68, 71, 77, 91, 113, 115–18, 145; risk perception 68–9, 72, 91; social affordance 73–5, 76*t*; structural processes 96*t*; trust 69, 86, 144, 148
Orthner, D.K. 30
Osland, J.A. 27

parent–adolescent conflict 32–7, 43, 64, 144
parental mediation 39–42, 43; parental style 41–2; restrictive mediation 40; social co-viewing 39–40; strategic and non-strategic mediation 40–2
parent–child closeness 122
Pasquier, D. 34
Patchin, J. 121, 124, 125, 126
peer relationships 9–11, 80–2, 137–8; activities 51–2; communication channel choice 92–5; online and face-to-face convergence 95, 96–8; popularity 122; as protective factor 121–2; proximity–similarity hypothesis 11, 81; social network effects in adoption of media 86, 88–91; time spent with peers 46, 53–5, 56–8, 57*f*; *see also* online communication; online relationships

Pellegrini , A.D. 52
personal information disclosure 28, 41, 66, 124–5, 129, 132
personality characteristics 66–8, 76, 117
Peter, J. 68, 77, 89, 91, 95, 118
Pew Internet and American Life Project 36, 55, 90–1, 101, 106, 124, 128
Pfeil, U. *et al.* 15
physical attractiveness 66–7, 86
play 51–2
Ploderer, B. *et al.* 98
pornography 27
proximity–similarity hypothesis 11, 81
Putnam, R. 21, 111

quality of life 110

race and ethnicity: autonomy 111; chat rooms 70–1; computer use 105–6; diversity 79; hate websites 27–8; internet use 104; online harassment 133
Rafaeli, S. *et al.* 111
relationships *see* family; online relationships; peer relationships
Rice, R.E. 64, 104, 108, 138, 145
Rivera, F. 28
Robinson, J.P. *et al.* 46, 103
Rodkin, P.C. *et al.* 122
Rosen, L.D. *et al.* 30, 41, 42, 128, 131
Russel, G.J. 33, 34

Sandberg, J.F. 51
school forums 65
Schouten, A.P. *et al.* 75
Seepersad, S. 71
self-esteem 52, 73, 133
Seoul 75
Seto, M.C. *et al.* 27
Shapiro, M. 71
short message service (SMS) 88–9
Shrum, W. *et al.* 11, 78, 81
shyness 66–7, 86, 134
Simmel, G. 110, 117
Singapore 33, 75
skills 102, 105, 141
Smahel, D. 98

Smetana, J.G. 34, 43
Smith, P.K *et al.* 52, 129
Smollar, J. 10, 12, 52
SMS (short message service) 88–9
SNS *see* social networking sites
sociability and internet use 5, 45–62;
  activities and social development
  51–2; activity displacement 53–5;
  displacement hypothesis 46–51,
  61–2; displacement or
  multitasking? 59–60;
  extracurricular and sports activities
  53–4, 55; integration with 'offline'
  life 46, 70, 71, 73–5, 148–9; internet
  use and network size 58–9; social
  activities 53–4; time displacement
  55; time with peers 46, 53–5, 56–8,
  57*f*; *see also* online relationships
social anxiety 52, 66–7, 71, 86, 118,
  134
social capital 109–13, 138, 145;
  bonding and bridging 73, 111–12,
  114*f*, 115, 116*t*, 117; costs and
  benefits 116*t*; relational quality of
  adolescents 115–17, 118, 147;
  social morphology 116*t*; and social
  networks 20–1, 73
social cohesion 110, 113
social construction of technology
  8–9, 21–2, 22*t*, 73–4, 109, 142
social development 51–2
social diversification 18–22, 25, 97,
  137–40, 141–2, 147
social groups 14–15
social heterogeneity 113, 127–8
social identity and deindividualtion
  (SIDE) model 85, 87*t*
social network analysis 14, 119
social networking sites (SNS):
  characteristics 89; closeness to
  friends 58, 65, 113; and
  employment 141; motivations for
  use 90–1, 113, 134; negative effects
  119, 124, 132; use 3, 86, 88
social networks 13–18; centrality 16;
  density 17, 114–15; effect of ICT
  on 21–2, 22*t*, 58–9; effects in
  adoption of media 86, 88–91;
  effects of online relationships on
  75–8, 93; homophily 15, 97;

multiplexity 15–16, 144–5; size
  14–15, 58–9, 147; and social
  capital 20–1, 73; structural
  characteristics 18*t*; tie strength 17;
  transitivity 97, 117; *see also*
  negative social ties
social policy 4
social presence theory 83–4, 87*t*
socoeconomic status 103–4
Soukup, C. 107
Spears R. 85
Spina, S.U. 79
Sproull, L. 65, 84
Stanton-Salazar R.D. 79
Steinfield, C. *et al.* 108, 113
structural holes 110–11, 112, 116
Subrahmanyam, K. *et al.* 34, 46, 47,
  88, 97, 117, 133
Suler, J. 129
Sullivan, H.S. 66
Sutherland, R. *et al.* 32
Sweden 107

Taipei 75
Talmud, I. 64, 65, 68, 69, 77, 78, 89,
  94–5, 108, 113, 116
Tapscott, D. 70
technological determinism 7–8, 9,
  21–2, 22*t*, 73, 142
telephone 89, 146
television 21, 38, 47, 48, 49–50, 55, 60
Terlecki, M. 106
text messaging 89, 90, 129
Tichon, J.G. 71
Tidwell, L.C. 85
time spent with family 29–32, 36, 43,
  46, 56–7, 57*f*
time spent with peers 46, 53–5, 56–8,
  57*f*
Tocqueville, A. de 111
trust 21, 69, 86, 144, 148
Tsai, C.C. 67
Tsitouridou, M. 104
Turkle, S. 6
Turow, J. 28

UK: bullying 129; family 32–3, 35–6,
  38; media adoption 86, 88, 91;
  online harassment 131–2; online
  relationships 64

USA: access to ICT 103–4, 105–6;
    activities displacement 55;
    cyberbullying 123–4, 128; family
    30, 32, 36, 38, 41, 42; gender 106,
    107; media adoption 86, 90–1;
    online harassment 119–20, 131;
    online relationships 64, 67, 71
utopian perspective 110

Valentine, G. 32, 35, 70, 72
Valkenburg, P.M. *et al.* 67, 68, 77, 89,
    91, 95, 118
Van Dijk, J. 100, 102, 105, 106, 107
Van Zoonen, L. 106
Verma, S. 10, 52
virtual reality 6
virtual relationships 6–7
Vryzas, K. 104

Wajcman, J. *et al.* 26, 38
Walrave, M. 126
Walther, J.B. 85

Wang, R. *et al.* 42
Wasserman, S. 111, 114
Watt , D. 24, 32, 34
web searching 60
Wellman, B. *et al.* 2, 3, 18, 38, 63–4,
    65, 72, 106, 112, 116
White, C.J. 112
White, J.M. 24, 32, 34
Wilson, B. 74
Wilson, K.R. *et al.* 108
Wing, C. 132
Wolak, J. *et al.* 11, 27, 64, 69, 72,
    131
Wolfradt, U. 67–8
Woolcock, M. 111–12
Wulf, W. 20

Yan, Z. 72
Yates, S.J. 38
Ybarra, M.L. 123, 127, 132
Yelsma, P. 49
Youniss, J. 10, 12, 52